Gale Ets Marie

Upstart

iUniverse, Inc.
Bloomington

Upstart

iUniverse books may be ordered through booksellers or by contacting:

iUniverse
1663 Liberty Drive
Bloomington, IN 47403
www.iuniverse.com
1-800-Authors (1-800-288-4677)

ISBN: 978-1-4620-8413-5 (sc)
ISBN: 978-1-4620-8414-2 (e)

Printed in the United States of America

iUniverse rev. date: 2/1/2012

Chapter 1

"In Belgium, that year it was truly a very bad winter there were any things going wrong for the mother and father of Prince Edlance. His father's health was the first and foremost important problem all were facing.

"Lady Chardinrey my devoted wife and the one who bore my children. You do not have to be here all day long in my hospital room,"said her husband.

"Yes, I do,"said his faithful wife.

"Then would you please, make sure that I have just one thing before you leave,"said the husband.

"Yes, what is it,"said the wife.

"I need you do get my slippers and I will stay in the chair,"said Ed.

"You have to stay in bed a few days but I will ask if you can get out of bed sooner,"said Chardin.

"Chardin, then may I have another cup of coffee,"said Ed.

"That you may have, this time if things to not go well with your chemo and we do stop pretending there are trips to Moscow. This is where you have had the chemo inside the Hermitage I will need to tell the family,"said his wife.

"Chardin, we have to first find out from the doctors,"said Edlance.

"Alright you win again and when there is no visits before we are going to Moscow they are going to think something is wrong, "said his wife.

"This is indeed good coffee,"said Ed.

"I know I had some,"said Chardin.

"There is something wrong but until the doctors say something that I am not going to be well again then we stay with this plan,"said Ed.

"Then we will wait,"said his wife.

"It will wait say did you see the nurse that is waiting on me,"said Ed.

"No, now this time when we leave Moscow and this Palace keeps quiet so your son Edmond and Paul are not aware of your cancer so the businesses can still go on,"said his wife.

"You did not see the new nurse on in the evenings, "said Ed.

"No dear, if it makes you happy hired her as a full charge nurse with some others when we are home,"said Chardin.

"You know I do need some nurses eventually, and she could use the extra cash and a good reference when she leaves,"said Ed.

"Ask her tonight,"said Cardin.

"I will and two others that are working here, ok,"said Ed.

"Yes, you need the help when you are home,"said his wife.

"Of course we will be staying here in Belgium,"said Ed.

"Yes, we are,"said Lady Chardinrey.

"That is good we promised my mother that we would stay,"said Ed.

"I also promised your mother we would live there and we will not be moving, we will never leave her alone,"said Ed's wife.

"I know we did and she loves us for that,"said Ed.

"Yes, she does, do you like this new nurse very much because I told you if the medication or your behavior was different I would understand,"said her Ladyship.

"Yes, I do but you are for me, she is just very polite than the others and they are all married,"said Ed.

"Ok, so she is a good nurse and a good person, so hire her,"said Chardin.

"This is what we had agreed that I would find someone to take care of me and help you out. Also that I was not going to return and there is no transplants,"said Ed.

"Oh, this is it and I will obey your wishes, we certainly have talked enough about this,"said his wife.

"Yes we did for hours in fact and I told you that you are going to be wealthy and the children, yet you are in charge of the businesses until you can get one of your sons to do it for you,"said her husband.

"I will you can be sure of that,"said her Ladyship.

"Now how about that coffee and some desserts that are left from my lunch,"said Ed.

"Sure here they are,"said Chardin.

"Do you want any.?"said Ed.

"No, thanks the lunch I had at home was very good,"said Chardin.

"What did you have.?"said Ed.

"Your mother and I had just soup, it was chicken and home made,"said his wife.

"I bet it was good,"said Ed.

"It was so good I waited until you were finished with your lunch and because you are still hungry here it is all for you to have and a clean bowl,"said Chardin.

"I did think that was a big handbag you had,"said Ed.

"Not that big, just handled correctly,"said his wife.

Chapter 2

"Now I know we discussed this but I need to go home and you can decide if you really like this girl then have her be your new nurse,"said his wife.

"Yes, I will but you are my Princess Chardinrey and I need you,"said Ed.

"Yes, I know you are my Prince Edlance I, Prince Edlance the first and only and I need a few nurses to help you, I can not do it myself,"said her Ladyship.

"I will ask and I will see you tonight, no I will see you tomorrow and let my mother and the children know I will have a few nurses. All this just because the doctor mentioned ten minutes ago that this is it, "said Ed.

"I will tell them and you ask the nurses, if they are on duty,"said his wife.

"See you tomorrow in the morning no the afternoon for the discharge.?"said Ed.

"Yes, at noon, then you get ready and we leave at one o'clock,"said his wife.

"Then at high noon it is, I love you dear,"said Ed.

"I love you too and see you tomorrow,"said his wife.

"Ok,"said Ed.

"These discharge forms I will sign tomorrow nurse.?"said Lady Chardinrey.

"Yes, we are very sad about the health of your husband,"said the Nurse.

“Thank you,”said the Ladyship

“Your welcome, I want to say we are all upset about your husband and what I need to tell you is we here the staff did not do this mistake, the media,”said the Nurse.

“I do not mean to interrupted you but does the media know,”said her Ladyship.

“Yes, we are very upset we just heard it now the news, and your chauffeur is in the direct tunnels to your home,”said the Nurse.

“I have to let all of you know I am very relieved to know this is in the news know I do not need an interview until he is home with me,”said her Ladyship.

“This is the elevator for your car and this security guard will go with you,”said the Nurse.

“Thank you guard for your help,”said Lady Chardinrey.

“Let me open the door Lady Chardinrey,”said the guard.

“We need to get home soon,”said her Ladyship.

“There is the underground door I will take the elevator in this part of the castle here so I can talk to the children and their grandmother,”said her ladyship.

“Very good, the car will be here if you need to go anywhere,”said the Chaufeur.

“Thank you, I think I will stay in for the rest of the evening,”said her Ladyship.

“Very good, we are very unhappy about all that has occurred,”said the Chaufeur.

“Thank you,”said her Ladyship.

“Hello, children and grandmother,”said Chardin.

“Hello, Mom,”said the daughter, the youngest named Lise.

“Hi,”said the smallest, son. Donald

“Why,”said the oldest son, Will.

“Then I will tell you,”said his Mother.

“Why can I see Dad I am older now,”said Will.

“Oh, alright,”said their Mother.

“Yes, your Mother will tell you lets all sit down,”said Ed’s Mother.

“Yes, grandmother is right lets all sit down, “said Ed’s wife.

“Ok. Said Don.

“Children first I need to apoligize to your grandmother,”said Chardin.

"There is not need you, are a good daughter-in-law and mother,"said Grandmother.

"When your father and I were going to Moscow so many times he was actually in the Hermitage secretly getting his chemo. Then this is the last time it is going to work. Also your father will only be alive for more than one year. I am so sorry to tell you this,"said the Princess.

"So that is why he cut his hair off about thirty years ago but he would do that when he was ten,"said the Grandmother.

"No, he did that just in case so we could confuse us all,"said her Ladyship.

"I do not know what is all,"said Lise.

"Dad is dieing.? "said Will.

"Yes, he is,"said his Mother.

"I do not want his to die,"said Donald.

"I know, now lets sit with grandmother and all of us can hug,"said Mother.

"Oh, grams,"said Lise.

"When your father is home show him your love,"said Grandmother.

"We will grandmother, again you use good judgement,"said their Mother.

"Yes,"said Lise.

"Now children go upstairs and get ready for bed and all of us will watch the tel and fall asleep on the floor, ok,"said their Mother.

"Come on, help, Will,"said Lise.

"That girl has the longest blanket in the world. Now I know why Ed wanted her to have,"said Lady Chardinrey.

"Now Chardin do not weep they are not all upstairs. You let them know something is wrong, say nothing after this,"said her Mother-in-law.

"That is right I need to get upstairs before the news start,"said Chardin.

"Yes, do I will follow in the elevator,"said her Mother-in-law.

"Good,"said her Ladyship.

"Now children will you look at the outside how lovely it looks Don do you want to go on the elevator with Grandmother.?"said his Mother.

"Yes,"said Don.

"Good, then go now,"said his Mother.

"See Mom, I am all ready,"said Will.

"Very good Will, we are getting ready for bed and then we will have snack,"said their Mother.

"Mom,"said Lise.

"Oh, you look so clean and are ready to have some juice or soda, milk what do you want.?"said Mom.

"Milk with cokies,"said Lise

"Why does she say cokies.? "said her Mother.

"That is what they all have on the tel,"said Wil.

"Oh Dear. "Lise this is another cookie can you say that,"said their Mother.

"Cookie,"said Lise.

"Very good here is another cookie, Lise,"said their Mother.

"Thanks,"said Lise.

"She sounds just like Don,"said their Mother.

"Here they are Don and grandmother,"said her Ladyship.

"Don do you want something to drink and eat some cookies or a some pie,"said Mom.

"A cookies and milk, but milk dark,"said Don.

"Oh, some chocolate milk and cookies does grandmother want something some coffee and a dessert.?"said the daughter-in-law.

"You get something for yourself and I will have something later,"said her Mother-in-law.

"Alright I have to get your son tomorrow at 12:00a.m, "said her Ladyship.

"Now tell me how many times did he have cancer,"said the Mother-in-law.

"Just twice,"said Lady Chardinrey.

"All those times you went to the Hermitage,"said the Grandmother.

"We did have to go for the sake of the business,"said Ed's wife.

"Now we do not have to go Moscow again, I guess,"said Lady Chardinrey.

"What kind of cancer,"said the Grandmother.

"First in the lungs and now it is no possible chance of recovery, did he ever do any work when I was gone from this house,"said the daughter-in-law.

"Yes, he did mention about cleaning out this castle basement,"said the Grandmother.

"Now we have a good lawsuit the government inspected this house and ours,"said her Ladyship.

"That is whay I stayed at your castle on the shore and then your castle a mile away from mine this one,"said the Grandmother.

"That now would explain this is why we are living here with you while our castles are both being painted,"said her Ladyship.

Chapter 3

“There is no law stating that he can not move that cancerous material that asbestos and also we still can sue because the government is suppose to get rid of that themselves in these buildings of these castles in the city,”said Lady Chardinrey.

“So I will start the proceeding tomorrow if Ed will not, “said his Mother.

“Good,”said her Ladyship.

“Now lets see if the children are asleep and we can see the tel of awhile,”said Grandmother.

“Are you tired I am,”said her Ladyship.

“They all went to bed.? No here is Donald on the couch,”said the Grandmother.

“Do you want to go to bed.?”said Lady Chardinrey.

“Yes, I am tired so lead the way I rroom is first so here it is good night,”said Grandmother.

“Good night, Mother,”said the Princess.

“Ok, Donald sleep, good night, and good night Will,”said her Ladyship.

“Night Lise,”said her Mother.

“Hello. Dear are you falling asleep Ed, pick up. Ok, then good night,”said Lady Chardinrey.

“Hello, children are you having your breakfast soon and all are washed up. Thank you nannies I will take them down stairs with you,”said Lady Chardinrey.

"They are all ready to go to school,"said the Nurse.

"I hope all of you had a good sleep. Good morning ?"said Grandmother.

"Yes, good morning,"said Will.

"Good,"said Don.

"Lise,"said Lise.

"Yes, we all have had a good sleep and a good morning too. Grandmother, "said Lady Chardinrey.

"I know they are good children,"said their Grandmother.

"While the nurses have placed them into the classroom I am going to leave for the hospital,"said her Ladyship.

"It is near noon time. The phone is ringing,"said Grandmother.

"Yes, I will take the call, Darling you are calling from the hospital, "said her Ladyship.

"What did he say.?"said the Grandmother.

"What, you are, that is good, so, ok until then my love,"said Ed's wife.

"What happened,"said the Grandmother.

"He has a ride home, the nurse he wanted to hire is giving him a ride home now and is going to sleep over with two other nurses to take care of him,"said her Ladyship."

"That does seem to work and he pleased with this,"said the Grandmother.

"Yes, just like the children will be too,"said Ed's wife.

"Then do we set anyone at the table,"said Grandmother.

"No need, they will have their meals with the staff as planned,"said her Ladyship.

"Fine,"said the grandmother.

"Here they are now, it is good the children are in the classrooms,"said her Ladyship.

"Yes, here we are, I hope nothing but just nursing is apparent,"said the Grandmother.

"Sure, he knows me,"said Lady Chardinrey.

"I hope so,"said the Grandmother.

"Now Ed, how are you, do you want to rest,"said his Wife.

"Yes I would for a few hours,"said Ed.

"Also the nurses should be introduced to the others.? "said Ed.

"Yes, they will be,"said his wife.

"Good rest for a while and then we can have dinner and talk,"said her Ladyship.

"I will, I am very tired, "said Ed.

"Now grandmother,"said Chardinrey.

"We can wait for him to wake up later, or do you want to talk to Ed,"said Lady Chardinrey.

"No, he should sleep and I will wait to talk to him later on,"said the Grandmother.

"There lets wait for them to get home, have some more coffee,"said her Ladyship.

"We can, if you want to,"said the Grandmother.

"All is looking satisfactory,"said her Ladyship.

"Things will work out,"said Grandmother.

"Yes, they are going to,"said the Grandmother.

"I put the nurses in with the nannies so they will know each others schedule,"said her Ladyship.

"I do think he needs a few large males to help pick him up if he can not walk,"said his Mother.

"That will probably never happen even in his last days,"said his Wife.

"The doctor discussed this with you.?"said his Mother.

"Yes he did,"said his Wife.

"Now I think Ed is up because I hear the children talking to him they are laughing and having a good time that is so good to hear, "said her Ladyship.

"Good evening Ed the children eat a few minutes ago and here is your food right here and I will join you ok, and your Mother also,"said her Ladyship.

"We can sit and talk a while or are you still tired,"said his Mother.

"No, I am awake and feeling very good and how are you two,"said Ed.

"Fine, thank you Ed for asking,"said his Mother.

"We are both fine I called the children, Ed and his wife Princess Ownsite they are both hoping you are ok,"said his Wife.

"They are not going to visit.""Or they should be here tomorrow before the press is at its worst,"said Edlance.

"Yes, they are going to be here in the morning or late tonight,"said her Ladyship.

"They are going to stay for a few days,"said Grandmother.

"No, they are both going to leave by the same Concorde jet that they own and the jet will pick up his brothers and sister for a visit to Bavaria to see them both,"said Chard.

"Chard is that a good thing to do,"said Ed.

"Yes, but for them both to be here, no, so that is why they are going to leave in one hour after they have arrived,"said her Ladyship.

"Then if the brothers or their sister want to visit they can do so,"said Ed.

"Yes, but I found out all are going to be here at the same time tomorrow and we will all sit down for a large dinner in this castle,"said her Ladyship.

"So if we go to bed early we can get enough sleep, any anyone is tired I know I am,"said her Ladyship.

"This has taken a toll on you, Chardin,"said Ed.

"I did get a lot of sleep last night we all went to bed early,"said her Ladyship.

"I know it can be tiring and I too am very tired and it was quite a day,"said Ed.

"This large dining room will be ready for tomorrow, I do no mean to have a different conversation but I would like to know,"said the Grandmother.

"Oh, I hope so too,"said Ed.

"Yes, this room will be used,"said her Ladyship.

"Good, we both Chardin need to rethink my jewelry, the last time I wore something in this house at this table, the children asked if I was going to be leaving right after dinner, "said the Grandmother.

"I know last New Years Will asked if I was going to get rid of my old man,"said her Ladyship.

"What did you say.? "said Ed.

"Yes, what did you say.?"said the Grandmother.

"Nothing, I went up stairs and put on a mesh head dress when the company left and he was very impressed with me, "said her Ladyship.

"What one is that,"said Ed.

"In your study on the second floor of our castle and we danced that night in front of them all,"said her Ladyship.

"There are ten of them which one did you know would work ok,"said Ed.

"The night before I looked and the first one I put on worked, perfectly,"said her Ladyship.

"I remember, then we finally talked you into having your photo done,"said Ed.

"It was a few years after Princess Ownsite had her photo done in her home in Newport, Rhode Island,"said Chardin.

"Right, they entertained in three building I remember they were very busy when they got married. She is a very good daughter-in-law, "said Ed.

"Yes, she is and today because of them both we did not have to live at the Breakers in Newport and they got all the tunnels done in the states,"said her Ladyship.

"They are a good couple you raised him correctly,"said the Grandmother.

"Yes, but he did not get that kidnapping from me,"said Chardin.

"Not me,"said Ed.

"Not my family, I do feel as if I was kidnapped at times,"said her Ladyship.

"It was on my mother's side of the family,"said the Grandmother.

"Are you sure.? "said Ed.

"I am not complaining at all I have had a perfect and beautiful time here and I love you and our children and I have a wonderful mother-in-law,"said her Ladyship.

"There, did you hear that Ed, and you did not want to live at home,"said his Mother.

"We are just visiting again, our castle should be finished soon, we did need a new kitchen,"said Ed's wife.

"Now we are all grateful for what we have, the children and our homes,"said Ed.

"That kitchen is going to be terrific I remember when I was living with all of you last year and I love my new kitchen. It did not take long to do,"said the Grandmother.

"No, but if you want it done right it does take time,"said Chardin.

"Mom, may I have some water,"said Don.

"Here you are,"said his Mother.

"Thank you,"said Don.

"Your welcome,"said his Mother.

"Dad are you going to the hospital again.? "said Don.

"No, but I may going to stay here for a while ok,"said Ed.

"Yes, good, Lise needs all the help she can get,"said Don.

"I know I will help her,"said his Dad.

"Good,"said Don.

"Where did she get that blanket.?"said the Grandmother.

"It was for the dining room table when it is open as it is now for 50. We had it delivered in the wrong material and she has had it ever since. She screamed so much that I gave it to her,"said her ladyship.

"That is because I promised her a ride in it when all of you were out of the room I would secretly carry her around in it, and then place her on my shoulders from the table itself,"said Ed.

"I know I could not part with it or compete,"said her Ladyship.

"So now it is hers,"said the Grandmother.

"Yes with a very large red covered wagon to pull it in, and the access to the elevator all the time,"said her Ladyship.

"It did make her take responsibility for that elevator, even with a crowd of people she was right there one evening blanet and all,"said the Grandmother.

"So there is not question about it we will have Mr. Question with us for maybe a few more years,"said Lady Chardinrey.

"It does appear to be that way for a while,"said Grandma.

"I could talk to her right now let me take this coffee into the living room and see to it that she is there in about a few minutes ok, dear,"said Ed.

"I will let the Nanny know I want to see her,"said her Mother.

"See that is all we need to do is for her to talk to her father, she loves him and will do the right thing,"said her Grandmother.

"Lady Chardinrey, your daughter, "said the Nanny.

Chapter 4

"Lise, your father wants to talk to you in the living room,"said Mom.

"Here is my daughter and how are you this evening.?"said Dad.

"Ok, I love you,"said Lise.

"I love you too, Lise,"said Dad.

"Now could you do me a favor, could you keep this blanket in the nursery and take another one and I will get you a lot of dolls to cover up with the old blanket,"said Dad.

"Ok, I do it now good night,"said Lise.

"Good night, my little baby, give me a kiss and I will see you tomorrow ok,"said Ed.

"Ok, dear that was done, now would everyone would want some more coffee,"said his wife.

"Do you have the phone,"said Ed.

"Yes, her it is,"said his Wife.

"Thanks, Nanny I want you to put the dolls from my room to the nursery when Lise leaves that room, ok, "said her Father.

"I am glad we took those dolls with us, while they painted the other house,"said Ed.

"When the boys see them they will think they were all here in this house anyways,"said his Wife.

"Now she can see the room if we all go upstairs right after our coffee,"said Dad.

"Tell Don I am waiting at the elevator, if he wants a ride,"said Grandmother.

"I will, when Don leaves why not show Lise the dolls and I will talk to will,"said his Wife.

"Will, do you want to sleep on the floor for a little while,"said his Mother.

"Children, we are going to sleep on the floor for a while,"said their Mother.

"Good night, children later I will put you in your rooms,"said Mother.

"See,"said Lise.

"Very good, now your dolls are very warm,"said her Mother.

"Do you like my new pink blanket it was in the closet where all the dolls were,"said Lise.

"The new blanket as pink is very nice and now the dolls are very warm and all together,"said her Mother.

"Now go to sleep and we can give all of you a very nice party because your father is home,"said Grandmother.

"Or we can have a small party and then we can get some gifts for ourselves and we all can celebrate,"said their Mother.

"Good night. Will try to encourage them to go to their own bed when we are in the other rooms, and thank you dear, "said his Mother.

"Mother and my darling wife some more coffee and cake before we go to bed,"said Ed.

"Yes, please darling I need a stimulus,"said Ed'swife.

"Yes, and thank you for the new pink blanket Ed,"said the Grandmother.

"Thank you, that was so nice and I let her know that her babies are all safe and warm now,"said her Mother.

"It did not take much to convince her,"said Ed.

"She also let me know that the blanket was in the closet and she decided it was time to use it,"said her Mother.

"The same closet where the dolls were.?"said her Grandmother.

"That is right and that is Lise for you she will take the gift right out in front of you if it is her birthday,"said her Mother.

"So what a card we have. Don is faithfully there every time I am on the elevator, he is such a good boy,"said the Grandmother.

"Also Will is for the second evening in a row putting the children into their own beds, he is such a good help to me,"said his Mother.

"We have very good children why I remember Ed before he left for the States he would put the children to bed for us,"said his Father.

"He and his wife will be the first to arrive tomorrow their sister and husband from then Norway and of course their brother is not going to join us from the their Breakers estate,"said their mother.

"The others will visit one sister living on the coast line of Belgium, and one other very faithful brother still getting the rolls industry in Europe, actually right now he is still in South America with that business,"said the Mother.

"That is right he has five franchises now,"said his Grandmother.

"Should we call it a night, my Prince,"said her Ladyship.

"Yes, good night. I will walk alone my door is open, "said Grandmother.

"Then is your maid right at the door good night, Mom,"said Ed.

"Night,"said her Ladyship.

"Good, dear my Princess and as a Countess in Italy, maybe a vacation.?"said Ed.

"No, we will stay here or let me think it over. I ask your Mother with the photos from last weeks dinner party to use them in the Versailles magazine,"said her Ladyship.

"She wants to.?"said Ed.

"Yes she will,"said Ed's wife.

"So let me wake up with you, then we can have breakfast together, it is nice being home again with all of you,"said Ed.

"Alright Ed, before we both know it we will be awake and talking to the children,"said Chardiney.

"Look at that here you are in your bathrobe and your hair is in a towel,"said Ed.

"We did sleep soundly and now I know why you were sent home from the hospital it was to have a good night sleep,"said his wife.

"Oh, this is the life, I smell the breakfast and for food is ready to be served,"said Ed.

"You are allowed to have any more chemo treatments at home if your like too,"said his Wife.

"No, that was it there is nothing else to do,"said Ed.

"I know I remember no transplants,"said Ed's wife.

"Thanks for that, I am going to take a shower, no a tub bath, "said Ed.

"I am getting dressed right now. Soon we can both go to the dining room,"said his Wife.

"I will meet you there the male nurse is outside tell him he can wait inside here for me,"said Ed.

"Ok, I will and I will see you in a few minutes ok,"said his wife.

"Go right in and wait for him ok, now Grandmother lets go downstairs together the three of us, look Don is waiting for you,"said her Ladyshgip.

"So here we are and the food smells divine and I know it is all set for today we will all be together at last,"said the Grandmother.

"We will, and now we can start, here is Ed,"said her Ladyship.

"Since I have been home I have decided to eat a lot of food,"said Ed.

"Good, and the children left a lot of extra food so go ahead and stuff,"said Ed's wife.

"I will, "said Ed.

"So we are going to have a busy day, and I hope many of them do start entering the house even right now,"said Ed's wife.

"Anything else, some more, Mom,"said Ed's wife.

"No thanks dear, I am going to go into the living room and later I will have some more coffee,"said Grandmother.

"Alright we will be there in a little while,"said Grandmother.

"We can go too, if you want, I am finished,"said Ed.

"Then here we go,"said Ed's wife.

"Look, the pink blanket has a new place,"said Ed.

"I can not believe what I see,"said her Ladyship.

"Why did she leave it on the bottom of the sit of iron,"said the Grandmother.

"His feet are cold,"said Ed.

"No, he is protecting it,"said Lise.

"Here we are starting a new puzzle,"said Will.

"Yes, we are, it is my brother's house in Boovaava,"said Don.

"Yes, he has a big castle like the one at the shore we were in last Christmas,"said Wil.

"Oh, that puzzle, is good,"said Grandmother.

"Yes, you are right Will, last Christmas was a lot of fun,"said their Mom.

"Look, Will I see a place for this one right here,"said his Dad.

"Oh, good thanks Dad,"said Will.

"The soldier is going to use my blanket if he calls,"said Lise.

"On the phone,"said her Mother.

"Yes,"said Lise.

"I think the soldier will be there only if it is an emergency, is that ok, Lise.?"said her Dad.

"Yes, then it is mine.?"said Lise.

"Yes, it is yours,"said her Dad.

"There she goes to watch her brothers and she will stay in her chair and watch them,"said Ed.

"This time there is a blanket, that all of us do not have a problem with,"said her Ladyship.

"I think because we helped her with she will be very good to her children and will remember we were very understanding of her situation and needs,"said Grandmother,

"She will be a very forgiving teacher and a compassionate doctor also,"said Ed.

"All I need is a good mother to her children,"said her Ladyship.

"Your right, and she will be a good teacher, many forget now a days it takes a human quality,"said Ed.

"Don would make a good husband and Will, they both are considerate,"said their Mother.

"I think they should go to Law school or at least work in the business in the main office here in Belgium,"said Ed.

"Lise, does show concern too maybe all of them could be lawyers,"said their Grandmother.

"I know right now with the others we did a good job of raising them,"said Ed.

"Yes, but I told you that having money did work,"said his Wife.

"These three will turn out all right we have many successful stories to tell them about their brothers and sisters,"said Grandmother.

"I know we do,"said her Ladyship.

"Everything is all right, they will survive, their sister lives in the palace at the coast and she is writing, that is going to calm them down at bit,"said Ed.

"They to can live on the coast and create some art work and be married,"said the Grandmother.

"It is not the end of the world for them there is still plenty for them to do,"said Ed.

"They will accomplish a lot in their lives,"said their Mother.

"Now we need to be grateful that the others are showing them a good example,"said Ed.

"This is true and when are they going to arrive,"said Grandmother.

“Soon very soon,”said her Ladyship.

“I can not believe it a message from Ed and his Princess Ownsite is at the airport and now in the tunnels as we speak. He is going to be here in about thirty minutes,”said their Grandmother.

“Oh good, kids your brother Ed is arriving in a few minutes,”said her Ladyship.

Chapter 5

"Here they are and I am so happy to see you both again,"said their grandmother.

"Grandmother, Dad, Mom, Will, Lise and Don, I love and missed you so much,"said Edmond.

"Hello, everyone one I brought with me because she is not to heavy for the plane. Grandmother would you like to hold your granddaughter, Belissa, her she is and I love you dear, "said Owns.

"My son, and daughter-in-law and you brought, Belissa. I can not believe it, she is a little taller,"said her Ladyship.

"Son it is good to see you and Owns and what about the other youngsters did they make a fuss, because they could not be here, "said Ed.

"I did the best thing a Mother could do I did not tell them we were leaving,"said Ed.

"I did that very last minute we left and they did keep quiet,"said Edward.

"Ok, then, we have everything under control. "said Princess Ownsite.

"Now, I have to know we are having a dinner at lunch time so we can go home about one o'clock,"said Ed.

"Yes, it is all set for 11:30 am ok. We are having a turkey dinner,"said their Mother.

"I can smell it right now, we are not staying over so can we say hello to the staff,"said Edward.

"Yes, you may both do that,"said his Father.

“They both will be awhile remember Pentilus went to the United States with the both of them, “said their Mother.

“With them, with the train, Pentilus did to help,”said Lise.

“That is right we were looking at their photos,”said her Mother.

“Why don’t we get the gang on the way back to the dining room,”said Dad.

“Here we are did you both see the staff,”said their Dad.

“Yes, and like Pentilus he shook my hand and we all acknowledge each other and then he dismissed us from the kitchen,”said Owns.

“I expected that from him he does not detain us while we are in his kitchen,”said their Grandmother.

“I guess Edward forgot about their domain,”said his Mother.

“Yes, I did, but we just did not seem to be the same,”said Edward.

“No, you to never were and that is his job,”said the Grandmother.

“He did not want anything to happen in his kitchen,”said Edward’s Father.

“So tell me how was it being the King of Bavaria, I know that Carl is enjoying himself ruling for the people,”said the Grandmother.

“It was delightful, to be the Queen of Bavaria, “said Princess Ownsite.

“Yes, it was, but it was better when Carl took over permanently,”said Ed.

“Now lets all sit down and enjoy this dinner. Pentilus prepared this dinner for you both, the breaded asparagus, just the way you enjoy his cooking,”said her Ladyship.

“Now your sisters can not be here both are having babies,”said his Father.

“I know I called them last night,”said Ed.

“Your brothers can not be here either it is to far away,”said his Mothers.

“I have little, Lise,”said Edward.

“Yes, and I just could not wait to see Will and Donald too,”said Owns.

“Don,”said Don.

“You are right,”said Owns.

“So we can still give out the gifts before we have something to eat right, Mom,”said Ed.

“Yes, of course,”said his Mother.

“Here are the gifts,”said Princess Ownsite.

"Oh, dear this is for us both, said Ed.

"A model of a ship, thank you ,"said Will.

"Look, Grandmother they bought us that old home in near the border,"said her Ladyship.

"Now we can visit our daughter this week,"said his Father.

"A new doll,"said Lise.

"Don what is it.? "said Will.

"A ports car, "said Don.

"Grandmother what is your gift.? "said her Ladyship.

"Why it is a monocle. This is easier than my half glass,"said their Grandmother.

"It is an antique also,"said Ed, her grandson.

"You are correct,"said Grandmother.

"It had a broken glass in it so we put in a very high powered lens,"said Owns.

"Thank you so much I will use this all ways,"said their Grandmother.

"So now lets all have an early dinner,"said Lady Ownsite.

"Look, there is a little charm on the monocle, it said. Oh, no, thank you both,"said Grandmother.

"What does it say, Grandmother,"said Will.

"With my new monocle can actually read it, very well too, "Hope you and my brothers and sister Will and Don and Lise will enjoy the cove beach estate too. Love Ed and Owns,"said Grandmother.

"You bought that old summer home too, you were the ones remodeling these two buildings, two castles, thank you dears, the both of you,"said their Grandmother."

"You four are right next to us,"said her Ladyship.

"How about all of us being able to use two buildings at once,"said their Father.

"Yes, we have been with grandmother for two years now and we are going into our own castle in two weeks,"said her Ladyship.

"You are use to living in here Owns with Grandmother before you both started "Grenaire"together,"said Lady Chardinrey.

"I know I owe grandmother my life, my world, my fortune because of her making me stay here while Ed and I dated,"said Princess Ownsite.

"That is right,"said the Father-in-law.

"Yes, it is true, Mother put down the law the day you two were together,"said her Ladyship.

"One year living here with Grandmother, then we were engaged, and then it did not look as if I was kidnapped,"said the Princess.

"That is right, my dear and I hope you are getting a check each month and each year,"said Edmond's Grandmother.

"Yes I do and from Ed also,"said Princess Ownsite.

"Good you deserve that,"said Grandmother.

"I know I am quite aware of this that it was the help of my wife too,"said Ed.

"This is the truth, now how about passing me some more turkey, Ed,"said his Dad.

"Sure, here you are,"said Ed.

"My goodness, I would not be here if it was not for my husband, Princess Edlance the second. My entire life became the envy of many girls, my age and still I am loved by many who I do not kinow,"said the Princess.

"It takes time to get use to these things, the media has been polite to you many times,"said her Ladyship.

"I know it was myself who was getting all the disturbing news in print,"said Ed.

"I do remember and you deserved every bit of what you received for that year." said her Ladyship.

"But he did become her hero Chardin,"said the Grandmother.

"Yes, he did and he still is,"said Princess Ownsite.

"He is,"said his Father.

"I am so glad and happy for you both. We will finish our coffee in the living room,"said her Mother-in-law.

"We can enjoy a few minutes more with my son and daughter-in-law,"said Ed.

"Oh, I love my two gifts,"said their Grandmother.

"Yes we do"said her Ladyship.

"Oh, I do have some information to appreciate all that Ed and his wife have done for the public. A friend of mine never sold her castle to a bed and breakfast firm who would give her a condo at any time, told me the following news,"said Grandmother.

"This is very good, listen to what grandmother has to say, sorry that I interrupted,"said Ed's Father.

"She told me that her condo was in the states and before these tunnels were in the government was going to charge her 4 thousand dollars per year for their van to bring anyone on the interstate highway system in Connecticut, "said the Grandmother.

"Can you imagine now what you two have done for the world,"said her Ladyship.

"Now all vans serving each client are for the state only and others have to call the cab services that each state now has, none are independent,"said Ed's father.

"Now on this happy note we need to say good bye to you Ed and your beautiful Princess, good bye my son and you my helpful and beautiful daughter-in-law,"said her Ladyship.

"Good bye my dear I love to you both and little Belissa who is so good you would hardly know she is here.""said Grandmother.

"I think she is still dazzled with all the gold baroque and the chandleirs, she looks all the time at home and now she points to them. Thank you so much and especially for my wonderful life with Edmond., "said Princess Ownsite.

"Your welcome, that is another thing you both have done the opening up to these buildings keeping the new born comma victims progressing everyday,"said their father-in-law.

"Thank you we need to go home now the plane is waiting and your staff on the place I know has enjoyed your turkey dinner also,"said Ed.

"Yes we all did and now I am walking you three out to the door and Ed will stay with the children and your Grandmother will watch them too, "said her Ladyship.

"No, I want you to stay with the children, ok, bye every one,"said Ed.

"Good then I will close the living room doors so you can concentrate on leaving and good bye, we love you both bye little Belissa ,"said Her Ladyship.

"Good bye,"said Grandmother.

"Good bye,"said their Father-in-law.

"Good bye, Don and Lise your brother is leaving,"said Will.

"Let them both sleep they both and you have new toys to open, you can wait until tonight to open your gifts,"said this Mother.

"Yes, Mother these are the gifts you promised us right,"said Will

"You are correct so let them get up, and play,"said his Mother.

"She will not sleep tonight, better wake them both up,"said their Grandmother.

"Don needs to sleep in the night hours only,"said his Father.

"They do not need any nap time,"said Grandmother.

"Here kids open up your new toys, "said her Ladyship.

"What a nice visit,"said Grandmother.

"Yes, it is a shame all of the others are far away,"said Ed's wife.

"No, it is not,"said Ed.

"Your right, they all need their privacy,"said her Ladyship.

"I told Edward and his wife that the awards will be given to them by the local organizations and they will be mailed, "said her Ladyship.

"That is sad but they do need to be watching their family and those who give can be visit. Giving them awards and to let the public know their doors are open is a sign of politeness,"said their Grandmother.

"I agree,"said Ed.

"Yes, they should be with their families, while the children are young,"said the Mother-in-law.

Chapter 6

"They are home,"said Grandmother.

"Good,"said her Ladyship.

"We can go ahead and use Lloyd's if the press starts with something that is not true,"said Ed.

"There will be something now that they have returned after all this time away from us,"said her Ladyship.

"I am positive there is going to be very foolish on the part of the press,"said their Grandmother.

"We can have our P.R. look at all the damaging media news, in fact he did that the last time,"said Lady Chardinrey.

"He worked very hard in fact, I saw all the articles and media footage and he sum up a good substantial sum,"said Ed.

"That is true he did get a good check for each of us and the children too,"said Grandmother.

"I will give him a call, because their photos of the visit were given to the media,"said Ed.

"Now we have a good chance of someone going wrong,"said the Grandmother.

"I know you are right, and I now know it is not going to be good,"said Chardin.

"The first thing mentioned in the news there were no awards given to them at all,"said Ed.

"Those things take weeks to do, they were only staying here for three hours,"said the Grandmother.

"I know and if I know the media they are in for one big lawsuit and I hope it is the worst of the tabloids magazines that actually when we win they do not mind being dismantled like all the rest,"said her Ladyship.

"Winning awards and winning the talbloids they are up against it all the time with awards being given out, I hope they know how to handle this one for their sake,"said their Grandmother.

"The media is suppose to know what to do,"said Ed.

"To make the conversation better did you like little Belissa she looks like Ed so much and I know she is the pride of his life,"said the Grandmother.

"You know he told me in a whisper there is a little baby on the ten floor in the nersury of the infants that they adopted and she and he have been with each other and they are having the infants in the main house with them more and more each day,"said her Ladyship.

"Yes, I do not mind that at all, they had no place to go but that nursery is a fully equipted they are also there for a good healthy life, "said the Grandmother.

"They had other there that occupy the seventh and eleventh floors in an their own apartments with their nannies,"said Ed.

"Their were ten nurses who aparted the children and live in the buildings with them. After they gave up control and now have dual adoption laws to help those children in case any thing happens to their parents as well,"said her Ladyship.

"This is alright I am not unhappy about that at all. There were three cases that the couples wanted to adopt and the staff still work there but are in the retriement section before it is used so the children still have a normal life with parents, "said Ed.

"Nothing is wronfg that children are close by and this is what they wanted and the government is pleased there might be some new employees as lawyers some day who were once children grownign there,"said her Ladyship.

"What about the children who do not want to practice law after a while.? "said the Grandmother.

"It is called rotating shifts and job responsibility a few days and many are happy to return or stay somewhere else for a little rest,"said Ed.

"Besides is that understood still today that all parts of Europe are to remain being very relaxed during the work environment, that is the biggest part of the tourists attraction,"said Her Ladyship.

“Yes, for the visitors no one rushes the Baroque Ro Co Co at all. For a long time now, it has controlled even when the buildings is empty,”said Ed.

“The government, scientists and the wealthy families new what to do to save this part of the world.” Said her Ladyship.

“This is true,”said Ed.

“Now the architects are trying to save the world with warm and comfortable buildings for the populations. Said her Ladyship.

“You two both have this down perfectly,”said Grandmother.

“This is the way we talked to each other when Ed and Princess Ownsite got married and moved,”said her Ladyship.

“That is right, now I remember walking in on you two and I left because I wanted to talk to the nursery children in a regular tone,”said their Grandmother.

“We envied you but we needed to do our homework for days like this but you again pulled us into the conversation and we appreciate you very much,”said her Ladyship.

“Yes, as Princess Ownsite mentioned you are our inspiration and motivator,”said Ed.

“With that I will ask for more coffee and desserts of the day,”said Grandmother.

“Right away you have earned,”said her Ladyship.

“Did I earn,”said Don.

“Yes you did, your brother said, “you were growing up. “He wanted to know where were the little ones were that were here years ago when he was living with us,”said his Mother.

“Their in boarding school,”said Don.

“Right, can you imagine you brother and sister look just like the baording school brothers and one sister you have that are not living at home at all,”said his Mother.

“They do look like all of your sisters and brothers,”said their Father.

“Go see if the snacks are in the dining room and we can have some food right now ok,”said his Mother.

“It is here,”said Don.

“Ok, Mother lets get some real snacks right now ok,”said her Ladyship.

“Mother we have some food waiting ok,”said Ed.

“Ok, I see it all ready and it looks, oh,”said their Grandmother.

"My some cake and cookies to help out but first I do see some turkey sandwiches,"said Ed.

"Oh, this is a good dinner not that early either,"said her Ladyship.

"Why not have the over turkey,"said Will.

"This is another one the first turkey is probably going into a stew,"said her Ladyship.

"Then this too sounds very good and I think we will have a bowl of stew tomorrow,"said Ed.

"Nice,"said Will.

"Now enough about the dinners and such what about your new toys,"said Ed.

"We do enjoy that puzzle and the models too,"said Will.

"My car,"said Don.

"My doll,"said Lise.

"All is ok, then, "said Ed.

"Yes, "said Will.

"My,"said Lise.

"Me too,"said Don.

"Every good,"said Grandmother.

"Yes, I am very proud of all of you children,"said her Ladyship.

"Yes, we are,"said Grandmother.

"Yes, we are very proud of all of you, so proud in fact that we will get more gifts for you, very soon indeed maybe tomorrow, ok,"said Ed.

"Yes, "said Will.

"Yes, yes,"said Don.

"Yes, Yes, Yes,"said Lise.

"I just forgot to mention to Edmond when he was here but I did call him about this,"said Ed.

"What.? "said his wife.

"That the Divas concerts are always here or in Versailles or the Hermitage and Chambord has its owe Divos. That this is the first year the males and females were two days apart, "said Ed.

"That is surprising even Gale in Versailles had to be reminded,"said his wife.

"Why is that,"said Grandmother.

"Because neither one of them remembered there are males groups that sing,"said Ed.

"That is hilarious for someone like to hear that,"said Grandmother.

"Also the concerts do space the males and the next day is the female then male this is the first time for that too,"said Ed.

"So what did the groups and agents do,"said Grandmother.

"Nothing to timid to call Versailles up and mention that the system does still have males singers,"said Ed.

"I do not believe my ears,"said Grandmother.

"Princess Ownsite never even thought of it nor Edmond when they wrote their first memoirs,"said Ed.

"What about Gale he certainly did not forget.?"said Grandmother.

"He did too and all the concerts for the males worked just that winter. All of them were in all the buildings before the winter ended,"said Ed.

"I did forget to mention all of them, just the ones we saw and all of them were visiting at least just once while we were here,"said her Ladyship.

"They have both had the groups in for a few hours before the shows start and after and some of them immediately went to another early morning performance,"said Ed.

"I do remember that they now have a strict law about how long the concert will be,"said her Ladyship.

"That is correct, for myself and Will we had a long concert in this backyard. Now they had to close at a certain time,"said Grandmother.

"Yes, that impressed Will very much being able to stay out very late,"said Ed.

"I know he was very please with the concert after Ed and his Princess married and we never did anything about that building. Then we were able to use the building instead of putting together a completed castle,"said her Ladyship.

"How many years has it been since they got married in that building.? "said Ed.

"Not to long,"said her Ladyship.

"No, it has not been long but now we have a more important thing to discuss do we finish that building or add to it,"said Grandmother.

"Lets add to it and keep they concerts going,"said Ed.

"Good idea,"said her Ladyship.

"Now we will give the public a brand new castle next the remaining building that we have never finished,"said the Grandmother.

"That is a great idea and we all can live in it when it is finished. We will make a few apartments there for the children when they are older,"said Ed.

"Yes, we all will live here together after the building is finished,"said their Grandmother.

"That is a terrific idea, we will enjoy that new home and the concert halls will not be seen anyways due to the architecture and the designers will be fantastic too,"said her Ladyship.

"So we are all in an agreement about this that is good, so lets celebrate and we can go ahead with the construction this week,"said Ed.

"Yes we are going to and I will call the designers too,"said her Ladyship.

"We all ready have the plans and the architects model is in the other room,"said Ed.

"So leave them a message right now so they are aware of it,"said her Ladyship.

"Chardin you are a genious and a wonderful wife,"said Ed.

"I know,"said Princess Chardin.

"As my Duchess you are the best,"said her Ladyship.

"I did think we were not using these titles, just Lord and Lady,"said Chardin.

"I know I just want to go be a good day,"said Ed.

"Yes, it is,"said Lady Chardinrey.

"This is a day,"said Lise.

"Good day,"said Don.

"A very good day we are going to move,"said Will.

"Yes, we are,"said Grandmother.

"It should all be done within a year all of the foundation is there we have been using the floors for a concert parking,"said Ed.

"Are you sure all the foundation is there waiting,"said Grandmother.

"Sure it is we did not cover it over,"said Ed.

"Yes I am,"said Lady Chardinrey.

"It is the small building that are up around the existing larger building and parking lot, right now,"said Ed.

"Now that all is settled. We can enjoy the food it is now is the last we are having tonight,"said Lady Chardin.

"We will have everything necessary in this new home,"said Ed.

"I know it does sound like a final dream come true,"said her Ladyship.

"We are going to have a few horses and ponies,"said Will.

"Sure we even have a stable there too,"said Ed.

"Oh, boy ponies,"said Lise.

"Horses,"said Don.

"We could start with the fast foods services in that part of the new building also,"said Ed.

"Right and a few shops too,"said Grandmother.

"Of course the usual sleep and loitering and Exile bank too,"said Ed.

"It is perfection and we need that all the time,"said her Ladyship.

"Great I will get on the calls right now, "said Ed.

"Good we still have the same architectural firm so lets get with these drawings and plans this afternoon, "said his wife.

"I will have the secretary get this done immediately so we can exspect great or better results soon,"said her devoted husband.

"All right, and I am ready to give a statement to the press,"said Grandmother.

"That would be nice,"said her Ladyship.

"No it would not, that is your job, Princess but you could use your title as Duchess now that your husband is ill,"said Grandmother.

"I should use the Duchess title, it will allow many to know we can be separated at the end,"said Chardin.

"Are you sure about this that you and he will be separated when he dies and you are going to take the children to the new building. I gathered that when it was finally mentioned,"said his Mother.

"We are using the South Pacific Island and Norman laws so if she and he moved when he is dieing they are married and we are divorced,"said Chardin.

"You know what you are doing yes, because I will owe all when he dies and she will a check each month,"said Ed's Mother.

"So she gets the house too in the near border of France the one you too stayed in to have Donald,"said the Grandmother.

"Grandmother do not have me use your name of Constance a removed Queen in a Finland marriage yourself,"said Chardin.

"I was young their brother was dieing and I kept the money from leaving the family and this family as well,"said Ed's Mother.

"That is just what I am doing for her as well,"said Chardin.

"I know I realize that right now as you said it,"said Granmother.

"I do not want surgery like you grandmother please forgive me, I can do it on my own,"said Chardin.

"I know you do and I am with you but I have a feeling that you want to leave us too,"said the Grandmother.

"I have children and I need you too so do not worry about anything,"said Chardin.

"Is the land and everything now in your name.?"said Ed's mother.

"Yes, it was when we first started the chemo,"said Chardin.

"That is right, I asked if he had a will and he said,"Yes."So that is good and everything is finalized,"said his mother.

"It is and if I go it is all yours and she is provided for with a small castle outside the border in France and a check each month. Then I am sure she would help out, and it will be at my request anyways,"said Chardin.

"Thank you I just wanted to know,"said Grandmother.

"She never has controll over our homes she is with you and a director of the finances each month,"said Chardin.

"So I control what happens,"said Grandmother.

"If you do not want her here then she goes to her home in France and she will be taken care of by the Director of the Finances that is appointed,"said Chardin.

"We are in an agreement,"said Grandmother.

"Thank you and we have to use her name as a very exciting thing for Ed and us in front of the children,"said Chardin.

"Yes, I did already I asked Don to call the nurse to have her help me this morning. While I gave her nothing but praises,"said Grandmother.

"Good that is a start and we need to work together on this,"said Chardin.

"Say we could invite her to dinner as she is representing the other nurses as well,"said Grandmother.

"I will in fact tonight is good but tomorrow night is even better,"said Chardin.

"So now we have a future friend,"said Grandmother.

"Yes, you know it is harder to win the affection of the children,"said Chardin.

"When they see us a dinner they will be more relaxed with her now than as a nurse,"said Grandmother.

"Right again, do you want anything to eat before dinner,"said Chardin.

"No, thanks I would like you to go an ask her now, and I will talk to Ed, he is here right now,"said Grandmother.

"Good I will leave at the back door,"said Chardin.

"I completed the work they are going to start this week in fact,"said Ed.

"Good and I thank you, I have something to tell you, the nurse you have have asked to visit and stay awhile and care for you Chardin is asking her to have dinner with us or maybe tomorrow evening,"said Grandmother.

"That's good and maybe for dinner this evening, that is fine,"said Ed.

"Here is Chardin now and she is going to tell us,"said Grandmother.

"She did reply and this evening is better for her, I also mention there are no photos because she is not purchasing a franchise,"said Chardin.

Chapter 7

"Good evening, Lady Chardinrey, please call me, Erica,"said Ed's new nurse.

"Thank you, and here is my Mother-in-law, Constance my older children have heard her introduce herself as a fugitive from Finland,"said her Ladyship.

"Of course, you know my husband, Ed,"said her Ladyship.

"Yes, I know my employer, who should be sitting down in the later afternoon and right after dinner then if he wants to walk around after one hour then he may,"said the Nurse.

"You are right, would you like a drink,"said Ed.

"I apologize for the instructions, it is important. I would just like a coke with ice if I may,"said Erica.

"Certainly, and he needs to be reminded we will be served in about twenty minutes,"said Grandmother.

"The children will not be with us, but you do not have to explain it is important at dinner to have the conversations very pleasant for your husband,"said Erica.

"It should be pleasant and calm at all times, and we quite agree with you, Erica,"said Grandmother.

"Yes, I told my children if they are going to act out then they can go in a watch the tel, "said her Ladyship.

"So how are you and do you like your apartment,"said Grandmother.

"Very lovely, thank you for asking,"said Erica.

"Erica has her masters and is writing a book comparing nurses to the states,"said Ed.

"You are from Florida and why did you want to live in Europe,"said Chardin.

"Why did you move to Belgium,"said Ed.

"I worked in Italy and in Spain and I like the lifyle style it's calmer and tranquity of both countries is ideal,"said Erica.

"Are we just as relaxed as the others.?"said her Ladyship.

"Even more so,"said Erica.

"Really,"said Grandmother.

"The hospital is busy but the society or its everyday people in the city are very quiet very calm and is very pleasant if one person is rude or is a hurry they go out of there way to apologize,"said Erica.

"But all of you need to use your automobiles, I do not have the status and I am sure all of you would gain a crowd of pleased people to see their royals in the city,"said Erica.

"That is something to hear, and you Erica may call me Grandmother,"said Grandmother.

"That you Grandmother, but I would not advice to go out into the public eye and never let your children. This surrounding fortress will never harm them at all, "said Erica.

"No, it does not,"said Ed.

"If they have an urge to go out they do visit there sister in her castle near the water,"said her ladyship.

"Oh, I ask Will one morning who lived there and he told me your daughter does and she writes children books I understand,"said Erica.

"Yes, she does, and she is having her first baby in two months,"said Ed.

"Now that I did not know if you want me to be there the last few weeks I could do that for the both of you,"said Erica.

"That is a good idea. So why not, let me call her and you can see her tomorrow and maybe visit for the last few days before she gives birth, "said Chardin.

"Alright, I could talk to her tonight if you want me to and maybe see her in the afternoon tomorrow or whenever she is comfortable with a meeting, "said Erica.

"I will call her right now,"said her Ladyship.

"Here she is, on the phone,"said Ed.

"May I take this phone call outside these French doors to the hallway,"said Erica.

"Sure you may, here please sit right here and I will close these doors,"said her Ladyship.

"I hope she is will talk to me too or I will talk to her tomorrow,"said Grandmother.

"Now that was a good desserts and we need more of them so I will let the cook know on my own phone,"said Ed.

"Oh, good I was going to suggest that Ed,"said Grandmother.

"How is she nurse.? "said her Ladyship.

"Yes, nurse how is she,"said Ed.

"Good,"said the nurse.

"I was just going to say I will talk to her right after you but I can talk to her tomorrow anyways,"said Grandmother.

"You will have your wish Grandmother, I convinced your granddaughter to live here in case there is some complications about her delivery because your home is closer to the hospital,"said Erica.

"When tomorrow,"said Ed.

"I convinced her the cauffeur who drove me and her father was the best friend I would ever have that can help her now, so if you let him pick her up there is not need for any alarm,"said Erica.

"Yes, I will let the staff know and go get things ready,"said her Ladyship.

"She told me her husband is in the service, he had met her when a ship patrolled this coast line of your five estates,"said Erica.

"Yes, he was here for three weeks and now he has been at sea for these last few months and should be home on soon, "said Ed.

"Yes, he has one of those positions when he can get the time he can come home,"said Grandmother.

"That is all right, he does not need to come home at this point in time,"said Erica.

"All is ready,"said her Ladyship.

"Thank you, "said Erica.

"No, we need to thank you,"said her Ladyship.

"She told me she loved him and yet this last week, it has been difficult and lonely so I insisted that she returns home for the delivery tonight,"said Erica.

"She does miss us.?"said Ed.

"Yes, but this marriage has made them even stronger being away and now the baby, this is making her a little sadder while they are separated,"said Erica.

"Now we have your daughter back," said her Mother.

"Wait she needs her rest and to be place into bed immediately for her own good and let her sleep,"said Erica.

"Yes, that is true they left me alone sleeping and they were all down stairs very quiet too,"said Grandmother.

"That is what happened to me too,"said her Ladyship.

"We will make sure this happens again letting her get a lot of sleep,"said Ed.

"Yes, we will,"said Grandmother.

"We should think about our other daughter if she is alright in Norway,"said Ed.

"I will give her a call right now,"said her Ladyship.

"It is so good to have both at home, me do agree that we need for security reasons, a new name for the nurses and for your daughters to protect the media from them in these times,"said Grandmother.

"Yes, quite a few times Gales own name was used by our Edlance,"said Grandmother.

"Your right and the nurses also during this time with, oh you said that all ready,"said Grandmother.

"Now is a good time to start, nurse you are Lady Urnlee, and the others nurses will be given theirs right now, "said Ed.

"My returning granddaughter will be called Lady Seebees," said Grandmother.

"She would want to call her husband up and let him know he is Lord Gavga,"said Ed.

"Yes, this will be good especially with the new building," said Grandmother.

"I cannot believe it my other daughter agreed to live with us and leave after the baby has been born, her husband can set will be here on weekends,"said Chardin.

"Good she is Lady Leavelets,"said Ed.

"Right the new building and to allow our staff to appear to be family,"said Chardin.

"I am now Lady Urnlee I did not ask for this title. I do not mind it at all,"said Erica.

"That is alright with all of us, we just do not want to use your name in case you were to go to the states and live for a little then you can to recognized while being in a secured environment,"said her Ladyship.

"So you do not mind if I have a title too.? "said Lady Urnlee.

"No, you have given me back my children for at least we do not have worry about the births of their children that much. It is certain now at least they will be delivered they are here with us,"said Lady Chardinrey.

"Thank you for the title and for your honesty,"said Lady Urnlee.

"You have given me back my children I am so happy and I will owe you for the rest of my life,"said Lady Chardinrey.

"None the my granddaughters left in anger they were living with their husbands so now they jhave very good coverage with you as there nurse,"said Grandmother.

"You have rightly earned your title and so will the other nurses watching for their deliveries,"said Ed.

"Now lets all celebrate with this fine desserts and another after dinner coffee,"said Grandmother.

"Listen Will has told the other two sometimes it does take them awhile here Lise, she thinks both of them have babeis right now, and Don just mentioned are they going to play football with us tomorrow,"said their Mother.

"I can not believe my ears again he wanted to know if the babies were going to play football in a few days,"said Grandmother.

"This is why I give them just one sentence and then Will help them out, he is becoming an adult very fast because of those two,"said their Mother.

"That is so beautiful, Will is such a good brother,"said Grandmother.

"I am going to the other room to talk to them again,"said their Mother.

"Now lets all have some coffee and listen to them,"said Ed.

"Now I know why Lise listens to them so much she is learning,"said Grandmother.

"Thank you for returning my two daughters,"said Ed.

"Yes, thank you I can not believe they are returning home,"said Grandmother.

"They are and we are all going to watch them and my other two nurses too,"said the Nurse.

"It all seems so possible now to watch them and to make sure all is medically correct for their deliveries,"said her Ladyship.

"I am so glad to be of some help now I need to tell all of you the conversation that was with Lady Seebees it was nothing to worry her about but I did tell her an untruth, "said the Nurse, Lady Urnlee.

"I know you did not lie but we do not mind at all,"said her Ladyship

"But it can happen, complications can set in when the mothers are alone and usually they do have families,"said the Nurse.

"So what you have mention does not need to be looked at with statistics anyways,"said her Ladyship.

"So let her think she had done the correct thing or the right decision on her part,"said the Nurse.

"Also she was having fun with her unborn child in the home where she and her husband once was,"said Ed.

"Right she does have an attachment there right now,"said the Grandmother.

"Right that bond with her home is now and always will be until she and her husband move into another building,"said the Nurse.

"So if he comes home before or after we can present them with a new house to rent or even that one,"said her Ladyship.

"We can do a lot, first we have to make sure those children are born with a safe and adequate medical facility right here,"said Ed.

"Or buy a new ambulance if needed, and then give it to the hospital,"said the Grandmother.

"All this is good, lets wait until they are both here, and let me suggest these things at the right time,"said the Nurse.

"She is not on a crusade like us let her do all the work when it is time too,"said the Grandmother.

"You are very wise Constance but I would not think it was a crusade for any of us but if I am on a roll then lets get it done successfully while I am,"said the Nurse.

"True she is an technically a visitor,"said Ed.

"I would mention it to anyone that I am an authority on good and proper health, and that is why your daughter do not question what I say or do,"said the Nurse.

"Right we can not do what we are not qualified for,"said the Grandmother.

"This is true I would never think any of your children would go up to me and sit on my lap other than Don who would like a female he can trust,"said the Nurse.

"That is a fact,"said the Nurse.

"Yes, he would,"said the Grandmother.

"Just like I would never ask the government or tell them their laws I am not qualified, while I was writing my books,"said Lady Urnlee.

"Two splendid decisions have been made tonight and we do owe you,"said Ed.

"Yes, we do,"said Lady Chardinrey.

"We are owning Lady Urnlee a great deal, for this has made us closer and we need to put this family together as soon as possible. For tonight a new individual of this family has done just that,"said the Grandmother.

"Yes, you do not know how important it is since we allowed Ed and his wife to go to the states. We all have benefited from it but we do miss our children,"said Ed.

"When we are apart, it is love that grows giving us strength,"said the Nurse.

"There now we can relax and enjoy the rest of the evening,"said her Ladyship.

"If only fussing I would do is if you have extra babies items strollers, cribs to have them ready when the new mothers have here and let them know you are prepared,"said Ed.

"They have lived alone or as with their husbands and having a child they might be a little annoyed at the slights things, so it is not any of you. "said Lady Urnlee.

"That could only be me if it is anyone here to be blamed,"said Lady Chardinrey.

"Slightly true but we have to remember she has been or they both have been given there freedom having a husband,"said the Nurse.

"It will work out I can remember when both girls wanted to be alone in their fantasies and were preoccupied, "said Grandmother.

"I am still reminded with these three little ones that I do not exist when the tel is on,"said Ed.

"May I suggest that we do this to ourselves unintentionally, by looking at the tel guide and inviting each other in to watch a favorite movie, this means each other are agreeing that this is quite time,"said the Nurse.

"They do not do this and they can not read and depend on us. "said their Mother.

"It would work but we give then enough time during the day to look forward to the movie,"said Ed.

“Then a favorite movie and a new show on the tel gives them that independence and one of them might watch the movie in another room,”said the Nurse.

“That I like because I would go in and check up on them and it makes them more older but not faster,”said their Mother.

“All of these situations will now make it easier on all of us when they new babies are here and other children will use the tel and so will we and the nannies will sit for us,”said the Nurse.

“We do have those new temperature kits to use,”said their Grandmother.

“That is very helpful the number one cause of problems today on are high temperatures that are not noticed, “said the Nurse.

“We are very fortunate, as you know now and are apart of Lady Urnlee yet we gave up one of our children, you met him today for a few minutes and for Lloyd’s and also by Lloyd’s our fortune is do to him,”said the Grandmother.

“Yes, we mean well, “said their Mother.

“You do not have to explain, he met your needs financially and gale also in Versailles and now I myself can use the tunnels in the United States and go to work tin New York and live to California if I want to,”said the Nurse.

“Yes, he did accomplish this, “said his Mother.

“Right he has given the world a lot with the tunnels and the traffic is now under control in the states and in Paris to Moscow,”said the Nurse.

“We owe him and you to,”said Grandmother.

“Do not forget you gave birth to him, now we need to use our recourse and get the babies into control of this empire so we can enjoy a good life to make sure that this is still done for all the world in the future years to come,”said the Nurse, Lady Urnlee.

“Thank you for being her,”said Lady Chardinrey.

“Yes, I are so grateful, “said the Grandmother.

“We have work to do and maybe I should at this time, this evening, call it a evening and very good evening and thank you for the title and being a part of your family too,”said Lady Urnlee.

“We could all go upstairs, together, and then it can be a morning time breakfast before me k now it,”said the Grandmother.

“Yes, I will be up early when my daughter arrives so I think I might even get to sleep right away,”said Lady Chardinrey.

Chapter 8

"Good morning, Mother,"said Lady Seebees.

"When did you get here it is so good to see you and this early that is wonderful we do not have to wait,"said her Mother.

"Have something to eat I just arrived about one hour ago,"said her Daughter.

"This is so good I am so please you are here early,"said her Mother.

"Did you bring anything with you.?"said her Mother.

"Yes, a crib that the driver put into the car and all of my belongings but nothing as furniture I did bring all the tels if the little ones want their own,"said her Daughter.

"That was nice I hope the both of you survived that moving, this morning,"said her Mother.

"Yes, we did there was another small truck and the men they work in the gardens for grandmother,"said Lady Seebees.

"That is fine we do not mind it was good of the driver to do that,"said her Mother.

"I ask them last night and he promised me I would be in without a sound,"said her daughter.

"You are so good and kind and looking wonderful you must be a good cook,"said her Mother.

"I learned how to cook before I went to college, right here in fact with grandmother,"said her Daughter.

"That right, you wanted a summer job so she gave you one,"said her Mother.

"I wanted that work,"said her Daughter.

"I know you did, and now your working, your having a baby, are you comfortable right now,"said her Mother.

"Yes, I am,"said her Daughter.

"Oh, Mother, this is why I left, you never act sensible with me,"said her Daughter.

"I know it but I want your life to be exciting for your husband not just be an employee,"said her Mother.

"That is true,"said her Daughter.

"Now have some more food, it is best that a larger meal be in the morning,"said Ed.

"I was going to ask that, good morning dear here is your daughter,"said her Mother.

"Good morning, to the both of you, my daughter it is good to have you home,"said Ed.

"Thank you Father it is good to be home and I missed you, the both of you so much,"said Lady Seebees.

"Seebees, my little girl soon you will be caring for a new baby,"said her Father.

"Did you know that today your sister is arriving and is going to stay with us,"said her Mother.

"No, that is good she and I both need your nurse to give us help and advice before we both help ourselves, "said their Daughter.

"Now dear do not say save your marriage, he is on a ship and will be at sea,"said her Mother.

"Yes, I know with all the free time I had I was thinking of some sort of observary on our coast line before his retirement,"said their Daughter.

"Maybe right next to our light house that is near bye and he can work,"said his Father.

"Oh, father do you think so that is how we met and he can survey the property again for them and watch it too,"said Seebees.

"Yes, we will arrangement the observatory but you must stay with us let them finish the building,"said her Mother.

"When he is home then go to the cottage with him and your baby for privacy,"said Ed.

"That seems to be ok, and will work out very surprisingly for privacy and his relaxation,"said her Mother.

"This is a fact, he is not going to want all these people in one building, "said Ed.

"I suppose your right even in spite of all those other people on board ship there is a difference when with a lot of children too,"said her Mother.

"Now did we will have something to eat, because your Grandmother will be here soon and the rest of the children too, "said Ed.

"Now any more coffee.? Just help yourself, "said her Mother.

"Are you going upstairs.?"said Ed.

"Yes, I am going to get the children up that are awake,"said their Mother.

"Ok, I am going to have more, a second breakfast in fact,"said Ed.

"Do you want any more, daughter you must keep up your strength, tell me, did your Mother start saying things like keep up your strength,"said Ed.

"No. We were talking about Gavga, and his tour,"said Seebees.

"There your message is in for the observatory. It is included with the new plans for the castle."Ed.

"It has to be where he was surviving on either side of the clifts or in the middle seeing the beach,"said his Daughter.

"Right they would know that or you may ask him, right him a letter only and he might be able to send you an answer,"said Ed.

"Thank you, I will,"said Ed's daughter.

"Please do not write his officers' unless he gives you permission too,"said Ed.

"He informed me even if I did they most likely when not be read, due to espionage,"said Ed's Daughter.

"This is very true you now live in a very exciting world with him, you will have your observatory,"said Ed.

"Thank you again, I think I will have some more food,"said Lady Seebees.

"Good let me get it for you I will just give you all the choices ok,"said Ed.

"Good morning. Oh, my Granddaughter and here is Don, Don it is your sister,"said Grandmother.

"Good morning, Don give me a hug,"said Seebees.

"Go morning,"said Don.

"Are you going to school today,"said Seebees.

"Yas,"said Don.

"Good study about the earth and stars and the sun too,"said his Sister.

"Look, who is here Lise and Will,"said Grandmother.

"My sister, Mom told me you would arrive today,"said Will.

"Yes, and I bought you a friend and you will be an uncle soon,"said Seebees.

"Sisster,"said Lise.

"Lise you look so beautiful. My two handsome brothers, I am so glad to be home with all of you,"said Seebees.

"What destroyer is Lord Gavga on,"said Will.

"He is on the U.S.S. Belgium,"said Lady Seebees.

"Oh, my goodness,"said Will.

"What What is wrong,"said their Mother.

"Nothing Mother that destroyer is so large no one has seen it at all,"said Will.

"Then it is safe,"said Lady Chardinrey.

"Yes, it is, and I have to talk to him when he is home, and I bit all of you he will not say one word about his ship at all,"said Will.

"You will not bit or say anything without permission,"said her Ladyship.

"Actually Mother this is my bit, and I won it first, we never talk about those things at all, Will ok,"said Seebees.

"Ok, you won this round,"said Will.

"Will apologize talking to your sister that way,"said his Mother.

"I apologize,"said Will.

"Accepted my brother,"said his sister.

"I am just going to let everyone have their lunch at eleven and we do finish up so most of us will be waiting for their sister and then we can be ready,"said her Ladyship.

"When will she be here,"said her sister.

"Leavly will be here after one o'clock she is on her way right now and her husband is driving her,"said her Mother.

"With her things.?"said her Sister.

"Most of them I understand that he packed as much as can and is going to go home and return on weekends, probably with more things as needed,"said her Mother.

"So he will stay here on weekends only,"said her Sister.

"I do not think every weekend Seebees, he has a business to run until he branches the final office is our capital. Maybe by the end of this year,"said her Mother.

"That will be fun we all can do things, like to shopping,"said Seebees.

"Yes, but lets wait until the baby is born, we do have excellent food here and lets keep the going to town available for later, until the babies have arrived,"said her Mother.

"Sure of course I do not intend to out outside at all until the delivery,"said Seebees.

"I know what you mean and it might be still be snow on the ground,"said her Mother.

"Just more snow,"said Seebees.

"Why do you go home after each holiday I know you were mitting and learned how by grandmother and the cook you had with you this year,"said her Mother.

"It was my first time away from home after college,"said Seebees.

"Of course it was, and you will be there again maybe in the newer building, something else to look forward too,"said her Mother.

"I hope he loves the idea of an observation building,"said Seebees.

"Oh, by the way when you write that letter thank him for that idea. We would have never done this without him and it is very necessary with a light house on one side,"said her Mother.

"This is will do right now and I will give you a copy to read it before it is mailed. So am going to my room, and I was wondering, "said Seebees.

"Yes, I will make sure the lunch is brought up top you this time you should make an effort to be here for every meal,"said her Mother.

"Yes, I will and I love you mother,"said Seebees.

"I love you, and if you late your name then be on the throne of France when it is at the highest for your father and me,"said her Mother.

"I am going too,"said Seebees.

"Good, so get some sleep a little nap and we will see you soon,"said her Mother.

"Oh, Seebees this is your nurse who spoke to you on the phone, she is just going upstairs right now for some sleep,"said her Mother.

"Good morning, that is a good idea getting some rest and a better one that you move in on an early hours schedule being early is very good for the baby," said her Nurse.

"Thank you, we need to talk today," said Seebees.

"It would be best maybe even tonight and try to get some rest ok,"said the Nurse.

"Thank you so much and for your help last night too,"said Seebees.

"It was my pleasure and there is more help later, first you should rest. Let me help you upstairs but we will take the elevator, ok,"said the Nurse.

"Yes it is, thank you Mother I will talk to you later,"said her Daughter.

"Yes, ok, and I want you to sleep, dear it is important,"said her Mother.

"Now Mother, did Ed say it is alright to have a large meal tonight only.? "said her Ladyship.

"Yes, he did and to start the lunches now was fine with him,"said Grandmother.

"Good, because I do not know when anyone is arriving,"said her Ladyship.

"I know it is difficult when these things happen but we have our family back with"us,"said Grandmother.

"She just mention that she liked living at the cottage because it was the first rent since college,"said her Ladyship.

"I know I am surprised that she is here and now there will be another daughter and a newborn, all due to the nurse,"said Grandmother.

"I wonderful if she will wait for him to return and then live there with him and the baby,"said her Ladyship.

"That is when it will happen as soon as he is home and you my dear are going to welcome it and give them furniture and a new home,"said the Grandmother.

"It does seem to be that way doesn't it.? "said Lady Chardinrey.

"Yes, it is and will be,"said the Grandmother.

"Don are you have for lunch,"said his Mother.

"Yesss,"said Don.

"Lise, are you hungry. Also will. ?"said their Mother.

"yesss,"said Lise.

"Yes, I am Mother,"said Will.

"Good, all of you sit down and we can begin. Constance I think I have been in this dining room all morning talking, "said her Ladyship.

"You have not left this room,"said her Ladyship.

"I know that,"said Grandmother.

"I have been here for three hours, and all of us have been just talking,"said Ed.

"This is an exciting day we will have your children back with us and having will have their children,"said her Ladyship.

"I forgot, oh it is good that Leavly will occupy that last room so she has access to the other rooms for you other three children two boys and one girl,"said her Ladyship.

"That is a lot to care for and we are going to use the carts after today, maybe just for the breakfasts and lunches,"said their Grandmother.

"What about that.?"said Lady Chardinrey.

"We can not want all that noise on this first floor, so we will use the carts for a little while,"said Ed.

"Yes, you are right we need too,"said Lady Chardinrey.

"Now that is done, I will leave it to the staff at the kitchen,"said Ed.

"I wonder what they will say.? "said Grandmother.

"Look, an answer,"said Ed.

"What did he say.? "said Lady Chardinrey.

"The chef, indicated that it is an excellent idea, the carts will start tomorrow. "said Ed.

"Good so we can start in as a lunch,"said Grandmother.

"I will bring this up to Seebees,"said her Mother.

"You know technically Seebees did sit on the throne of France last year just before she moved,"said her Grandmother.

"She did and she has to do it again to get a better name she can sit for the photo right here in the new part of the building when completed,"said Ed.

"Oh, good I will let her know all of this. Also that the throne is in the new building,"said Grandmother.

"After she has her photo, the room is painted and is given a new chair,"said Ed.

"Good I think at that time in my life and the new building done with my 150 room apartment I will use my old title as Empress." said Grandmother.

"I am glad you said that." said Ed.

"I am looking forward to it,"said Grandmother.

"It will be given a first while we use the building as just Prince and Princess or Lord and Lady as usuall,"said Ed.

"You know you both sat on the Belgium throne for Gale and you could use the name of Duke and Duchess." said Grandmother.

"I will think it over,"said Ed.

"Give it some deep thought,"said Grandmother.

"I will like Shakespeare,"said Ed.

"Yes, give it some deep thought, Shakespeare,"said Grandmother.

"Yes, indeed as I am Will, himself,"said Ed.

"Good however, we do not need to get into this to intensely seeing all the British men are on the stage, then I wonder if I am in the best seat in the house,"said his Mother.

"I do not know about this in that day and age, but in the new castle we are building we have a proper theater,"said Ed.

"That is promsing even for me when I have my photos,"said his Mother.

"Good, now the children have finished their lunch do you want any more.?"said Ed.

"I am fine, thank you,"said his Mother.

"I apologize we will be back to normal using the carts, it is just this evening and then you will have your upstairs maid to help you again. ok,"said Ed.

"I do not mind it just this one day, in fact we have to keep down the noise and the children running in each room once again, "said their Grandmother.

"I know especially when we are all here under on roof,"said Ed.

"It was only a lot of noise on the weekends when they were not in a class room,"said Ed.

"That's right it is like a holiday, with the girls arriving,"said their Grandmother.

"There Seebees is having her lunch, and she thanks you for the message,"said her Ladyship.

"Now for your lunch,"said Ed.

"It seems the entire morning and now afternoon is in this dinning room,"said Chardin.

"Same with the both of us,"said Grandmother.

"Yes, but I have been here two hours before you wanted breakfast,"said Chardin.

"As Lise would say, we can use her new blanket,"said Ed.

"I do have something to tell you and it is very confidential it is just between us ok,"said Chardin.

"Sure you know you can trust us,"said Grandmother.

"Yes, sure you can, now what is it.? "said Ed.

Chapter 9

"Do any of you remember, no first do we still have that Section 8 where a family can live in the building with you and learn about a charity,"said Chardin.

"Yes, it was started in the states and then went to the buildings with the tunnels and then the large estates,"said Ed.

"Yet the original owner can go to another building, unless the others want to ,"said Grandmother.

"We did not do this why.? "said Ed.

"Because Seebees has a friend that stayed with her in college and she invited her if the program is still available,"said Chardin.

"Why we did not ask for this and it is not possible but we can give them a building alone instead,"said Ed.

"She had mentioned if that was possible it was all right,"said her Ladyship.

"So let us know the name tonight and we can have Seebees call them,"said Ed.

"Good, I will just as soon as I see her,"said Chardin.

"Great then that is good, I did think I was going to hear something distressing,"said Grandmother.

"I apologize I should of mentioned I had some good news. I am so embarrassed I did not mean to get you upset, Grandmother,"said Chardin.

"You know you can not do anything wrong my dear,"said Grandmother.

"Thank you,"said her Daughter-in-law.

"No you can never do that my dear that is why we both love you,"said Ed.

"Yes,"said Grandmother.

"Thank you both and I love the both of you and my children too here is Don I wonder Grandmother you are being told to go upstairs or not,"said her Ladyship.

"Here I am Don lets go upstairs right now, he certainly gives me a good amount of time to finish my breakfast,"said his Grandmother.

"Yes, he is very polite I noticed that,"said Ed.

"Now my dear, now that Don took Grandmother upstairs I need to discuss something with you,"said Ed.

"I will get some coffee and what is it, dear.?"said Chardin.

"I need to set up an account in an island in the South Pacific and one with the Mormon Church so you and I are married so then when I leave with her she and I are,"said Ed.

"You are going to have the lawyers draw it up, soon,"said Chardin.

"No, as soon as I know she wants to date and then marry,"said Ed.

"As soon as you can marry then write it up, marry and then both of you leave for another building ok,"said his wife.

"We are going to do just that,"said Ed.

"All right,"said Chardin.

"Then when we are gone you and I are still married of course it is public when we are together so we will not do that. I will see the children and they will think she is just a nurse for a little while,"said Ed.

"True but when you are married we will never see each other because I want her to take care of you alone ok,"said his wife.

"She is going to and she has the help of the other nurses too,"said Ed.

"That is perfect,"said Chardin.

"So when does this all take place. Said his wife.

"Soon, lets not think of that right now,"said Ed.

"Here is our other daughter and her husband that is good timing dear, they arrive and we are all finished with breakfast and lunch, I will ask them if they still need a lunch or a dessert and coffee,"said his wife.

"My darling daughter, how are you and look here is her husband, Lord Roffster and their lovely children my children give me a hug,"said her Ladyship.

"Now give me a big hug too kids and here is my daughter, and hello son-in-law,"said Ed.

"My grandchildren and great grandchildren,"said Grandmother.

"Grandmother,"said the children.

"My babies,"said Grandmother.

"So you go have given it a go and all in fine at home,"said Ed.

"Darling it was not in Siberia and a severe winter,"said her Ladyship.

"I know, "said Ed.

"But you two did work in Finland how was it,"said Grandmother.

"It was in the city,"said Grandmother.

"Yes, each time we moved we were always in the cities,"said the Son-in-law.

"That was good, and now you are both and we need to get you situated we gave you the last apartment with three extra rooms as for the children on the right and at the end of the hall,"said Grandmother.

"Also we have several nurses here to help you with watching your progress,"said Ed.

"We are all so pleased to have you here with us,"said her Mother.

"Yes, we saw your home and how country it was but you both need some time in the city too,"said Ed.

"I quite agreed,"said Lord Roffster.

"Yes I agreed too with my husband,"said Lady Leavlets.

"So let me get all of you some food and the children as well,"said Chardin.

"All right we can use another meal after that long ride,"said Lady Leavlets.

"Oh, by the way dear, if you do not like your name your father wanted me to mention to you that just sit on the throne of France at any time for a new name,"said Lady Chardinrey.

"How about you mother, do you get a name again too.?"said her Daughter.

"No the last time he tried that I divorced him, for three months,"said Chardin.

"You did.?"said Lord Roffster.

"Yes I did but the children were very young,"said Chardin.

"I took her back after three months,"said Ed.

"Sure it was that or be on the curb the next morning,"said Chardin.

"I know,"said Ed.

"That was too funny,"said Lord Roffster.

"After that I did not think so,"said Ed.

"You love Mother to much than to fool around like that,"said their Daughter.

"I know that was the last time and it was a good thing I told her about Lloyd's,"said Ed.

"It was a triumph right dear,"said her Ladyship.

"No comment,"said Ed.

"That is even good,"said her ladyship.

"Now are you two going to have coffee and grandmother too,"said the Granddaughter.

"We all will, providing that your father just listens,"said her Ladyship.

"Yes, I will dear I am all yours,"said Ed.

"All yours,"said Don.

"Who said that,"said Ed.

"Me,"said Don.

"Where are you,"said Ed.

"Under the table,"said Don.

"Ok,"said Ed.

"Here I am,"said Don.

"Oh, there you are,"said Ed.

"Where is Lise,"said Don.

"Lise where are you,"said Ed.

"Under tabler,"said Lise.

"Seebees here is your sister,"said Ed.

"I saw them up stairs,"said Seebees.

"Here is my husband, Roffster, my sister,"said Leavlets.

"Dad just let me know if I did not like my name to go to France and sit on their throne, how about are you I am,"said Seebees.

"Seebees your friend can owe a house that I have now if your sister and her husband does not mind,"said Ed.

"We do not mind staying here father because of the business in the capital yet we have sold ours bought new and put all our stuff in it that we do not need,"said Roffster.

"That is not a problem, I will buy and her friend can rent,"said Ed.

"Now our castle is in the Netherland at the shore is ready to be rented or sold,"said Leavlets.

"It is near the inland I know it very well husband and I rented it for three days,"said Seebees.

"Three days, I told you it was them, Rofster, "said Leavlets.

"Then it is a deal,"said Ed.

"Will the check be in your husband's name,"said her Ladyship.

"Yes, "said Leavlets.

"Please, write out a check mother to Rofster,"said Ed.

"I do need to know and I apologize do you both want this check to be divided. "said Grandmother.

"No, Rofster bought it on his owe for going to business each day,"said Leavlets.

"Yes, and also I gave the other sell to Leavels because it was your gift to her when we were married, "said Rofster.

"We took advantage of your wedding gift because we need to get out of his apartment with the press, "said Leavlets.

"Oh, and thank you for the house to use and my name,"said Rofster.

"Well good and you welcome and Gale will be pleased with the decisions of the names soon too,"said Ed.

"They will like the castle I was looking forward to returning each weekend but it is fine right here too, thank you too for the apartment it is very comfortable. "said Rofster.

"Yes, thank you both it is very pleasant upstairs,"said Leavlets.

"When the other house is ready Seebees can have Grandmother's house and the three of us and the children will live in the new building,"said Ed.

"Where do we say,"said Leavlets.

"In our old house with a brand new kitchen,"said Ed.

"Thank you Ed but I will stay right here in my home with Seebees and her husband and child,"said Grandmother.

"Sorry, Mother you know that you are the only target here to be picked on,"said Ed.

"I think that is Don who enjoys me we are on the elevator everyday together,"said Grandmother.

"Yes, me,"said Don.

"Opened your mouth to wide this time and got it closed too,"said her Ladyship.

"We have talked our way into an early dinner so why not have it now,"said Ed.

"I ask the chef to prepare a ham dinner this evening if it is ready we can sit down,"said Her Ladyship.

"What Don,"said Ed.

"What Lise,"said Lise.

"It is here the food, what a house keeper you have mother,"said her Ladyship.

"What happened to the staff in the other house,"said Leavlets.

"Seebees had the chef and cook and a new gardener too,"said Ed.

"Dinner,"said Don.

"I am with you,"said Grandmother.

"Don will stay with me,"said Grandmother.

"Yes,"said Don.

"Lise is with me,"said Ed.

"An me,"said her Mother.

"Will, what about you,"said Seebees.

"I want the cottage,"said Will.

"I know it, I knew he was going to say that,"said Seebees.

"Thank you, Seebees you are truly a Princess,"said Will.

"Thank you, me Lord and you are truely a Prince, Prince Wilfred Ets Marie,"said See.

"Now shall we go into the dinning room,"said Will.

"Yes, we shall thank, my Lord,"said See.

"My Lord, "said her Ladyship Chardinrey.

"Me Lady,"said Ed.

"Me Grandmother,"said Don.

"My lord, thank you,"said Grandmother.

"My Ladies,"said Rofster.

"Me,"said Lise.

"Me,"said Leavlets.

"Now all seated then I will say prayers,"said Ed.

"Dear, here is your napkin, Don,"said her Ladyship.

"We can now have some music,"said Ed.

"All are forgiven if you do not want a turkey again tonight is ham,"said their Mother.

"Maybe again,"said Lise.

"Remember Will and Ed and we went to the cottage and will would not go home at all,"said Leavlets.

"I forgot all about that but I remember going home and Ed was getting his mopid to give him a ride home,"said See.

"He went up to the house and got the mopid and then we walked back,"said Leavlets.

"I remember because I ask if you wanted me to pick you up in the car,"said Grandmother.

"I said no, because I though we were all going to have a ride,"said Seebees.

"You mean we walked. Now I know why we walked,"said Leavlets.

"Yes, that is right I did,"said Seebees.

"Seebees you did think we would all have an individual ride home,"said Leavlets.

"Yes,"said Seebees.

"Now children lets have dinner and not so much interuptions with laughter calm down and lets enjoy our first meal together,"said her Ladyship.

"I do have one thing to say, I did in fact pick all of you up because your brother ask me too,"said Grandmother.

"That is right,"said Leavlets.

"Ok, Ok, I was wrong but we did walk a little bit,"said Seebees.

"Me,"said Lise.

"Yes, you Lise do you want more food,"said her Mother.

"Yes, please,"said Lise.

"Does anyone want anymore or another coffee.?"said her Ladyship.

"We will help the children, Mother,"said Leavlets.

"Good and I will get the coffee, I need the tell all of you, this is the last meal together until Sunday evening is our only meal as adults alright,"said her Ladyship.

"That sounds delightful and I do need someone to help me alright,"said Seebees.

"Yes, you and Leavlets will have a staff to help you, remember we have the staff from two buildings also,"said her Ladyship.

"So the meal plan will go very well,"said Leavlets.

"Yes indeed and if you have any medications the Nurse will give them to you,"said her Ladyship.

"I am sure she will pick a time to give them out individually too, so that does not lead to any accidents with the little ones,"said their Grandmother.

"I agree, just later on tonight the nurses are going to be in the living room to explain to many of us individually about medications and the procedures,"said her Ladyship.

"They are aware of the size of our family right now and you can invite them in to see all of you in your apartments this week, so they can observe the children as well,"said Ed.

"Good so we can see them tonight too, I need that,"said Leavlets.

"Then it is all settled and the three nurses have titles for the sake of the family right now,"said her Ladyship.

"For me, ok, they all are,"said Ed.

"Yes, dear we know and now I hope we all can go into the living room, and if anyone who needs the power room, please do so,"said her Ladyship.

"Great meal,"said Rofster.

"It was devine,"said Leavlets.

"Yes, mine,"said Lise.

"Alright Don, we are going into the living room right now ok,"said Grandmother.

"Yes, "said Don.

"That was a good meal Mother, thank you Rofster did you see the puzzle we are doing,"said Will.

"I saw it earlier but I did not know which building it was, is this where your brother Ed lives, "said Rofster.

"Not any more he duplicated it for himself and Owns, you met Princess Ownsite his wife. ?"said Will.

"Yes, several years ago at that building,"said Rofster.

"Leavlets look at this building, you two once visited,"said Will.

"Lets see I think this one goes right here, it looks like the foundation what do you think Ed is that right,"said Rofster.

"I think it is, is it Will.?"said Ed.

"Yes it is,"said Will.

"If we are going to build this we have to have it on a table that we do not need, this one right here is perfect, so check with your Mother,"said Ed.

"That is fine there Will,"said her Ladyship.

"We can do this even tomorrow, or do you think we will have it done by tonight,"said Will.

"It does mention in the directions it takes a while,"said Rofster.

"That is at least a week or two,"said Ed.

"Maybe even three or four months,"said Rofster.

"My dear here is some coffee and cake and cookies,"said her Ladyship.

"Thank you dear, do you want to help,"said Ed.

"No thank you dear, now Seebees I think you should talk to the nurse. Lady Urnlee," said her Mother.

"I will go upstairs and talk to her,"said Seebees.

"She has an office around the corner for anyone during the day who needs a nurse. So let me know when you are finshed and Leavlets can talk to her, ok. "said her Mother.

"Dear, how is everything going,"said her Ladyship.

"Thanks for the coffee and the cake to terrific too,"said Rofster.

"Everything is home made and staring tonight all of our rooms have coffee and snacks also all are home made too,"said her Ladyship.

"Oh, we can have a snack at night if we need one, we started doing that just a few months ago, and it works out quite well, instead of going to the kitchen,"said her son-in-law.

"That is good, all of these apartments have kitchens in them,"said Ed.

"Are any of you on a time schedule for this or do you give yourselves several hours to get it done,"said her Ladyship.

"No amount of time but I think this takes a couple of days we do not want to know the time it is in an envelope and we will look later,"said Will.

"Oh, the time was put there by the company, the manufacturer put it in an envelope,"said her Ladyship.

"No, I put in insde that, that is yours,"said Will.

"What, look, he is using my best stationary, Grandmother. "said their Mother.

"Oh, no you are very clever, Will,"said Grandmother.

"I did not think you would mind it,"said Will.

"That is alright, I do not mind it at all,"said his Mother.

"Thank you Mother, you are quiet helpful,"said Will.

"Thank you dear, I do mind a bit. Have a good time with the puzzle,"said his Mother.

"Mother I am back from talking with Lady Urnlee,"said

"Leavlets please go see the nurse, a left and the first door,"said her Mother.

"Alright, I will return soon,"said Leavlets.

"Then we might want to go upstairs for the rest of the evening,"said Lady Chardinrey.

"We can start right now Don and Lise and myself,"said Grandmother.

"I am going to stay in Lises room until all of you are upstairs alright.,'said their Grandmother.

"Thank you so much Mother, and the nannies will get them all ready,"said her Ladyship.

"Will we need to stop this puzzle soon,"said his Mother.

"We can stop now,"said Will.

"Good lets call it a night,"said Ed.

"Yes, it is late,"said Rofster.

"Here we are Lise we are right behind you. Are you going with Grandmother too.?"said her Mother.

"Yes, bye,"said Lise.

"There goes the elevator we could all take the ones that are connected to our rooms,"said Ed.

"Alright that might be a good idea,"said Lady Chardinrey.

"See you all very soon,"said Ed.

"Right,"said Rofster.

"There Ed we are here and now we might want some snacks, but first I will check up on the children and Grandmother,"said her Ladyship.

"Ok, I will get things ready and now look at that cake,"said Ed.

"Will is in the shower, Don and Lise are and Grandmother is too, "said her Ladyship.

"They are almost all set for the night,"said Ed.

"Yes, I will check on them in a little while,"said Chardin.

"Here are your choices this evening,"said Ed.

"Fine selection,"said Chardin.

"All the children look good and healthy,"said Ed.

"Yes, and I am glad the two mothers to be are in good shape too,"said Chardin.

"I am glad we have enough apartments in these new castle it should be finished in a few months and am glad I did the work constantly even as it was extra longer than I did plan on,"said Ed.

"I know it was a long time and yet all of the inside a done except of gold trim on one floor,"said Chardin.

"I am putting an extra wing on so we can get some privacy, they are going extra fast with overtime too,"said Ed.

"It is expensive,"said his wife.

"No, I do not mean overtime just two extra shifts and men,"said Ed.

"It does seem to be a large project that we have but Ed did his home in record time,"said her Ladyship.

"The coliseum seems to always have a profit for the building so I think we can go ahead with the construction costs,"said Ed.

"I know it will go up fast, it is more than three-quarters completed inside as it is,"said her Ladyship.

"I know when we took away the floors from the coliseum to finally complete the house we did not loose any parking spaces,"said Ed.

"I know,"said her Ladyship.

"When Edvard did the house and duplicated it he made enough parking lots under and above the ground and so did I,"said Ed.

"This I am aware of but we are nearly completed, do we need this other building,"said Ed's wife.

"With our growing family this will stop anyone from leaving if they wish to,"said Ed.

"We will do it,"said his wife.

"Thank you,"said Ed.

"If they want to raise the children away from us that is allright as long as they are here,"said Ed's wife.

"I did do want you told me to do, I ask her out,"said Ed.

"When are you two going out.?"said his wife.

"I know you have aright to know, but she informed me she would never do this unless I was on my death bed,"said Ed.

"What do you mean,"said his wife.

"She will live and take care of me when I am on my death bed and only then,"said Ed.

"What is she going to do,"said his wife.

"She will nurse all of us and when I am on my dealth bed then we can move if you do not want the children to see me that way,"said Ed.

"No, I do not want them to see you in bed,"said her Ladyship.

"Because you are aware of us, with my intentions then she thinks we should wait for the time of my health being impaired to be somewhere else"said Ed.

"I god, I do not believe this, she is thinking of the children,"said his wife.

"That is what she repeatly said."according to Ed.

"I am so grateful I need you here and I know she can endure this but I can not,"said his wife.

"I told you the will is all set and for you, her and all the children, and also the business too,"said Ed.

"I did sign that will you know that,"said her Ladyship.

"I know and so did she that when we are living together in my new home and hers, it is hers when I die,"said Ed.

"Thank god now I can be relaxed in my owe home and not worry about the way you are going to die,"said Ed's wife.

"I will not die in front of them, I promised you that,"said Ed.

"Thank you, now lets have some more food,"said her Ladyship.

"That is the best idea I have heard all night,"said Ed.

"I do not mean to be insensitive to you but I need to know when this buildings will be done,"said his Wife.

"Inspire of the newest addition we could be in the main building on the second floor only and they work towards the top or attic where we will live,"said Ed.

"Yes, and how long,"said his Wife.

"We can be living on the first floor in three weeks but due to the noise if we wait until they are in the other building working it could take six months,"said Ed.

"We can wait,"said her Ladyship.

"The new building will have its own foundation in one week,"said Ed.

"We do need that building done and to have extra space is a God sent just like you,"said his Wife.

"Thank you dear,"said Ed.

"You welcome I guess this is it for the snacks,"said his Wife.

"No, there is more in the right here. Oh, now the paper work was submitted last week and I forward it off to the lawyers right now, "said Ed.

"So then what.?"said his Wife.

"My approval on the computer will start the work in the Mormon church and in the South Pacific,"said Ed.

"What Island.?"said his Wife.

"That is for the lawyers to know and if you want to know it is best to ask when my will is read, but there will be an island somewhere,"said Ed.

"This is then no one can find out so easily.?"said his Wife.

"Right and it is important to you and the family,"said Ed.

"I know,"said his Wife.

"Good so we have another discussion I found out today the doctor called and he visited today to tell me that my death will be fast,"said Ed.

"He did not want to disturb me or the children,"said his Wife.

"No, he just spoke to me only,"said Ed.

"Ok, that is alright,"said his Wife.

"I will know when I am going to die and I have plenty of time to leave and to be in my other house by the shore,"said Ed.

"Ok,I just do not want anyone along here unless I thought you were going to be confined to your bed for months at a time,"said his wife.

"No, but I want you to know there is someone who has an interest in me and will look after all the children when I am gone if you die too,"said Ed.

"Right I forgot we have to make it look that you are returning soon for my sake as well as the children,"said his Wife.

"Even inspire of the funeral all the children will anticipate you returning deep inside them,"said his wife.

"Why not have the funeral in the new castle and live there and I am buried there and the children would not have to know for awhile,"said Ed.

"Good, but we will live here all the time and when you are ready to die you and all of your nurses can be there,"said Lady Chardinrey.

"That is a great idea,"said Ed.

"This will have to do, and I will appreciate that house even more,"said his Wife.

"Why I can visit when you are in your grave,"said his Wife.

"Good, and here are the rules I what quiet and no noise, and this masoleum will be in the new building.

"Yes, of course I will make sure of that I am there,"said his Wife.

"Remember no one enters without signing the book and bring flowers and no radios. I do not even want someone talking in that part of the house,"said Ed.

"That even goes for Edvard when he lives here when we die he does not control that part of the house,"said Ed.

"Then you are going to have to use your title of King Edlance I as of now,"said her Ladyship.

"Ok, we do have a throne here that looks like Versailles,"said Ed.

"That is not good enough, use Belgium they are friends and give her respect and your small children, dieing as King,"said his Wife.

"Yourself, are you all right being Duchess Chardinrey,"said Ed.

"Yes, my brief time being Queen Chardinrey is a better balance to know Lady Urnlee is now Queen making me even more, less annoyed about anything,"said his Wife.

"Good, so we agree and I sent a message and the computer showed me my recent photo and I will use it and it should be on the tel tomorrow,"said Ed.

"Now does this avoid Versailles.?"said his Wife.

"No, I will be there for one day and then in the Belgium throne room only as a photo, then many others might do the same.?"said Ed.

"We are due for this again, this project has been on hold for some time now,"said her Ladyship.

"Also it is the legal premise of an assination attempts, so it does not occur again. We have three volumes with peoples names not wanting for this happen so why not do this again,"said Ed.

"We are going too and so will Lady Urnlee before and after my death,"said Ed.

"Now that is alright so we only do it by photos.?"said his Wife.

"Yes and give does give an opportunity for another volume,"said Ed.

"Oh, it is now a little bit upsetting,"said his wife.

"Remember, no radios and complete silence,"said Ed.

"Very funny,"said his Wife.

"Who is this why it is Lise,"said her Mother.

"Sorry, Lady Chardinrey,"said her Nanny.

"Ok, she can sleep within us,"said her Mother.

"Now who is this.?"said Ed.

"Lise,"said their Daughter.

"Ok, sleep right here and we are going to talk for awhile,"said her Dad.

"She is so good, taking the extra bedroom next to us,"said her Mom.

"It is your room as a living room or sitting room so this is the only way in so I think she knows that,"said Ed.

"She does, and also "No doors please "this was her statement the last time,"said her Mother.

"So it is true she does fear another entering,"said Ed.

"No, she wants to sleep with us so she knows we are here and will listen for someone in the morning so that is why I turn on the light immediately,"said Lady Chardinrey.

"She does not have any fears of strangers, entering,"said Ed.

"No, remember the firemen and the time the police entered her room and it was a bat,"said her Mother.

"I remember what she did,"said her Father.

"She got up and went into our bedroom,"said her Mother.

"That is right she did and she did not say one word when she woke up,"said her Father.

"Not even one word when she walked into our room,"said her Mother.

"With this we need to get some sleep,"said her Husband.

"Right, as late as it is, it is going to be morning time very soon,"said his Wife.

Chapter 10

"Hello. Good morning Lise, lets let your Daddy sleep this morning and we can go down stairs for a while,"said her Mother.

"Mommy,"said Lise.

"Good morning. There is Grandmother, you are up early, and you had breakfast,"said Lady Chardin.

"Good morning and Lise let me take her while you get her food ready,"said her Grandmother.

"She was sleeping with us and that is why she is with me,"said her Mother.

"Yes, why so early.? "said her Mother-in-law.

"I heard her talking to herself so I did not want to disturb Ed,"said her Ladyship.

"Lise did the two of you almost wake up Ed your father.? "said her Grandmother.

"No, "said Lise.

"That is good your Dad needs his sleep, right,"said her Grandmother.

"No,"said Lise.

"Ok, here is your cereal and some toast if you want it,"said Grandmother.

"Maybe some milk, Lise,"said her Mother.

"No,"said Lise.

"Here it is,"said her Mother.

"And you dear, are you going to have some food at all.? "said her Mother-in-law.

"Yes, I have my plate right here,"said Chardin.

"Now we have two others, I will get their food,"said their Grandmother.

"Don and Will, good morning,"said their Mother.

"Good morning, I will get my own grandmother thank you,"said Will.

"Thank you Will and good morning to you too,"said his Grandmother.

"Goood Mronning,"said Don.

"Donald, good morning here is your food,"said Grandmother.

"Chardin, they are fed and I am going into the living room to finish the newsapaper,"said Grandmother.

"You could use the computer it is cleaner,"said Chardin.

"That is true, I think Ed said he was going to leave the computer on the newspapers sections for us and give the staff the papers,"said Grandmother.

"It is already for you Grandmother I saw it was on before I decided to have breakfast,"said Will.

"Nice, then I am going with my coffee to the other room and send them in when they are ready, ok,"said their Grandmother.

"Sure they just can not wait to get in their to finish that, "said her Ladyship.

"The puzzle, may I Mother be excused,"said Will.

"Yes you may, I see you have had enough,"said his Mother.

"Oh good, Thank you, Mother,"said Will.

"Grandmother look two buttered hard rolls and some pastries and a very nice,"said Will.

"Don and Lise do you want any more food,"said her Mother.

"Yes, eggs and bacon two please,"said Don.

"Here is two of each,"said his Mother.

"Good,"said Don.

"What,"said his Mother.

"Than you,"said Don.

"Lise, "said her Mother.

"Eggs and baco,"said Lise.

"Here they are,"said her Mother.

"Thank boo,"said Lise.

"Your welcome the both of you, and you both eat so much food,"said their Mother.

"Here is dad,"said her Mother.

"Good morning and my two babies,"said Ed.

"Good morning Dear, "said chardin.

"Good morning, I had breakfast upstairs and gave the rest of the food the children,"said Ed.

"Good you were asleep and I smelled the food down here, so here we are,"said his Wife.

"There is some let so I will have some more,"said Ed.

"We are going into the bath and wash up and we will be with Grandmother she is reading right now,"said his Wife.

"See you all there very soon babies, in the living room,"said Ed.

"Good morning, Edward,"said his Mother.

"Good morning, Mother, I need to tell you something,"said Ed.

"What is it,"said his Mother.

"The main house is completed enough for me to stay there with Lady Urnlee as my nurse, "said Ed.

"You know she is your wife and you can not return here,"said his Mother.

"Yes, I know but it seems to be ending I did not tell her the pain is very severe and the male nurses have been waiting for me so I can have my me next shot in the hallway,"said Ed.

"She does not know this.? "said his Mother.

"No, I use the excuse that I am going to sere the children down the hall,"said Ed.

"So tell her now and go to the other building,"said his Mother.

"Please have my clothes and all of my belongings in the new house, ok,"said Ed.

"Yes now here she is and tell her so you can stop your next painful moment or I will,"said his Mother.

"Here is Grandmother Lise and Don and your dad,"said her Ladyship.

"Dear I have to tell you that I need to go with the nurses to the completed part of the building and stay there and the other nurses will check up on the girls progress. Right now my progress is getting worse,"said Ed.

"Let me walk you to the door that is attached to the your autos,"said his Wife.

"Daddy,"said Lise.

"Oh, a hug for me,"said Ed.

"Don, I want a hug too and so does your Dad,"said his Wife.

"Now all of you go sit down with Will,"said their Father.

"Will how about a hug too,"said his Father.

"Sure I do not mind and of course Mom,"said Will.

"Now lets talk in the other room, Ed,"said his Wife.

"Ed, let me tell you something and you can meet Chardin down the hallway, ok,"said his Mother.

"Bye dear, I hope you know how happy you have made me,"said his Mother.

"Me too,"said said Ed.

"There ain't a tribe in the whole that has made me more happier than yours, "said his Mother.

"I am so glad to hear that, it has made me very proud to have you as my Mother,"said Ed.

"Thank you son, now go Lady Chardinrey is waiting for you,"said his Mother.

"Bye Dad see you in a little while. Say good bye and wave to your Dad, Lise and Don,"said Will.

"Yes, good bye son, we love you,"said his Mother.

"I saw his photo in the computer he made a fine King of France,"said Will.

"That photo, is it in the newspapers.?"said his Grandmother.

"No, it is tonight,"said Will.

"Look I am going to turn the computer around and see he is in his red soldier uniform,"said Will.

"He looks very handsome, that is why I always loved your Grandfather who looked just like him, you are older and have to know I married your Grandfather brother first and became Queen of Norway,"said his Grandmother.

"He was dieing and my marriage to him saved the money in the family and your uncle became King after he departed,"said Will's Grandmother.

"So when Dad is Duke in another day who is going to be the next King,"said Will.

"Maybe no one until they apply,"said his Grandmother.

"I would for the assignation book volume number four, but I do not want to take away from his picture you love so much, Grandmother,"said Will.

"Thank you but I think you should wait until you are maybe eighteen alright, let your brother-in-law have his as Lord Rofster,"said his Grandmother.

"Do you think he would be up to it,"said Will.

"Yes, just like you are very strong right now,"said his Grandmother.

"Thank you, Grandmother I think being a soldier can wait a little while longer,"said Will.

"You are a stronger soldier,"said his Grandmother.

"Thank you Grandmother, here is Mother right now, look Mother, Dad is on the computer and he is in the newspapers this evening.!"said Will.

"Yes, he looks very handsome in his soldier's uniform and it is in the newspapers tonight.? "said his Mother.

"It is a very good photo,"said Grandmother.

"Yes, it truly is,"said Ed's wife.

"Now how about some more coffee, Mother.? "said her Ladyship.

"That would be nice,"said Grandmother.

"Is this newspaper just for us or is it international,"said her Ladyship.

"All for the world to see. All are listed right here. Is he going to have a copy tomorrow for himself.? "said Will.

"Sure,"said his Mother.

"Now that Lise and Don are out of the room getting the other puzzle for me. Is he going to return again,"said Will.

"No will he not,"said his Mother.

"Here is Lise and Don with the new puzzles, thanks kids,"said Will.

"Ok,"said Don.

"Oda,"said Lise.

"Now children do you want some lunch, it will be here soon,"said her Ladyship.

"Yes, "said Don.

"Yessss,"said Lise.

"What are we having.? "said their Grandmother.

"Here is the menu,"said her Ladyship.

"Thank you, I forgot all about these things are in print everyday,"said their Grandmother.

"Did you realized that Rofster went to work and the two sisters are walking outside their all the children,"said Chardin.

"Good routine, bye the way tonight you will be the Queen of France,"said Will.

"That's right, my Norway lasted just one evening,"said the Grandmother.

"Daddy,"said Lise.

"Where,"said Don.

"Stop crying Lise,"said her Mother.

"Don, stop that,"said his Grandmother.

"Stop acting like Upstarts the two of you,"said their Mother.

"Yes, oh Lise that's not you or Don, that is so funny,"said their Grandmother.

"Ok, said Lise.

"I stip,"said Don.

"Yes, you are stip,"said Grandmother.

"The nurse called, Lady Urnlee,"said the Duchess.

"How is he.? "said his Mother.

"He was looking at the paper and saw the tel, and his photo on the evening news and it is 7:30 p.m. and he died a few minutes ago,"said the Duchess.

"Now what about her.?"said Grandmother.

"They were both married the minute they got into the building a ceremony was done and a new license was given to them immediately,"said her Ladyship.

"She is now the Duchess,"said the Grandmother.

"She let me know there was some enjoyment so she does not know if there will be another baby soon or not. This I did not mind hearing. "said Lady Chardinrey.

"She was nice enough to let us know there could be another child soon,"said the Grandmother.

"Call her back and let her know after the burial, to move back in for the girls need her to watch over them and your future children,"said Grandmother.

"We discuss that earlier yesterday and she did plan to return after the funeral, "said her Ladyship.

"Just remind her,"said the Grandmother.

"I could not stay said Lady Urnlee I was talking to you from the auto. I brought the uniform you wanted to the funeral home so he would be ready to be in the new castle tomorrow morning or tonight it is up to you,"said Lady Urnlee.

"No, we will begin tomorrow and I am glad you decide to stay here with us,"said Lady Chardinrey.

"I am glad to that you returned to us,"said the Grandmother.

"Now dry your eyes and we will get some sleep, or just rest for a little while."The hallway here looks quiet and the children I can here are watching the tel, I will let Seebees know and you two go to your apartments, ok,"said her Ladyship.

"Alright,"said Lady Urnlee.

"Now Leavlets I need to tel you and your husband something. Now grandmother I do not think anyone is going to leave their own apartment so I will talk to you when the service tomorrow is over,"said her Ladyship.

"Yes,"said Grandmother.

"Yes, Edmond the service was exciting and wonderful and he is buried in the new building and the entire cemented structure is waiting for the building completion and his placement too,"said her Ladyship.

"Thank you, said Lise.

"Lise gave me some flowers I think they are from the hallway.This is what your Father wanted that your lives are not interrupted. Yes, thank you, good bye. I love you too. Now Lise look at all these flowers lets put them into this vase,"said her Mother.

"Oh, those flowers look so beautiful and dear so did this empty spot in this arrangement so why not put them all together,"said their Grandmother.

"Why not it is better this way, see Lise they all look so nice together,"said her Mother.

"Don, look,"said Lise.

"You, did,"said Don.

"Don, it looks very nice,"said his Mother.

"Ok,"said Don.

"Now the will was read and Lady Urnlee is going to stay here and still watch for those new born babies and to help out so we have all the help we need and nannies too,"said her Ladyship.

"It does same a bit warm in here,"said the Grandmother.

"I am going up stairs for a second ok,"said Chardin.

"Will, play with the puzzle again, ok, help me,"said Grandmother.

"Grandmother we have over half done and it seems to be endless,"said Will.

"It is and it is difficult, it is not the kind of puzzle you put together on a flat table,"said his Grandmother.

"Here, this goes right there,"said Grandmother.

"Well I am back and it looks as if I am going to have a baby,"said Lady Chardinrey.

"Oh, my goodness dear, you are in good health so why not and what a good memory of Ed,"said Grandmother.

"Yes it is, I did have something to share with you what about Lady Urnlee would that be good news too.? "said her Ladyship.

"Yes, need need little feet running around especially in the new castle,"said Grandmother.

"That is for sure we do need that to happen,"said her Ladyship.

"Yes we do, right Will,"said the Grandmother.

"Yes, a new baby brother,"said Will.

"Or me,"said Lise.

"Yes, Seebees you are going to have a sister,"said their Grandmother.

"Mother here sit down, I am so pleased,"said her daughter.

"Leavlets you are going to be a sister. She said she is resting and tired but this news did wake here up and she loves you,"said Seebees.

"Now let me tell Edvard, hello, dear I need to tel you are going to be an uncle. Yes, thank you and I love you too,"said his Mother.

"What did he say.? "said his Grandmother.

"He said that I just called. Owns here this,"said her Ladyship.

"Are you going to let the press know,"said the Grandmother.

"It is already there see the tel, here I am on the tel kids,"said her Ladyship.

"Yes, you are,"said the Grandmother.

"Mom,"said Lise.

"Mom,"said Don.

"Mommy you are correct,"said his Mother.

"They discuss the death and separation and the new wedding very nicely, as a helpful part of his silent death,"said Grandmother.

"It was silent and that is the way she watching me or someone that she recommends, whoever I need you with me Grandmother are always with her children,"said her Ladyship.

"Thank you dear but I have no intentions of going right now,"said their Grandmother.

"Good I am counting on you to help and you always do and have,"said Chardin.

"The rest of the children are upstairs for the afternoon and we need to sort of some the Ed's things. Everything in here stays here, is there anything that you want to bring to the new house.?"said her Ladyship.

"No, nothing in this house is going and if it does it will be in my apartment. I thought of that myself a few days ago and there really is nothing to be moved,"said Grandmother.

"So now all we need to do today is look at the antique we have in our parts of the cities such as Paris and buy them from our own shops and place them into our new castle,"said her Ladyship.

"I do appreciate Ed and Owns for staring us on our very own antiques shops and we still do have an update on the computer too,"said the Grandmother.

"We need to first find out about the Belgium shops first,"said her Ladyship.

"Hello, again, said Lady Urnlee.

"Hello, Dear,"said Grandmother.

"We are just discussing our new antiques for the other home,"said Chardin.

"I heard antiques and I did check up on the girls and faithfully many times during all these sudden events so I am sorry that I forgot when I was doing my nursing,"said Lady Urnlee.

"The first day I was with Ed he told me that in the old warehouse that was for the children Ed and Owns took care of, he said he ordered this last month many antiques from the towns in Belgium and from Paris too."Sorry I forgot,"said Lady Urnlee.

"That is wonderful news,"said Grandmother.

"When he told me he said he did think that the corrective behavior would help him,"said Ed's wife.

"It did,"said Chardin.

"I let him know it would on a temportay basis for that particular time and place and the therapy of doing things to make someone else happy is just what it does and his illness was still going to take over,"said Ed's Nurse.

"He is still thoughtful and helpful,"said Chardin.

"He did indicate that the warehouse did not have all of the antiques and new will need more,"said Lady Urnlee.

"He is helpful even when we do not exspect it,"said Granmother.

"How many pieces do you know,"said Chardin.

"There is seventy-five and they are all on the first floor and it is very crowded,"said Urnlee.

"All should be alright there we do not need the heat on and all should be removed before the winter is here, so I guess we are alright,"said Chardin.

"He mentioned the gardener looks at them everyday and opens up all the windows,"said Urnlee.

"Good, I will find the receipts and the gardener later, I left a message to the housekeepers, so thank you Urnlee it is good to know all this because anything else is bought,"said Chardin.

"Yes, that is correct and thank you so much, now we do not have to spend any more money getting this castle furnished,"said the Grandmother.

"I hope I was a help,"said Urnlee.

"Yes, we saved a lot of money,"said Chardin.

"Yes, now we can buy for the bedrooms,"said the Grandmother.

"Making all the rooms look lovely instead of that instilled look the public always think these castle have,"said her Ladyship.

"It will look nice if you do use anything Ed had purchased that was what he wanted to happen,"said Urnlee.

"Yes, he did want that,"said her Ladyship.

"You know Lady Chardin if you were to furnish that new castle you will make the magazines and home issues, "said Urnlee.

"You must call me Chardin, the press will do a lot of damage if they though we were not friends and you are like a sister to me,"said her Ladyship.

"I never thought of that I will for now on,"said Urnlee.

"You are right I could win a few awards too,"said Chardin.

"Yes, you could Chardin, and Urnlee it is still Grandmother to you, ok,"said the Grandmother."

"Thank you I will,"said Urnlee.

"This could make a big difference in our lives, this new house.?"said Grandmother.

"Yes, it will and buying more for the bedrooms is very true it will enhance the building,"said Urnlee.

"I heard from the housekeeper, the receipts are written and will be mailed to us,"said her Ladyship.

"Good I hope he did not spend to much,"said the Grandmother.

"He did not say,"said Urnlee.

"I did not think so,"said her Ladyship.

"He might of,"said the Grandmother.

"What is this now. A message.? "said her Ladyship.

"What is it, is there something wrong,"said the Grandmother.

"It is from Gale. In Versailles,"said her Ladyship.

"I do not believe what I am reading, our son Ed has been removed from working and being in charge of the businesses so now it is for Edlance or myself to be in charge of the corporations,"said her Ladyship.

"I do not know what to do I can get my son from Newport, Rhode Island to do it,"said her Ladyship.

"He is doing such a good job of it so far in the states.! "said the Grandmother.

"He will have to leave and enter on another name so for using another passport is never a problem for us,"said her Ladyship.

"Remember when Versailles had the alien web and there were parts of it yet unable to see the roof of the tunnels or caves it was called. At times it would be there and Ed did mention that they had found at few people there from governmental offices,"said her Ladyship.

"Your not looking for Ed,"said the Grandmother.

"No, he does not want to return we discussed this in detail,"said her Ladyship.

"Then what,"said the Grandmother.

"Do you remember Sean as his Passport is written up for Paris only, and how his wife just lets him visit Versailles and he does what he wants and his very moody and his wife is afraid of him,"said her Ladyship.

"Yes, he did not even show up for his own father's funeral,"said her Ladyship.

"That part of just his mood and behavior that can not be stopped,"said his Grandmother.

"Yes, but I do need to other brother who showed up his Paris passport is under Detva Dovbonovich. I need to get my hair done in a cornrow and with an extension helmet for only the back to below my neck all of black diamonds, "said her Ladyship.

"You are going to the caves to find Michael if he is the real one,"said his Grandmother.

"I heard of a statesman was found there and returned,"said Urnlee.

"You would need to have a gift, besides the duplicate of Michael, can you imagine having a stranger in the house,"said his Grandmother.

"He is not a stranger he went and is part of Michaels' life,"said her Ladyship.

"Oh,"said his Grandmother.

"I need that group of people who investigated the caves, I do have the three females doctors names because I wanted them to look under these buildings,"said her Ladyship.

"You were, Oh.?"said their Grandmother.

"I can call them right now and have them meet me tomorrow at Versailles, and I will leave right now, tonight,"said her Ladyship.

"You need a gift,"said the Grandmother.

"I have one it is your black diamond head dress. I need that gold mess from the hallway soldier,"said her Ladyship.

"I am insured for others who do not return,"said the Grandmother.

"I do not think the aliens can. Get my maids and yours in here right now and they can start on my weave,"said her Ladyship.

"All of the maids are going to weave my hair now, you are a good staff and I know you can get this done, I am going to visit Versailles tonight,"said her Ladyship.

"I know how to do the front part,"said Urnlee.

"Good that is all I need, then I can put the back into extensions I have myself,"said her Ladyship.

"Sure I can start right now,"said Urnlee.

"Thank you, get all those wigs and extensions from my dresser, please,"said her Ladyship.

"Yes. My Lady "said the Maid.

"Your going to have to sit right here and do not move at all,"said Urnlee.

"Mother call Detva and have him here in an hour in this house, please right now. Thank you,"said her Ladyship.

"I will, I should have never told you I was a real blonde since that time it has been, please right now for everything,"said her Grandmother.

"Is there an answer to the page, "said Detva's Mother.

"Wait, now what did he write. Yes, he will be here in a few minutes with his brother,"said Grandmother.

"Mike knows he is leaving do not say anything about this all of us are discussing the business and how to run it for Gale,"said her Ladyship.

"I know this is not proper or ethical but do you want two sleeping pills that were Ed's in case something goes wrong and Mike does not want to go into the tunnels or is to frighten,"said Urnlee.

"Yes, I can give them to him saying it is good to have these pills when in the tunnels only,"said her Ladyship.

"I hate to do this but he has not never been the same to me and is very impolite to me and others,"said his Grandmother.

"It is the best thing to do before he has someone harm him,"said his Mother.

"I called Gale and let him know about the female doctors who will meet me there and he said he might not be awake but to go with his butler and then he will only see us leave,"said her Ladyship.

"I bet he mentioned a gift for the aliens, right,"said the grandmother.

"Yes, he did something that is of jewels or gold,"said her Ladyship.

"The black diamonds are attached to black gold and those jewels shine all the time,"said the Grandmother.

"Better get the gold mesh from the soldier, alright please take another maid. Ok. This is very important we need that in good condition,"said the Grandmother.

"The housekeeper is here,"said Urnlee.

"My Lady, Do you want any dinners prepared for now and some sandwiches for traveling,"said the Housekeeper.

"Yes, we do and you do not have to return again, just have a few more maids here alright and thank you I will be gone for about one day,"said her Ladyship.

"Thank you, I will be at the end of the hallway at the front door Lady Chardinrey, and of course I will inform the butler to open the door,"said the Housekeeper.

"It is Peter and he will be using the tunnels,"said her Ladyship.

"Very good I will let the security guards know and automobile and ready and some of your belongings as well are there and a gift for Gale a large ring. Thank you My Lady and please have a safe journey,"said the Housekeeper.

"Yes, I will,"said her Ladyship.

"You do not get any better than her Chardin if the enemy was in here she would be the first to take a bullet for you,"said the Grandmother.

"I know and I know her for the last so many years she was crying in the other room and I did want to dismissed before she broke down again,"said Chardin.

"She did take it badly,"said the Grandmother.

"Why did you not cry so much,"said Urnlee.

"My mother-in-law and I had an occupation of asthma and we do not cry so easily, because of our youth as a child it for us was a full time job, as an asthmatic,"said her Ladyship.

"Do not so funny on my creativity I am ranking over you remember,"said the Grandmother.

"Ranking, that was rather funny Oh, I am so sorry here I am thinking of a militarian position, yet as asthma a disease I never heard of it used that way,"said Urnlee.

"It was Mother has many titles in Europe due to that disease,"said Lady Chardinrey.

"I apolgize,"said Urnlee.

"Accepted, but what you are doing to my hair right now is making up for what we did not set you up for it was not intentional. Look at the good work she is doing. "said her Ladyship.

"If she does mine right now I will pay her for the both of us,"said the Grandmother.

"Yes, that is right. How about using and in your name Ed's auto his rolls we do not need it at all,"said her Ladyship.

"Thank you,"said Urnlee.

"Now here is your son Peter and he is ready and the auto is filled up with food too,"said the Grandmother.

"Hello, Mother,Grandmother and Urnlee with your mother it looks so nice,"said Detva.

"Yes, I need to look proper and jeweled as an appreciation to get your brother returned to me,"said her Ladyship.

"He will be here soon, and is getting ready, and will be driving up and place an overnight bag in the car,"said Detva.

"Do you want a dinner I think I am going to have some food as soon as he arrives.Ok,"said his Mother.

"Michael is in the tunnel now and will be here very shortly,"said his Grandmother.

"Why don't all of you go into the dinning room and I am going upstairs for the rest of the evening it was good to see you again Detva. Good night everyone,"said Urnlee.

"Right we should just start to have some dinner so Likus will join us,"said his Mother.

"Good idea I will have something too,"said Detva.

"Michael, we are going to sit down right now, for something to eat,"said his Mother.

"Hello, Grandmother, Peter and Mom,"said Likus.

"My little Likus, you must see me more often,"said Grandmother.

"I will,"said Likus.

"Mike, do you have your bag in Mom's car,"said Detva.

"Yes, I do, "said Likus.

"Good, I will bring the car around to the back I mean the driver will,"said Detva.

"So lets have some food,"said Grandmother.

"This all looks so good,"said Detva.

"Mom, can you tell me what this is about.? "said Likus.

"I have to take over the businesses and you two are going to listen to Gale at meeting at Versailles tomorrow morning. Said her Ladyship.

"So we are given a position in the company and you are in charge is that what this is or are you working in the building or another one, what? said Likus.

"I am in charge of the entire business and you get can work with me if you want too,"said their Mother.

"Sure,"said Detva.

"Yes, of course,"said Likus.

"So now that we had something to eat and drink I think we can be on our way. Here is the car"said her Ladyship.

"I will drive Mother,"said Detva.

Chapter 11

"Now we are here wake up Michael,"said Detva.

"Now Doctors here are my two sons and I would like to get this done right now "said her Ladyship.

"Versailles, I have been here many tímes, yet it always is exciting,"said Detva.

"Here is the elevator, now we need to go here to the bottom to get some credentials first boys, ok.?"said their Mother.

"Now we will go into this large gold door, and the doctors will wait here,"said Detva.

"Now it looks very foggy, here we are and the web is taken out of sight, see a few of us are here do not be afraid,"said their Mother.

"It is father, and I could not see who was next to him. Did you see? "said Like.

"Now we wait,"said their Mother.

"Mom it was me next to him Likus just left us, now he is here again,"said Detva.

"Yes, he should be placed right next to your father it is all right,"said Mom.

"Mom, I am cold here put these on and now this shirt. Now this jacket and shoes,"said his Mother.

"Now there we are ready to go,"said Detva.

"No, wait I have to do something. I am placing this black diamond head dress on this little one,"said Lady Chardinrey.

"Oh, that is why, and you still look good and the baby alien does too,"said Det.

"There now we must close this door, we will go upstairs with just one scientist and the others may explore or all of you might want to, we will see you upstairs,"said her Ladyship.

"Your ladyship you must keep a bedroom door open about an inch or a window so and let the air in,"said the Butler.

"Thank you here is a gift for Gale it is a ring I am sure he would like it. This was Edward's my late husbands ring. It is also brand new."We must leave right now,"said their Mother.

"Very good my Lady I will give it to Prince Gale immediately,"said the Butler.

"The scientists are staying for a few days and then will see you at your home, is that true,"said the Butler.

"No, they are going to leave late tonight and then be with me,"said her Ladyship.

"Very good, I will let Prince Gale know, Good bye,"said the Butler.

"It has been a while, three years ago you were with us. Hope all is fine. Go Detva we need to get home soon and do not speed. Bye and take care,"said her Ladyship.

"Bye,"said Detva

"Good Bye,"said Likus.

"I am going to sleep and Detva you are going to drive very carefully. ok,"said his Mother.

"Yes, officer I will the next time thank you,"said Detva.

"What, what is going on.?"said his Mother.

"Nothing the officer saw a blinker off and we have one day to get it fixed,"said Detva.

"That means we have to have this stamped or pay for the crime,"said his Mother.

"That is right, and we are home as of right now see the tunnel ahead, and Likus has been asleep all this time,"said Detva.

"I know where we are hear is the back stairs thank you Detva for getting us home all right,"said his Mother.

"Good driving, Pete,"said Likus.

"You drive the next time when the three of us start working in Paris,"said Detva.

"Oh, no I did not think of that,"said his Mother.

"I did, it is just for a few days and let the staff know are yourself, Mother, you are working from the home,"said Detva.

"That is a good deal and we can go into Paris for two days to do what you need right, and your new office can be in the new building itself,"said Likus.

"I am so proud of the both of you, you are thinking all ready about what to do,"said their Mother.

"So it is a deal Mom, we can do it and remember there is enough money for us to buy out Ed,"said Detva.

"We can be as responsible as Edvard and Ownsite themselves,"said their Mother.

"Yes, we can,"said Likus.

"So lets all get some sleep and we will talk in the morning and by early afternoon we can be in Paris to talk to the staff,"said their Mother.

"So go to bed the and we can have a good breakfast in the morning and leave if they do say we do not need to go in then we will not ok,"said their Mother.

"That is fine with me,"said Detva.

"Yes, that is all right and I do not mind it at all,"said Mike.

"Good night,"said their Mother.

"Mom,"said Lise.

"Mommy,"said Don.

"Hi, babies I did sleep, I did right Oh, just five hours,"said their Mother.

"Lady Chardinrey, here is your cart and there is food downstairs anyways,"said her Maid.

"Thank you, go children because I hear the nannies preparing your breakfast ok,"said their Mother.

"Hello, good morning, Likus,"said his Grandmother.

"Good morning, Grandmother, we had a wonderful visit at Versailles and we saw the tunnels, I do not remember to much of the building,"said Likus.

"That is all right your Mother needed instructions for the business, so there was not much time even to do any shopping in Paris I understand,"said his Grandmother.

"No, there was not,"said Likus.

"No, there was not. Good morning Likus and Grandmother, "said Detva.

"Why did we not stay longer at Versailles, Detva,"said Likus.

"Mom had to get some papers and Gale was a sleep so she did not want to intrude,"said Detva.

"Also she wanted to be home she is not one for socializing when in mourning,"said Grandmother.

"I see,"said Likus.

"There will be plenty of times to see Paris when you are working there at Versailles or wherever the business is located in France.?"said Grandmother.

"In Paris and in Versailles I would imagine,"said Detva.

"Yes in both and I will take one day in Paris and then at Versailles,"said Likva.

"I think both of you would have to needing to receive interviews and sign important documents,"said Grandmother.

"This sounds like fun to me and I am enjoying it already,"said Detva.

"Yes, I am sure the both of you will enjoy this business,"said their Grandmother.

"Here are the children and there goes the children I guess they are in school today,"said Detva.

"There they are in the preschool for today,"said their Mother.

"I did see that,"said their Grandmother.

"I did not want them to talk if they were awake and knew about Versailles,"said her Ladyship.

"I know that and they will not even remember it tonight, "said their Mother.

"I sure they will not,"said Detva.

"I brought these games for them that were at home, "said Detva.

"One look at those games, and they will be interested,"said Likus.

"They are good games too,"said his Mother.

"Yes, that is a good idea, "said their Grandmother.

"Thank you,"said Detva.

"Likus I have two gifts from you so just leave them here and they will take notice,"said his Mother.

"When you two boys visit one should call the other to see if there are any gifts, or if someone is to bring some food, just the way us girls do it so can you too,"said Grandmother.

"Oh, Grandmother I brought Gale the gift from Edward and he will like it when he visits and stays in the Octver building,"said Lady Chardinrey.

"That ring Ed told me was Gales's new gift,"said the Grandmother.

"It resets with new stones that are not sealed in a ring permanently,"said her Ladyship.

"Phone call,"said the Butler.

"Yes, hello, Gale Yes, thank you all is fine. Your welcome and I am sorry I did not see you but there will be others times. Yes, I will talk to them tomorrow morning. Yes, ok, thank you and good bye, Paul. Say hello to all for me, bye, "said her Ladyship.

"What did he say,"said Grandmother.

"He could not talk long. He said hello, Mother and to boys as well. He wanted to thank us for the gift,"said her Ladyship.

"Then he liked Ed's gift,"said the Grandmother.

"He did he like it very much,"said her Ladyship.

"Apparently Ed found another ring like that one so he saved it for him,"said Grandmother.

"This family does not need to of them I even put back jewelry that was duplicated as purchases,"said her Ladyship.

"I do know this one by heart because one of the packages I did the wrapping, they all went to Exile jewelry shop in the Ludwig castle, "said Likus.

"That right you wrapped up two packages if I remember correctly. This time Ed took home a lot of jewelry to sell at a discount,"said their Mother.

"Just being curious Mother did you get any payment for what you gave to Ed,"said Detva.

"No, I just listened them as stolen,"said his Mother.

"Very funny you were allowed to use Lloyds' and be paid for what he sells them as,"said Detva.

"So that means he gives you a check when he is home or how does that work,"said Likus.

"Our insurance payments are high each year but we get paid, especially when giving something away,"said Mother.

"We gave Urnlee Ed's Rolls to her, so we got paid for that kindness, so it is in the family but she did marry him for a little while,"said the Grandmother.

"So I would have to buy it and because she was his wife she could receive the car and then you get paid,"said Likus.

"Right, that is the way it would work and if your Grandmother purchased the car, then I would not get a thing. So Dad has thought of this very clearly, so we were able to get rid of that automobile,"said Detva.

"Yes, it was a sportive car,"said their Mother.

"I did not want it,"said Detva.

"Nor did I, we are both very please with our rolls,"said Likus.

"So did you boys have a good dinner. Because right now we are going to have some snacks and refreshments,"said their Mother.

"With this business, it is our time to manage it, so why don't you have an office right in the new castle,"said Likus.

"I am until it is necessary to go into Paris,"said his Mother.

"I understand it is in the middle of Paris,"said Likus.

"Yes it is and we need to go into the office in my, our new castle and soon,"said her Ladyship.

"If all of you do not mind I am getting some coffee does anyone want some,"said their Grandmother.

"Grandmother are you going to have some photos done or work in the office in the new building,"said Likus.

"No, I will go in there to talk to all of you or at least see how busy all of you are, nothing more than that,"said Grandmother.

"Then you will probably be with Lise most of the day,"said her Ladyship.

"Yes, I am sure I will,"said the Grandmother.

"So just what do you want me to do Mother, "said Likus.

"Watch the office when I am not there the two of you , and make them wait on the line until I return and there are many things that need to be done,"said their Mother.

"Of course for the men there is a representative positions as sales of the franchises too,"said Grandmother.

"That sound good but could we have many or all the sales here to be able to entertain too,"said Likus.

"Excellent idea,"said his Mother.

"Yes, it is,"said the Grandmother.

"Yes, I do agree that is excellent so we can entertain our future franchise owners here in our new castle and soon I hope, "said his Mother.

"I could call many people and find out if they are interested using a proper list that is, from the start,"said Detva.

"This is getting very interesting we are putting ourselves in front and thinking of the public, that is good,"said the Grandmother.

"Remember the commissions should go to our purchasing new stocks to obtain as many as possible,"said her Ladyship.

"I know it is important to own more than the public so we do have control and their best interest at heart,"said Detva.

"Yes, that way the price control will remain as it is now,"said Likus.

"Ed his wife Owns were the first to first start this business so we do have to show them that we do care about what they have done for us and Gale also, "said their Mother.

"This does sound like a plan to me so I guess all of us are in the main building and this new wing will have the business in it too,"said Grandmother.

"If and when my other son is with us, I would like him and his wife and children to return to a new building where our offices are, "said Lady Chardinrey.

"We can work there in the day time,"said Grandmother.

"Good, we will all be there and I think your son our older brother will live with us in the main house for a little while,"said Detva.

"If I hear all of you correctly from down the hall, if you want Lord Cregill and his wife and children to be with us, he might want some freedom at first,"said Seebees.

"That name is also very good but still identifiable if you want him to not travel he need a name like Lord Bleeford ,"said Likus.

"We will have all under control when and if they move back home, at least for the time we need to do this for Gale,"said her Ladyship.

"Yes, but wait until we finds out and he visits so there is not a message or even a phone call for anyone to know that they have left permanently,"said Detva.

"Coffee and this lunch was upstairs that why I am here for more food,"said Seebees.

"Good, finish it, we have had enough,"said Likus.

"Yes, please do,"said her Mother.

"So I know what I can do and Leavlets we both can have about ten children each to help out,"said Seebees.

"Oh, you card you hearing that, we need you to work not get yourself sick so much,"said her Grandmother.

"Remember Ed and Owns had stress and they enjoyed their company because they were in a foreign countries since their marriage being alone and we were not there,"said her Mother.

"Ok, I was only joking. I only want two more and that is it,"said Seebees.

"Three is a good size family I think, what do you say Mother,"said Chardin.

"Three is fine even two if the both of you are pleased with two children,"said their Grandmother.

"Are you ok, Grandmother,"said Seebees.

"I am all right It just has been a busy day could you take me upstairs for a while I would like to lie down for a while, Seebees, please,"said her Grandmother.

"Sure Grandmother I will,"said Seebees.

"Donald, your sister Lady Seebees and I are going to the elevator could you show her how to use it, he is my good chaperone and body guard,"said their Grandmother.

"Will you return later, Mother, I will have Urnlee look at you,"said Lady Chardinrey.

"I will stay with Grandmother for the night ok, Mother,"said Ladys Seebees.

"Please do that would be very nice, and thank you dear,"said her Ladyship.

"Welcome come on Don show me how to use this elevator, ok,"said Seebees.

"Grandmother and Seebees,"said Don.

"Ok, first I close this door,"said Seebees.

"There gone for the evening Detva and Likus, I hope the nurse Urnlee can see them right now. Good Urnlee can you visit Mother and Seebees. Yes, in her room,"said Lady Chardin.

"She will let you know if anything is wrong,"said Detus.

"I know what is wrong, many grieve in different ways, We should of talked about Ed your father more to her and I think that was the reason,"said their Mother.

"No, I think she was just tired,"said Detva.

"Maybe both reasons are good,"said Likus.

"Indeed they are, now would you like some coffee, please help yourselves, "said their Mother.

"Grandmother is relaxing with Don they are watching the tel and she said that you do not have to visit that she is fine she just wanted to get out of those shoes and rest,"said Seebees.

"You are quite sure now,"said her Ladyship.

"Yes, Mother they are both on the couch and her feet are up and her maid is there and she wanted a soft cold drink,"said Seebees.

"So the maid is there.?"said her Mother.

"Yes, and now the nurse, Urnlee,"said Seebees.

"Let me go up stairs and I will find out if we should all see her one at a time,"said their Mother.

"I hope she is all right,"said Seebees.

"I know she misses Dad but these lights in this large dinning room and the dinning room are very bright,"said Detus.

"I know this is still one of the many first days and evenings Dad is not with us. If anyone knows this it is Grandmother,"said Likus.

"You are right Likus and we will notice this in a few weeks and it is all right to think that he will return. You know inside yourself and to say those things, there is nothing wrong with that,"said Seebees.

"That is true, we can pretend it is not wrong at all, especially because of the little ones, so do we say in about ten months from now, I just saw Dad walking into the garage and let someone drive off.? "said Detva.

"Knowing Lise she will stay at the window all day long,"said Seebees.

"That is right, so we do not want to her, just let her know that we will talk to Mother,"said Likus.

"Good idea, "said Seebees.

"Yes, it is,"said Detus.

"Here is Mom, now lets tell her what we have discussed,"said Seebees.

"What is it,"said their Mother.

"If Lise gets to upset months from now we are going to let you handle it,"said Seebees.

"Thank you, she knows he is dead, but if he is to return then I will deal with it, but I have not seen or heard anything from her or Don and every morning they are with me,"said her Mother.

"How is grandmother.?"said Detus.

"She is fine, these are never on in this room or the dinning either. So if you want to visit one at a time, Detus why not be first being the oldest here she already has seem Leavlets, "said their Mother.

"Is it these lights being the bigger part of all her discomfort.?"said Likus.

"Yes, it would have made her more relaxed, but she might decide to go upstairs earlier each night,"said his Mother.

"Now that is alright,"said Likus.

"Just this last week your Grandmother went upstairs early,"said his Mom.

"Now Likus it is your turn just for a few minutes, ok,"said his Brother.

"Now Detva what did Grandmother say.? "said his Mother.

"Nothing much Don was tired so I brought him to see his Nanny, and Grandmother knows that Mike is going to see her in a few minutes,"said Detus.

"Alright then we will have some more food and then go upstairs to our bedrooms for the night, ok,"said his Mom.

"That does sound good, I just can not wait to stay in the tub for a little while,"said Detva.

"Good and instead of going in to see if you are out of the tub you will call me before you are asleep, alright,"said his Mom.

"Sure I will, Mom,"said Detus.

"I have the nanny with me Detus,"said Seebees.

"That is good,"said Peter.

"Just a little bit more coffee and then I am ready to go upstairs,"said Seebees.

"Me too,"said Detus.

"That sounds great,"said Likus.

"Good the Nurse had helped place her into the bed and so I only gave her a kiss good night,"said Likus.

"That was all, she did not say anything.?"said his Mother.

"I ask her if she was tired.?"said Likus.

"She said,"She was very tired,"said Likus.

"I can just imagine it was a busy weekend and today was too,"said their Mother.

"Ok, a few more ideas about the business and we have to make sure it does not bother Grandmother,"said Detva.

"I guess you are right, we are excited about the business because of this as an adventure. We have never done this before and she is the only one mourning,"said their Mother.

"But Mother we are doing this to keep busy, all of us, and on that note I suggest in that large building we have a portait room so we can at least go into different part of the buildings not to be reminded if it going to be upsetting of anyone of us, "said Seebees.

"Death can do that and there is already a place for a portrait room. All the family does need to sit for a portrait very soon, right after we all move in,"said their Mother.

"I know not to confuss Grandmother why don't we let her know in case we start to talk about very subject at once, why not let Donald go get her when we are done,"said Likus.

"She would like that very much. good idea, "said his Mother.

"She and Don can stay in her room while they are watching the tel and we can let them know if they want to be with us, they can be. I like that a lot,"said Seebees.

"You know that my will and your Dads and our Grandmother states that Lise and Don will probably get more money and your children as well and only in case the economics of life is more difficult,"said their Mother.

"Mother you have done so much excepting my husband and now a child and you both gave me a house too,"said Seebees.

"I love my apartment in the city and now I am making some money on it living at home,"said Detus.

"Yes, and the estate on the shore in France has given a yield that is very good for my future,"said Likus.

"I am glad you all agree, this extra money includes Likus's two children also,"said their Mother.

"We all agree Mother and I am sorry that my marriage did not work out,"said Likus.

"I know you are and we do include your children if they want to live here with you but we as a family need your children all grown up to return to us when they are older,"said his Mother.

"Yes, I understand and maybe my wife will be married again, and my children can visit a few times during the year,"said Likus.

"Who knows Likus you might remarry.?"said Seebees.

"Yes, and if Detva does we will have enough grandchildren to take over and make sure that this business is making money,"said Lady Chardinrey.

"Mother this is probably a good time tho ask and I can tell Leavlets, do you want to remarry, knowing how much in love the two of you were. You do want need to answer and I also do apologized for this question,"said Seebees.

"I know you are thinking of my own interest, but what is best is that I keep busy with this business and if someone does introduce himself to me all of you will be the first to know if I am going to have a day,"said their Mother.

"Ok, we just want you to be happy and I think this business is the best thing that could happen to me because these last few days I receive a phone call from my husband.

Instead of giving him a call,"said Seebees.

"That is progress, and I am sure the navy took notice,"said Detva.

"Is that a good thing.?"said Seebees.

"Excellent it is showing you are giving great concern for your baby and all that you are with right now,"said Detva.

"Right, and you can tell your husband for me that we are taking care of you and when and if he asked how am I and if I wanted to remarry.?"said Lady Chardinrey.

"What should I say.?"said Seebees.

"What.?"said Mike.

"Yes, what.?"said Detva.

"The answer is she is thrilled to take care of this business right now and does not need to have another franchise at this time,"said Lady Chardinrey.

"I know I would not make the same mistake twice, is something that I would say,"said Seebees.

"Your father did hold the patent on himself and it was enough for me to stop staring every minute of the day until all of your children were born then I had something to do,"said their Mother.

"That was nice to hear,"said Likus.

"Yes, it was,"said Detva.

"I love you Mother and I hope I have twins to keep us all busy,"said Seebees.

"That would be fantastic but one is enough to handle,"said her Mother.

"I know especially when living by ourselves on the shore, "said Seebees.

"The shore might be his next commission, permanently,"said her Mother.

"That will be good,"said Seebees.

"You are Lady Seebees your choice of who your husband is, is wonderful to me and your late father and the both of you men will do the same and we will get far in this business together, ok,"said their Mother.

"When Gavga is home we would like to use the beach home,"said Seebees.

"Yes and if you return to us and not be alone there I would appreciate it, he you just watch your children it is fine,"said their Mother.

"Oh, ok, oh, I understand,"said Seebees.

"I would like to stay for a while and I can give you some rent,"said Detva.

"I will too,"said Likus.

"I can not,"said Seebees.

"All ladies are exempted, just the men, and we do have a few good afternoon for a picnic at the new house. Might not be to bad after all we do have that new barbeque in the backyard,"said Chardin.

"We could go there next weekend,"said Seebees.

"That is a good idea, "said Likus.

"Yes,"said Detva.

"Then it is settle we will go this weekend, but we will not stay there over night,"said their Mother.

"I would like to stay there when it is all completed,"said Seebees.

"We will,"said their Mother.

"We can still rent the properties.?"said Detva.

"Yes, they are your good investments, "said their Mother.

"Now, I am your guardian so I went to have the will read to me alone, there is a copy of it I will let you read it tomorrow. While one of you read it in your apartment then the next ok,"said their Mother.

"We are going to do that, for you Mother,"said Likus.

"Thank you all of you, now alright, it does state each of you besides the properties you were living in there is one extra for each of you,"said their Mother.

"Seebees you will have the next new observatory and on both sides of the cove. On the ocean front,"said her Mother.

"Thank you, Mother,"said Seebees.

"One an observatory and one a new castle, with about one hundred rooms, both can be used as a military if war, "said her Mother.

"Yes, thank you so much,"said Seebees.

"Now Peter, you may have because of your name if you want to live in Russia you may or just rent that devine home next to the Hermitage,"said his Mother.

"Thank you, Mother. Said Detva.

"Now Likus you have the French estate near us by the shore. You like so much,"said his Mother.

"Thank you, Mother, "said Likus.

"Now Lise and Don are to young yet we do have a house for them. When our Grandmothers dies, Leavlets will have her house being the oldest daughter,"said their Mother.

"Does she know,"said Detva.

"I told her about four hours ago to make her more happier,"said her Mother.

"Seebees you and your husband have a choice to put the houses on the ocean front or the river bed peninsula at a cove only,"said her Mother.

"I will let Gavga know this might give him a new leave home, "said Seebees.

"Go ahead if you want to end your marriage,"said her Mother.

"Then what do I say.? "said her Daughter.

"After the will was read I have an opportunity to use land at the ocean front for an observatory and a new castle or the same thing on the river bed front near our cove,"said her Mother.

"Good help me do this message,"said her Daughter.

"After the will was read I have an opportunity to use land at the ocean shore for an observatory and a new castle or the same thing on the river bed at our cove. Which is a good idea for the militaryian observatory and of us the castle too, in case of a war. Love you a lot and so does the family,"said Seebees.

"That is nice he will enjoy this so much maybe he can come home, or maybe then it is a divorce. So I will let him decide,"said Seebees.

"Remember and let him know this right now, we are building it not the navy but they may approve of the plans for the observatory. The navy are certainly approved of for the plans for the castle in case of any difficulties,"said her Mother.

"Do you want me to send this message,"said her Mother.

"Yes, I am to excited and this one you can sign it, so his superior officer will see it,"said Seebees.

"Now you are a good ruling Queen like your Grandmother giving out orders and telling many to do good things just like me when I sent this message. Very good, you are my daughter that is for sure,"said her Mother.

"Yes, you are, just like Catherine the Great,"said Peter.

"Yes, she did.'said Mike.

"Now my Dear, as thinking as a good queen, I think you have allow your husband to return right away as he surveys the property again,"said Lady Chardinrey.

"Oh, my goodness Mother I did, I think he would not mind it he is working when he returns,"said Seebees.

"Know I do not think he would mind but do allow him to go back,"said her Mother.

"They might not be called to a war they are mainly patrolling the shores,"said her Daughter.

"That is excellent, my dear,"said her Mother.

"Yes, now I remember you telling me, that is good news again,"said Detva.

"Yes, I do too remember you saying that this is good news,"said Likus.

"He might have to stay home after the baby is born or only to out for a few days at a time each month,"said her Mother.

"Right only in a major world war then it does not apply,"said her brother Detva.

"That is also a written fact,"said Likus.

"So he is going to have leave soon,"said Seebees.

"Yes, he should be. I know we talked about this before but now I am certain he will return to you,"said her Mother.

"I feel so much better,"said Seebees.

"Good and when the baby is born you are going to let him know that he can have another tour of duty. When you feel fine and are ready to let him go. Just give him a suggestion that is all,"said her Mother.

"I should feel much better by then.?"said her Daughter.

"I guess that is part of being a good Queen too.?"said Likus.

"Yes, it is my sister, I do have to say it if you are depended upon a man and letting him go on another tour there are many men who see this. As you have become a good candidate for a new husband, I have to say this because I do worry for you also,"said Detva.

"It is a lot to ask him to do and yourself but he just might enjoy that new observatory,"said her Ladyship.

"Thank you and Detva and Likus and Mother you are all so good to me,"said Seebees.

"Then we have done and are true in our beliefs that are good,"said her Mother.

"I know it is very different now,"said her Daughter.

Chapter 12

"Remember, and Mother and Likus will agree you had a wonderful vacation at the beach after your wedding with a lot of time to think so that part of your life is now interrupted with all of us,"said Detva.

"I guess that would pertain to anyone who moved in,"said their Sister.

"Everyone,"said Likus.

"Yes, but the diffence is eventually after moving in and have a nice apartment, a few days of not seeing anyone, there will be a person to see how you are,"said their Mother.

"That is alright I do not mind a visitor,"said their Sister.

"Now you see that when I gave Gale his gift because he prefers to be alone and just have a few guests at a time,"said their Mother.

"You needed to get some files anyways and instructions, you can return another time it is not as if you two do not know each other,"said Detva.

"Actually he was your Father's friend in hight school and college and then I met him after your Father and I started dating,"said their Mother.

"I did not know that, maybe I was told,"said her Daughter.

"Right before your Father graduated I met Gale,"said their Mother.

"So you stayed friends because of the business,"said Detva.

"Yes, Gale wanted Edvard to create the tunnels systems in the States and in all of Europe too. Now look what we all have "said their Mother.

"We have these new homes because of Gale that is coorect right Mother.? "said Detva.

"Yes, of course I did not give Ed and his wife a home in Bavaria and you can do this now for Gale and earn all three of you, just help me out,"said their Mother.

"That is right the King Ludwig castle has two franchises now and the building has all condominiums in it and is one itself too,"said Likus.

"Yes, we could do the same,"said the Sister.

"Yes, and your own husband would enjoy that also,"said her Mother.

"So how do we divide it up to do the same as Ed,"said Detva.

"A central building for certain areas for such as Russia and France and then one in Norway, Finland, Italy and Eqypt also,"said their Mother.

"This is getting better every day,"said Likus.

"Why each one of us and me at the new castle for Belgium can control and make sure the prices stay where it is for all citizens,"said their Mother.

"I will take Egypt. Said Detva.

"We can rotate every six months. I will take France and Finland since Russia our older brother would never part with it,"said Likus.

"Then if we want Likus and I can rotate the four countries every two years,"said Detva.

"Of course, I do suppose your sister Leavlets would return to Norway and run Finland as well."

"What about me,"said Seebees.

"We do need you here with the observatory because if I not mistaken this will give us a stipend to help us out and be comfortable the rest of our lives "said their Mother.

"You do not think this means we can stop working and just use all these houses for rents,"said Likus.

"We could in fact use them for a littlle while and move in and use the positions for extra money and to make sure the prices stay low for the Euortrain and the tunnels do not have any tolls, "said Detus.

"Yes, but the fast tunnels there are any two in one direction only and there is a toll that is paid once a year,"said their Mother.

"Right I pay that going to Moscow or Bavaria only when I visit I have a book of ten visits only,"said Detus.

"I gave you those books for Christmas, each ticket can be used at any time,"said his Mother.

You did and I thank you again,"said Detva.

"No, thank you I am going to purchase some more in case Rofster wants to return to their last house in the Netherlands,"said her Ladyship.

“I think they have a one year rental there and then the renter will decide to stay,”said Seebees.

“All this is getting better, Mom can stay at home and eventually we can use in the new castle as a central office instead of in France,”said Mike.

“This is better because of leaving an employee at each building in charge with a good income he can send each month with a computerized report here,”said Detus.

“That is what Ed did in the states and in each town or city they lived in and the same people now will send us a report starting each month to us,”said Seebees.

“Right those reports should be transmitted now, who will call Ed,”said Detva.

“I will, then he will know I am doing my work so let me get that done right now,”said their Mother.

“This is exciting,”said Seebees.

“You know you at those new summer cottages or your new castle and the observatory should have the payroll for the entire productions of our employees due to the navy guards that will be guarding those buildings,”said Detva.

“Your are correct, we should transfer the employees who would want their same job there too,”said Likus.

“Seebees you are becoming more and more important as a new Queen,”said her Mother.

“Ok, we all need to say good night and all go upstairs and we will meet each other in the morning,”said their Mother.

“Mother may I talk to you alone for a few minutes,”said her Daughter.

“Yes you may, and boys make sure your own food is taken out before the staff returns,”said their Mother.

“Mom do you think he will be home soon.?”said her Daughter.

“Yes, dear especially when we have an observation building for them two in fact. From what I understand is he returns to fullfill his agreement,”said her Mother.

“So if he asked for a transferr to do the surveying then he might have a leave for that too,”said her Daughter.

“This leave is over in two days so I do think the priority is first would be the next surveying so he might leave the ship from here or in the next port. I am not sure how this works,”said her Mother.

"You can call him tomorrow when he did not call it is because there were no phone calls being made this evening. Do not call that ship and talk to anyone other than him,"said her Mother.

"I will not, and thank you Mother and good night. I love you, the three of us do,"said Seebees.

"Oh, you soon will have your baby,"said her Mother.

"Yes, and if it is a girl I will name her Chardinrey or even if it is a boy,"said her Daughter.

"Thank you dear and good night you need your sleep, oh look who is here Lise come on lets get some sleep. Good night dear,"said her Ladyship.

"Good night Mother and Lise,"said Seebees.

"Night,"said Lise.

"Good night,"said her Mother.

"Lise now go to sleep you are with me, now,"said her Mother.

"Night,"said said Lise.

"Good night. Dear,"said her Mother.

"Good night,"said Lise.

"Oh Lise, you jump right on me,"said her Mother.

"Hello, Donald,"said Mother.

"Good morning,"said Don.

"Good morning the both of you, my too babies, "said their Mother.

"Goo morning, "said Lise.

"Now Don I want you to go and see Urnlee she is going to take your blood pressure. Ok, go right now and Lise will follow after her breakfast,"said their Mother.

"No, you do it,"said Don.

"You do,"said Lise.

"Now the both of you stop acting like upstarts, Don go right now ok,"said their Mother.

"See Lise there is nanny and she will return for you ok,"said her Mother.

"No, "said Lise.

"Now what did I tell you do not act like an upstart, now finish your breakfast,"said her Mother.

"Ot,"said Lise.

"Here is your dress for school. Ok,"said her Mother.

"Si,"said Lise.

"Oh, good you are going to hear a Spanish book today last week it was French right,"said her Mother.

"Si,"said Lise.

"That is alright I know you like those short stories,"said her Mother.

"Good morning,"said don.

"Donald. Good morning, you decide to return so how about another hug,"said his Mother.

"Now that you are here and Lise is finished can you bring her to see Urnlee,"said their Mother.

"Yes, "said Don.

"Very good now both of you look very nice, handsome and so beautiful,"said their Mother.

"Bye,"said Don.

"Bye,"said Lise.

"Thank you and go see Grandmother down stairs when you are finished with Urnlee, alright,"said their Mother.

"Yes,"said Don.

"Yes,"said Lise.

"Good morning, the food was put away and it was a very good according to my children I am going to have breakfast downstairs with their Grandmother,"said her Ladyship.

"Very good, Lady Chardinrey,"said her Maid.

"Good morning Mother, Constance did you see Lise and Don,"said their Mother.

"Here we are,"said Lise.

"Right here,"said Don.

"You were hiding from me and you won, do you want any more food,"said their Mother.

"No tas,"said Lise.

"Yes, some milk,"said Don.

"It will be ready soon,"said his Mother.

"Thank you, Mom, "said Don.

"Here, Don you want the more.""Let me know,"said his Mother.

"Ok,"said Don.

"Do you want milk or something else,"said their Mother.

"No, tas,"said Lise.

"Lise just some milk for me, ok,"said Grandmother.

"No, tas,"said Lise.

"They both had a good breakfast upstairs with me, "said Chardin.

"You know you have put on a few pounds yourself,"said Grandmother.

"Oh, no, here children the bus is here by now go with your nannies. Please give me from my home a… thank you,"said Chardin.

"Were you going to say something.? "said Grandmother.

"Yes, I have a test upstairs the maid is going to get it and I think I am going to be a Mommy again,"said her Ladyship.

"Good, you will keep you busy too but you are not sure.!"said her Mother-in-law.

"Here is the maid, thank you and please stay outside the door,"said her Ladyship.

"So go into the bathroom now and you better tell me first, its just like my son to start leaving misses, after he is gone,"said the Grandmother.

"Do you want anything, Lady Constance,"said the Maid.

"Maid, please come in here now, thank you. You please for give with never saying your name for security reasons, you should know about this because you gave her the test,"said Lady Constance.

"Mother, you are going to be a Grandmother again, oh, good, let the maid inform all the others alright, "said her Mother-in-law.

"Yes, please tell the staff,"said Lady Chardinrey.

"That is so wonderful,"said Grandmother.

"I did say in front of your maid that Ed did it again as soon as he left and still made messes,"said Ed's Mother.

"There will not be any mess at all we have enough nannies,"said Chardin.

"Nannies, for what.!"said Seebees.

"I am glad all of you are here, I just took a test and told your Grandmother and then the maid to tell the staff that I am going to have a baby,"said Lady Chardinrey.

"Mother, thank you I love you so much for this,"said Seebees.

"I do not know what to say but I love you too,"said Leavlets.

"Same for me,"said Rofster.

"Here is Detus and Likus,"said Seebees.

"Yes, my two boys can here this right now, I am going to have a baby,"said their Mother.

"Mom, I can not believe this, are you ok, right now, here sit down,"said Detva.

"Yes, please sit down this is so wonderful I am going to be an Uncle,"said Likus.

"Yes, you are. Than what am I going to be.? "said Detva.

"Both to you are going to be brothers again, when the baby is born,"said the Mother.

"You two are so funny early in the morning, but you Mother are you alright are you ok, "said Seebees.

"Have you been sick in the morning, Mother we are here to help you and there is a three nurses here too,"said Leavelts.

"No it just was very sudden and I did think it was the funeral and being worried about Lise and Don,"said Lady Chardinrey.

"I was going to ask you last week, but I did not want to,"said their Grandmother.

"I would of indicated a, "no"immediately,"said her Ladyship.

"Lets all sit down for some coffee and something lets just relax the children still do not understand so we will all go,"said their Grandmother.

"Grandmother, I apologized for interrupting I have been here every day and I do not intend to say anything,"said Will.

"We always forget Will some of the time he is out of the room and is always getting another toy for the children to use. My little Will,"said his Mother.

"Now we do need to let the nurses know,"said Grandmother.

"They do know and I wanted them to discuss some sort of a plan for each with them checks our vital signs, with an office on each floor,"said Lady Chardinrey.

"Urnlee will always be in charge right.? "said Lady Leavlets.

"Yes, she will one male nurse had to leave and another is taking his place that is the way they do these positions and it is a she and her shift started today,"said Chardin.

"May I speak for a minute, I do not want to start a different conversation, but my wife and I are going to be in the news as an temporary owner for the throne of France in the Palace of Versailles,"said Rofster.

"We let the press know last night and gave them our photos, so we had to tell you right away,"said Leavlets.

"Let me see the computer and that was very good to do but the rest of you we want to know it anyways even if it is at the early hours in the morning, ok,"said their Mother.

"Is it there I did not look this morning,"said their Grandmother.

"Yes, it is true and it was just what I though it was Rofster and Leavels. So then that is all right and many will be confused until Gale or we take over. Thank you both very much, "said their Mother.

"When should I have my name changed, I know when I have the baby."The newspapers are going to have a good time of it using Seesaws, that's ok,"said Seebees.

"You are a good sport but what about this she gaining a new country business and a baby from the dead the news is really going to do us, like a person that does not deserve all this money too,"said her Ladyship.

"Sure they will rip us apart and we need to get ready for a good fight if the press goes to far,"said Rofster.

"Yes, they will, I do not have any surprising news for anyone just yet. Unless Grandmother you and I want to get married today, "said Detva.

"You are so funny, oh my goodness, Detva did you say no.?"said Grandmother.

"I do not mean too,"said Detva.

"I am not a witness,"said Likus.

"This is a good time for all of us to have a refreshment of some kind,"said her Ladyship.

"No one can not say for the two of you, three of you do not make life exciting while in the news,"said Seebees.

"I can not even imagine the things that would be put in the news about the both of you ,"said Leavels.

"Oh ya, well Leavels or Leastrung, I read shortly afterwards that you had married the gardener,"said Detva.

"They will say they are all young and handsome the last time I saw as my interview. And the rest have book work to do before retirement so she probably had a good selection. Not all are here for the summer only too,"said her Ladyship.

"I read that the two of you were in a classroom here and did not know how to use the computer while the commuting professor was from France, now who can answer.?"said Likus.

"I can to protect the family and in a hurry too, I registered under my old name,"said Leavels.

"Good and Peter, for the same of the family, what would you say.?"said Likus.

"I would have to say, no comment,"said Detva.

"Both are excellent answers and could only lead to a cartoon and we did make a fortune with slander, "said their Grandmother.

"This is becoming very good as a group and remember we make more money on slander when we are not together and I want it to be in good taste, please,"said their Mother.

"Yes, and for Lloyd's and the record I want it written up that she was stacked, for the sake of the family,"said Likus.

"Very good, and I hope the cartoon is helping us,"said Grandmother.

"It does or I am going right back to her,"said Likus.

"If she does then why did you not call the one a gave you, everything was alright with us we did not mind breaking up,"said Detva.

"I need her phone number again. "said Likus.

"Better than that, here is my phone and I remember her number too,"said Detva.

"Ok, my conversation will be in the other room, "Hello it is Likus Hi ...,"said Likus.

"That should be him busy for an hour or so, maybe he might leave tonight for Lloyd's. Said Leavels.

"That was cute,"said Rofster.

"What, what did I say wrong,"said Leavels.

"Leavels you are my wife come over here and I will whisper,"said Rofster.

"Thank you Detva for helping Likus can on the right,"said his Mother.

"Track, and a more preferable avenue, than whatever his wife saw. This one will stay with him and I do not even care about how much money this new girl wants for her family if they are married.,"said their Grandmother.

"What was wrong with his life,"said Leavels.

"Other than his wife also put into the newspapers. He was a vampire"said Char.

"What is wrong with a vampire,"said Leavels.

"Nothing but the alcoholics a fighting is the same as them that have taken away the Euro train and its tunnels form the states. Yes, I know that the engineering and technology was not new. But the work was half completed and stopped during their reign,"said Lady Urnlee.

"Your Mother is correct and all the families were at that particular time in life would receive a social security for the child that was somehow it looked as if the tunnels were not in all would be paid. Yes and thank you Peter for Likus's recovery." said their Grandmother.

"I made a decision we need a better satellite to use and there is a scientist I am allowed to have as a transfer from a shuttle but he will only leave one shuttle to the next with seeing his soon to be divorced when he meets his wife at that moment. This is only to see if she is alright,"said Ladys Chardinrey.

"Do they stay here any of them,"said Detva.

"Not at first,"said his Mother.

"Why,"said Rofster.

"Stop that, he is just being funny. Sorry to interrupt, please continue, why.? "said Leavels.

"She was given an assignment as a model and there are two guests, one who will steer the shuttle and another experience lady that will help her see for husband to be identified. This is so the other can watch the transfer and his wife does just what she is told, "said their Mother.

"It all sounds so dangerous,"said Seebees.

"I talked to this model on the phone last night named Outhall and she is going to talk to Gale in Versailles to arrange her modeling shoot with his photographers, "said their Mother. "

"Oh, we did go on the wrong day,"said Detva.

"We left early and always will,"said his Mother.

"You can meet her, "said Seebees.

"Then you go and take a few photos for me. She is my favorite model anyways so it will even not fool her for a second. You will go the day I tell you to and come fright home after then when she is back at Versailles you may call her up and visit her again if she agrees. "said his Mother.

"Yes, this is terrific and I will return when you say,"said Detva.

"I will tell you right now I want you to visit her one week before she meets her husband so the next one she thinks of is you. Also you will call her is just before she goes into the shuttle, do you understand me, Detva,"said his Mother.

"Yes I would never go into Versailles unless I called for an invitation first and that would have to pertain to the Euro train and it is to soon for that,"said Detva.

"Yes, it is to soon, and you will receive your invitation,"said his Mother.

"Good, thank you so much, I am going to date Outhall, I going to date Outhall. Lord Bleeford, I have her now,"said Detva.

"What , what is this.! What I thought we had a pack no name calling in the house,"said Likus.

"Wait one minute, I want everyone to hear this now and I do mean this do not ever call Versailles without my permission or go there, thank you,"said their Mother.

"No, we do,"said Don.

"No, said Detva.

"No, never name calling without permission a guest present, we go ours,"said Likus.

"Stop that the both of you,"said their mother.

"No, not even call without permission,"said Rofster.

"No, said Seebees.

"No, but I want to go there the next time, ok,"said Will.

"Yes, you may,"said his Mother.

"Thank you, Mother,"said Will.

"Now that all is seem to be ok why not go to our apartments and have dinner and be back about six alright, "said their Mother.

"Yes, I could use a nap but if Don wants to visit and Lise that is fine with me,"said their Grandmother.

"Then lets all go upstairs and rest a while before dinner,"said their Mother.

"Don, do you want to stay with me for a while,"said his Grandmother.

"Lise, you can stay here with me ok,"said her Mother.

"Si,"said Lise.

"How was your Spanish lesson.?"said her Mother.

"Good, uno, dos,"said Lise.

"Good, do you want the tel on.? "said her Mother.

"Yes,"said Lise.

"Si,"said her Mother.

"Si, "said Lise.

"Very good here is your show,"said her Mother.

"Mom,"said Lise.

"What is it.?"said her Mother.

"Dad,"said Lise.

"Oh, let me turn the set to me and I want you to just wait for one minute, ok,"said her Mother.

"Now,"said Lise.

"Not yet I will tel you ok. "said her Mother.

"Si,"said Lise.

"That is a very good, I enjoy listening to your Spanish sentences,"said her Mother.

"Gracias, Lady Chartiney,"said Lise.

"Oh, you are so good and here is the tel, just in time Lise for you to see,"said her Mother.

"Oh, my tartoons,"said Lise.

"Are they your favorites ones,"said her Mother.

"Si,"said Lise.

"Mom,"said Lise.

"See,"said Lise.

"What, good that is your favorite show,"said her Mother.

"Now do you want to nap for a while and I will watch the tel.?"said her Mother.

"Si,"said Lise.

"Stay here and I will get your dinner ready and my own too,"said her Mother.

"Mine,"said Lise.

"Yes, all yours. You and I are going to have dinner together, ok,"said her Mother.

"Yes, Please. Where is Dad.? "said Lise.

"Your father is not reurning he is dead and you know that but I am here,"said her Mother.

"Ok,"said Lise.

"Here is some more juice,"said her Mother.

"Si, "said Lise.

"Now we can talk like a good little girl and did you know you need to speak in English when others do not know Spanish. Did you know that.? "said her Mother.

"Yes,"said Lise.

"Are you finished.? Or do you want some more meat and potatoes,"said her Mother.

"No, how about another slice of this cake with me I want some more, too,"said her Mother.

"Yes, please,"said Lise.

"Yes, please. You are so polite, Lise,"said her Mother.

"No,"said Lise.

"No, Yes you are. This is good, and enjoyable,"said her Mother.

"I know, me finished,"said Lise.

"Ok, I am going to wash your hands and face.?"said her Mother.

"We see Don and Grandmo,"said Lise.

"Yes we are. Now lets go downstairs and there is food there if you want anything else ok, "said her Mother.

"Gramother,"said Lise.

"I am afraid, she has a good appetite but lets she if she wants another plate of food.? Lise what do you want here point of it,"said her Mother.

"Lies, pick out what you want, dear,"said Grandmother.

"Very good that is perfect,"said her Mother.

"Good,"said Lies.

"Thank you for being in the dinning room, Constance,"said Chardin.

"Yes Constant,"said Lise.

"Very good Lies, now finish your dinner ok,"said her Grandmother.

"Ota,"said Lise.

"I see what went wrong, what is on your mind Chardon. With me is the time for a long discussion, "said her Mother-in-law.

"I need to tell you something and the others tonight, I am going to keep this baby you realizes that even if I am not a good mother at least they are protected,"said her Ladyship.

"You are a good mother and you will have this baby,"said her Mother-in-law.

"Thank you,"said Chardon.

"You are a good mother and you will have this child and do not get me angry,"said the Grandmother.

"No, I will not and thank you again,"said Chardon.

"We will not discuss this with anyone else alright, we do not want the other two here being upset when they are, you do follow you,"said the Grandmother.

"Yes, I do and I will not say another word,"said the Daughter-in-law.

"Good, now have some more coffee or something to eat,"said her Mother-in-law.

"Good evening, Everyone,"said Seebees.

"Good evening, Rofster and still napping with the children. "said Leavels.

"Or are they letting him nap you might want to wait him up or he might not sleep or maybe up at two o'clock.?"said the Grandmother.

"Thank you, Grandmother I will go see him right now, Will do you want to go upstairs with me,"said Leavels.

"Sure I need to get another game too,"said Will.

"Everyone help them selves ok,"said their Mother-in-law.

"We started the business today and the fax and emails are important and I looked and read each one and my secretary has been helping me do this right now,"said Chardin.

"That is not me.? Started the busins,"said Don.

"Oh, I am so sorry you remember that, to us is still something funny, ok,"said his Mother.

"Don that was alright, you need to calm down and not get so excited. Also Lise did not understand, "said their Grandmother.

"Did you understand that, how about some homemade cookies, and I will turn on the tel for your favorite show,"said her Mother.

"Yes, Pease,"said Lise.

"Getting to be yourself my Daughter now that is the way we do things,"said Lise's great Grandmother.

"Here is Rofster, he will stay awake,"said Leavels.

"Thank you, Grandmother for the advice,"said Rofster.

"Your welcome you should get your sleep at the right hours, are you very tired,"said the Grandmother.

"No, I am not and please wake me up again,"said Rofster.

"Ok, now everyone has something to drink,"said the Grandmother.

"Here is Will,"said Leavels.

"Good, you gave Lise, Don and yourself another puzzle,"said Seebees.

"It is another building see,"said Will.

"Very nice, lets start,"said Lofster.

"Let them finish it,"said Leavels.

"Yes, of course,"said Rofster.

"Now who wants to know what happen in the world, we according to many of the newspapers in the computers, have stolen the media,"said Seebees.

"Does it have everything we listed including the cartoons,"said Detva.

"No, but just about all of them and we should do what now.?"said Seebees.

"Just wait until the media gets to nasty and rude and the truth that is printed as an error is still a good lawsuit and now we just wait and see,"said their Mother.

"That is correct and if you want me to read all that I think you should not see then let me know right now,"said their Grandmother.

"I do suggest that Seebees, Leavels and myself we all do not attempt to read the worst about your lives it is really for the audience of the tel,"said their Mother.

"Oh, and another thing when anyones sees Gale Ets Marie in Versailles now that he is married in the home he goes by the name of Paul as in Duke Paul,"said Chardin.

"So they children are all set for the understanding of the exile,"said Seebees.

"Good thinking,"said Rofster.

"Yes, when he was going to Austria with Queen Marie Antoinette and the children. He did use the name Duke Paul. Now Gale would be ordered back to Belgium and then the States. He only used the throne for the Euro train just like very patent that has been used since the 1900's,"said Lady Chardinrey.

"So we do call his Paul in the house, to himself so the children will understand later,"said Leavels.

Chapter 13

"That is right so he was just here in his building two days ago. So now we have to look for something that is questionable in the news. He does help us out and always has, these are his businesses,"said her Ladyship.

"He gave them to Edvard to use,"said Seebees.

"That is correct and Ed and his wife were paid very well many many times in fact,"said her Ladyship.

"Now the patents are ours to build up the same fortune as Ed and Owns,"said Detva.

"Then where do the patents go back to Ed.?"said Likus.

"It is not Italy, where most of them were placed by society. Including the aqueducts that was the only place the Christians could pray, now we have proper churchs,"said their Grandmother.

"It should go to your brother in Newport, Rhode Island who has worked there just for a salary and he should come home with his family. Then Detva may take over in the states,"said Lady Chardinrey.

"Then I go to the states for a salary, and Detva works and is in charge here,"said Likus.

"Then it is my turn in the states and then Rofster, "said Will.

"I am going to miss you sweetheart you have been anything to me, Leavels,"said Rofster.

"Oh, shout up maybe it will be me,"said Leavels.

"That is a good idea and I will put my franchise in for the Eurotrain Exile pharmacies where I think it needs it,"said Rofster.

"Now we are thinking like a family and still having a good sense of humor,"said Lady Chardinrey.

"Also there is another franchise that no one has done it is the total Venice canals with tunnels underneath the water allowing small craft too. We had, we have one inquiry and a law firm mention or demanded and they are still negotiating after two years,"said her Ladyship.

"For digging all that mud out and then put the tunnels in, it might be more time than just two more years, "said Seebees.

"I would like to go see them myself,"said Likus.

"You would,"said his Mother.

"Yes, we never gave up that property and it was never effect by the floods so why not Detva you do not mind that do you,"said Likus.

"No, not at all,"said Detva.

"You just committed yourself to seeing this girl you use to date,"said Seebees.

"I am not going tommorw I will present by the company formal letter to visit the Mayor and other officials, I know it was started by Ed but it still needs someone to run it is way behind schedule,"said Likus.

"Good so you might leave in about a couple of weeks, or months, just first make sure they know you will arrive and wait for an answer,"said his Mother.

"I will let the Mayor know or the officials that I will set up an appointment when I arrive there,"said Likus.

"Or better an appoinment in three weeks while you are there and invite the officials one family at a time before their appointments start,"said their Grandmother.

"This would be so much fun and excitement for you, Likus,"said Leavels.

"You do not mind Mother me leaving and you do need all of us to help,"said Likus.

"No, this way you are helping,"said his Mother.

"Likus, Mother has Seebees and myself when we have our babies,"said Leavlets.

"I know I just do not think of myself as a necessary person here and I do believe I can do more good in Venice,"said Likus.

"You will do more no matter where you are, the main thing right now is are you going to live with her in Italy or I think your first date is tonight. So go see her and invite her out, maybe to Ed's restaurant Usa in the City,"said his Mother.

"I will call in the other room if I return she can not leave,"said Likus.

"Just go there Likus and do not say would you like to go to Italy with me unless she she mentions she is tired of living with her parents, joking say, "I am going to Italy to work you should go with me,"said her Mother.

"That is a good idea, I will just to see her.Bye,"said Likus.

"Have fun,"said Grandmother.

"Bye,"said Lise

"Bye,"said Don.

"Bye,"said Likus.

"Don't do it,"said Will.

"Oh, said Leavels.

"Oh,"said Will's Mother.

"Will apologize,"said his Mother.

"I am sorry, I apologize,"said Will.

"He was only being funny,"said his Grandmother.

"I know but if a stranger was here it would not look good,"said his Mother.

"Sorry Mom, please do not be angry,"said Will.

"I am not angry, please do not let that happen again, "said his Mother.

"Ok, "said Will.

"Now I see that the press has put us in the front of the news, so things are working, yet some we should be getting a salary or something put into our accounts,"said the Grandmother.

"Oh, I found out about that thye keep their individual accounts yet the largest check is going to us in a few days,"said her Ladyship.

"You mean the account of the total business.?"said their Grandmother.

"Yes, that we get and then they keep their own personal account, and when we are not in charge we do to,"said her Ladyship.

"We keep our own accounts,"said their grandmother.

"These are the people that are working Grandmother. You and I do not have accounts right, Mother,"said Leavels.

"You get an account being in the news that is the largest account going once it is at its highest and we are all involved,"said their Mother.

"So if we start out, not working and just waiting for the news to give us some coverage, would that be a small amount all the time.? "said Leavels.

"That depends on what we want you to read,"said their Mother.

"It could be one or a group,"said Seebees.

"Then we have to give it a try when it happens,"said Rofster.

"Yes, now lets stop this and we can have some refreshments,"said their Mother.

"So me,"said Lise.

"Do you want some juice, or soda.? "said her Mother.

"Juice, very good,"said her Mother.

"Thanss u,"said Lise.

"So I hope these years are good to us all,"said her Mother.

"Of course, all the years,"said their grandmother.

"Detva, do you want to stay and work here,"said his Mother.

"Yes, I do not want to take away what Ed and his wife had started,"said Detva.

"So it is alright, about Likus,"said his Mother.

"Sure it is, and I will make sure he does, I just did not want to say that right now,"said Detva.

"That was nice and you do appreciate him for doing this,"said his Mother.

"Yes, he is doing the work that many of us do not want to do,"said Detva.

"Many of us can not go to Venice and the states so he is very valuable, yet Ed has several books about there life together and Likus will only have two,"said his Mother.

"So Ed and his wife will always be more popular for their work,"said Detva.

"Yes, I understand that you would not want to interfere with that,"said his Mother.

"No, I do not mind if Likus does this,"said Detva.

"When we are popular with this advertising of us being in charge we will in fact be seen and noticed,"said their Mother.

"Taking away from everyone that is not living in this house just like Ed and his wife for years but they were chosen to do this now it is for us,"said the Grandmother.

"So we will be more popular than anyone and for us in this house to gain the popularity many of us will have to be in the news together,"said their Mother.

"So we are taking away the press, from Ed and his family,"said Seebees.

"He has won a lot of awards and I will not be the first to be in his way when he is to receive another as an elder,"said Detva.

"Gale, Paul will be in charge so we who are not in the news triumphly with Ed resume and do the work that Gale does not want to do,"said her Ladyship.

"Anyways I trust all of you and here we have another person who came into our lives that I trust so much who has decided to come out of retirement to help us all, "said Her Ladyship.

"Did Lloyd's of London start already,"said Urnlee.

"No, but we have been testing ourselves and Likus is going to move to Italy and we are just waiting to be insulted buy the media, "said Chardin.

"Well thank you for the warning and preparation to a worst media I do not want to read about, even with me. Now I need to take all of your vital sign. "said Urnlee.

"Sure, me,"said Don.

"I have to tell you there was water running from the third floor and I let the staff know they have now cleaned it up, the children and nannies are safe and many of the children are asleep,"said Urnlee.

"I need to go upstairs,"said Leavels.

"That is why you are first,"said Urnlee.

"Now Chardin,"said Don.

"Why not Mom,"said Cahrdin.

"He is the new Doctor on call,"said Urnlee.

"That is nice,"said his Mother.

"Doctor what about Lady Seebees,"said Urnlee.

"Yes, nurse and Grandmother,"said Don.

"Very good Doctor, is there anyone else.?"said Nurse Urnlee.

"No Nurse,"said Don.

"Very good, and now I hope someone can let out to Lloyd's there are a few illegal degrees on the premises,"said Urnlee.

"No, he is the best Doctor in the world,"said Will.

“I know he is. Then if there are any complaints we can ask the Board of Directors Lady Chardinrey is in charge of that and I think Doctor, Lady Lise too,”said the Nurse.

“That is good,”said the Doctor.

“In that case, I will not let them out of my sight until we have to finished,”said their Grandmother.”

“I am so delighted, Lise and Don took charge of that,”said their Mother.

“Si,”said Lise.

“The children are asleep,”said Leavels.

“Vitals,”said the Doctor Don.

“Yes, doctor,”said Urnlee.

“Thank you, Nurse and Lady Urnlee are you going to return after the rounds are done,”said Chardin.

“Yes, I will thank you and thank you too doctor,”said the Nurse.

“Hurry back Urnlee,”said Will.

“Yes, and when you do you and I will be playing cards, at least I know how to keep one of you calm,”said Grandmother.

“We can play bridge,”said Chardin.

“Yes, said Leavels.

“Alright I will be back in just a few minutes,”said Urnlee.

“I remember she put down cards on her application so why not start a good thing and besides Chardin you have to much money anyways,”said their grandmother.

“I last time we played for money in a winter I lost and I had to wait for the snow plow because we had to rely on the city.Why was that.? ”said Chardin.

“It was only two years ago, and we are still included with them because we gave them are new ones and if the others do not start we have to call them,”said their Grandmother.

“That is right I hope these winter will be mild thank goodness the the Finland dam we were the first to notice the different snow storms that stated in the year 2010,”said Chardin.

“I know I like the fact that the scientist that is being released from Norway that he will help us with the new satalite to be reused since the Emos project was completed,”said their Grandmother.

“What was he in for.?”said Seebees.

"He gladly took the rap for a colleague to not hurt his family or wife, and has been doing work for the government and also keeping order in the prison because he was a lawyer,"said their Mother.

"He is in a building the government build for him and with a staff under him this time to the work on research when the computers were just in every home,"said the Grandmother.

"So why did he not leave,"said Leavels.

"This was his law suit and what he had discovered the government place him there with staff in one month time and they are still building homes for the staff and a Eurotrain train for them that brings them to Belgium only,"said his Grandmother.

"Why doe she not see his wife,"said Seebees.

"The wife requested him to have the Catholic church run the building and to have research there at all times,"said Chardin.

"I feel so unimportant and awful to want my husband back,"said Seebees.

"Don't last year Dr. received his title and the Noble Peace Prize,"said Will.

"They had this planned and they believe the other doctor was dieing and he wanted his wife to be rich with the insurances. Thank you, Will,"said the Grandmother.

"Your welcome,"said Will.

"Seesaw now to wait and great things happen to great people of mine. Just think with a nick name you might get to Lloyd's again,"said Will.

"Mother, we do have a PR in the house,"said Seebees.

"He is just doing his share and even I never thought of that,"said his Mother.

"I will not take my 10% now,"said Will.

"Getting back to the doctor he will not be here and we need him to be in the new satellite station in the Netherlands, "said his Mother.

"Why the shuttle,"said Will.

"His parole is now and he wants his wife to be divorced from him at 12:00 p.m. in space seen by the personnel transferring him,"said Lady Chardinrey.

"This was an agreement he had made for this work he is about to do, "said their Grandmother.

"It was, and I do not know about the financial but his wife is set for life when he to out and so are the children,"said his Mother.

"That is not to bad for demands,"said Rosfster.

"What are you saying that all of them think I had a good supply of our the counter drugs when we were dating,"said Leavels.

"No, dear I can not even bring them home, I am sorry,"said Rofster.

"Let that be a lession to you before you try anything again,"said Leavels.

"Good one, you even had me going for a while,"said her Ladyship.

"I just wanted everyone to know I do not play favorites,"said Leavels.

"I love you,"said Rofster.

"How cute, but not here,"said their Grandmother.

"If anyone wants to leave now and go upstairs they may, are you tired Leavels and Seebees, "said their Mother.

"Yes, we will,"said Leavels.

"Good night and do not be angry,"said her Ladyship.

"I'm not angry mother, I just like to be in charge,"said Leavels.

"Good night, everyone,"said Rofster.

"Night,"said Grandmother.

"Night, I am going to watch the tel,"said Will.

"Lise and Don do you want to sleep on the floor and we can go upstairs later, ok,"said their Mother.

"Si,"said Lise.

"Yes, pleease,"said Don.

"Good night, everyone. I am going to call Gavga,"said Seebees.

"That will be good for you and give him my love, and good night,"said her Mother.

"Grandmother, do you want more coffee,"said her Ladyship.

"Yes please, and even in front of the children you can start calling me Constance,"said her Mother-in-law.

"Ever since Ed was sick I do not want to say that, just Mother,"said her Ladyship.

"I know I will whisper how about them at Monte Carlo,"said her Mother-in-law.

"The steps are fine and they want to have their own life,"said her Ladyship.

"They do not want to be responsible and medically, I am doing the right thing and they are too,"said her Ladyship.

"They have a good business and I want it to be the best, they started with the patents and they are going to be more successful. Besides she had two,"said Chardin.

"Repairing and putting new tunnels along the shore, just giving them money and no one seeing what they are doing,"said her Mother-in-law.

"I know but they both want to help so this way they eventually have more in common, and they have done more than their share of the work,"said Chardin.

"That is true a good and true test of strength,"said their Grandmother.

"I told them both I would be very pleased and honored. But if my son can go to the states than so can they go to Monte Carlo and do the same work as him,"said Chardin.

"You knew what you were doing and Ed did not suspect a thing you told him and to mind his own business and that it was another government and maybe they appointed,"said their Grandmother.

"I know and when he was home he never asked,"said Chardin.

"There are almost finished with the new tunnels by the sea, I think you could have them go see Ed and his wife, this weekend and have them visit us in two weeks, "said the Grandmother.

"All right I will, the children are asleep, Hello Ed, yes hello Dear my I please speak to Dad, hello, yes it is me yes now I want you to both go see Ed. This weekend I will call him right now, ok bye,"said Chardin.

"Hello, Ed remember you ask me if I knew or your father knew who was in Monte Carlo, will you father arrange it for them to work there and they are going to visit you both. Yes, they are your grandparents. Good they will be there and give them some money for there work. Thank you, wait, "said Chardin.

"Let him know you are pregnant so he understands your sharp tone,"said his Grandmother.

"Grandmother wanted me to tell you, she reminded me to tell you I am pregnant and that is the reason for the sharp tone and attitude. Ok, thank you, I love you too,"said his Mother.

"Hello, dad he does exspect you both this weekend and he id delighted he has and she has two people they both can talk to about what they have doen for a living.

"Wait, remind of your sharp tone,"said the grandmother.

"Also my Mother-in-law wanted me to tell you my sharp tone is because I am having a baby, ok. I can not talk anymore. OK, bye,"said Chardin.

"Excuse me Lady Chardinrey. I had a call from your Father he has a very good butcher with there own truck and he ask about the measurements of the freezer so I gave him all the necessary information the food well be arriving about in the afternoon in about two days, "said the Housekeeper.

"Oh boy that is so nice of them, we could use the extra food right now,"said their Grandmother.

"Yes, I know,"said Chardin.

"I know you are not in the mood, but think of it this way at least now one might have left your husband my son but there are so many in our lives we are going to be very busy these next few years and it is all by Gale it is our turn to be very rich,"said Grandmother.

"I know if I died he would force Ed to run the business and Gale is correct it is our turn to do this and we have taken our time about it,"said Chardin.

"It is good that we are doing this we did not have a heavy price to pay our family returned to us and only in a new castle could we get this done,"said the Grandmother.

"You mentioned not a heavy price to pay why not at the shore at the end of that large river entering Belgium is our land why not take Edvard's franchise and duplicate for the family the King Ludwig building then we actually have enough space,"said Chardin.

"What type of plan, by the water for the castle.? "said the Grandmother.

"I know that area, Ed and use to drive there when we wanted some space or just to drive instead of going into the city,"said Chardin.

"Here is is a large wall that can hold back the wall in case of a flood it did happen and then inside is our living space and it will be raised up to the height of the castle,"said Chardin.

"Oh, then with a bottom of the other side of the wall towards the inland is the parking lot and above it a new colisum and the building over looking that roof as a lovely baroque garden,"said the Grandmother.

"Just like the other one and we can get a family into the castle. We will move into the other only for a little while until the other building is completed.,"said Chardin.

"That is marvelous exciting I love every minute of it,"said the Grandmother.

"I know wait just one minute I remember Ed putting this on a blue print for me. I think it is in the library watch the children and I will be right back,"said Chardin.

"Alright it will give me a chance to finish this coffee and snacks,"said Grandmother.

"Sure ok, there is more in the bottom of the cart if I want any I will get it, no, here there might be some other kind of pastry for you to choose,"said Chardin.

"Some coffee,"said their Grandmother.

"Here it is,"said Chardin.

"Look an email address to the architects. You two thought of everything one day,"said their Grandmother.

"I guess we did that day, he did he help me,"said Chardin.

"I am not going to say one anything at all, here have some coffee and a new pastry,"said Grandmother.

"I will, until I can think of what to say, other than you are involved do what does happen happens to all of us and I will not say anything at all any more,"said Chardin.

"Good one, but I will take the email address and send it off to the architects right now,"said her Mother-in-law.

"Constance if I remember you have about a twelve room suite to yourself,"said her Daughter-in-law.

"Yes, I remember you telling me that, and I responded to letting you know I needed about eighteen rooms then with I do believe there was about three children running into my bedroom each morning,"said her Mother-in-law.

"Yes, that is right how did we stop that,"said Chardin.

"Puppies, that all died in our own road by different cars,"said her Mother-in-law.

"Constance, we did have, have our hands full,"said Chardin.

"No, we had many nannies,"said their Grandmother.

"Do you want two puppy for the children.?"said Chardin.

"Let them out at night, who is going to do it.?"said their Grandmother.

"I know,"said Chardin.

"We have an anwer on the property, It will be started next week,"said their Grandmother.

"Good, now we can move in there in about six years that all,"said her Ladyship.

"By then we will need the privacy and room,"said her Mother-in-law.

"I am sure we will,"said Chardin.

"Have some coffee,"said her Mother-in-law.

"Right I need something and it is better than a drink,"said her Ladyship.

"Well I well have my last one for the night, please make me in one,"said her maid.

"You have that and I will have these children moved to their rooms,"said her Ladyship.

"Yes, please call the nannies alright,"said their Grandmother.

"Thank you for agreeing,"said Chardin.

"We need to talk, so they need to leave,"said their Grandmother.

"Nannies please take them upstairs And Lise casn stasy in my room and please stay there until I come up alright,"said Chardin.

"Yes, I will, "said the Nanny.

"Now we can talk easier,"said Grandmother.

"Constance we do need that new building and maybe the obsevation can be a part of it for Seebees sake,"said her Mother.

"Yes, this would work but it is up to the Navy first,"said her Mother-in-law.

"I know it should,"said Chardin.

"Is it on the same land as they originally surveyed,"said Constance

"No, that is on the shore,"said Chardin.

"Then build them both,"said Constance.

"Yes, even another castle would not hurt right there on the shore too,"said Chardin.

"My house is for Leavels, Detva has the castle Will has the new castle on the river with Don. Seebees has Lise and the new baby if something happens,"said the Grandmother.

"Likus might stay in Venice, and Creg in Newport he might return sometime,"said Chardin.

"Moscow will always have Ray he might even take Urnlee and her child, for a time so she can meet them,"said their Grandmother.

"Not for a long time,"said Chardin.

"As it is she will only stay there for a few months anyways,"said their Grandmother.

"That is true according to his will,"said Chardin.

"If that is all of them not to mention that all the small homes or estates we have in Belgium can accommodate them all later,"said Grandmother.

"We are providing for our families children and they still may live where they want to, but Ed had a reason for employment and it must be told to them they may live near by but they are needed here in Belgium,"said their Mother.

"I do not think there would be any reason to leave there is always employment of some kind for them to enjoy,"said their Grandmother.

"We have never stopped them from doing something on there own, Seebees does enjoy her art work, and she has done quite well for herself, but I need them all here,"said their Mother.

"You are correct but at this point in time it is only the baby talking to you so talk to him and let him know things are all right,"said Grandmother.

"You are right again,"said Chardin.

"You are worry about a lot of things, but we are wealthy and if anything happens the law states we are allowed to live in another country that does need us, "said Grandmother.

"We did put in the Euro train.! "said her Ladyship.

"Yes, that does increase your own value while living there,"said Grandmother.

"That is why our children were there,"said her Ladyship.

"Now there are more and this is why you raised them to help uis out they do not forget and there is property for them to undertand themselves, too,"said their Grandmother.

"We did just that, we gave away Ed, and he returned,"said her Ladyship.

"No one gave him away, we sent him away, and he is living with the one he wants,"said their Grandmother.

"It is alright to think Ed is still here and he sent him away for a little while, that is all,"said her Mother-in-law.

"Use your inner thoughts and talk to Ed, just do it for yourself the children do not need to hear the conversation,"said their Grandmother.

"We do need their in the open to find out what is wrong or right, so I will keep it inside,"said her Ladyship.

"Also with your step father and real mother you have been very unselfish now,"said their Grandmother.

"Thank you,"said her Ladyship.

"Giving them some thing that they can relate to, the Monter Carlo new tunnels is just what we needed for Ed, he will be so thrilled to meet them,"said their Grandmother.

"Just think they put in the Monte Carlo tunnels and now he has something to common with them,"said her Ladyship.

"That is why you are there Mother,"said their Grandmother.

"Also when they have Urnlee it is only a visit, she knows she is a good nurse and she is in charge and will earn that money too,"said Grandmother.

"Your right again and I need some more coffee,"said her Ladyship.

"We can stay up another hour, so I will have more myself. I do have to admit these Italian pastries are delicious, we have a good cook,"said Grandmother.

"Oh, I figure you and with pay anyone that does not want to duplicate anyones dinner as a chef they are allowed to cook and visit for the evening with extra pay so that will keep everyone happy in all the buildings,"said Grandmother.

"I will write that down right now the chefs will like the overtime,"said her Ladyship.

"Mention to supervise only so there is not to much stress, "said Grandmother.

"I will put down surpervisor or whichever works for them.? Ok,"said Chardin.

"Good to me,"said Constance.

"Now that is completed,"said her Ladyship.

"Constance you I love you and we have never had any words to each words that were unkind,"said her Daughter.

"I know you do and I love you and all of you. You have made a life enjoyable but you must realize we did not live with each other until these last three years,"said their Grandmother.

"Ed never told me about the cancer until he did think it would be obvious,"said Chardin.

"He never told me at all until you both came home and then he was dead one month after, and I forgive both of you he must have known I could not take it,"said Grandmother.

"What I am asking is if something happens to me please you would save the baby.? "said Chardin.

"Yes, now stop getting yourself so worried,"said Grandmother.

"One question for my sake, he did not take his life.? "said her Mother-in-law.

"No, he had one month or it would have been two,"said Chardin.

"I just had to be sure,"said Grandmother.

"I understand, it was not pleasant and lieing to was not easy. But you do see Don and Lise who are not realizing it just yet,"said Chardin.

"Yes, I think it will take a while that is why I do not mind that I did not know it because it would be worse for us if the both of them saw many of us crying,"said their Grandmother.

"I know I do not think I could go along with to much of that with this baby,"said Chardin.

"I can just imagine,"said their Grandmother.

"Your situation you did not have anyone nearby,"said Chardin.

"I know but it was war times, you did what you were told,"said Grandmother.

"We are here now in better times,"said Chardin.

"That is what is so nice about being alive in this world, a wonderful family,"said Grandmother.

"We do have a lot to be thankful for,"said Chardin.

"Yes, we do and your children are beautiful, your still a beautiful woman why not start dating after a year,"said Grandmother.

"Maybe after one year,"said Chardin.

"Your not the kind that sits all day long,"said Grandmother.

"No, I am not but I will wait one year,"said Chardin.

"Good, now you sound like my Daughter-in-law,"said Grandmother.

"I do, I really do, I must be getting back and in charge of things again,"said Chardin.

"That is what we need to see and hear,"said Grandmother.

"Now I know of a good, many antiques shops to explore on the computer again for this new castle,"said Chardin.

"You ought to know we started them with Ed and his wife,"said Grandmother.

"Oh, know look at you Don,"said his Mother.

"Sorry Lady Chardinrey,"said the Nurse.

"We are all going upstairs, in a few minutes, nurse,"said her Ladyship.

"Yes, Don show me how to use the elevator,"said his Grandmother.

Chapter 14

"Lise, wake up you do not want to miss school your Spanish lession is today,"said her Mother.

"Si,"said Lise.

"Don go downstairs and visit Grandmother, ok,"said his Mother.

"Si,"said Don.

"Lise we can have breakfast downstairs with Grandmother,"said her Mother.

"Grandmother good morning,"said Lise.

"Now she is awake she was sleeping even during her bath, and when I was dressing her,"said her Mother.

"Good morning, everyone,"said Grandmother.

"Good morning,"said Chardin.

"You need to use exercise for the baby Lise has a nanny in the day time and evening,"said their Grandmother.

"I know I was just getting use to it so when the baby is here I will be a little prepared,"said her Ladyhip.

"Good now let the nanny do the rest ok,"said their Grandmother.

"I will,"said Chardin.

"Now have some more breakfast if you want too,"said Grandmother.

"This week I go into the office on the third floor with Likus who is leaving for Italy tomorrow and is going to bring his girlfriend,"said her Ladyship.

"That is news, are they going to wait for six months,"said their Grandmother.

"They are and they intend to get married there so we do not have to be so concerned,"said his Mother.

"It is his second and hers so we will let the kids go,"said the Grandmother.

"No, she does want a very private ceremony just with a priest and themselves,"said his Mother.

"It sounds more romantic, less stress and indeed privacy which is the key to success which Likus do not use for his first marriage ,"said his Grandmother.

"From what I remember either did she there was to many outside forces for her first marriage to survive, "said his Mother.

"Now look at all that food, are you sure you do not want anything, some more Lise,"said her Mother.

"No, thank you I have had enough,"said Grandmother.

"Good, then I will have some more,"said Chardin.

"Yes, please do, I did have enough you can tell how much I had, it was enough, for me, "said their Grandmother.

"What do we have inside the new castle.? "said Chardin.

"Besides the satelite at the shore on the ocean front and we can be on the river bed with our Central office there while we are all living there who want to,"said Grandmother.

"Then we have everything in its placed with the proper security and also this satelite head quarters could never be purchased from us,"said Her Ladyship.

"Or stolen, it will always be there,"said Grandmother.

"Always be ours that means we have the best security systems in the world for the Euro train,"said Her Ladyship.

"We are very fortunate indeed and it is all Ed's work,"said his Grandmother.

"Should we divide the Europe into two parts for them to watch too,"said his Mother.

"No, I talked to Ed about not working on this project and he agreed with me to watch their family and it is about time they both did,"said his Grandmother.

"Your are right again, especially the media did start to notice that and so did we,"said his Mother.

"Now they have enough Nannies to help out,"said his Grandmother.

"Yes, they do and so do we,"said Her Ladyship.

"I told them to hire many times and they did,"said his Grandmother.

"I guess we are then allowed to do this business starting this week,"said Her Ladyship.

"Yes you will and bring the two girls and Urnlee with you and do not have anyone stay alone upstairs and I will make sure you have a food cart to that floor right now, "said Grandmother.

"For now it will be referred to as the Family Food Service,"said her Ladyship.

"That does sound professional and needs to be approved,"said Grandmother.

"Good morning, Seebees and I are going shopping,"said Leavels.

"You are going to use the computer upstairs.?"said her Mother.

"We did not mean to deceive you but you do not think we would go outside like this,"said Seebees.

"Oh, no, but you both had me there for a second, just one thing no more up in the air talk. Don't let us have to think of what you two are going to do, ok "said their Mother.

Right, and because of your enthusiasm of going shopping and no hard feelings about what your mother and I agree on, there is another 5 thousand for each of you,"said their Grandmother.

"Yes, and did not buy anything as everyday shopping item we do have a store in this building for groceries and such. So have fun today, the both of you. "said their Mother.

"Thank you Mother so much,"said Seebees.

"Yes, thank you both,"said Leavels.

"I guess we should by things on the computer for Don and Lise maybe a size bigger, or at least they have something else to wear if not for only a few times,"said their Grandmother.

"Do you want to do that, I am just being lazy and want some more food,"said Chardin.

"Sure I will and if there is anything that you would want for them I am going to leave it on the same page. Said their Grandmother.

"Lady Chardinrey we will be on the third floor if there is anything we will call you or transfer the calls, "said their two Secretaries.

"Thank you and make sure all the rents show up for each building and are in the accounts, thank you,"said Her Ladyship.

"With that I feel so much better, I forgot to ask them, did you,"said Chardin.

"No, but remember they can still open the mail and write your correspondence for the day, "said Grandmother.

"Yes, it is nice for them and they can get a lot of work done, we will still have their offices on the first floor too along with yours and mine,"said Chardin.

"Good bye, Mother and Grandmother,"said Will.

"Bye Dear and hug your Grandmother,"said his Mother.

"Good bye Dear enjoy your lessions,"said Grandmother.

"Bye,"said will.

"Bye said his Mother.

"He returned and I saw him leave,"said Grandmother.

"He put something into the car, then he returned, "said his Mother.

"How it was, his gym bag, he one day took a porcelain doll of mine for show and tell,"said his Grandmother.

"I will call him on the phone,"said his Mother.

"Hello, Will, I am going to blame this on my pregnancy but do you remember you took Grandmother's porcelain doll to school for show and tell. Yes, and ok, then I will wait, and have a good day and return it today or I will get it myself,"said his Mother.

"No, something from the safe this time,"said Grandmother.

"You are too funny this morning. He took Don's teddy bear and they have to write a report on a younger brother or sister's toy. Then have their picture taken and given to each one for their birthday,"said his Mother.

"Something like a message that they are sorry if they did rank on each other,"said Grandmother.

"That is correct just like we gave the girls 5 thousand each but they needed it,"said their Mother.

"You right this is very true now look at this page and should I have them delivered. Here is the paper and instructions of the returning the item for their photo,"said their Grandmother.

"Did he say it was there.? "said his Mother.

"No, my guess is that Lise had something missing and so did I it was my favorite dish, I thing it was easier for him to take these things out then to let all of us about it,"said Grandmother.

"What did he take of mine,"said his Mother.

"My dish is back,"said his Grandmother.

"I know what is going on, he is doing a project for all of us, and we, the both of us would not mind it if Ed were alive. So we must be patient and not make a big deal about it and I will let him know again about

Edvard's last will and testament. Hoping that nothing else goes out of this house,"said his Mother.

"Now I do not think anything is missing and we do have a schedule of things that we display so why not ask the staff to locate all the belongs as an inventory. Especially after Ed's departure we have a good account of everything before we move,"said their Grandmother.

"Good idea, and we need one right now anyways,"said Chardin.

"Yes, it is a good idea since his death and before we all moved. There I put reguest in to the staff and housekeeper "said Grandmother.

"Thank you, Constance this almost had me shaken up,"said Chardin.

"We are in luck all morning long thinking of this and here they are they all had a half-day today,"said Grandmother.

"Will, I was wondering if these are all the items you took out of the house because now with the last requests of your father we have to listed all of the things in this house Is there anything else you need to do.? "said his Mother.

"No my teacher said for me to make the computer presents for their birthdays and add my own photos if I want too,"said Will.

"So these are the only ones you used and all these are in the house right now, "said his Mother.

"Yes, now I need to use the computer for the other gifts, "said Will.

"Good and do not submit or email alright,"said his Mother.

"No Mother I will not without your permission and when I am finished with the first one I will let you look at it alright,"said Will.

"Yes, it is alright,"said his Mother.

"Show us as soon as you are finished alright or you know my secretary can show you how,"said his Mother.

"That is alright now we have the inventory done,"said her Ladyship.

"What is this, we said our good byes and now it is you Mother and Grandmother and Don and Lise we are leaving for Venice now, "said Likus.

"Goodbye and Likus and I know dear and as your name is Princess Clayfee we know in a distance land anything will be fine for the both of you,"said Lady Chardinrey.

"Yes, please have a good time and enjoy yourselves,"said Grandmother.

"Bye ,"said Don.

"Bye Ikus,"said Lise.

"Are you sure you both have everything and I know there is not need of a car, so we will give you a check Likus and Seebees and her sister can use it,"said her Mother.

"Bye dears,"said Grandmother.

"Bye,"said his Mother.

"Hear Detva yelling,"said the Grandmother.

"No, what Lise was asking me something.?"said her Ladyship.

"I heard Detva, yell to them, "I want good reports about you too,"said Grandmother.

"I want good, they are to humorous I know I am going to miss them, but there are three more on the way,"said Chardin.

"We still did not hear from Urnlee. Did we.?"said Grandmother.

"I know I wonder when.? "said Chardin.

"It should be soon,"said Grandmother.

"So we are going to have a few more little ones and now I am sure all of us will be staying of course our soldier at sea will be here soon to survey,"said Chardin.

"So two leave and maybe five will be here soon.? "said Grandmother.

"I hope so I do not think Seebees will enjoy of thinking of her husband as a new born,"said Chardin.

"That is right there are four babies and one large adult,"said Grandmother.

"One large, one very large, I think that is why he left and we will allow her to leave with her sailor when he returns,"said Chardin.

"Yes of course and if Leavels wants to leave she can stay right here and we will be going to live in the new castle, anyways,"said Grandmother.

"They both know he will be needed as a survivor and to watch the progress first hand,"said Chardin.

"He can serve at a part-time basis at sea and they would want him here,"said Grandmother.

"Maybe just here on land to see the project underway while many a ship sets anchor in our river bay and ocean,"said Chardin.

"That is what I mean he can stay of ship while it is here and work there until they leave,"said Grandmother.

"He should be given a command in the castle as an full-time job and continue his career in that building and the other,"said Chardin.

"Your right that is perfect,"said Grandmother.

"That does sound to good to be true, yet he could start at the bottom and then near his retirement they can keep him on in charge of something important,"said Chardin.

"That does sound humble enough,"said Grandmother.

"I wonder if Seebees and her husband will go alone with all these plans,"said Her Ladyship.

"It is not her or him first it is the navy and then he must decide to leave his peers and take a desk job here,"said Grandmother.

"I know,"said Chardin.

"I do not think you do many of these men choose careers not to be home and to hurt the children and their wife,"said Grandmother.

"I know they are isolated and only call each other, "said Chardin.

"Do not go making plans for those two, only when he returns do they leave for the cottage,"said Grandmother.

"Now I understand yes, they are probably the only ones that when they settle down it would be for good,"said Chardin.

"Not if he has an extended leave and has assigned for a life time to retirement,"said Grandmother.

"What do you mean.? "said Chardin.

"I think what he did after he got married and used all of his time and vacation and stayed here for a few months was this. He used up all of his time and probably asked for a position here at the observatory,"said Grandmother.

"Then what.?"said Chardin.

"He showed that there was no accumulating time for shore leave and probably asked to be here when they needed a survivor,"said Grandmother.

"So then what, I am still confused.?"said Chardin.

"He is now a VIP or a hero to them he has made a significant contribution to his Navy and service not to mention that he is a Dad,"said Grandmother.

"I do know this part he outranks many when he is on dry land, for the rest of his life,"said Chardin.

"But if something happens to Seebees and he can not get back to his ship and job he is lost among and somehow would not what to fit in, or could not. This is reality,"said Grandmother.

"What do we do.?"said

"So lets get Seebees a new name and just say her husband is on patrol of the high seas. Here it is my secretary did this today,"said Grandmother.

"Why that is wonderful it is beautiful she will be so trilled to see this before dinner and look her gown is fantastic and so is she,"said Chardin.

"Do you like it, it goes into the magazine tomorrow and will be out in one day,"said Grandmother.

"Her Royal Highness Princess Baitlym, "said her Mother.

"Look what else has been written, "She awakes her husband on broad a ship patrolling the high seas and as his leave is concerned I am home just like many other wives, but the arrival date is soon,"said Grandmother.

"Protecting our home is essential and we will be waiting,"said Grandmother.

"If this does not send him home then I do not know what will do it. "said Chardin.

"Chardin you are in a dream world, I was interviewed and I said,."She is waiting along with a new arrival, soon to be,"said Grandmother.

"So what if I had everything printed maybe it will work,"said Chardin.

"Right and look at my photo for the high seas, The Royal Highness Queen of,"said Grandmother.

"Those titles should get him home now,"said Chardin.

"Look, I think she is so beautiful, that baby has taken up most of her time and I am so glad she got her hair and nails done the other day, "said her Mother.

"We have the people right here but it is hard for her to walk a great distance, she certainly did that before she moved in being alone,"said Grandmother.

"I wonder if I hear her talking to her sister,"said her Mother.

"Yes, I think they are both talking,"said Grandmother.

"Seebees are you awake could you please come down stairs right now your sister may too if she wants too,"said her Mother.

"No, Mother I am going to bed and too check on the children if Seebees or you want to tell me you both may tomorrow alright. Ok, Good night,"said Leavels.

"Good night,"said her Mother.

"Now Dear your Grandmother and I have this ready or rather she did it today and I just approved of it, it is a wonderful idea, "said her Mother.

"See the computer, your own article in Versailles and the Hermitage this week, and you on the throne alone,"said Grandmother.

"Yes, Dear and your name is Princess Baitlym does that sound better,"said Lady Baitlym.

"You understand that we could not include you and your husband because he is on board ship,"said her Mother.

"Do you like your gown and the jewelry we picked out of you will be in your safe in your room, or better it can be in the ususal place it is in now, "said Grandmother.

"They can remain there, I do not want them in my room, it is to dangerous,"said Lady Baitlym.

"Oh, my goodness look,"said her Grandmother.

"What, oh,"said Chardin.

"Good evening dear I am home for good this time, "said Gavga.

"My darling, I love you and you are home for good,"said the Princess.

"I love you too,"said her Prince.

"Why not go to the other room the dining room and we can get some dinners for all of us and give them a good amount of time enough to be alone. For a while Chardin,"said Grandmother.

"Thank you Constance I did not think of that at all. Yes some food for all of us,"said Chardin.

"Yes, some food I have told the chefs already, about twelve dinners,"said Grandmother.

"Oh, no do you think she wants to leave with him,"said Chardin.

"No, not even after the baby is born,"said Grandmother.

"Mother we are going upstairs and Gavga is not hungry, good night,"said Lady Baitlym.

"Good night Mother and Grandmother. It is good to be home, my commission is in the new building both of them, if I need too,"said Gavga.

"That is wonderful should I bring up some food for either one of you, the maid has it ready right now,"said Chardin.

"Sure that would be nice having dinner just the two of us,"said Gavga.

"Good I will tell the chef,"said Chardin.

"I already told him,"said Grandmother.

"Oh, it is so nice to have him home,"said Chardin.

"She would survive but Leavels is much stronger to be alone,"said Grandmother.

"You think so.? "said Chardin.

"Yes, but Leavels is much stronger,"said Grandmother.

"I guess so,"said her Mother.

"Do you want a dinner join me and have something,"said Grandmother.

"I will,"said Chardin.

"There all is well, did you notice how the security was he did not tell us in advance he was returning,"said Grandmother.

"Now that you mentioned it. All is very quiet,"said Chardin.

"start eating you can use the strength yourself,"said Grandmother.

"I hope they have enough food,"said Chardin.

"They do I sent up four trays. Now they can pick at what they want,"said Grandmother.

"Very good he probably has a good appetite,"said Chardin.

"Now he is not going to leave this house with this service, he got tonight, let them and the others have their dinners upstairs for now on, all their meals,"said Grandmother.

"That is a good idea,"said Chardin.

"I already put in the request to the housekeeper,"said Grandmother.

"Good, Thank you, you think of everything,"said Chardin.

"Just to make things smoother,"said Grandmother.

"I know it does,"said Chardin.

"Thank you,"said Grandmother.

"This dinner is good, will there be food in this dinning room every day and every meal,"said Chardin.

"Yes, of course I am going to date the general in Austria but he has to move here if me get married,"said Grandmother.

"What a good idea,"said Chardin.

"Yes it is,"said Grandmother.

"It is late give him a call tomorrow,"said Chardin.

"Nonsense it is not late watch this. Hello Shawn, hello goods and you why not visit this weekend. ok, good night. Thank you Prince Shawnif?"said Grandmother.

"That is perfect and good,"said Chardin.

"What do you think I do when I am upstairs,"said Grandmother.

"What? "said Chardin.

"I talk to Shawn for a last two months,"said Grandmother.

"I do not believe this, but you know what I do,"said Chardin.

"I know you worry to much and you should eat more,"said Grandmother.

"Your right,"said Chardin.

"Then date, meet secretly,"said Grandmother.

"Do You.?"said Chardin.

"No, I just talk for a few seconds and I mean seconds so it is not traced,"said Grandmother.

"Clever, I can not believe what just happened in a few minutes my daughter is now happy to have her husband home and now you are dating. Now I am going to ask you,"said Chardin.

"Yes, I will and when I am on the throne of France I am going to be 34 years old, "said Grandmother.

"Constance are you going to stay that age.?"said Chardin.

"Yes, I will after all it is good for Lloyd's and I can bring in more money that way than being myself, If that makes any sense to you.?"said Grandmother.

"It does make sense, it does,"said Her Ladyship.

"This might even happen within a few months, he is arriving this weekend,"said Grandmother.

"You are going to sign the necessary papers and agreements,"said Chardin.

"Dear, I need to tell you something when we are married everything of his is mine. It always was. "said Grandmother.

"Yes, I guess so,"said Chardin.

"He is another from the same branch of male offspring wanting my hand when I saved their fortune marrying their dieing father,"said Grandmother.

"I know,"said Chardin.

"Stopping the World War I and II from taking the money and saving it in England and the States, so it is still mine and all from the thrones too,"said Constance.

"It just did not stay there in the banks,"said Chardin.

"As soon as it matured like the cd's today it was invested in program and always insured at all times,"said Grandmother.

"Constance, what about the others.?"said Chardin.

"The people on the thrones and their families they are California and on the stage and in the movies, "said Constance.

"I was Belgium able the live in the Boston and they all went to New York then out west,"said Constance.

"So why was that not discovered,"said Chardin.

"Do not worry if some one mentioned that they registered their child in a French boarding then a visitor would then see a like-a-like, a twin,"said Constance.

"So they left a few at a time, "said Chardin.

"Espionage it not stupid, these thrones had brilliant handsome and beautiful people on them and their families and they were clever and could act, "said Constance.

"So the world did not know,"said Chardin.

"The world was to frightened. There was only a few thrones at a time and a few families all was not done at once,"said Constance.

"That is very true and history,"said Chardin.

"I know why many do not start a new relationship with a twin or a look-a-like there is to much of a price to pay and a new hardship that could not be endured again because it could be to painful,"said Constance.

"Life is painful at times,"said Chardin.

"Remember that regardless of who is who in the news the ones who do the work do this work are looking like others but acting like them,"said Constance.

"We need to work on the sorrow to do things are good for us and others,"said Chardin.

"You hear mentioned I might look like him but I wish I had his money for his acting but I could not do that type of work, "said Constance.

"I am here and so are you,"said Chardin.

"Yes, that is right, but just mentioning painful, sorrow and doing for others. I am really surprised that our Gale who his wife calls him Paul, that he is now married. For someone not wanting to be hurt. Oh, but I did find out his wife is in excellent health,"said Constance.

"She is and he is now over that, and I do not think anything is going to happen badly to them, after all it is Versailles,"said Chardin.

"This is ture and there really is not a stigma attachment this building, all one needs to do is refer to it as Versailles, "said their Grandmother.

"Mom and Gram,"said Don.

"Look who is here, do you want to sleep here for a while and then we can all go upstairs very soon,"said Don's Mother.

"Don are you still tired,"said his Grandmother.

"Me,"said Don.

"Lise did not return so I guess she is asleep,"said Grandmother.

"I hope so, her Donald sleep on the couch for a while,"said his Mother.

"Here dear sleep by me,"said his Grandmother.

"Grandmother is so good to you,"said Chardin.

"Now you do understand I know we covered a lot of topics, "said Grandmother.

"So all of them had their own accounts in California, Boston and New York, "said Chardin.

"That's put it another way there is money for them to return in those homes to rule,"said Constance.

"So they managed, who did not want to die,"said Chardin.

"They had a choice and were forced to take,"said Constance.

"Towards the states,"said Chardin.

"Now as far as their own money I had the states so it would not go as far as to the World Wars,"said Constance.

"Where is it,"said Chardin.

"I am not in control of it, it is in gold in the each countries and it is for their returning of the ruling families only,"said Constance.

"So it is for someone new to rule,"said Chardin.

"Now how does one touch money from European banks that close just open up in another country and move all the time until the wars are over,"said Constance.

"All that gold, "said Chardin.

"No, in drafts, that others invest in buying what is there and the companies invest in its citizens once again,"said Constance.

"That is right the gold does stay there it usually does,"said Chardin.

"That is right the people invest they are insured which is the law and the investments to go on,"said Constance.

"Yes, the banks are insured and the businesses go on as usuall,"said Chardin.

"The banks that forget their own insurances these countries have it a little bit harder the next time, until a new investor comes along,"said Constance.

"So we can call it a good night, and it has been a successful afternoon and evening,"said Her Ladyship.

"Then you are not angry at me,"said Will

"You were there all night,"said his Mother.

Yes, I just woke when I heard you say call it a good day and night or some thing,"said Will

"Do you want to go upstairs right now, do you want some juice just a mouthful at the most,"said Grandmother.

"Yes. Please, "said Will.

"There are you hungry maybe a large soft cookie to take with you you do not need to finish it leave it on a night stand,"said his Mother.

"Good night,"said Grandmother.

"Night ,"said Will.

"Night Will, you your my good boy, ok,"said his Mother.

"Look around the room for more children,"said Grandmother.

"No, no one is here, it is a good thing he did not stay here alone,"said his Mother.

"Good, no one is here, because I have something to tell you and I forgot it many times tonight and the last three days also,"said Grandmother.

"What is it.?"said her Ladyship

"Do you remember the morning Lise was all dress and ready for school.?"said Grandmother.

"Yes, I do she was in my room and she did not eat to much food,"said her Mother.

"Well, I came down stairs for breakfast and I found her snoring and the two large dogs were with her by her feet when I came into the room,"said Grandmother.

"The dogs I do not mind she is the only one that lets them in. But being here alone sleeping in this room is not good,"said her Mother.

"We thought of dogs and completing ignored them, thinking of having puppies in this house, no it was directed for our new house,"said Grandmother.

"That is right and I need to remember to look at this place more carefully before I go to bed,"said Chardin.

"Yes and I will too, so that is how the dogs get in,"said Grandmother.

"I can not believe I forgot them the other day this is how much stress I have. I went to the garage just to see how many autos there were and I recognized that I alone had three and then four years ago there were seven,"said her Ladyship.

"That is right you took my two and I wanted to get paid, and have my own chauffeur too,"said Grandmother.

"Yes you did, but to forget Will and Lise,"said their Mother.

"I know but they were in the house,"said their Grandmother.

"Your right again,"said Her Ladyship.

"This is not a good time to get upset,"said Constance.

"Your right I do need some coffee,"said Her Ladyship.

“Let me see there is enough for the both of us and I am going to take up this food and the rest of the coffee as well,”said Chardin.

“Ok, here put mind in this large carry all and we can go up stairs right now and relax in our own beds. Maybe not you if someone runs into your bedroom, maybe Lise,”said Grandmother.

“She is ok, then I know she did not sleep down stairs,”said her Mother.

“You are to hard on yourself. Thank you for using my elevator it makes things very easy,”said Grandmother.

“If you in about two months are looking like thirty-five years old for your photo many things should be easier for you,”said Chardin.

“Your right and I could do this all in about one week, marriage and all,”said Grandmother.

“That is good I will be grateful, good night, “saidChardin.

“Good night, dear,”said Grandmother.

Chapter 15

"Lise, What time is it.? Ok, go to sleep,"said her Mother.

"Si,"said Lise.

"Mom, can I go to the movies today in the study or the film study room,"said Will.

"Sure can we all go together, Will,"said his Mother.

"Thanks,"said Will.

"Then sleep here for a little while with us,"said his Mother.

"Ok, I am,"said Will.

"Good,"said His Mother.

"When are we getting up,"said Will

"In about one hour,"said his Mother.

"Ok,"said Will.

"Mom. Food,"said Lise.

"Here is some,"said her Mother.

"Si,"said Lise.

"Now lets sleep ok,"said their Mother.

"No,"said Lise.

"Finish first, then sleep,"said her Mother.

"No more,"said Lise.

"Do you both want to go downstairs, now that you are ready we have a lot to do today and Gavga is home,"said their Mother.

"Baitlym. "said Will.

"How do you know.?"said his Mother.

"It is right here on the your computer,"said Will.

"Oh, that is something else,"said his Mother.

"I know, "said Will.

"So take your sister down stairs and your Grandmother should be there and there is more food ok,"said his Mother.

"Bye,"said Lise.

"Bye I will see you both in just a few minutes,"said their Mother.

"Ok,"said Will.

"Ok, "said Lise.

"Ok, "said their Mother.

"Constance I have sent downstairs to you Will and Lise. Ok, you see them now I will be there in a little while. "said their Mother.

"Why, Will and Lise, good morning,"said their Grandmother.

"Good said Lise.

"Good morning, Grandmother I love you,"said Will

"Good morning, I love you too the both of you,"said Grandmother.

"Love you,"said Lise.

"I love you too, Lise. Said Grandmother.

"Did you see Baitlym in the newspapers,"said Will.

"Yes, I did I sent that last night and they ran it this morning,"said Grandmother.

"The picnic was last week before Likus and his future bride left for Italy. So I think we will have the staff prepare steaks on the grill outside and bring them in for us ok,"said Her Ladyship.

"Before things get to cold that is a good idea,"said their Grandmother.

"We should and we will it might be very few after that,"said her Ladyship.

"A request the corn put on the fire first and leave them alone do not clean them, and the chicken some of it can be placed in Italian sauce Lise and I love it that way. "their Grandmother.

"I will not need to ask the others how they like there because the food was delivered and the freezers are filled now, we will do many dishes today, "said her Ladyship.

"It is a good treat to look forward to, just like last weeks picnic,"said Grandmother.

"Yes that was fun, I want everyone together today for dinner, but I want the chefs to prepare the staff foods first,"said Her Ladyship.

"Now lets see what the computer has for the company right now,"said Grandmother.

"All is ok, the same amount of rent is in for each year and is up-to-date,"said Chardin.

"That is right, there are no errors,"said Grandmother.

"We have done an excellent job the first two weeks,"said her Ladyship.

"I can remember when Likus went to Italy and they did not want to do the project then. Why is that.?"said his Grandmother.

"They wanted fortified once again in front do to the Northern cold waters,"said Her Ladyship.

"Then this is it and we can continue without it closing,"said Grandmother.

"Yes, this is it finally,"said Chardin.

"I remember when Ed and his wife were very disappointed when they could not star over just when the work was done as a very good barrier,"said Grandmother.

"I have the apology here see it is from the Mayor of Venice and the committee they started the second enlarged barrier and did not want to make it official that Likus was to young to help with the work,"said her Ladyship.

"I know, he was but so was Ed,"said Grandmother.

"I know that but Venice is Venice and it was much more dangerous then the Connecticut 1-95 Interstate tunnels there was no possible running water or streams to have problems with,"said Chardin.

"This is a fact and I am glad he can do this now, and also his Grandmother and Grandmother should be able to visit Venice right after seeing Ed and his wife and the children too,"said Grandmother.

"Oh, I told Likus that they are going to visit him in Venice because he knew that Ed was entertaining them and he understood,"said Chardin.

"Then there was no problems about not knowing,"said Grandmother.

"No because he did not want anyone at his wedding because she is very shy and it did not work out for his first marriage,"said Chardin.

"What else did he say.? "said Grandmother. "Due to our attached feeling with them while they were living to close to us,"said Chardin.

"What else.? "said Grandmother.

"The pregnancies are to remain in this house,"said Chardin.

"Chardin there is one more thing I need to hear.? "said Grandmother.

"There is no broken romances or divorces when living away from home,"said Chardin.

"So they all need to move soon,"said Chardin.

"All the four castles will be done soon and we will all being moving,"said Grandmother.

"Then we will not have any divorces.? "said Chardin.

"No we will not,"said Grandmother.

"I know we were to forceful,"said Chardin.

"No, with these new homes we will do fine and the Family Food Services will continue,"said Grandmother.

"So it was our fault.?"said Chardin.

"No, we have the money and the necessary government building to build now and now we will take those steps,"said Grandmother.

"So we did not cause their divorces,"said Chardin.

"No, we now can build and we al were at one time living here,"said Grandmother.

"So I am not to be blamed at all,"said Chardin.

"No, I told them too, because it was the only way out,"said Grandmother.

"You told them to divorce,"said Chardin.

"Yes,"said Grandmother.

"So did I,"said Chardin.

"I know Ed did he told me,"said Grandmother.

"Yes, and their sisters and brothers too,"said Chardin.

"Including Will, he has been by your side ever since,"said Grandmother.

"I can imagine, I need to buy him clothes and quite a few puzzles and some toys that only he would enjoy lets look right now ok,"said his Mother.

"He is mature enough to have his own laptop, and the others,"said Grandmother.

"Then those will be for Christmas and let him use this and he will appreciate and so will the others to,"said his Mother.

"This is a good idea, we should wait until Christmas,"said Grandmother.

"There are seven laptops to buy,"said Chardin.

"Excuse me Lady Chardinrey and Princess Constance, Prince Shawnif has arrived,"said the Butler.

"Oh, Constance I want you to talk in the living room and Lise and I will be in the dining room for a while, it was good to see for again we can talk later, Shawn,"said Chardin.

"Mom I am leaving her Versailles again and I do not know when I will return ok,"said Detva.

"Sure son, just say Hello to Shawn in the living room and you can leave right after. See you soon good bye say good bye to Lise. Lise here is some more food,"said her Mother.

"Good bye, Mother bye Lise. Hello,----- grandmother ----------,"said Detva.

"Hear him Lise, now you can not hear Detva he is in the living room right now. Then he is going to Versailles that is so good, but you are going to be with me ok,"said Her Ladyship.

"Si, "said Lise.

"My Lady there is some one to see you,"said the Butler.

"My dear Lady Chardinrey, I am one of the scientist that will be on the shuttle and I need an audience with you so I may please have an appointment with His Royal Prince Gale Ets Marie in Versailles, "said the Scientist.

"Certainly and whatever your name was it is now Lady Stelbee and you are invited to have your photos done here using the French throne and even before you arrive to see Paul who we and you will address in his house alright."The photos are done as we speak see. Now lets get an invitation form this building to Versailles. Ok, in three days,"said Chardin.

"Thank you so much. I need to tell you of the discovery that might be true. I think from where the web is the it automatically and others throw out water dirk and rocks very large boulders that might be placed in the air causing severe tornadoes,"said Lady Stellbee.

"Called me Chardin, this is interesting yet if it is in the caves or tunnels could we control them,"said Her Ladyship.

"Yes, you are correct. I think we already do,"said Lady Stelbee.

"That part someone does probably is not very good,"said Chardin.

"Not only we can but with a new tunnel of morter we could have another wall of China and a very large one that is worse,"said Stelbee.

"You need time these three days will help you get your report together and we are staring a new observatory for our own satelite. If it is up to you when it is control by the navy and the other the air force if you want to give them a report please just return yourself,"said Chardin.

"I will be delighted too, thank you again,"said Stellbee.

"Stellbee you need time to present this and if you need to go now let me see the appointment for today in Versailles. You may have an audience sooner so why not let our chauffer drive you now it is alright and the drive is relaxing,"said Chardin.

"Thank you so much again and for all that you have done,"said Stellbee.

"There see that auto you will be in it in twenty minutes with some food to have and a new chauffer that will wait for you to return here and not with my son Detva who just left for Versailles minutes ago, "said Chardin.

"That Limo is so elegant,"said Stellbee.

"You need to be there immediately but first have something to eat in the limo and go over you report and Paul will let you do some work there maybe even a report,"said Chardin."

"It does not seem possible so I am going to Versailles after all. And thank you thank you, I will leave now so you do not have to go outside and thank you again. Bye Lise. Good bye Chardin and thank you,"said Stellbee.

"See Lise se is going to see Paul in Versailles and Detva,"said her Mother.

"Grandmother, did you hear and see I just sent a good scientist to Versailles,"said Chardin.

"Good and I will do one more I am going to clear the way in the tunnels for Versailles so they can get there in minutes,"said Grandmother.

"Here let me Shawn by troupers are just in the border of France because I am here. Hello Sargent the limo heading for Versailles see that plate on you screen do you see them, make sure and tell the chauffer they are on their way to Versailles. Lady Stellbee in a very important scientist, in minutes now. Air force too and troups at the exists and entraces to be blocked, ok,"said Shawn.

"That was impressive,"said Grandmother.

"Well my troups need something to do and this is an emergency you did the right thing Charin you deserve an award. Is there anything to add to the message Chardin,"said Shawn.

"Yes, tell her when she returns this way there is a three week vacation for her as our guest,"said Chardin.

"They got it loud and clear,"said Shawn.

"Now Paul has these same orders and he has people there right now as we speak." said Chardin.

"This is so exciting, we can be apart of the observing audience and Shawn is invited to speak, look Paul apologized if we want to speak we may,"said Grandmother.

"I do not want to. "said Chardin.

"I do not want to it is an emergency what do I have to say, you go ahead and talk Shawn we will be in the other room and these doors will be locked, "said Grandmother.

"Yes. Let us know when it is over, Shawn. I want him to do everything on the phone, we can wait right here,"said Chardin.

"Alright, everything is done and we can observe on the tel,"said Shawn.

"Good, now we can find out if she had arrived safely,"said Grandmother.

"Here she is on her way,"said Chardin.

"I need some coffee and something to eat anyone else.?"said Grandmother.

"Yes, please,"said Shawn.

"No, thank you, Constance,"said Chardin.

"Here she is in France now look at that auto go why they put here into another car and very fast police car,"said Shawn.

"They must of decided to do that when we just put on the tel,"said Grandmother.

"Their look she is in the Versailles front door what would you say about eight minutes doing over a hundred,"said Chardin.

"A little bit more maybe eleven or more,"said Shawn.

"She is inside, look who answered the door and brought her to the reception room was Detva,"said Grandmother.

"Here we see them talking to Paul. They are sitting, and the picture is off,"said Chardin.

"See there is a brief message and we will be right back,"said Grandmother.

"No, it was one announcer to another they just switched reporters but what is this,"said Shawn.

"We have to wait thirty minutes or more and she will be introduced but we are, no they are going to let her announced her own discovery,"said Chardin.

"With this discovery I believe that the web has collected debree and rocks, water and has cleaned out the tunnels for further use,"said Shawn.

"We missed part of it,"said grandmother.

"This station gives her introduction,"said Shawn.

"Good afternoon, I am a scientist my name is Lady Stelbee I would also like to thank His Royal Highness Princess Gale Ets Marie for this sudden audience and Her Royal Highness Princess Chardiney of Belgium,"said Lady Stelbee.

"You, Mom,"said Lise.

"Who arranged this meeting for me. Also that extraordinary ride to the Palace of Versailles I really did not want to fly and with our police forced they actually proved me wrong, "said Lady Stellbee.

"Would you take a place or helicopter now,"said the Press.

"I think I do not have any fear of flying and do please do this please obey the law. Thank you, "said Lady Stellbee.

"We know how ergent this meeting was and you did not want to fly, is it because the meeting was within an hour that this is a controllable issue by man,"said the reporter.

"I am allowed to answer this being in an abused relationship and as a young girl saw hurricanes. If the debris is dumped on the people can pick up and move and start all over again. Or if the debris was put there first and there is nothing that can be done but first understand how it is being controlled. Then by who,"said Lady Stellbee.

"Then you saw as a young girl, would you say by an act of God and knowing these regions it was a listed priorities with suicide and by proxy itself,"said the reporter.

"Once this occurs and then the parents find out something.? They are there now due to fact of funds to return and they might have had a pleasant year or more. Enjoying their new surrounds of their country side or their farms that are very quiet and it is an enjoyable place to grown up in,"said Lady Stellbee.

"She did just what she wanted someone to ask her these question to her,"said Chardin.

"Thank you so very much, and please drive carefully,"said Lady Stellbee.

"Thank you. Said Detva.

"Look Detba,"said Lise.

"Me,"said Don.

"A call for you Lady Chardinrey,"said the Butler.

"Hello, why thank you so much for mentioning me too, yes today will be fine but do not drive first ok, and tell my son oh, ok, thank you, Detva you enjoy yourself and cooperate yes, and say hello to Lise and Don. Ok, bye,"said Chardin.

"There all is fine and it went quite well,"said Grandmother.

"Yes, I think so and I was so pleased she thanked me in public it not everyday I female gets to decide on these things that are important to mankind,"said Chardin. "Now we can sit down and relax all is fine with many of us,"said Shawn.

"She forgot Shawn who arranged the transportation,"said Chardin.

"No she did not they will put that is the newspapers or I can have an interview as long as it is not on an international level for all to here,"said Shawn.

"What did Lady Stellbee say,"said Grandmother.

"She is going to return in about one hour so she can type up a report and I think she wants to use the small cottage by the sea for her research for three weeks,"said Chardin.

"Or maybe work there during the day and return and enjoy her title here with the rest of us,"said Grandmother.

"That probably is true but she might need a few days alone to get it written so she may have my secretary to help her, "said Chardin.

"My secretary is married with a little girl and yours has a baby so she is going to have to fax over all of her work during the day,"said Grandmother.

"She will not mind that she just wants to be alone until the work is completed,"said Chardin.

"So she will be here within the hour good so lets have a good lunch for, but we will meet this Sunday, we can have a grilled foods every night too,"said Grandmother.

"Now she maybe in the last two rooms near the corner looking out of the back yard,"said Chardin.

"She would like that it is nice and quiet,"said Grandmother.

"Thank you, Constance I was wondering why I should leave her there,"said Chardin.

"That is the number one reason, quietness,"said Shawn.

"She does need to get all of those reports done,"said Chardin.

"Yes, and soon with accuracy too,"said Grandmother.

"Then she must be given the cottage if she wants it and return when she feels that her work is done,"said Chardin.

"It would be nice if she returns in the evening time to have refreshments with us,"said Constance.

"I sure she will and I could suggest if she wanted to write another P.H.D. on her new subject,"said Chardin.

"That is a wonderful suggestion, many people could write over six hundred or more pages on a new subject, I think she will be thrilled,"said Shawn.

"When she is here I will ask her, she should be arrive very soon,"said Chardin.

"Now for the sake of the families reputation what did you suggest for lunch,"said Constance.

"We are going to have a large dinner of an oven roast due to the fact that it is home made gravy and toast is very exceptional. Scientists some things do not cook enough food for themselves and she is single,"said Chardin.

"She might even get a boyfriend with her title, a her new career and our recipes, should do it,"said Constance.

"It will be more than three things I am sure,"said Chardin.

"I know that Lady Stellbee is here, you watch the children and I will introduce Shawn to her at the door. I might even say hands off. "said Constance.

"Here Lise some more fruit, there is no school today, no schooling at all, today Lise,"said Chardin.

"Guess you received your answer to that remark, Constance. "said Shawn.

"Lets go and talk to this scientist now that she represents this house,"said Constance.

"Yes, you both should, here Lise,"said Chardin.

"Hello, Chardin thank you for having me here,"said Lady Stellbee.

"Your welcome, Constance thanks you too and so do I d for all your help,"said Chardin.

"Now you I rushed Lady Stellbee with her title and neither one of you remember this Austrian preventing a scandal and you are here today because of this wonderful woman,"said Chardin.

"Yes, how are you both doing.? May did try to get here before me but I got here first Shawn so she would not interrrupt the you too of you,"said Stellbee.

"I do not believe who I see, shawn she pretended to date you and the court order was never given to May as long as you were in Austria she would not persue you, thank you dear so much for thinking of me again,"said Constance.

"The same young lady who told us that she May was to get married anyways,"said Shawn.

"Thank you so much, for this second rescue,"said Shawn.

"So what has happen to May,"said Constance.

"She is going to start her chemo as planned and not to interrupt others,"said Lady Stellbee.

"As soon as I heard your voice Stellbee I put you into Versailles to give her full recognition because she did help us out again,"said Chardin.

"So she would have not told you Shawn about her cancer,"said Constance.

"So I did,"said Stellbee.

"Also Stellbee took away the name of Lady Baitlym too,"said Chardin.

"We owe you quite a lot,"said Constance.

"You owe nothing and now her husbands knows it is very serious and he has placed her. It only gets her more upset with many visitors, "said Stellbee.

"What about you,"said Chardin.

"May, She had him as a fiancee and went ahead with the plans when they back fired with Shawn. She was not even a friend she was trying to get my job and this appointment, I honestly thought she read all of my notes even about the tunnels and its webs making tornatoes, "said Lady Stellbee.

"Back then we just discovered them a few months ago,"said Chardin.

"That is how long ago I wrote it down, way before the tunnels and its webs were discovered,"said Lady Stellbee.

"You waited a longtime for this discovery.? "said Chardin.

"Yes, I did but when I read in the news yesterday that Shawn was going to be a guest here, I immediately told May's husband not to let her leave and I did not, "said Lady Stellbee.

"Such as long time to keep an idea or discovery quiet,"said Constance.

"I helped May out and her husband out as much as I could I even told him to listen to what she says as write everything down, "said Ladys Stellbee.

"What awful ordeal for him,"said Chardin.

"He mentioned she was talking out loud and yelling so he put her in the next day she will never be here and anyplace else again,"said Lady Stellbee.

"What a hardship for all of you,"said Constance.

"Remember Shawn when she was married and I called you and told you if she ever goes to your house to call me,"said Lady Stellbee.

"Yes, but she did not I called up at all. Then I called Constance and told her that I had my last commission at sea that year, and we have been calling a few times each year,"said Shawn.

"Right well she married someone I did not know but he stayed with her and was ture and loved her a grewat deal, so I was tolded by a few friends that knew him,"said Lady Stellbee.

"Now everything is done and if you want to use the cottage by the shore let us know and you could even write another P.H. D. on your new findings, "said Chardin.

"Right now I do need to rest so I will see all of you tonight about seven is that alright with you I do need to rest a while,"said Lady Stellbee.

"Yes, you may and also Paul does exspect to see you there again for an award even before your new honoraries,"said Chardin.

"My goodness all of you think of so much, I am going still spinning,"said Lady Stellbee.

"It is a good thing you did not take the helicopter, needing to be on the news." said Chardin.

"Please take a nap and if we see you even tomorrow early in the morning I will personally bring you to the cottage so you can look at it, then we will return for lunch,"said Constance.

"Thank you I would like that every much even if it looks as if I will be sleeping around the clock after all this,"said Lady Stellbee.

"What you have done today for mankind it would make me sleep for another day with all that good stress of the day,"said Chardin.

"So all this time you have directed yourself to us,"said Grandmother.

"I had help May was not truly a rude person she knew I had a discovery and she figured out how to get me here, I would imagine,"said Lady Stellbee.

"That is probably the beginning of the cancer perhaps,"said Chardin.

"It could do something,"said Constance.

"I do have a call it is May's husband excuse me,"said Stellbee.

"Constance more food it is our last big dinner of the night and is the barbeque is later on this evening. I hope everything is alright,"said Chardin.

"May died just before her first treatment of chemo about an hour ago. There is no funeral at all she drove to many away and the casket is closed.

He wants it very quiet letting everyone she was just his house and nothing more,"said Stellbee.

"I am so sorry,"said Chardin.

"You do not have to be she and I did not have enough time to even be friends after she did steal her husband from me,"said Stellbee.

"Then neither one of you knew each other well.? "said Constance.

"I just knew her to know what she was capable of you, she took my boyfriend away my job and its promotion she had his child and it died before birth so she just gave herself and unpleasant life, "said Stellbee.

"We will pray for her tonight in our prayers before we go to sleep,"said Chardin.

"I am having a large package of her notes as discoveries sent over May's husband is giving me them so I can read them,"said Stellman.

"You could find out some important discoveries of hers and maybe there is a story in it for her as a book,"said Constance.

"I think I can get it done, I should go to the cottage tomorrow so I can think of things to write,"said Stellbee.

"The package we will send it right down to the cottage and it will be delivered by the same messenger,"said Chardin.

"Thank you I feel the way I have been treated I am like family,"said Stellbee.

"What you have done for Constance and Shawn there is no possible way we could send you home without showing some gratitude,"said Chardin.

"You mentioned gratitude why not give her a house to rent where she works, I know where you work there is a very nice little castle near the Belgium border. Said Shawn.

"Did Leavels renters leave her small castle it is closer to where you work. After all you are of noble rank and you have earned it with a P. H. D. "said Constance.

"Good, but does it have a drawn bridge and at mut, it might sound funny but now May's husband is not the move I need to be away from him for a more than a year,"said Stellbee.

"Then it is decided you may live there, I will call Leavels now, instead of getting here to the stairs case. Hello, is you home available. Good there is a new renter,"said Chardin.

"Why you are able to move in tomorrow, we will have our movers move you in in three days but please stay with us for the three or six weeks we want you here with us,"said Constance.

"Do let them help, they work here and do mnay things but furniture and placement is there specialty, "said Shawn.

"It would not hurt to have a free year on us,"said Constance.

"I will do one more thing the paper work will come from the Grenaire Real Estate so why not have her listed as disabled as stress related and tiredness, "said Chardin.

"But I have never been using Grenaire, I have always had my own rent,"said Stellbee.

"Nonsence we have already placed the land as our own Grenaire and while you care here I will have the application as an email for you and you will have a new home for about one-hundred and fifty dollars a month. But the first year is for free, so you can have freedom to do your work, books and degrees, "said Chardin.

"You just put all of that into your phone, just now,"said Stellbee.

"Just now, my dear you are a Princess and as Lady Stellbee you need a perfect housing and Grenaire is,"said Constance.

"That is correct you have earned every bit of it, you have allowed Constance and I to be together. "said Shawn.

"I guess I have earned,"said Stellbee.

"I am not surprised if she receives many checks and grants, but do not buy that house get something else and keep that castle for visits,"said Chardin.

"I just wonder, Hello Paul, what about Lady Stellbee does she get a very large check even with the Noble Peace Prize.? Good I will let her know. Bye thank you. "said Chardin.

"What did he say.? "said Constance.

"You are getting a very large check to help you out which has nothing to do with work and a check so that your work,"said Chardin.

"My goodness,"said Shawn.

"That is more,"said Constance.

"A company contacted Paul just after you left and they are mailing you a check and permission to observe or just read your work at your convenience only,"said Chardin.

"How wonderful,"said Constance.

"Yes, it is,"said Shawn.

"There is another company to do the same, but both want to give you a monthly check with no ties, you are still on your own,"said Chardin.

"Heavens, and it all happen right in front of me,"said Constance.

"These checks are going to be given to you by messenger, according to Paul who had a lot to say to them so they did mention that there companies will put something together, for you, "said Chardin.

"This is history in the making and the best kind of history a positive,"said Shawn

"Paul has all the phones numbers and all the company names so they will make a good presentation to allow you to get use to the idea, "said Chardin.

"I do not know what to say, when I told May's husband not to let her enter the country. He said,"I deserve being praised,"said Stellbee.

"Yes you do. Paul is also going to send you a list of all the companies and the correspondence that he has received most of them he has forwarded to your home, and now are going to be here and at the cottage too,"said Chardin.

"I can not believe I was a part of history, a written document given to Versailles that could make a big difference to the world,"said Constance.

"The military too, I think I will call a few generals and let them know if they need to talk to you I will let you know Stellbee, "said Shawn.

"What Shawn.? "said Constance.

"Here is one person that is very interested,"said Shawn,

Chapter 16

"Hello, President. Yes, you may investigate,"said Stellbee.

"Good, now she nust work in that cottage before anything else gets in the way,"said Chardin.

"Stellbee, did he say anything about you leaving soon,"said Constance.

"No, he did not,"said Stellbee.

"I think he is waiting for a P.H.D. and a few awards because that is how people know about these things,"said Shawn.

"I dear I am going to do this and it might not seem fair at first, but I am going to put you into the cottage right now, so you can work on your P.H. D.

"That is a good idea, it is only way to be recognized,"said Constance.

"The maid just told me when we were discussing properties she had the cottage cleaned and it is filled with furniture and food, "said Chardin.

"Chardin is right you must go now and give it a try,"said Constance.

"If it does not work then return and we will think of something else,"said Shawn.

"Now we are preparing a lot of food chicken, corn and steaks and we will sent the down to you and each meal of the day and a staff to stay with you our maid right here her name is Dab, "said Chardin.

"You should go now and there will be enough food for the both of you each day and four times a day,"said Constance.

"So here is the car I told I am determine to make sure you work on that P.H.D. and your books as well,"said Chardin.

"I do not know what to say all of you have been so good to me,"said Stellbee.

"We are the ones that still need to thank you for you have allowed us to be together and and have decided in three months to be married,"said Shawn.

"A very small wedding only you and Chardin as witnesses, "said Constance.

"See you are bring us luck all the time,"said Shawn.

"Now hurry and get into the car and we just might be there the three of us with a preacher in three days and just might get married in that cottage and then into your new building you are renting for a honeymoon,"said Constance.

"Those are wonderful plans I will wait for all of you to arrive then,"said Stellbee.

"Why not,"said Shawn.

"Whay not in three days it is and we will arrive at 11:00 am,"said Constance.

"Why I was always wondering when this would be so perfect and her home is delight according to Leavels,"said Chardin.

"This is wonderful we did we actually did it. "said Constance.

"See you in three days Stellbee we will order you some clothes and they will be arriving tomorrow,"said Chardin.

"This is what I have been waiting for, for many years Constance, "said Shawn

"Me too,"said Constance.

"So now that we are in the computer lets get a preacher and some things delivered and just a small lucheon at the cottage then you to leave with the chauffer to Stellbees castle,"said Chardin.

"Good"said Shawn.

"Why not go upstairs and be alone for a while,"said Chardin.

"Alright but I want to have my honeymoon in the new building the first and seond floors are heated,"said Constance.

"Alright at Edlance Castle it is fine and lovely,"said Chardin.

"This is the call that I was waiting for, it is Stellbee in the automobile. Hello, I first want to tell you that Constance and Shawn are having their honeymoon in the new castle the first two floors are heated and are done. Ok, we will see you in three days,"said Chardin. "

"What did she want she is driving there so there is nothing for her to report that is wrong with the building,"said Constance.

"Nothing is wrong and there are two things to report. The drive is very exciting to the cottage and the country is lovely, and she requested to having long pants outfit to your ceremony as something that she can wear to work too,"said Chardin.

"She is a smart woman and she is your size you do have lovely things you do not need at all, "said Constance.

"At this time I need to have a drink but that is a splendid idea in that castle,"said Shawn.

"I did think you would agree,"said Constance.

"I need to go upstairs and you entertain Lise if she waits up, she had an early lunch,"said her Mother.

"Maids come with me and I will tell you both which things go to the laundry down stairs and for the seamstress to iron after the cleaning,"said Chardin.

"Dear, we are going to have such good fun together and we can stay in that building for a few days and return as soon as you want too,"said Shawn.

"Very good lets see how much we miss this place first. Do you want to live somewhere with privacy,"said Constance.

"No unless you want a full staff and I will tell you now that the only time I ever heard you laught and enjoy life was when you had a lot of little infants in the house.

"What a wonderful idea and with a staff to help,"said Constance.

"We can do it with a staff in our own home, if you want too,"said Shawn.

"If anything happened to both of us there is Detva and Likus to help and I am sure the girls would not mind,"said Constance.

"There I gave her some of my furs, and jewelry as well I let the maids know there was a bonus soon, so they would not be left out,"said Chardin.

"What about mind there really is nothing to give her,"said Constance.

"You girls are very kind with your valuables,"said Shawn.

"After a funeral it is a larger deductible so I did not want these things going just to no one,"said Chardin.

"What about your daughters.? "said Constance.

"Not these things, I have all of others furs for them upstairs,"said Chardin.

"Then you have met a true friend with Stellbee, just as a precaution if she does not want anything to return it and the both of you can go shopping,"said Constance.

"She will let me know. Now here is the food and we can enjoy ourselves and the maid called me to let me know that she heard typing on the computer just after Stellbee had her dinner,"said Chardin.

"Good then I am glad it is working for her in that building, it was not wrong of us to do that, she could get here P.H.D. done or a book in the building,"said Constance.

"I told her that if she can not concentrate wthat she may return.? "said Chardin.

"She should give it a try, maybe the circumstances are better here than at home,"said Shawn.

"There see, we are almost finished with our dinner and she is still typing,"said Chardin.

"Good now we do not have to worry and tomorrow Chardin and go see her if there is no typing and she if things are working out,"said Constance.

"That is final then we have our P.H.D. and a Nobel in the works,"said Shawn.

"Yes, we have accomplished for ourselves a start of something controversial and militarian too, that could work in our favor for mankind,"said Chardin.

"It will be so, it is just going to take time but the military will not let this stop, and will give her full control with backing for the project,"said Shawn.

"It is so exciting to think we were knowing about when it first happened,"said Constance.

"Will and Don were very interested maybe we have a new scientist in the family,"said their Mother.

"Could be. You know I have a friend that Will and I can go see him at the Naval base and Air Force base too,"said "said Shawn.

"Mom could I soon,"said Will.

"Soon and if Don wants too he is still to young,"said their Mother.

"I hope so it sounds like fun and very exciting too. Thank you, Sir,"said Will.

"Your welcome will, it is going to be exciting and fun for me too,"said Shawn.

"Then you too may have your trip next Friday. Don and I will be here having fun putting his game together using those little block,"said Grandmother.

"Will you know Grandmother and Shawn will be home from their honeymoon next week,"said Chardin.

"We better make it in about three months from now, besides I have exams right now,"said Will.

"Then it is soon very soon I promsie you,"said Shawn.

"May I have some coffee with all of you.?"said Leavels.

"Yes, and please have some more food, you know you need your strength,"said her Mother.

"Yes, all of the girls in this house know they have food upstairs and come down stairs for more food when having a baby, it is my law,"said their Grandmother.

"You know you do not have to ask. Just have enough food upstairs then come on down and I will fill you up again,"said her Mother.

"Thank you, Mother. Did you get anything done with Stellbee, I heard she is in the cottage working on her books,"said Leavels.

"Or it could be her P.H.D. one of them I told her if it does not work she can return and just do these things in her new home,"said Lady Chardin.

"I am glad everything worked out ofd her and her discovery is extraordinary too, Grandmother when are you two leaving,"said Leavels.

"We are both leaving Thursday afternoon,"said her Grandmother.

"Then your gift should arrive by then,"said Leavels.

"Thank you, dear, Here is the blood work from the city,"said her Grandmother.

"Yes, thank you and think of it I will be called Grandfather, "said Shawn.

"That does sound delightful, I want to say something none of you have to buy us anything,"said Constance.

"Oh, yes they do, I am going to be a Grandfather and on my birthdays they need to buy or even make a gift, that is a lot of fun,"said Shawn.

"That is right too I love a home made card and enclosed there is one large penny, in it,"said Grandmother.

"That sounds like a very good gift too,"said Lady Chardin.

"Now how about some more coffee and we can snack on chicken tonight and have some sandwiches too, "said Grandmother.

"Next we have to do this evening is to see what was done in the building by the computer, "said Lady Chardin.

"Do the staff know that are working there that we are going to use the building and travel during the days they are there working,"said Constance.

"Yes, they do and is one section that is completed for you to stay in if there is to much noise then just visit us,"said Lady Chardin.

"Ok, but I understand that the part that is completed is quite sound proof so we can stay there during the day to evening or just stay there all the time,"said Constance.

"What a rare treat to have a wonderful place like that completed for your honeymoon,"said Chardin.

"Yes, it is,"said Shawn.

"Yes, you are both correct and it is very private,"said Constance.

"Grandmother because your bedroom is right next to us we are going to move to the end of the hallway and Shawn and you have three extra rooms, ok,"said Leavels.

"Yes, that would be nice an extra living room would be nice, thank you,"said Grandmother.

"Then that is settled because I had the maid start doing the packing this morning, Ok,"said Leavels.

"Yes, I saw her and they are finished, is there more food,"said Baitlym.

"Help yourself there is plenty,"said chardin.

"Now I am ready for seconds too,"said Leavels.

"See that Shawn your food is very good I think I will have more,"said Grandmother.

"Yes, her Lise and Don some chicken,"said her Mother.

"That good,"said Don.

"Good,"said Lise.

"So lets go to the living room in a little while and we can have snacks there later on. Here are the children's games and new clothes and a new outfit for you, myself and Stellbee,"said Chardin.

"Nice, then all is ready,"said Constance.

"Mother I want you to know that not everything was delivered for us, ok, "said Leavels.

"Why is that some things were tailored. No what I have had seconds I am going up to see my husband,"said Baitlym.

"Good dear tell him I said,"Hello, and I am glad most of your things have arrived,"said Chardin.

"Yes, dear have a good evening,"said Constance.

"Good night,"said Shawn.

"I must go see my husband, too,"said Leavels.

"Good, and if you are hungry each evening please be down right away for more food, ok,"said Chardin.

"Night Love,"said Constance.

"Good night,"said Shawn.

"Now we need to talk a little while about your wedding tomorrow at 11:00am. in the cottage. Do you want your surgery first.?"said Chardin.

"No, we are married then a small luncheon, and we both leave immediately to the new building Edlance castle,"said Constance.

"Then we have an early dinner at the cottage and the Priest and I leave. This is to give Stellbee and lot of extra food to have later,"said Chardin.

"Then while we are driving into the front gate of the castle, you should be home with your children and we will be having dinner in the new dining room,"said Shawn.

"That is splendid Shawn and Constance the first to use the new dinning room and on your honeymoon, it is so romantic,"said Chardin.

"Constance is the first to go into surgery, then it is my turn,"said Shawn.

"When we return that is right, what a good plan,"said Constance.

"So we agree. Now we can both look 35 to 55 years no one will know,"said Shawn.

"I can not wait it sounds exciting,"said Constance.

"Yes, and in one year we can renew our vows in the new castle and have everyone there and take a lot of pictures,"said Shawn.

"Sure and the ones who can not make it will be with us at some other time during the year,"said Constance.

"This is quite good in fact I will have to notify my son in Russia with his family that he has a new couple to do his add, it is us,"said Shawn.

"What business does he owe.? "said Chardin.

"He runs the extra sleep they wanted,"said Shawn.

"That is right too, why am I thinking he was in the auto business, "said Chardin.

"Because your son wanted him to buy it out so instead he put in sleep because your son said,"It was needed,"said Shawn.

"That is right too because of anything happening I did not think of Alex still keeping the car business,"said Chardin.

"Because of your son my son is doing quite well and has bought out of Russia and Bavaria and soon as he is going to give the business to me then you can buy me out so you will own all the territory and now Venice which is last,"said Shawn.

"Why thank you Shawn,"said Chardin.

"Actually the sale and the proceeds go to my wife as a wedding gift,"said Shawn.

"Why Shawn you are so thoughtful,"said Constance.

"This money is a gift, you can not give it away,"said Shawn.

"No, I will not,"said Constance.

"How can we repay your son.? "said Chardin.

"He would like to take your place some day just like you did when Ed and Princess Ownsite in Bavaria gave the business to you from Gale who said,"It was your turn,"said Shawn.

"Sure it will be a while then we can give it to him and then it will go to Likus when he lives with us,"said Chardin.

"What he really wants is to make a lot of money on the insurances by the media that do make a lot of mistakes and he is willing to pay Lloyd's for what ever it takes." said Shawn.

Ok, but you too will be living here with us and in a the new home and he is going to look like the enemy or in this case a true Russian who will stay right where he is. And so do the both of you or he will not make, much at all,"said Chardin.

"I understand and I told him that but there are a lot of businesses he would like to buy out in Russia,"said Shawn.

"I think Shawn is prepared to know that his son is wealthy and to be that way all of us will have to sacrifice for what we want,"said Constance.

"If he works hard and must live there anyways so it is not a big deal. Having him wealthy and knowing his family is taken care of then this is what it does cost,"said Shawn.

"Just like Ed and his wife Princess Ownsite, they are happy now,"said Chardin.

"They are very happy and so will my son to help us out,"said Shawn.

"Very good so I put in for a news to pick up his anger and sold the business. But he will run it. The media will say he is not happy about what you have done,"said Chardin.

"The media will certainly do that because no one is invited and we have our two witnesses. Today at 11:00 a.m. is my wedding,"said Constance.

"We can think of dozens of things the media would say what we need to do is to get ready and have a nice drive to the cottage. See you both in one hour,"said Chardin.

"We will meet at the front door, "said Constance.

"Yes, we are,"said Chardin.

"There is was a good drive and I think it is a beautiful morning for a marriage. The two of you look like such as perfect couple,"said Chardin.

"Good morning all of you,"said Lady Stellbee.

"Good morning. This is our priest, Father Miare,"said Constance.

"Constance and Shawn are standing before us in this beautiful garden to be married,"said the Priest.

"Now is there any one present.....

"Now you may kiss the bride... you are now man and wife,"said the Priest.

"Congratulations, Constance and Shawn,"said Lady Chardinrey.

"Congratulations, the both of you,"said Lady Stellbee.

"This is a fine day for me marrying the two of you,"said Father Miare.

"Luncheon is serve,"said the Butler.

"All looks so lovely and table looks devine,"said Constance.

"Yes, it does indeed,"said the General.

"Here are a few gifts right here I did cover them over earlier last night,"said Stellbee.

"I am delighted to see both of you took great care in preparing this reception for us both,"said Constance.

"Now I need to give a toast,"said Lady Chardinrey.

"This gift is beautiful. And so were all the others. Now it is time to go to our home and is still a beautiful place as a honeymoon too,"said Constance.

"You will both enjoy yourselves,"said Chardin.

"You know if there is not so much noise we might just stay there and wait for all of you to arrive when the building is completed,"said Constance.

"I know I will certainly visit all of you very soon,"said Stellbee.

"Say hello, to all of them for me my dear. Good bye"said Constance.

"Good bye,"said Shawn.

"That was lovely and they are so good to each other,"said Lady Stellbee.

"A lovely couple,"said Father Miare.

"I hated to see her go, but he has made her so happy over the years,"said Chardin.

"You can tell the way he looks at her,"said Stellbee.

"Now we get right into the dinner for the three of us and then father and I need to go to our homes right after dinner,"said Chardin.

"I need to get to work on my book. A copy of my P.H.D. is done,"said Stellbee.

"To think that I was a part of it,"said Chardin.

"Wish you luck and God's praise and we are apart of your safety that is what we can do,"said the Priest.

"Yes,"said Stellbee.

"You have been given something wonderful and let Lady Chardinrey and Gale be apart of it so you can continue your work,"said the Priest.

"I will and I have allowed her to help me and Constance so I am in good hands and I do know I could have done this without Chardin and Constance, "said Stellbee.

"Good, so now we will have success and to let the world know of your discoveries it is every important and I thank you too,"said Father Miare.

"So the dinner was excellent, and we need to get one your way. So my dear, this is for you and I need to make sure Father gets into the right auto, so good bye,"said Chardin.

"Good bye, Father here is a check and another one just for you. When you get home please call me,"said Lady Chardinrey.

"I will good bye,"said Father Miare.

"Now hello, Leavels I am on the phone and I am in the drive way entering the front door, so I will see you soon,"said Chardin.

"Good afternoon, "said the Butler.

"Good afternoon, I will be in the living room in case anyone is home,"said Chardin.

"Mother how was the wedding.?"said Leavels.

"I had a chauffeur to take the pictures,"said Chardin.

"How was the food, we hare having everything this evening including the same cake so Don you may tell Grandmother when she returns. Hello, Lise,"said their Mother.

"Hello, Mother will we be contracting them I mean the staff to do shopping for them while they are away,"said Baitlym.

"Hello you two, Savga and Rofster both can be here to listen, they have staff there and they will return maybe next week,"said Chardin.

"Everything went all right,"said Rofster.

"I guess we will see them when they return,"said Savga.

"Yes, that is just what is going to happen we will wait for them to return,"said Chardin.

"See me,"said Don.

"Yes, you,"said his Mother.

"What about the photos,"said Baitlym.

"Now we can sit for awhile and I sent the pictures off and we should be getting them back by my secretary soon,"said Chardin.

"What about our gifts,"said Leavels.

"They loved them all of them, I need a drink a good drink to relax even as it never does,"said Chardin.

"Did you get something for Lady Stellbee.? "said Rofster.

"Yes, a ring that she was wearing before the lucheon and dinner, "said Chardin.

"That was nice,"said Leavels.

"Yes, the gifts were open while we had our luncheon,"said Chardin.

"It all seems as lovely and beautiful,"said Baitlym.

"When the dinner was over I gave Stellbee and the priest a check,"said Lady Chardinrey.

"I know I was very short of the births and deaths. Yet my child and Urnlee's will be apart of your father's and my continuation and especially with Urnlee as your new Mother someday. We are all getting along. Said Chardin.

"I know no one has talked about this at all. It was a miracle you and Urnlee survived and you both did even the both of you having a baby,"said Baitlym.

"I wanted everyone to be happy and enjoy life that is what your father wanted,"said Chardin.

"I know that, it is what he has mentioned many times with a missing grandparent,"said Baitlym.

"I think that the South Pacific and the Mormon religion the two did work very well for when he had died and Urnlee got married the document did create an easier departure with us and you just a few days in fact, "said Baitlym.

"Yes when they left for Austria, while he was dieing that month all reverted back to Catholic and she was recognized as being married and my divorce was official, "said her Ladyship."

"Now that it is over we do enjoy Urnlee and it was nice of you to give her, her own home,"said Baitlym.

"Thank you,"said Chardin.

"Now Mother that we are all Catholics began, With must of these houses completed are we all going to meet here for the holidays.? said her Daughter.

"Yes we will, there is more room and it will work out for your grandmother too,"said Chardin.

"This is true,"said Baitlym.

"Now what if I were to asked you to talk about you.?"said Chardin.

"I have everything and now we can enjoy our families together. I do enjoy the preschool of Versailles in this building too. "said Baitlym.

"Yes, and it has been three days since the return of your grandmother's last vacation and Urnlee seems to enjoy beign here and has not returned to her house,"said Chardin.

"I know, and I think they are going to rent out soon,"said Baitlym.

"That will be good, it will be nice to have all of us together this Christmas,"said her Ladyship.

"Yes, this is true and the preschool does come in handy,"said Baitlym.

"I knew you would put some humor in this some how and you are correct,"said her Mother.

"Mother the children are arriving, I just want to say how much I love you and for all of help you have given us,"said her Daughter.

"Thank you but what about all of help you have given me back with employment of the business. The sleep, loitering, preschool and the Euro train on both continents is the best ever today because of my children, "said her Mother.

"Thank you and we have all worked hard everyone one of us have a good trust fund for our children,"said Baitlym.

"Also we are the talk of the world today with two new castles at the shore that are making money on tourists alone, not to mention the navy the naval value both have on the shore and one the cove too,"said her Mother.

"There was quite a lot of press and both are exquisite inside,"said Bailtym.

"The gold inside takes away from our other buildings, creates another value to the property and is available to time of war, thanks to the government who wanted to invest in each room,"said her Mother.

"It does give another step into helping many governments. I like the fact this gold is the surounding of the molding yet is the new electrical batteried heating system and can be given back to the government when they need it, "said her Daughter.

"It would only look like we are redecorating the rooms one at a time,"said her Mother.

"It is better because when the solid gold molding it take off the the wood is replaced and painted gold it will look the same,"said her Daughter.

"It will be the same,"said her Mother.

"Your right and dad would be pleased with us,"said her Daughter.

"This is dad, and he would insist on a fee, and we got one a yearly fee too.

"Did you agree it goes toward the gold and the Euro train so be compliments a government and considers the people first and a true value towards a nation who did invest,"said her Mother.

"Did you find out who they were the nations.? "said the Daughter.

"No, this is all locked up with the navy who uses both buildings while we are not there,"said her Mother.

"That is good for security foir us and it is best that we do not know,"said Baitlym.

"It is just known as investors, and any country may apply,"said her Mother.

"Why even we can or my children's funds can be invested there,"said Bailtlym.

"There is a country that wants to sell,"said her Mother.

"If it is on payments we can do to large ones and maybe the others will invest too,"said the Daughter.

"This will happen, we must give our clients another investment when they want the gold again,"said her Mother.

"Good, I will tell the others if I see them before dinner,"said the Daughter.

"I will too, it looks as if the children were rerouted to another part of the building,"said her Mother.

"It looks that way,"said her Daughter.

"It guess they are having snacks,"said her Mother.

"I am sure for it, it has been a while, Mother I am glad we talked and now I have some thin to invest the money in that is completely secured and insured." said her daughter.

"It is, very safe and secured and the insurnace is automatic and is not expensive at all." said her Mother.

"Good I will let every know immediately. See it was sent as we spoke." said her Daughter.

"Great, you are perfect." said her Mother.

"That's because I have a perfect mother, and a perfect dad too." said Baitlym.

"I am so glad we all introduce our children our new borns to the public." said her Mother.

"I am delighted I got my family into the news and we had a very large photo of all of us together too." said her Daughter.

"Now we all can enjoy these holidays and we will have another large photo in the living room with a tree." said her Mother.

"We could put it up right after the first of December due to this living room being new and is just completed. Tell me Mother when the other buildings require you to say a long time are you returning sooner than the others." said her Daughter.

"I will returned because of my children have to remember they will be guests only. I know your grandmother will live there in the cove." said Her Ladyship.

"Grandmother did say she enjoyed her new start with her husband so I she will visit every day." said Her Daughter.

"That is good, I want her to be happy, the both of them." said Lady Chardinrey.

"I knew you do and here are the little ones." said Baitlym.

"Watch them, all of them, even yours, walk right by and go to the snacks." said Chardin.

"Even my too, they were told not to interrupt." said Baitlym.

"Here are the nannies and they both closed the doors." said Chardinrey.

"They can do no wrong, we might have had important guests." said Baitlym.

"I know and I am going to stay here and see them go out the living room doors again." said Chardinrey.

"They will, as long as we do not give priviledges that the nannies do, I think they are going to ride their bikes for a few minutes." said Baitlym.

"So now we can get ready for dinners and soon we will all to be in this living room and appreciating this evening as a family." said Chardin.

"Good I think we can order a cake." said Baitlym.

"I already did and a few pies for snacks and coffee, the usual routine." said Chardin.

"I do think we have to should include Grandmother every day." said Baitlym.

"She is on her honeymoon and as soon they are comfortable with each other, they will stay for awhile." said Chardin.

"That would be nice." said Baitlym.

"Yes, we need her but she and all of us need our privacy, especially her right now." said Her Ladyship.

"I guess I am like her that wants all of us to be with each other." said Baitlym.

"That will, go away the more years the children are in school. All of us that leave for school then it appears to be correct even with the preschool here." said her Mother.

"Housewives are expected to stay home." said Baitlym

"I do no think so, you yourself can run that Versailles Preschool franchaise." said her Mother.

"Maybe some day." said Baitlym.

"You have a long time before that happens, and remember your book about your marriage, someday many will want to read it." said her Mother.

"We do have interesting lives and many things have happened." said Baitlym.

"This is all facts about us and I know you will make be lovely, beautiful and courageous too." said her Mother.

"I know I promised a great evening with all of you but I am going upstairs and when you are in the living room with the otherrs I want to restt his evening ok." said her Mother.

"Yes, sure Mother are you all right." said Baitlym.

"I have a little headache and I want to stay upstairs with the children then I will send them down stairs with all of you." said her Mother.

"Ok, I will start getting everyone upstairs with you for dinner and I will stay here with mine and and the others." said Baitlym.

"Thank you dear we will talk later this evening." said her Mother.

"Children we are going to have dinner know and all of us are going to be in the living room this evening so lets have dinner right now ok, all have washed up we all look clean,"said Baitlym.

"Good evening everyone I looked at Chardin and she is sleeping the children and her had dinner, "said Urnlee.

"Thank you Urnlee I do not know what I would do without,"said Baitlym.

"Are we all going upstairs now.?"said Urnlee.

"Yes, we are,"said Baitlym.

"Good I am very tired,"said Urnlee.

"So am I , Good night, "said Baitlym.

"Good night,"said Urnlee.

Chapter 17

"Good morning, Urnlee,"said Grandmother.

"Good morning, I am so sorry I have tell you that your Daughter-in-law, Her Royal Highness, Princess Chardinrey died early this morning. She called me and did not want me to disturb anyone until they woke up. I am so sorry the doctor did say it was a painless and peaceful death, "said Urnlee.

"She did not wat to stay,"said Grandmother.

"I never told you or anyone else the both of them did not want to be apart form each other. If there was something like cancer then they would separate,"said Urnlee.

"Here is Baitlym,"said Grandmother.

"Your Mother died this morning Baitlym I am so sorry,"said Urnlee.

"Where is she, I did think she was with the both of you,"said Baitlym

"She is in the funeraltory room right next to your father's grave,"said Urnlee.

"This is what she requested, Baitlym, "said her Grandmother.

"Yes, she did she wanted to be placed there next to your father immediately and she did not want me to wake up anyone,"said Urnlee.

"I will wait here,"said Baitlym.

"Thank you, "said Grandmother.

"Did any call my brothers,"said Baitlym.

"Yes, she wanted the staff to do everything,"said Urnlee.

"Mom, why, oh, I know it was because of Dad,"said Baitlym.

"Will I love you and little Lise too we are going to get very busy and be ready for our private funeral alright,"said Grandmother.

"Yes, grandmother I love you too," said their Grandmother.

"Love you, said Lise.

"What are we to do.?"said Will.

"We all are going to manage and pray for them both in the chapel,"said Urnlee.

"Then we bury them both together,"said Will.

"Yes, we are, and I love you both, you know that right.?"said Urnlee.

"Yes, I know,"said Will.

"Love you,"said Lise.

"Now lets have some breakfast, we need to eat some food to keep up our strength,"said Baitlym.

"That is a good idea,"said Grandmother.

"Yes, we should,"said Urnlee.

"I do not want to see the visitors in the chapel right after breakfast,"said Will.

"Will, it is not right after breakfast, but the reception apartment is all completed, up to this evening I am sure of that,"said Urnlee.

"Alright I apologize, "said Will.

"You're a good man, Will,"said Urnlee.

"You are and I do not want any upstart ideas from you too little Lisa."You are Lady Alisan today,"said her Grandmother.

"No, I won't "said Lisa.

"Do I have be Lord or Prince Willbrence,"said Will.

"Whatever the visitors say, said Grandmother.

"Now are we all ready to go into the apartment, then we can be seated for the first guests to arrive and later on the photographers are taking pictures, only when we are not seated. "said Urnlee.

"It looks as if the autos are approaching right now, "said Will.

"Then lets get seated right now or director as indicated as the door is open now,"said Grandmother.

"This is going to be a few hours,"said Baitlym.

"How do you know.?"said Grandmother.

"Because when we entered the guests were just around the other corridor, and those side doors on the left-hand side were being closed,"said Baitlym.

"I will tell all of you right now that we are in the apartment alone, and the children are having their, anyone of us especially Urnlee may right a book about this and her marriage,"said Grandmother.

"Yes, of course,"said Baitlym.

"Yes, please do,"said Detva.

"Yes, that is your new job, and not mine,"said Likus.

"All do agree,"said Constance.

"Thank you so much,"said Urnlee.

"Now we need to go back into the room right now and he will be buried tomorrow morning, "said Grandmother.

"I hate today,"said Baitlym.

"I know what you mean,"said Seebees.

"We need to rest this evening I have never talked so much in all my life,"said Constance.

"That is for sure, my throat is dry,"said Seebees.

"An understate I believe,"said Likus.

"How is Venice,"said Baitlym.

"Lets here from you,"said Detva.

"Ok, it is wonderful, you all know I managed to receive the beautiful place in all gold for my work and I live there now,"said Likus.

"What did Gale say.? After all it is his business,"said Detva.

"Yes, what was the answer,"said Baitlym.

"That is our boss in Versailles, what did he say.?"said Urnlee.

"He said, He did not mind al all that I owned."Also if do not I sell it to any of you he will purchase it instead of a stranger,"said Likus.

"Good, so I know you enjoy the building, are you going to stay a while,"said his Grandmother.

"Yes, there is very little to do now, but I enjoy the fact that not to many visit and all the errons and shopping is done by message due to the residence, "said Likus.

"Have you had an offer.? said his Constance.

"Many, but I promised Gale and then it will be apart of the unique business itself, of the origin that is,"said Likus.

"Good idea Likus, you have the right attitude,"said Detva.

"Yes, you do,"said Grandmother.

"You do,"said Lise.

"Here is my, baby and how is my sister.? "said Likus.

"Good,"said Lise.

"Now we should all go upstairs to our own apartments and get some sleep,"said Grandmother.

"This is very good,"said Urnlee.

"Urnlee, you out did yourself today with the arrangments,"said Baitlym.

"I am glad you agree, I know this is your house now, but I know I could help, the flowers are artificial, yet all the proceeds do go to the usuall charity the lost Eurotrain runaways as your parents requested,"said Urnlee.

"Thank you, and the runaways or stranded adults is the decision of Gale in Versailles if his clients agree, "said Baitlym.

"That is a good idea,"said Urnlee.

"Yes, it is,"said Likus.

"We did it and I did think something would be wrong but we got by without a problem,"said Grandmother.

"What I know Lise does not understand that her Mother is buried, what would happen,"said Urnlee.

"What is therew something that you know,"said Seebees.

"I think Grandmother is just a little releaved, I am that everything went smoothly,"said Baitlym.

"We will know now, hello, Lise and Will,"said Seebees.

"Grandmother can we go get Mommy now,"said Lise

"We can go see where Mommy is alright Lise and Will, come on and we can go get a hot fudge Sunday at the little shop it is still open and we can buy a toy, ok,"said Urnlee.

"Now that Lise is in the bathroom Will I want you to say tomorrow if the three of us or anyone else wants to go to the shop we will go everyday for one week to get a favorite new toy ok,"said Urnlee.

"Right and we will not visit the graves, until she is older,"said Will.

"You are such a good brother,"said Urnlee.

"Thanks Mom come on Lise we are going now,"said Will.

"I want a large chocolate bar, ok,"said Grandmother.

"All of you think of a soft drink and a sandwich and I am going to call you up and then give me the orders alright,"said Urnlee.

"That is a great idea, how about ten steak sandwiches and a bag of onions and ten chocalote bars and ten sodas all for cokes, right,"said Detva.

"Ok,"said Baitlym.

"No one different,"said Detva.

"I think the chocolate is good to have for energy at this time,"said Seebees.

"Here we can still all be in the dining for this all agree lets go,"said Likus.

"Yes, lets see them enter I want to ask Lise, if she needs any help while waiting for them in the hallway,"said Grandmother.

"It will be fun, a very good snack to have in this room and a reminder that we can do this again,"said Detva.

"Do you think there is a charge for this,"said Seebees.

"No, we will just replace the steaks during our own orders, for a month, "said Likus.

"You did not put in a short order, in that Palace in Venice, did you Likus,"said Seebees.

"Yes, remember I had them major companies out in their short order staff and business but call it Versailles,"said Likus.

"That right, it is in Italy, England and France and will be in the States and Belgium next year,"said Detva.

"I remember this, this was what you were talking about and wanted all of us to own and you had to be conviced by Detva to do it yourself,"said Seebees.

"Yes, and likus turned over the patent to Gale and the company receives a service fee as an innovator of the Patent and for each franchise also he receives cash,"said Detva.

"So he bought the patent,"said Seebees.

"Yes, but I am allowed to start all of Europe and in the States if I want, do you want to help there,"said Likus.

"I should, just for a new start in life, let me think it over,"said Seebees.

"It is a good idea, but it is not for me,"said Baitlym.

"What is not for you Baitlym, if I may ask,"said Urnlee.

"Mother, Likus ask me if I wanted to start the franchise in the states of the Versailles fast foods service,"said Seebees.

"Why that is wonderful you can live in Newport near your Brother right next door in fact in any of the Mansions,"said Urnlee.

"Leave it to her to live in a good place and after all, your brother has lived there since the tunnels of 1-95 started. Now there is no place at all that looks like I-95 since the tunnels were finished and all the buildings went up,"said Grandmother.

"Good, you family can be there in three months and I will buy you a building, just fine out which one is available immediately,"said Urnlee.

"Oh, thank you,"said Seebees.

"Thank you so much all of you,"said her Husband.

"See you woke up your husband who never says a word and I think you are restless and need this, the both of you,"said Urnlee.

"We will go and it is going to be successful,"said Seebees.

"Maybe this what the restlessness was.?"said Urnlee.

"Yes, it is, just the other day she wanted to do this new for the company and I said,"I was with her,"said her husband.

"Good, it is settled. You both will leave for Newport within a week,"said Urnlee.

"Great, now I, we will contribute something too,"said Seebees.

"Your going away, how wonderful to be able to bring to the family another part of the business, "said Grandmother.

"How good of you, I do not have the drive or guts to do this and you do,"said Baitlym.

"I will miss my sister,"said Will.

"Miss me,"said Lise.

"Yes, especially you,"said Seebees.

"So lets have some of the snacks for tonight before we leave the dining room and soon we will tomorrow morning start preparing for this trip to Newport,"said Grandmother.

"When do I leave,"said Will.

"We need you to start all the businesses in Finland to Russia where they are needed,"said Grandmother.

"Ok,"said Will.

"Me,"said Lise.

"Yes, you, you may work on the coast of Belgium,"said Urnlee.

"Helping me,"said Will.

"Good,"said Lise.

"Here some cut of fruit, Lise. Have some more pie Will,"said Urnlee.

"Thanks Mom,"said Will.

"Thanks Mom,"said lise.

"Your both welcome, the two of you,"said Urnlee.

"I need another coffee,"said Grandmother.

"This is very good cake,"said Baitlym,

"Yes, the chef is always out doing himself,"said Urnlee.

"This is true the steaks the other day were the best I have had in a long time,"said Seebees.

"We can do that this weekend, if it snows there is a canopy there,"said Urnlee.

"That sounds good and he will not mind,"said Constance.

"A barbeque to two days to send off the pioneers to the west and we will have a formal dinner their last evening with us, with photos, allright,"said Urnlee.

"We would need a send off photo in the newspaper and just let the press know we are staying in Newport for a little while,"said Seebees.

"Yes, just make it look like a visit,"said Grandmother.

"And me,"said Lise.

"I need you with me, ok,"said Urnlee.

"Yes, I need Lise and Don also and Will you do not leave just yet,"said Grandmother.

"This is true no one leaves unless we give them permission,"said Urnlee.

"You should watch Lise tonight, or I will,"said Granmother.

"We can let her decide,"said Urnlee.

"Right idea,"said Grandmother.

"Is everyone finished, there is food upstairs, why not start to go to your apartments now.?"said Urnlee.

"To the staircase, Don thank you and here we go,"said Grandmother.

"Meet you upstairs grandmother,"said Will.

"Meet all of you upstairs,"said Grandmother.

"Upstairs,"said Urnlee.

"Upstairs,"said Lise.

"Night,"said Seebees.

"Night,"said Baitlym.

"Night,"said Detva.

"Night, "said Lise.

"Good morning,"said Urnlee.

"Goo Morning, "said Lise.

"Let me get your breakfast then your bath and we are downstairs and if you hungry there is more food to have, alright,"said Urnlee.

"I love you,"said Lise.

"I love you too, very much,"said Urnlee.

"Good morning you too, I will wait in the sitting room and all of us can go downstairs together,"said Grandmother.

"Don,"said Lise.

"We can meet both of you in the dining room, alright,"said Grandmother.

"Alright,"said Lise.

"Alright, Urnlee you look beautiful both of you girls do,"said Grandmother.

"Thank you and so do you, Constance,"said Urnlee.

"Thank you, see you both,"said Grandmother.

"Good morning, "Baitlym.

"Good morning, come on Don, lets go to the elevator,"said Grandmother.

"Good morning, Baitlym, what took you so long.? "said Don.

"While you Don ride your bike I need the exercise and use the stairs, and your so funny this morning,"said Baitlym.

"Good morning, everyone staying upstairs, "said Detva.

"That is alright. But I think we are going to have some of the children with us "said Grandmother.

"Here is work we are going to do today we need a photo of all of us this evening by the graves and chapel and then we are in the living for awhile just before dinner.I am sorry but we need these photos ok, "said Urnlee.

"Then Craig his wife and children are going home. They are taking with them Seebees her husband and children, "said Baitlym.

"They are leaving tomorrow instead of waiting another week,"said Urnlee.

"You just found out this a few minutes ago,"said Grandmother.

"Actually thirty minutes ago, apparently the four of them were talking last night and decided to leave at 10:00 a.m. tomorrow morning,"said Urnlee.

"Good for them to do something that they want to do, what adventure I am so glad she will be with our brother Craig in Newport,"said Baitlym.

"Yes, and she should get people to work for here as representatives for the project,"said Detva.

"Yes, so she and her family will be safe in Newport, I hope it will be that easy,"said Urnlee.

"Me, too "said Lise.

"No, you are staying with me, ok,"said Grandmother.

"Ok,"said Lise.

"Lets have some breakfast Lise. Come on Will and Don you too,"said Grandmother.

"Finished,"said Don.

"I never have to tell you at all, Donald,"said Grandmother

"Never,"said Don.

"Seebees you leaving tonight, my only advice is to get others to sell the franchises and enjoy the safety of Newport,"said Baitlym.

"It is tomorrow morning, and I will be safe in Newport,"said Seebees.

"Good, I love you, but I am not jealous you enjoy your work all of you please,"said Bailtlym.

"I sure do,"said Craig.

"Good, now all of you start your breakfast and we then we will get ready for the photos, "said Urnlee.

"Does this mean I get the corner room on the left,"said Will.

"I need that apartment. Bailtlym is in my other apartment and you can be next to her on that right side at the end, you are grown up now to protect all of us, "said Grandmother.

"I need to look out and see the front of the building,"said Grandmother.

"Good and I need to watch the backyard that goes into the woods,"said Will.

"Yes, you are but you need to be inside and away from the window, you can not let anyone see you,"said Urnlee.

"And me,"said Don.

"You will still be near Grandmother, ok,"said Urnlee.

"Ok,"said Don.

"Me too,"said Lise.

"Yes you are,"said Grandmother.

"Now does anyone wish to go upstairs now to get ready and we will meet in the chapel at 4:00 p.m, "said Baitlym.

"Here you are Urnlee I was wondering if you and the children were in here,"said Grandmother.

"Baitlym is in the Grave room and many are in the apartment, we wanted it is be as casual for the childrens' sake so I did not call you,"said Urnlee.

"That is alright,"said Grandmother.

"Thank you for this, this entire process of being in one place to another is for Lise and the others to know we do not wander off, I hope that never happens,"said Urnlee.

"The front doors have an alarm of it and the security, staff and outside guards are notified. You do not need to worry so much,"said Grandmother.

"Look at her and is small, and tiny and beautiful, I do worry,"said Urnlee.

"Don has schooled her and has even taken away her dolls she know who to trust and why, right now,"said Grandmother.

"That all seems to be a comfort,"said Urnlee.

"Strange it does to me too,"said Grandmother.

"Lets go to the graves and talk about how beautiful the flowers are for the photos,"said Urnlee.

"Grandma,"said Lise.

"Come on, stay with us Lise,"said Grandmother.

"Now here is where the family picture will be, the flower arrangements are excellent, do you think so Constance.? "said Urnlee.

"Yes, all of them look so lovely,"said Grandmother.

"See Lise here is your, flowers,"said Urnlee.

"Yes, they are exquisite,"said Grandmother.

"Exquit,"said Lise.

"Don now that you are here please go get anyone ok. Go help him Will alright. Thank you. "said Grandmother.

"Boys please get the others alright, thank you,"said Urnlee.

"Baitlym, Seebees here is something of your Mother to keep in your handbags, it is a handkerchief. All of you have things belongings of your Mother and father are your own beds and chairs, I wanted the photos done first so you may all go and look now or after dinner,"said Urnlee.

"We should go up now,"said Detva.

"Yes, we should,"said Seebees.

"This is not the will,"said Baitlym.

"That is tonight,"said Urnlee.

"What time tonight,"said Baitlym.

"After 8:00 p.m. when the children are asleep, the lawyers are arriving in the evening time only,"said Urnlee.

"Why at the late evening time,"said Seebees.

"So there is no obligations to stay, just for a late coffee only,"said Urnlee.

"We are near that time when the lawyers are to arrive,"said Constance.

"Lets be in the living room to talk to them,"said Urnlee.

"This is not what I expected!"said Detva.

"Mother, Grandmother myself and all the others in charge and having our own homes,"said Likus.

"I can not believe if we want to move out we have a home, I have a new home in Newport,"said Seebees.

"We all have our own homes or we can stay here and collect rent,"said Baitlym.

"This is the largest house one of the newest it is for anyone to return too,"said Urnlee.

"I will stay here and on the weekends we can all go to my new house if we want too,"said Constance.

"We can collect rent while we are here and help our children,"said Baitlym.

"This is all so wonderful, you are aware that this large new home does go to Lise,"said Urnlee.

"Yes, and I am going to return to Venice soon. So I will rent the smaller house on the beach,"said Likus.

"We are going to take that money, anything that belongs to Belgium stays here,"said Constance.

"Yes, I know or maybe one of us would want to live there,"said Likus.

"That might be possible for Will too,"said Detva.

"We know yet there are other things now,"said Urnlee.

"Yes, the autos there are four,"said Constance.

"If you live here permanently, then you use one, if here for a short time then you use the older autos,"said Grandmother.

"All of the jewelry was given out earlier.? I thank you Urnlee and Grandmother for the selection,"said Seebees.

"All of her minks that were six and each one of the wives received one,"said Baitlym.

"Did Lise get jewelry.?"said Seebees.

"Yes, she has her own jewelry when she grown up with the Exile jewelers and a few that your others bought her,"said Urnlee.

"I bought her a few rings,"said Grandmother.

"So did I,"said Baitlym.

"Here is a list and photos of all that she received. All are in the safe upstairs. One at a time anyone may see everything tomorrow if you want too,"said Urnlee.

"So it is done, mother wanted to be with dad and now she is,"said Baitlym.

"What did the autopsy report indicate.? said Seebees.

"There was a heart attack and she did not suffer,"said Urnlee.

"That is good to know,"said Baitlym.

"She called me on the house phone when I got there she was dead,"said Urnlee.

"She told me they were not going to be given operations of any kind,"said their Grandmother.

"Dad mentioned that to us one day,"said Seebees.

"They are at rest now and have each other,"said Constance.

"This is correct we should not be in the way of their happiness,"said Baitlym.

"No, I should not, they loved each other,"said Detva.

"Lets stop talking the children have returned,"said Likus.

"Mother I did what you tolded me and we have the home open in England we can be there is an hour so goodbye and bye everyone, we are off the England for one day and then we are in Newport for quite some time,"said Seebees.

"Bye,"said Baitlym.

"Wait why not drive them over, and return with the car, and Craig can take all of our luggage to the States. Said Detva.

"Sounds good we will all leave England in two tomorrow,"said Seebees.

"Ok, I am ready, you do not mind Grandmother or Urnlee,"said Baitland.

"Why not make it very romantic in England for your selves and the six of you leave now and let Craig and his wife take the children,"said Urnlee.

"Ok, children your parents are going to go to England and give Seebees her very last vacation for one day and then they are going to be working in the states, "said Grandmother.

"All of us say good bye, "said Urnlee.

"Lets see them off upstairs and then we will get ready for bed,"said Grandmother.

"See look at all of them from Lise's room,"said Urnlee.

"Now lets use Bailtlym's room or yes we can see them very well in fact I see the last part of their car now,"said Will.

"We are going to see a new film a cartoon called, "Versailles"it is one of the best for children,"said Grandmother.

"Great a new film for kids,"said Will.

"Oh, boy,"said Lise.

"All are watching and there is no one wanting their parents so far so good,"said Urnlee.

"That is good and I hope everything is exciting for them, in England,"said Grandmother.

"Nice and romantic, you did not want to go did you,"said Urnlee.

"No, I can create romance right here with a private dinner for two these sudden trips are not for me and anyways Seebees and her husband are going to start working so they need some excitement,"said Grandmother.

"They do and they deserve this,"said Urnlee.

"That is right now lets go and see the movie I heard this was quite good for children and adults who want to enjoy a good film,"said Grandmother.

"I do have to admitt these films that are released by Versailles Studios are excellent. They have even done the classics all over again. Many times with many different stars,"said Urnlee.

"Each classic has been done ten times already,"said Grandmother.

"What do you want, he started Versailles cable he might as well include everything,"said Urnlee.

"Could he think of something else,"said Grandmother.

"There is nothing else, I guess,"said Urnlee.

"Versailles is truly his now, he did not say when he wanted to run the business again in the headquarters building in France,"said Grandmother.

"No, but I bet the publicity is not really going to be to outrageous,"said Urnlee.

"No, it will not so lets see if the children want any snacks,"said Grandmother.

"The nannies are in here, most of them, they have been going on breaks in twos,"said Urnlee.

"Did you want to see the movie.? "said Grandmother.

"No, this is the time I am going to go to sleep early, right after the movie I am going to bed so is my little baby,"said Urnlee.

"She must be asleep already.?"said Grandmother.

"She is. After her birth, I have been getting a lot of sleep. As soon as she is walking and talking all of that rest will go away,"said Urnlee.

"It did when I got married,"said Grandmother.

"Anything that is new and not part of a routine would have an effort,"said Urnlee.

"Oh, did I say get more sleep, it is less,"said Grandmother.

"Sure, this is a difference, from the routine,"said Urnlee.

"We need some coffee and snacks lets help ourselves before the movie is over,"said Grandmother.

"I see your husband wanted to see the movie,"said Urnlee.

"He did want to see this movie with the children. I have a man for you to date, he is my husband's nephew, he is your age and very rich,"said Grandmother.

"We do have to wait a year. Besides is he as handsome as your son, that is another reason why I married him,"said Urnlee.

"He is in fact, I have a photo of him he could not be at the wedding,"said Constance.

"I do hear something that your husband was the only child,"said Urnlee.

"He was, his mother remarried, after his father died. Then she remarried and had two children,"said Constance.

"So how did they remain away from him,"said Urnlee.

"They divorced, he died and she took care of those two and my huband remained with his mother,"said Constance.

"Sure they would they are used to seeing just one mother,"said Urnlee.

"You might know of the daughter, she is with the royals all the time in Denmark.

She married Count Neargauled, "said Constance.

"I know who she is, is lives there in the Palace and they both have a small castle near time,"said Urnlee.

"She called me up when we got married, and when your husband died and called me up again, she wanted you to date her brother, "said Grandmother.

"Did you think if this when they all left and wanted to tell me this,"said Urnlee.

"I did think of it a few hours ago and gave them $ 2000.00 cash to push them out the door but no one knows in this house just you and I,"said Constance.

"Oh, just your husband's know.?"said Urnlee.

"No, he thinks she called to wish him and I happiness because of our marriage,"said Constance.

"No one knows,"said Urnlee.

"No one just you and I know,"said Constance.

"Then I give you permission to call him and invite him here and her at the same time so it does not look as if I am interested, alright,"said Urnlee.

"Good for you get back into life,"said Constance.

"Ok, but do not tell him anything let me tell you that I approve of him, ok,"said Urnlee.

"Alright, I think the movies are all over, here they are, I will call tonight,"said Grandmother.

"Maybe tomorrow instead, it is getting very late in the evening,"said Urnlee.

"Good, I am going to take your advice,"said Grandmother.

"How was the movie, lets all start going to our apartments good night anyone,"said Urnlee.

Chapter 18

"Good night, was the movie good, Don and Lise did you enjoy it.? "said Grandmother.

"Yes,"said Don.

"Yes, said Lise.

"Yes, said Will.

"Good, Urnlee I am going to help the nannies with the others, ok,"said Grandmother.

"Good idea, I am going to see that Lise is in bed,"said Urnlee.

"Good night, Don, "said Grandmother.

"Night Mom,"said Will.

"Night, Will thank you for helping,"said Urnlee.

"Now, her is the baby and she is asleep, Lise did you want to sleep in here tonight,"said Urnlee.

"Yes, I am tired,"said Lise.

"Ok, go to sleep,"said Urnlee.

"Good night ,"said Urnlee.

"Good night,"said Lise.

"Mom,"said Lise

"What is it, are you ok,"said Urnlee.

"It is time for my breakfast,"said Lise.

"It can not be we were just watching a movie,"said Urnlee.

"Good,"said Lise.

"The nanny, has you all ready,"said Urnlee.

"Wake up, that advice and chat we had last night made you sleep until ten,"said Grandmother.

"Lets go, Grandma,"said Lise.

"We will be down stairs,"said Grandmother.

"Good morning, did you call last night.?"said Urnlee.

"Yes, they are going to be here and the royals are to be here to for a few hours then they are going to be at our new castle by the shore for a few weeks,"said Grandmother.

"Oh,"said Urnlee.

"Seebees left that house vacant so they can stay there for a vacation,"said Grandmother.

"Good so we have guests,"said Urnlee.

"They need to be spoiled,"said Grandmother.

"You mean the sister and brother are staying here, right,"said Urnlee.

"If they want to, other than that, they may want to stay at the shore,"said Grandmother.

"Suggest that they may stay there with us for a few days alright,"said Urnlee.

"That does sound better,"said Grandmother.

"It is and we do not want them to be alone,"said Urnlee.

"Are we going to the beach,"said Will.

"We might, but let me mention it to our guests,"said Grandmother.

"Sure, this is our first guests in this new castle,"said Will.

"I know you are right about that Will,"said Urnlee.

"There has been a reason why for everyone since the house was buildt,"said Urnlee.

"I know it was mainly for funerals too,"said Grandmother.

"This time is is different we are having people who are relatives of Grandfather,"said Will.

"Your right, how do you know this,"said Grandmother.

"With the second entrace to the pantry and the dining room the wall is here against the dining room , I know I was not suppose to listen but I was protecting us,"said Will.

"Here is a door, the cook told me to tell you this last night but we were all very busy, he said, "It is a good place to hind from some strangers and in case of an emergency, "said Will.

"This is a door that opens up,"said Urnlee.

"Why for goodness sakes, here we are at the end of the pantry,"said Constance.

"Are there any others Will, because we might need them in case of strangers entering,"said Urnlee.

"Did I do anything wrong,"said Will.

"No, the cook was right and you did tell us,"said Urnlee.

"You are a good boy Will, are there any others,"said Grandmother.

"Yes, upstairs there are staircases,"said Will.

"Here we can get to the second floor right from this room,"said Will.

"Where is this door.? "said Urnlee.

"Here right here. Just press this and the door opens up right here in the corner,"said Will.

"Goodness sakes. Look a stair case. Where does it go? said Grandmother.

"Right next to the library door, but inside the library,"said Will.

"We need the plans of this house,"said Urnlee.

"Does any of the staff know, besides the cook,"said Grandmother.

"No, the cook mention these doors were for the family and he was not going to tell the staff,"said Will.

"How are they cleaned.?"said Urnlee.

"He did, the cook cleaned them and told me when you found out he would clean them so the others would not know,"said Will.

"Alright tell him he may do it secretly,"said Urnlee.

"Now what.? "said Grandmother.

"Well, this was my house and I gave it to Baitlym when her mother died it was official, but with these doors it could be dangerous,"said Urnlee.

"When she sees these doors she is going to give you back this building,"said Grandmother.

"She could have the house at the shore, right after the guests leave,"said Urnlee.

"That does seem to be a good idea. But is she going to object,"said Constance.

"No. she is going to be in shock,"said Urnlee.

"She might, but I think she will just give the building back to you and take the other,"said Constance.

"It will not to the sence of spying, it will be the idea that one of the children might have been missing and hurt,"said Urnlee.

"She is not the only one, how did Ed forget.?"said Constance.

"That is just finders keepers.?"said Urnlee.

"Your correct.!"said Constance.

"He was ill and never did think of these things at the end,"said Urnlee.

"My dear, you have had so much happening in your young life you deserve to this man and marry him, I am sure he is going to ask you,"said Constance.

"Thank you,"said Urnlee.

"But hat, I know he might not be a good as Ed but you need someone,"said Constance.

"Mom, I told the cook and he is going to clean the hallways and he will not tell anyone,"said Will.

"Very good you have done us a great service now we have a secret escape route,"said Urnlee.

"Yes, thank you Will,"said Grandmother.

"I need the architect's name and address do you know who they are I forgot if Ed told me,"said Urnlee.

"Sure I do there office is in town,"said Constance.

"Is it all right to call right now.?"said Urnlee.

"Sure I will ask him right now,"said Constance.

"He mentioned that the doors that are secret he is going to fax them right now and the blue prints,"said Constance.

"That is good,"said Urnlee.

"All will be sent to you within the hour and he does apologizes,"said Constance.

"I am glad this is finished,"said Urnlee.

"Are you upset,"said Constance.

"No, I am glad no one was hurt,"said Urnlee.

"He did say men do not discuss, these things with their wives in these types of houses. This is very true of my husband also,"said Constance.

"There are the floor plans,"said Urnlee.

"See all leads into the hallways, as this memo suggests,"said Constance.

"Good we have to do some other time look here are the guests and the royals do not know they are going to stay here,"said Grandmother.

"Good morning,"said Urnlee.

"Good morning, your Uncle is somewhere and now all the children are not here either,"said Constance.

"Now I can not believe it Baitlym and Detva and Likus and all their wives and one husband are now descending. They are on their own,"said Grandmother.

"All of you are going to introduce yourselves to make it as informal as it should be ok,"said Urnlee.

"Yes, it is not fair to impose we should have called first hello I am Likus and lets all go to the livingroom,"said Likus.

"Now that the cook has this orders we can begin to sit down at the table, and talk and have a good lunch,"said Grandmother.

"I hope that Seebees has a good time in Newport and works very hard,"said the Countess.

"Will your ex husband return here before he goes back to Denmark,"said will.

"Thank you, will I was just thinking of that we would like to see him and his new wife again if it is possible,"said Urnlee.

"They will return she and he just needed some time alone and to know us so there is not terrible and bad feelings between any of us,"said the Countess.

"They needed a little vacation that's all,"said Grandmother.

"Hello, everyone continue to have your lunch, sorry I am late I will sit down right now and be apart of you,"said the Uncle.

"Titles are for given as long as there is some rewards to be forgiven and accepted uncle one more time after this it is ok too,"said Will.

"Will, you are to secured and is this blackmail,"said Grandmother.

"Oh,no they had this planned already Uncle as gifts for all of us,"said Urnlee.

"I do not believe this, what I nice gift,"said Urnlee.

"You know the four of your could pay back Urnlee who gave you cash before you left the other day,"said Grandmother.

"No, that is alright they may purchase something for the children." said Urnlee.

"Thank you, from all of us and we will do just that,"said Baitlym.

"I hope your husband and his wife get long they seem to be a good pair,"said Likus.

"Oh no, Constance do you think of what just happened,"said Urnlee.

"It is a good thing Baitlym and Detva or at the head of the table so we can compare notes, "said Constance.

"What is he doing.?"said Urnlee.

"What do you exspect he is home from Venice for a little while he gets divorced here and then remarries here and now divorced again he gets rid of her and now another,"said Constance.

"She is going to get rid of that Count and marry again, These kids are leaving for there own homes and they can do this on there own time,"said Urnlee.

"They are enchanted, this is a better deal than the first,"said Constance.

"You are right as usual. So they all can stay,"said Urnlee.

"Good, and now maybe we can pick someone else if anything goes wrong they the others, the men will think twice about cheating on our women,"said Constance.

"Great idea, I think that this has saved a few marriages,"said Urnlee.

"An now what about the brother of the Countess,"said Constance.

"Now do not say anything else, and enjoy what just happened,"said Urnlee.

"I will, and I know you are too,"said Constance.

"Now do enjoy this yourself too,"said Urnlee.

"If my husband can take himself away from the table we are all going to the living room,"said

"Sorry my dear, I have been ignoring you,"said their Uncle.

"Don lets go upstairs for a few minutes,"said Grandmother.

"Ok, said Don.

"We are all going to stay here is the living room for awhile and we can all start on having some more desserts if any of you want too,"said Urnlee.

"This is so wonderful Urnlee. This house is lovely and so large if must have been a while to have it build.? "said the Countess.

"It took six years from a small castle to a very large one,"said Urnlee.

"It name is grand too, Grenland unlike the other in Bavaria,"said the Countess.

"Thank you, It is like Grenaire where Ed and Ownsite live, but it is not as tall,"said Urnlee.

"May I take him home with me to Denmark, I do not want to let anyone else hear this,"said the Countess.

"He could visit but He needs to return to Venice in three weeks,"said Urnlee.

"I will ask him but I will be whisper only,"said the Countess.

"You have returned and Don too,"said Urnlee.

"Yes, I needed to rest and he woke me up after ten minutes,"said Grandmother.

"What do you think your have missed.?"said Urnlee.

"I hope it was she if he did nothing,"said Constance.

"She is asking him to visit Denmark and then he is going to return to Italy in three weeks,"said Urnlee.

"I just want him to be happy and enjoy someone,"said Constance.

"It looks that way right now,"said Urnlee.

"I hope so, He needs someone to love him and to be with,"said Constance.

"Is that why you want upstairs to make sure something did happen, or hoping it would,"said Urnlee.

"Would and did, and it worked,"said Constance.

"Yes, you are right,"said Urnlee.

"Now you go over there , to her brother the Prince and ask Prince Needo if he needs anything else maybe another coffee or you, "said Constance.

"Need anything else Prince some coffee,"said Urnlee.

"That would be nice thank you and yourself,"said the Prince.

"For both of us,"said Urnlee.

"Thank you,"said the Prince.

"Would you like to walk into the hallway and talk.?"said Urnlee.

"Yes please, I was going to ask if you to show me a few of the rooms on this floor,"said the Prince.

"It is my pleasure too,"said Urnlee.

"Thank you,"said the Prince.

"Here is the library off the Great Hall and the staircase in the other floors, it is quite nice, most of the wood was taken from two old churches which are now replaced for each communities,"said Urnlee.

"I remember hearing about the churches all agreed with the foundation and its existing walls would be leveled to the height of the windows,"said Prince Needo.

"Yes it did please all and we now have a lovely kitchen floors and several feet to the back kitchen door to the outside where the staff my sit and are hidden by the same wall,"said Urnlee.

"I understand there were no windows left so it was easier to decide on the a new approach instead the traditional,"said the Prince.

"Yes, it was their own decision to purchase and then use a new material for the walls, both were in the news of how they used round and square and a star effect for the windows,"said Urnlee.

"So tell me about yourself do you live in the Palace too,"said Urnlee.

"Just on formal occasions now I live in my sister's house since she separated from her husband,"said the Prince.

"I know you are very busy with your child and I am so sorry about your husband dieing both of us could not leave Denmark do to a formal appearance that same evening and I did not attend due to a severe cold,"said the Prince.

"Thank you and you are alright now? I heard it was a cold and a severe allergy too,"said Urnlee.

"I am now fine,"said the Prince.

"You and your sister must rent our two homes so then she can avoid her husband too,"said Urnlee.

"That is a terrific idea for her she needs to leave Denmark to avoid them, they visit the Palace and with her leaving they might move in,"said the Prince.

"This could work out,"said Urnlee.

"Here we are at the living room again, thank you for tour. Would you like to go into the city with me tonight and we can shop too besides having a dinner,"said the Prince.

"Yes, that would be very nice, I will go get ready even if it now late evening, I did not mind it at all,"said Urnlee.

"I will wait at the front door,"said the Prince.

"Constance he is waiting at the front door we are going shopping and to have a small dinner,"said Urnlee.

"Good, buy just one thing and then have dinner at Ed's restaurant it is called Ownsite,"said Constance.

"We are, so give them a call,"said Urnlee.

"I am right now. Hello my daughter-in-law would right a table for two she will be there in a few minutes,"said Constance.

"Grandmother they went out,"said Will.

"They are dating now, I told her to date him if he asks, so we must to very good,"said Constance.

"Sure if they need a place to crash, they get stay on the second floor I just can not wait to date and then the restaurant is all mind,"said Will.

"Goodness,"said Grandmother.

"Are all of you going upstairs I quess I will too are you going with me Don,"said his Grandmother.

"Ok, up we go,"said Don.

"Good night Don, good night everyone,"said Grandmother.

"Grandma. Is Urnlee going to let stay here tonight,"said Lise.

"Would you like to have the suite of rooms right next to mine,"said Grandmother.

"Yes,"said Lise.

"That's good,"said Grandmother.

"How they are still a variety instead of a fish place,"said Will.

"Good night Lise, good night, Will,"said Grandmother.

"Good night,"said Will.

"Hope you had to good evening and did you get home after one,"said Grandmother.

"Yes it was one thirty, by the way how do I get my name off of the restaurant door.?"said Urnlee.

"What would you like it is say.?"said Grandmother.

"Right now, maybe Lloyd's,"said Urnlee.

"This is too funny, I was wondering why Will wanted to date and did say it could not be named as a fish place,"said Constance.

"I do not know why you think it is so funny after it was called Consee and before my name it was apart of trunk,"said Urnlee.

"Oh, Indian food no wait right there, hello Edvard what did you call the restaurant, oh, I will buy it all right you will have a check in the mail. Today,"said Constance.

"I will be called, Will,"said Constance.

"It will be called Likus favorite name, Countess for Lloyd's remember always think of the business,"said Urnlee.

"How about my Grandson's naval,"said Grandmother.

"No, that is not Lloyds's remember the press, it is now Countess. What was it did he say.?"said Urnlee.

"Yes, for Lloyd's when I was dating and then just married it became Urnlee but before that it was King, "said Grandmother.

"Yes,m grandma your husband is.! "said Will.

"King size, why I think I should give him a bonus for that maybe a 5 hundred thousand dollar bonus,"said Grandmother.

"That is good,"said Urnlee.

"Now I heard I am on the sign,"said Likus.

"It is called a sign to everyone,"said Grandmother.

"It is called Countess,"said Urnlee.

"It is a sign, that is what it is,"said Grandmother.

"Boy, am I glad I have home school,"said Will.

"Now wonder why Ed insisted we have the Versailles preschool and home school too,"said Grandmother.

"My dear, I hope you are not upset to much,"said her husband.

"Just think Likus all of that cash they took in and it has not been spent,"said Detva.

"Was this your idea,"said Likus.

"No, I think Ed wanted someone to buy and this is part of the game to be played,"said Detva.

"I do not appreciate it,"said Grandmother.

"It is for Lloyd's, we are there for the good and bad, lets hope that this is the last of it,"said Detva.

"This should be the last of it maybe we missed most of this, we have been very busy all of us,"said Likus.

"Did anyone check the news maybe we should sue the tabloids,"said Urnlee.

"We can see, maybe we the cook or some one has all the papers,"said Grandmother.

"There was nothing so far, I have watch everything,"said the Countess.

"See we have nothing,"said Urnlee.

"Now we need to get that business, to start on me and within the company I can take it away and give it to Likus. He can then run it ,"said the Countess.

"Right now we are in the hands of the company we need it back right now,"said their Grandmother.

"You can ask them for it right now being Lloyd's,"said Urnlee.

"I will,"said Likus.

"Good and I will approve it,"said Detva.

"Alright, so you two get the papers from the secretary and we can get this done right away,"said Urnlee.

"You are very much in charge when something happens,"said Prince Needo.

"We just had to funerals so I want everything cleared up in a few minutes for the sake of the children,"said Urnlee.

"We need to have my grandson right here,"said their Grandmother.

"I do believe it was very funny when my name was there too,"said Urnlee.

"I know I will get over this very soon,"said their Grandmother.

"Good now have some food. Now let the day begin,"said Urnlee.

"It just is not fair,"said Constance.

"Would you consent to it if you were asked,"said Urnlee.

"No, I guess I would have argued,"said Constance.

"Now, it is over,"said her Husband, Shawn.

"It is done.so it will be left alone starting right now,"said Urnlee.

"Grandmother is this, as we would be call an upstarts,"said Will.

"No, it was just done to ourselves no to a stranger,"said Grandmother.

"I understand we really did not try to hurt anyone did we,"said Will.

"It is a good thing you whispered it, it will be our little secret, ok,"said Grandmother.

"Our secret, ok,"said Will.

"We have plans today, and she is getting a divorce from her second husband that is why she is here,"said Likus.

"Alright, just give her the kindness that she deserves and help,"said Urnlee.

"I will,"said Likus.

"Now can we do something today,"said her Prince.

"We can take a ride or a walk I would like to be here allday, is that allright with you, I know, we can go to the city tonight when the children are asleep,"said Urnlee.

"We can go tomorrow night we you want to, lets see what tonight brings,"said Needo, her Prince.

"I am going to tell you this if she marries me I am going to let her be Princess Baylib she may keep her name but her title will be from me,"said Likus.

"Good now go away before Needo returns with my coffee and be good to her,"said Urnlee.

"With this advice I should do fine,"said Likus.

"Allright I give up, where did I go wrong what made him turn against me,"said Constance.

"I have to confess, he called me up and ask if he should do this and I mention to him to do it now,"said Urnlee.

"All of you are against me,"said Constance.

"No, I made it up and you need to get a hold of yourself,"said Urnlee.

"Your are right, I guess so, where is my husband,"said Constance.

"Ed you must call your Grandmother she is taking this very seriously about the name you put on the building and with hers too,"said Urnlee.

"My goodness you are working every minute, as you indicated earlier,"said Needo."

"I has to be done or we would all be in a turmoil,"said Urnlee.

"You can help me,"said Prince Needo.

"All right I will,"said Urnlee.

"Thank you, I really do enjoy your company, Urnlee,"said the Prince.

"Thank you, but what is happening to Likus,"said Urnlee.

"He has fallen in love, like myself,"said the Prince.

"That is not being funny, we going to date for one year,"said Urnlee.

"I will obey you, I love you, the first time I saw you with Ed,"said the Prince.

"When was that,"said Urnlee.

"You had just left the hospital and I visited alone then my sister arrived within the next hour,"said the Prince.

"Oh, my dearest, excuse me, I was given a tour of the building and I still want to stay and owe my I please,"said Baitlym.

"Yes, it is yours now that Seebees has moved to Newport I am going to allow the Prince and his sister is use both building,"said Urnlee.

"Thank you,"said Baitlym.

"You may use the house tonight if you intend to stay for awhile,"said Urnlee.

"You and Ed were very proper with your marriage decision and I respect you for that,"said Needo.

"Why not let my sister rent Seebees house and I can rent the gatehouse sort of your personal body guard at your front gate. I promise to enter this house, only with your permission,"said Needo.

"That does seem like to good idea and you tell let your sister that tonight,"said Urnlee.

"It is a deal then, I will sign the rent agreement,"said the Prince.

"Your sister may stay here or use the house and you can use the smaller house on the right it is not attached and there is no need of taking rent,"said Urnlee.

"Thank you, you are must kind and I will respect your year of privacy, I know it must have been difficult and it still is,"said Needo.

"It was difficult I did not think I would have a baby and I did,"said Urnlee.

"Now you have me and I will help you, so it will not be difficult anymore,"said Needo.

"There is some coffee for you two,"said Constance.

"Good thanks, I just want to let you know that Needo is staying in the guest house on the right and his sister can use Seebee's home if she wants to. Would you like to tell her that ok,? "said Urnlee.

"I will tell her right now. Good news, Needo, very nice, Indeed,"said Constance.

"Thank you we will talk to her later could you tell her that for me,"said the Prince.

"So we have made progress yet set up boundaries for ourselves,"said Urnlee.

"It is very important for the young children living here to see that,"said the Prince.

"I know it would not be right or fair to them now that I am their only mother,"said Urnlee.

"No, it would be very cruel to these little still including Will, "said the Prince.

"I hope Seebees understands that I hope she left, only for a new start for her and her family,"said Urnlee.

"She did, she would never leave if things were unsafe,"said the Prince.

"Your correct she would stay, now I need to lock up thse trap doors before anyone gets hurt,"said Urnlee.

"They have to have a safety lock on them,"said the Prince.

"There could be,"said Urnlee.

"I am sure the architect would tell you how to lock them, and show you how,"said the Prince.

"Good, I will write a memo right now,"said Urnlee.

"That is perfect now lets go see my sister,"said the Prince.

"I heard the news and I have something to say too. We are going to get married soon, when her divorce final,"said Likus.

"Good luck old man and my sister too,"said the Prince.

"Thank you, Urnlee and for the house as well to use, but I would rather stay in the apartment next to yours, would that be alright.?"said Princess Baylib.

"Sure, it is alright,"said Urnlee.

"Good, then that is settled and now I can return to my own house with my husband if he does not mind,"said Constance.

"What Constance, you can purchase anything you like my dear,"said Grandmother.

"There now we are all on the same page, I think,"said Constance.

"Grandmother you are always creating something for us to think about, with laughter, "said Likus.

"Good, now how is that dear what Likus was talking about,"said Constance.

"You may purchase in Venice, I do not mind it a bit,"said Grandfather.

"He is not to far off, I will say thank you to confirm this,"said Constance.

"If you want to, we can buy out Likus or move right next door,"said Grandfather.

"Here is a call,"said Urnlee.

"This really made my day,"said Constance.

"So did this phone call, do you know Ed's boss? "said Urnlee.

"Yes, we did meet her here a few years ago, she married Ed and Ownsite's uncle on my side,"said Constance.

"He just died and left her everything except for his,"said Urnlee.

"What,"said Constance.

"I do not know, her phone went dead,"said Urnlee.

"Probably she did not give it a charge, she just gave us one. They have no children so I do not think she is dropping anyone,"said Will.

"Will behave,"said Urnlee.

"Yes, please do,"said Constance.

"But did he, and his first wife died,"said Baitlym.

"He did have a few children they now must be, the youngest is sisteen now,"said Detva.

"We always did think of him as being single, and without children,"said Likus.

"When they got marry it was her that got them into the house while at their boarding schools,"said Baitlym.

"Seebees went to school with one of the daughters,"said Likus.

"Then she got them all together again,"said Urnlee.

"They were here about of three years ago, just when they were married,"said Baitlym.

"That is why they were not at the funerals,"said Detva.

Chapter 19

"So much as happened with us, I did not think of calling them,"said Constance.

"It is not your fault,"said Urnlee.

"Why no, there has been a lot happening right here among us all for the last two years in fact,"said Likus.

"No one is to be blamed, I will call her right now and ask if they would like to vacation here this week.,"said Urnlee.

"We still do not know if Detva is gay,"said Likus.

"Stop that, "said Constance.

"I could smack you a good one Likus, but I will not,"said Detva.

"Thank you, Detva my love,"said Likus.

"Very funny,"said Baitlym.

"Grandmother control him and keep her quiet, I have one marriage and I do not intent of have another and father a lot of children,"said Detva.

"Here is the situation for all of them. They are going to use the new beach house and we or a few at a time can us. We may stay a few days to get to know our new cousins. Does that sound like a good idea, to all of you ? "said Urnlee.

"Good, said Will.

"A few at a time. is all right,"said Bailtym.

"Excellent and maybe they might join us here,"said Constance.

"Exactly she wants to rent the building for a long while,"said Urnlee.

"Could I stay in her house with my family,"said Detva.

"I will let her know she is looking for a rent, this will be very good and when she returns maybe you can,"said Urnlee.

"Great I can start working for the company in the main building,"said Detva.

"It is a deal, the contracts will be mailed from her lawyers office,"said Urnlee.

"Detva I did not mean it, please do not leave because of what was said, "said Likus.

"No, I just told you and everyone else I now can work from the mean office in Paris,"said Detva.

"They put in in their new building, it is the one that looks like a large Shoe,"said Likus.

"When did this happen.?"said Detva.

"It was two days ago, or it was delayed I am not sure,"said Likus.

"That is right too,"said Detva.

"So you are going, anmd now I am going to Venice again,"said Likus.

"Both of you should go and help this company we are running, do not worry about us the securing is very good,"said Urnlee.

"Also I am at the front gate,"said Needo.

"Ok, everyone is safe and that is good,"said Likus.

"If this was run down and we had to sell everything and we would have to and also let go of the staff we would all of us would be going out to work everyday,"said Grandmother.

"Do not forget me, I have enough to help and we do not need to worry about letting people go and needing to go out to work every day because that is reality right now as it is,"said Grandfather.

"I know this part but do have each other and we must work with this company until Gale takes it over again, he is allowing us to have our share,"said Grandmother.

"That we will have I am going to leave tonight and the children will follow and so will my wife."I am sure she will want go,"said Detva.

"She has been contented to stay in your palace while you work things out here, do you think she will go with you,"said Urnlee.

"I am sure of it, but I will return with an answer right now in a few minutes, she will understand,"said Detva.

"I least this time we are all leaving under good terms and it is not death, Constance do you agree things seem better,"said Urnlee.

"Yes better, but I still wish I had Edvard right here,"said Constance.

"What happened,"said Likus.

"She said "Yes,""She was crying and laughter was present when we got off the phone, she was also going to tell the children,"said Detva.

"Now see we have three families leaving and the rest are going to stay here. There is enough to do in this building for the company, are we all in agreement now,"said Urnlee.

"Yes, my husband has always ready sent go franchises for your business in the states,"said Baitlym.

"So we have decided to go with what has been presented to all in favor, good it is 100% for the company,"said Urnlee.

"I second it,"said Grandmother.

"I agree,"said Baritlym.

"So do I, and we need Grandpa here for fast foods,"said Will.

"Very good, what an excellent idea and I will send out for Pizzas, sodas and desserts right now,"said Grandfather.

"But it is only lunch time,"said Grandmother.

"Then chicken it is for dinner, we need to celebrate,"said Grandfather.

"It is a right occasion,"said Urnlee.

"Urnlee may I speak to you in the other room, please,"said Needo.

"Yes, you may,"said Urnlee.

"I have something to say,"said Needo.

"What are you doing,"said Urnlee.

"Will, you marry me,"said Needo.

"Yes, I will. But we will wait one year and plan everything ok,"said Urnlee.

"Grandmother and the rest of you I have an announcement to make,"said Urnlee.

"Yes,"said Constance.

"Prince Needo and I are engaged,"said Urnlee.

"Congratulations, the two of you,"said Constance.

"That is wonderful,"said Baitlym.

"Graduations,"said Likus.

"Yes, you deserve someone,"said Detva.

"May I call Seebees.and tel her,"said Baitlym

"Yes, you may and thank you, all of you,"said Urnlee.

"That deserves tonight fast food as well, do you agree Don and Will. And congratulations you two,"said Grandfather.

"I will say for the entire week, right Grandfather,"said Will.

"Then ok, for a week or more,"said Grandfather.

"You do not have to do anything else,"said Urnlee.

"Just this week,"said Grandfather.

"That is so nice Grandfather. Said Will.

"Imagine, another family in the building,"said Constance.

"You may,"said Urnlee.

"But not out loud, I know,"said Constance.

"Now lets all have a toast to the new couple. May they both love each other and have great success, "said Grandfather.

"Now we should all go into the living room or library which ever alright,"said Urnlee.

"The children want to go upstairs to their playroom for the evening Grandfather bought them new toys for them,"said Constance.

"I think he wanted some quiet time in the study for a few days do you agree,"said Urnlee.

"Lets talk and this is what we do, we have made arrangements for four of ours to leave and two new people to stay,"said Constance.

"All will be good I assure you Constance,"said Urnlee.

"The others wanted something to do,"said Baitlym.

"They were unhappy,"said Urnlee.

"They wanted to feel needed and important with the business, children are like when they see the adults working,"said Constance.

"So we leave the doors open, available of those who like that excitement,"said Baitlym.

"That is why I choose to be a house wife twice,"said Constance.

"You are fortunate as a nurse you can run the house and we always want you to be paid for that, however I choose to raise my children only,"said Baitlym

"So Seebees wanted to work too,"said Urnlee.

"No, she told me she wanted her husband helping us and she wanted to live in Newport,"said Baitlym.

"She had a home here,"said Urnlee.

"She wanted to know how is was to be away from us and to know what it was like to have her own home,"said Baitlym.

"She and the others just wanted to be working for us and to be on their own,"said Constance.

"So maybe the little ones are to lawyers or doctors,"said Urnlee.

"I hope so all of them to be lawyers is fine with me,"said their Grandmother.

"That is allright with me too,"said Baitlym.

"Sounds like a good plan to me,"said Urnlee.

"You know Gale and Edvard adopted children and they are in two different countries. Maybe Shawn and I could adopt too.? "said Constance.

"You have a new wing right near your apartment,"said Urnlee.

"Good then I will call the lawyers and the school right in town, they are little babies right there that need a home,"said Constance.

"Give a call now and maybe the director is there or get an appointment for tomorrow,"said Baitlym,

"Oh, I thank Ed and Ownsite this is what they did when they just got unmarried,"said Constance.

"This is so exciting, please go on call right now Grandmother, the last of the little ones went with Ed and his wife, to Bavaria.,"said Baitlym.

"Dear I just called and made an appointment with the school, we are going to take in the little ones this week,"said Constance.

"That would be nice dear, after all Ed did take them all with him and he did feel obligated,"said Grandfather.

"So now we have an appointment at ten in the morning and the director mention their furniture goes with them and this gives a chance for more residents at the new and improved school,"said Constance.

"Did you mention to them that we can do the new improvements for them,"said her husband.

"Shawn, I did and it is all set they can move in tomorrow,"said Constance.

"How many.?"said Shawn.

"Sixteen,"said Constance.

"Ok. "said Shawn.

"The sooner the infants are out they can start the repairs,"said Constance.

"You are their boss you sign their checks and talk to them and visit, so you are in charge,"said Shawn.

"Then they will be here in the morning so I have told the children and staff. The first time Ed took them all. These children are mind and the others that are now in the our boarding schools,"said Constance.

"Yes, we are aware and the few that remain with us so far are in the accounting and legal profession,"said Baitlym.

"Sure the others know we can provide with housing accommodations in buildings or like this one,"said Detva.

"I placed six adults one year of ours in Venice buildings and no one has ever complained that they can not stay with us, but all of them are using the formidable buildings using Grenaire Realty,"said Likus.

"They are so deeply appreciated for such a beautiful castle in live in when raised in them by our staff, all of them work for us,"said Bailtym.

"There are two artists but they work fulltime, and would never starve and love their work in the business,"said Likus.

"We are very fortunate that they were raised by good staff,"said Grandmother.

"I will never forget the time I worked in the Belgium castle and a little boy sat in my lap and asked how his Grandmother was, "said Likus.

"You mean, Mother,"said Constance.

"I told him you were his mother and yet he looked at me and said,"I only take other from her,"said Likus.

"He still does, he calls or writes and lets me know if he had moved, "said Grandmother.

"You never tell us about them or their names do you,"said Baitlym.

"No, he worked at a bank and was in charge of it, then moved to the country at another bank that just opened and still runs it today,"said Constance.

"That is one of the fun moments or good times or the best memories of our work in the castle,"said Baitlym.

"Yes, I know , when I went into town alone, to see him he had his right leg taken off due to cancer and now he is fine,"said Constance.

"That was the only thing that ever happened to any or them,"said Baitlym

"Even with Ed there were three children that died of natural causes, yet two of them had serious problems with mental health so we gave them a small brick apartment with medical services inside, year round,"said Grandmother.

"No name of the facility other than the name of the building, it is very private,"said Likus.

"You can not save the world Constance,"said her husband.

"No, but tomorrow there will be little feet running in the house on the second floor,"said Constance.

"They will all be in the wing, I guess that is correct,"said Detva.

"When they move in they are going to my old house next door I want them in know it is me who will be there for them,"said Constance.

"From the last that I heard Seebees is not willing to return since her purchase,"said Baitlym

"There is still the house near the town line,"said Constance.

"She would probably want to move in here when she arrives, "said Constance.

"This is going to present to the media a new ridicule,"said Likus.

"The children will not read it at this last time, I said we do have lawyers, and the next time I said."It would be the press and photgraphers that this family needs,"said Constance.

"With the photography today with its cameras, even I became a photographer is a few minutes out of anger and they have left us alone,"said Baitlym.

"It will work out most of them understand and finally approve of what we have done giving them a good building and staff ,"said Constance.

"I will check up on them in a eight hour shift and we need three of four other volunteers,"said Baitlym

"Constance you can be evening for the first eight hours then me and the night shift visiting the children just twice one at two and then at four,"said Urnlee.

"From eight a.m. to three could be Likus and I,"said Baylib.

"We can work it out,"said Grandfather.

"That is an agreement.We start tomorrow,"said Likus.

"Well we had a busy day and soon we will hear busy feet or little voices,"said Baitlym

"I need some more coffee and then I will look at the children they are watching another movie,"said Urnlee.

"We will get at started on the building tomorrow I do not think anything is needed and the maids were looking after everything this last hour,"said Constance.

"This was coming eventually we do give ourselves a great deal of work and then allow the press to give us some hope after they do take their share,"said Shawn.

"I hope they will be kind,"said Constance.

"Remember the children will not read anything at all,"said her Husband.

"This is true we are in for something,"said Constance.

"Good we need a wakening and it is too us and no one else so that is a plus,"said Baitlym.

"Yes, we are ready and this is not the big one is it,"said Likus.

"No, if it was we would be in an Austrian house right now,"said Detva.

"Your right the biggest fear we have is the sleep, loitering and the train strike,"said Constance.

"So we have brought on a little problem, soo that is what it will be called, immediately,"said Baitlym

"Grandmother will have her picture in the papers explaining we are using our house so the repairs can be done in the other building,"said Detva.

"So then we will let the press do what it wants when they do not return and the building has other little children there,"said Urnlee.

"Lets see how they handle this,"said Likus.

"Constance they could not be that cruel to us could they,"said Baylib.

"Yes, they could but it will work in our favor not theirs,"said Detva.

"So all is settled then,"said Grandfather.

"We do need our sleep, so why not lets all go up stair and we can get some sleep and we can be up when the infants arrive,"said Urnlee.

"We should and their staff will bring them in and the same staff will stay with them,"said Constance.

"Constance wake up, the childrens have arrived and they are so cute,"said Urnlee.

"I forgot to set the alarm it is my turn for this morning it will give everyone something to look forward too,"said Constance.

"Now that you saw them and helped you must go there in three hours this way they will not be frightened,"said her Husband.

"Yes that is right we should not touch them all the time at least not all of us all at once,"said Constance.

"Lets wait for our shift, then they themselves have something to look forward too,"said Baitlym.

"We need to have our visits very spacious because we are the outside bring in the colds and flus,"said Urnlee.

"This is a fact of life,"said Constance.

"We have to treat that part of the building like it was a hospital,"said Urnlee.

"Right again,"said Constance.

"But we do not have to being our own children in they all can meet outside at the playground. This is just for a little while,"said Urnlee.

"You are our nurse you know what is best,"said Constance.

“There has to be a certain amount of time as a quarantine procedure and no one that young would understand or know what is happening,”said Urnlee.

“They all look so cute, handsome and beautiful too,”said Baitlym.

“Urnlee is working with the doctor so we will know what is going on with their health,”said Constance.

“Yes, I am and the doctor told me that all of them are in good health,”said Urnlee.

“So now all we can do is wait for our turn,”said Likus.

“It is not so difficult,”said Detva.

“No, they will be walking soon,”said Baylib.

“And talking too and screaming, they are on your end of the building Grandmother,”said Will.

“We probably be hearing allof them soon enough,”said Constance.

“Now we need to prepare ourselves,”said Grandfather.

“Yes, here are the names and they do where a small bracelet on their ankle with their name on it,”said Constance.

“We must not give out any information,”said Urnlee.

“Nothing, we have to protect them, “said Baylib.

“Right we need to keep quiet about them,”said Detva.

“Soon they can work with you in Paris, France,”said Grandmother.

“I would like that very much, but not all of them want to work there,”said Detva.

“I would like to see most of them or all of them using Grenaire Realty and working at home,”said Grandmother.

“That is what Ed does they have a choice of going to a Grenaire building or they were the condo next to them,”said Baitlym

“It is good to know there is an old castle they can stay in if they want one,”said Likus.

“Out of the four hundred and seven-five children only three wanted to stay home and after their college studies many were placed in the Grenaire buildings,”said Baitlym.

“Yes, Edvard has a good track record and has done a fine job placing and educating our own future lawyers for the business. Said Likus.

“Each of his chefs were raised in the Bavarian castle and work in his restaurants,”said Detva.

“Our chef told me he can not wait for one of them to take over,”said Baitlym.

"The children are a good lot and when you are good to them they are good to you,"said Constance.

"So now it is done and final and we have a job to do fitting these children into professions layers, doctors or something they do enjoy with our company, it is routine and it is apart of us,"said Grandfather.

"Our money is enough to take care of them and to help out the business so just save your money for yourselves and we can do the rest,"said Grandmother.

"Yes, and all of you are cared for and you all controll when we are not here,"said Grandfather.

"We know you love us,"said Baitlym.

"Yes, and these children will be provided for. If a few of them fall in love we will make sure if they were in the living in the city working with us and a good home will be provided,"said Detva.

"There is not that many children it is easy to find there where abouts and to make sure al,l of them are using Grenaire Realty,"said Baitlym.

"We have to fill these Grenaire or Exile Real-estate castles and palaces,"said Likus.

"It will be done our wills as reassuring for all and the staff as it is want for themselves so all will be done correctly,"said Shawn.

"Each one of us is a staff to this type of building and all of our offices are a type of building like this so as a family we can still live there,"said Detva.

"We are not the only lived in business, nor did we do it ourselves the fast food industry has a home it back of it too,"said Likus.

"Our homes are now next to Exile Bank behind it and it has been looking out very well with its own security too,"said Detva.

"That is work I want on my estate in France and with Exile Bank at the end of the property, and now I must leave you to meet my wife and family in Paris,"said Detva.

"I is a good idea,"said Grandmother.

"It is time to go now to say good bye everyone. I love you Grandmother all of this is because of you,"said Detva.

"I am leaving in a few minutes too with Baylib for Venice. My good grandparents who gave me everything, bye Mother and sisters and little brothers, "said Likus.

"Detva was never any good on good byes,"said Grandmother.

"He is shy,"said Urnlee.

"Even just on going on a vacation he would just walk away. Go say good bye to him at the car, we will all stay here,"said Grandmother.

"I will, right now and I will take Lise with me,"said Urnlee.

"Good, he always thinks it is the last time to see us,"said Grandmother.

"Urnlee will say good bye he is the shy one,"said Grandfather.

"I know and he does think the worst will happen when he is not here,"said Grandmother.

"So the children are upstairs they arrived in the court yard where it is a little warmer,"said Baitlym.

"Here is Urnlee, "said Needo.

"He gave Lise another kiss and I got one on my lips and from Likus too,"said Urnlee.

"He will not show warmth to a female that is married,"said Grandmother.

"He is good to have around,"said Needo.

"Yes he is, and Likus would flirt with a new female and joke with them but if there is someone that he is interested in he would return married,"said Grandmother.

"Ed would not do anything to help or they would have to decide themselves,"said Grandfather.

"The days of being and staying with someone, Detva would work hard to get his wife and family back and Likus would just move on,"said Grandmother.

"This was an interesting day, at least they all know there are nannies and they would return knowing they can help us,"said Urnlee.

"I would write them and let them all know they can return and always feel as if they can help, but they are working for the company and I can never do that,"said their Grandmother.

"It is not hopeless we have a very good staff of nannies and a doctor who visits once a week,"said Urnlee.

"So are all set and are and always have been grateful for this new house and our others homes and we are willing to share,"said Grandfather.

"Did you know there are two girls two little babies with the first name,"said Grandmother.

"May I say something we can call on a Princess and the other a Countess. "Grandfather.

"Why sure we have a Countess in the family as a matter of fact there are four, so one of them will give her title to her,"said Grandmother.

"Ed started them with titles so they would know they are included and would stay with him,"said Grandfather.

"I know I gave him their first home next to mine,"said Grandmother.

"That is right, so things will work out,"said Grandmother.

"Here you are,"said Urnlee.

"Thank you,"said Constance.

"This is good coffee,"said Grandfather.

"Thank you ,"said Urnlee.

"From night time to day break, coffee to coffee, that is what we should call to new day here,"said Baitlym.

"Baitlym that is what Likus would say,"said Grandmther.

"I know it is catching, when someone is not here,"said Baitlym.

"Good morning dear you could go to Paris and work or just live there for a few years,"said Grandmother.

"Good morning, Grandmother I know I can yet I want my children to have an uninterrupted education,"said Baitlym.

"You were always attached to whomever stayed with us,"said Constance.

"I know,"said Baitlym.

"Why not take a trip to the house on the cove and stay for one week or only two days,"said Constance.

"Good morning, you two, "said Urnlee.

"Good morning, I wish I could go away and work or maybe just college,"said Will.

"Yes Will, maybe just college instead and we need new lawyers,"said Grandmother.

"Ok, I will for you Grandmother,"said Will.

"Thank you Will, what a good boy,"said his Grandmother.

"I am going to see the children in a few minutes, "said Constance.

"May I see Jacob at the window,"said will.

"Yes, you may,"said his Grandmother.

"Windows,"said Will.

"Windows, click next. Then me "said Lise.

"Ok, very soon the two of you,"said their Grandmother.

"So Baitlym, this is a great difference, I am so glad you stayed,"said Urnlee.

"Grandmother asked if I wanted to take the family to the cove,"said Baitlym.

“That is a good idea it is still warm in the afternoon,”said Urnlee.

“I might go I do not know,”said Baitlym.

“Ok, kids lets go upstairs,”said Grandmother.

“Here do me a favor and take this test, you know I keep them in this draw,”said Urnlee.

“Good morning, so where is everyone going,”said Baitlym’s husband.

“The children and Grandmother are going to see the infants and Baitlym went to the bathroom,”said Urnlee.

“Baitlym did you see this test, you have to tell him now or I will before you get any depression over all that has happened in the last 24 hours,”said Urnlee.

“Darling did you see this test I took, Urnlee wanted me to before any depression got any worst than it is right now,”said Baitlym.

“You have pregnant, I am so happy for us both,”said her Husband.

“I would like to go upstairs for awhile,”said Baitlym

“We will go upstairs and stay there all day if you want to,”said her Husband.

“I need to talk to you Constance and is your husband in the Library,”said Urnlee.

“Yes, he is,”said Constance.

“Here is are what is something wrong,”said Grandfather.

“No, I need to tell you both that Bailtym is suffering from a a little depression because of her brothers’ leaving,”said Urnlee.

“I hope she is going to be alright,”said Grandfather.

“Yes, I hope so,”said Grandmother.

“But that is not what brought it on,”said Urnlee.

“No,”said grandmother.

“No, I am a nurse and I told her to take a pregnancy test and it is positive,”said Urnlee.

“Oh, my goodness,”said Constance.

“There is one more question, it might have seem very cold to you both, but being a nurse I had to find out what was wrong,”said Urnlee.

“No, it is good for the baby so now the doctor may visit her while he is here,”said Grandmother.

“Right, I let him know, and you my visit them now if you want too.” said Urnlee.

“I will first then Shawn you follow in a few minutes, ok,”said Constance.

"Urnlee why are you crying I just saw Constance and she gave me the good news,"said Needo.

"I am just a little happy that's all,"said Urnlee.

"You are a delight, you thrill me, then I will say to the ends of the earth,"said Needo.

"Thank you, it is just a great weekend here five people leaving and sixteen little infants taking their place,"said Urnlee.

"There must be more.?"said Needo.

"Yes, there is there is you now and I did have a little bit of nursing a few minutes ago, and compared to what I make in this building being in charge of the nurses and nannies I would never get the salary any where else.?"said Urnlee.

"You are an assett to this building, you knew enough to get a test for Baitlym before any real harm could have happened, you prevented this,"said Needo.

"When everyone is aware of this, you will be very valuable to all of us and especially me, I love you,"said Needo.

"Thank you, I needed to hear this and with you I am not alone,"said Urnlee.

"No, and when we are married we are not blood relations so the past is not repeated so I never want to hear that, will I,"said Needo.

"No, my nursing skills is very excellent and so is my judgment and reasonsing,"said Urnlee.

"Next is what is needed to be said,"When anyone else is worried that their husband has not done his share remember that all of us here are hear for the grandparents and you need to remind others of that, "said Needo.

"I know we must both stay for them, I think that is why Seebees left for her husband so she can be proud of him,"said Urnlee.

"This is correct, and I have enough money to invest yet I interested most of what I had and bought out the Denmark family that is why I was there, I am a controlling share holder,"said Needo.

"I have also a controlling shares by my late husband,"said Urnlee.

"I think the others knew of this and were a little intimidated,"said Needo.

"Does your sister know.?"said Needo.

"She knew that is why I was there if might know if the deal was successful because I had left with her,"said Needo.

"This is all so amazing,"said Urnlee.

"Then my Uncle Shawn probably does not know,"said Needo.

"Either does Constance, I am so surprised we will mention it to her when we are all together,"said Urnlee.

"She probably does not know,"said Needo.

"Does not know what.? Is there more of that dessert here.? "said Constance.

"There is some more Constance, did you know that Needo bought out the Denmark royal family of their own Euro train stock,"said Urnlee.

"Yes, I did that is why I gave him you, and if my son was alive and Chardin had died first I would insist that Ed would remarry."Constance.

"That was nice of you, Constance.!"said Needo.

"Do not worry my dear just like you as a nurse mad sure that Baitlym took that test, I to made sure that you would not be unhappy also,"said Constance.

Chapter 20

"Now we are all here to witness the marriage of Prince Needo and Princess Urnlee,"said their Uncle.

"He is making a speech,"said Constance.

"We hoped that you have had a wonderful time and we want to see all of you tomorrow just before you leave ok,"said their Uncle Shawn.

"I am so glad he did not say and we hope we do not see Needo and Urnlee here in the morning,"said Seebees.

"You are so right,"said Constance.

"How about me Grandmother do you think I would say that,"said Don.

"You are to funny the three of you, good speech up there Shawn,"said Constance.

"Thank you, Dear,"said Shawn.

"Your welcome, it was not like the party last night joking and laughing said Constance.

"Yes, I was good but not like Gale who entertained us last night and started this with his sense of humor at the parties. He said,"He was not going to give away the money, Urnlee. After all that last night I knew I was going to be sincere,"said Shawn.

"Yes, you all were and I hope I brought some laughter for us all last night."But I need to leave for Versailles good bye and all of you remember to stop by and stay for a few days I do exspect to see Ed and Ownsite there and I mean it and remind the others too when you see them that are leaving,"said Gale.

“Bye Gale we love you this is all yours it s all because of you,”said Constance.

“Yes, thank you and now I know I have to leave right now, Constance before things get to sentimental, I love all of you. I did not forget, it is because of this big strong man and his beautiful and lovely wife Princess Ownsite that did all the work for all of us,”said Gale.

“Bye, said Baitlym.

“Leave it to Gale that gave the credit where it should,”said Detva.

“He is correct, we would not have all this if it was not for Ed and his wife,”said Likus.

“We Gale we will visit soon,”said Detva.

“Yes, and I will be soon be arriving to Versailles,”said Likus.

“Good, hope to see you all,”said Gale.

“Now Likus you need to wait here for a few days if Detva is going to visit Versailles, “said Grandmother.

“We are going to visit for one day and sleep over because he might have a property for me to buy,”said Detva.

“Gale would appreciate that and what he offers you take it you might need that building for one of your children some day,”said Grandmother.

“Or you when you visit Gale, you can see me and I will buy another from him so you and Shawn may stay as long while if you both want too,”said Detva.

“You have a good plan for your family I like that,”said Grandmother.

“Grandmother I am leaving tomorrow morning, ok !”said Detva.

“I know you are and I hope you enjoy Paris,”said Grandmother.

“I will,”said Detva.

“So many went upstairs to get into something easier for this evening and all the guests decided not to stay over why,”said Grandmother.

“Other commitments and it was mostly work, as the final reason,”said Detva.

“You are going to embark on the new frontier and to find out if we are not being cheated or Gale. Just a few years there and now this promotion”said Grandmother.

“I can hardly wait and I hope we are not being robbed,”said Detva.

“I hope we are not too,”said Grandmother.

“Did you hear from Seebees,”said Detva.

“She is doing allright she is going to have her fourth child very soon,”said Grandmother.

“It must be very soon or she would have been here,”said Detva.

"In one more day because Urnlee asked her not to go to the wedding because of its journey to Belgium would be an ordeal,"said Grandmother.

"Hello, look we are going to have a little one in two weeks,"said Likus.

"What a coincidence, we were just talking about Seebees is going to have her child tomorrow, Baylib would you like to have your child, here in Belgium,"said Constance.

"I would like that but I want to be able to go home once she is born,"said Baylib.

"I understand and you enjoy Venice so I think the both of you and your many children will stay there for along time,"said Grandmother.

"We will indeed, and it is so nice to entertain in Venice,"said Baylib.

"I know there is so much gold in that house I am surprised that the government allow you to purchase,"said Grandmother.

"We did not purchase it was based on the tunnels and the publicity was to go to the home we live in for tourists day, so it became cheater to buy while living in there,"said Likus.

"So you are not allowed to leave for a few years,"said Grandmother.

"Why would I it is my house and I love being there,"said Likus.

"That is true, I would live there myself but I do missed walking on land,"said Grandmother.

"I do not miss anything other than all of you,"said Baylib.

"Thank you dear, we miss the two of you and we talk and wonder what you are both doing every day,"said Grandmother.

"She calls you every day and still wonders what you two are doing,"said Shawn.

"The construction is done and the tunnels are in yet there is still a small section are is being connected,"said Baylib.

"If is the section to connect into the homes in tasks time and a lot of correct decisions where to cut into the buildings."Likus.

"It is quite a project,"said Baylib.

"Each house has three cars each and underwater in the tunnels is parking spaces the tunnel on the top is for traffic to leave and the bottom is to enter and park,"said Likus.

"All have a stairway yet now by law they are getting an elevator,"said Baylib.

"It sounds so wonderful and the films on television is what everyone is talking about here in Belgium,"said Shawn.

"He has won several awards to for this work and now they gave one to the both of you,"said Detva.

"We are very happy together and I enjoy his work very much,"said Baylib.

"Oh, did I tell you both that Detva is leaving tomorrow so you need to give him a few days at Versailles and then both of you may leave, ok,"said Constance.

"I am only staying for tomorrow then the next morning I will be gone about 9 a.m,"said Detva.

"Good and we can arrive late that morning,"said Baylib.

"All of you will be leaving soon and then Urnlee and Needo will return in two weeks from today,"said Constance.

"She wanted to return early, so she mentioned,"said Shawn.

"They will be in Austria and then in Northern Italy for their last week so I will be getting probably just a few cards,"said Constance.

"Knowing my brother she will be doing all the cards for him,"said Baylib.

"That is how it is when you are married,"said Constance.

"You have cards of this place in your little shop,"said Likus.

"That is how we decided to use cards for our house in Venice,"said Baylib.

"That was a good idea,"said Likus.

"The last few times I have been here I always mailed yours home,"said Baylib.

"Oh, Detva I hope you are just looking for the payroll and keep away from the espionage of the company,"said Likus.

"That department is attached to mine and I just forward what I have learned,"said Detva.

"Good do not do anything to implicate yourself just give the information to them and move on to the next case,"said Grandmother.

"Nothing to dangerous I am sure of that, besides we do not have any secrets, everything is known to the world about all of our businesses,"said Detva.

"So here I am this morning, ready and I am leaving right now for Versailles,"said Detva.

"I can not believe it is so, we just get to enjoy one another and then we are leaving each other again , please you and your family must return soon and I hope everything works out for all of you,"said Grandmother.

"It will, and I love you,"said Detva.

"I am the only one up, and we both had just six hours of sleep, so I hope you have a safe trip to France and say,"Hello."to Gale for me when you get to Versailles,"said Grandmother.

"Bye Detva. Said Lise.

"Here she is here is my little baby sister, good bye,"said Detva.

"Lets both say good bye, at the door,"said Grandmother.

"Bye,"said Lise.

"Bye,"said Grandmother.

"Bye,"said Lise.

"See he is waving good bye,"said Grandmother.

"Bye,"said Lise.

"There and in a few days Likus and Baylib are going to leave for Versailles,"said Grandmother.

"Me too,"said Lise.

"Lisa, if you work hard to school you might be invited there to work for Gale, that would be fun,"said Grandmother.

Me,"said Lisa.

"Yes you, oh, I do enjoy entertaining in this large living room this great room has been so helpful for my guests,"said Grandmother.

"My bed,"said Lise.

"Yes it has been, this hallway is very good and nice to get to the dining room,"said Grandmother.

"Here we are again and the dining room is all ready to use, here is your breakfast,"said Grandmother.

"Good morning, some food, I did not miss, Detva.?"said Baitlym.

"No,"said Grandmother.

"I walked to the rotunda and open the door right as he had to stop for the gate and we said Good bye,"said Baitlym.

"You did, that was nice of you,"said Grandmother.

"Do not worry I was on the drivers' side entrance to say good bye to him at the door,"said Baitlym

"Then you did take your time to say good bye,"said Grandmother.

"Yes, I did and good morning Lisa,"said Baitlym

"I thought I heard the car stop again after the house gate opened,"said Grandmother.

"Yes, I gave him my travelers checks to use and he is going to send me a check for them, so now all are officially finished,"said Baitlym.

"You have some money to save,"said Grandmother.

"There was only two hundred dollars, something to use while on the road,"said Gbaitlym

"Knowing Detva he is going to stop and purchase something for the children before he gets home,"said Grandmother.

"That is why I gave him the checks, this breakfast is so good,"said Baitlym.

"More, thank you,"said Lisa.

"Eat of lot of food you both need your strength, how are you feeling this morning Baitlym,"said Grandmother.

"I am fine this morning, "said Baitlym.

"Good and you should rest today all day in fact and exercise just by walking in the house,"said Grandmother.

"I would like to eat a lot of food all day, that is the way I feel right now,"said Baitlym

"That is just morning hunger. We need to give you a busser to use and wear,"said Grandmother.

"I hope it looks nice and in many colors,"said Baitlym.

"It does have many colors and it looks like mine,"said Grandmother.

"Ok, I do not mine that thing around my neck,"said Bailtym.

"Good, here is a new one. Nurse, this remote goes into the security office, would you please give this to them thank you,"said Grandmother.

"Yes, Lady Constance,"said the Nurse.

"How many are in that draw,"said Baitlym.

"Just three are there,"said Grandmother.

"Are there any others in the security office,"said Baitlym.

"I think so I just broke it yesterday so I am sure there is enough,"said Grandmother.

"Here Lisa wipe your hands and face,"said Baitlym.

"Yes, what a good girl you are,"said Grandmother.

"Here is Shawn and Likus. I am going upstairs for awhile bye everyone. Said Baitlym.

"Bye, food looks good and Detva left,"said Likus.

"He did and Shawn there is the paper,"said Grandmother.

"Thank you, it is the computer for now,"said Grandfather.

"We are leaving tomorrow morning and it has been fun Grandmother,"said Likus.

"It has been fun and a lot of excitement this weekend,"said Grandmother.

"Have you heard from Urnlee,"said Likus.

"They are in Austria right now at Shawn's house and they are going to use the castle for a week,"said Grandmother.

"That is wonderful,"said Likus.

"It sure is, I am so glad she has someone,"said Grandmother.

"We both are fortunate and glad of this marriage,"said her Husband.

"They do look like a cute couple, and as for myself she is an excellent nurse I might have been very sick for a long time with this pregnancy, that is why I am grateful and I hope these two weeks go by very fast,"said Baitlym.

"Yes, they will and you are ok, now. She was with me during all of my surgery, so I am very grateful too,"said Constance.

"We all have reasons I think she made it very easy for wonderful for Dad and she helped out with Mom when her baby was born,"said Likus.

"We have a lot to be thankful for,"said Shawn.

"Now lets sit in the largest living room in case the children want to join us,"said Constance.

"Now here is another thing to be grateful about this amazing great hall and now the great living space for a lot of friends it is almost as big as the ballroom,"said Likus.

"We only have one more hour to stay and then we are need to leave for Versailles,"said Baylib.

"We have packed food for you and a gift for Gale along with a food basket we will enjoy some evening while in his Octigon building,"said Constance.

"I can not wait until we are in the Euro train," said Baylib.

"I did not tell the both of you we are having the same food now for a fast and easy lunch right here and then you may use it when you are hon the road going home,"said Constance.

"Boy, I wish I was going away to have something good to eat,"said Will.

"Me too,"said Lisa.

"Don is just laughing he heard it all, we are having the same lunch that I packed for Likus and Baylib right now,"said Constance.

"Did Detva get this too,"said Likus.

"Yes, he did and here is the same amount of money for you two that I gave Detva, everyone knows I treat all of you equal,"said Constance.

"You were the one who gave me Venice and now Baylib you have always been good to me,"said Likus.

"I did not get Venice."Shawn.

"Very good,"said Baillym.

"Likus, darling I need to tell you that I called my Uncle when he got married, then I spoke to your Grandmother so if there is anyone who gave me to you it was myself,"said Baylib.

"My goodness Likus you never did think of that did you,"said Baitlym

"No, I did not., and I am so happy you told me, I love you so much,"said Likus.

"I love you to dear and we do need to get going now I know we just eat but it is important what if Gale wanted to show us something outside of the building,"said Baylib.

"Alright we should leave right now, good bye Grandmother and Granddad,"said Likus.

"Good bye everyone hope to see all of you again and thank you Constance and Baitlym take care of yourself,"said Baitlym.

"Good bye, Uncle,"said Baylib.

"To make it easy all the children said "good bye."I sent then all upstairs,"said Baitlym.

"Bye Uncle and look Baylib see there they are all waving, good bye,"said Likus.

"Oh, they have their own private balcony when we pass bye them, "said Baylib.

"So there they go, and I hope they wiiill return in a few months. Do you really want Venice? "said Constance.

"Oh, stop maybe the both of us can have Versailles,"said Shawn.

"No, he did not offer that when we helped with the business, he will never leave that house,"said Constance.

"I know but I can not believe that new Versailles is right near a 25 century building for him or for the President,"said Shawn.

"As long as he is in the older building the Lloyd's goes sky high with financial help and cassh as well,"said Constance.

"If he becomes King of France then the Euro train expenses go to him and we all have a price increase to use sleep and loitering,"said Shawn.

"That is why we help until he wants to take over,"said Constance.

"Good idea, and we will continue giving him help,"said Shawn.

"I was a good visit for them and I enjoy these last few months, I did not mean to ignore you Shawn but I am tired are you.? Also we will help for years. ?"said Constance.

"I am not tied, and we will help him all the time ,"said Shawn.

"So how about some more food and lets enjoy today and we need to get something fun to do all of us is there a good movie,"said Constance.

"I just received the equalient to Versailles as a cartoon but it is in Ed's house in Bavaria,"said Baitlym.

"What is it called,"said Constance.

"It is called Grenaire, just like the name he gave to his house,"said Will.

"Ok, I heard of that it is being advertised today,"said Shawn.

"So we can all see it now that dinner is done,"said Constance.

"I had a wonderful nap for myself,"said Baitlym.

"You need your rest, dear,"said Constance.

"I know I do,"said Baitlym.

"Now the movie started,"said Constance.

"Good, I am glad we received it this morning,"said Baitlym

"Do you want some more snacks, maybe something to drink,"said Constance.

"Please a new drink nurse. thank you,"said Baitlym.

"This staff does not mind waiting on us. It does seem wrong but the children are quiet,"said Constance.

"They are all watching, I insisted that they do,"said Baitlym.

"It does work, look at them in the front two rows, no one is talking,"said Constance.

"All are seated, and that is what I want,"said Bailtym.

"Where is your husband.?"said Constance.

"With the baby. If she is quiet he might bring her in,"said Baitlym.

"Did you know that this movie has been the most popular cartoon since Gale did his first cartoon movie last year,"said Constance.

"You would think they are going to run into Versailles for more,"said Baitlym.

"That is why he is in Versailles,"said Constance.

"Here is my husband now without the baby,"said Baitlym.

"Lets go to the living room for some coffee and we can talk, "said Constance.

"Dear we are leaving for the living room for a chat and coffee,"said Baitlym.

"Don and Lisa you did not want to see the movie,"said Grandmother.

"What is this Don another movie instead,"said Baitlym.

"Which one is it,"said Grandmother.

"It is the same one they are here for more food. Here Lisa, "said Baitlym.

"Here Don some warm pudding,"said Grandmother.

"There when the both of are finished you may sit on the floor if you want too,"said Baitlym.

"Baitlym sit down and have some coffee,"said Grandmother.

"I am going to ask the kitchen to send in the same kind of food in the theatre,"said Grandmother.

"This warm pudding is so good on this wintery evening,"said Bailtym.

"There, all is fine with them and the children are ok upstairs,"said Constance.

"It does seem quiet in here, even the nursey is,"said Baitlym.

"I know, but we never could hear anyone upstairs,"said Constance.

"A lot of people left us,"said Baitlym.

"I hope you do not mind they are doing this work for me and you too,"said Constance.

"No, it is just not as busy as it was in the evening time,"said Baitlym.

"It is very calm and unusual,"said Constance.

"I am very aware of that, just a week ago many of us were in this room,"said Baitlym.

"Also, the tel is low this evening too,"said Constance.

"Here are the gentlemen now, have some food the movie was not what you expected,"said Baitlym.

"We both saw it last night on the tel, paid for I might mention that too,"said Shawn.

"So both of you wanted to be with us,"said Constance.

"Thank you for both joining us we were just saying how silent it is now that many have gone away,"said Baitlym.

"When Urnlee returns her sister-in-law might be here so that is four more,"said Baitlym's husband.

"That is good we will have a few more with us,"said Constance.

"It is my turn to see the children upstairs dear,"said Shawn.

"I can see what my husband is going to do right now,"said Bailtym.

"He did bring over some food to them,"said Constance

"Yes, I did and now he will watch the movie and he is gone for the evening,"said Baitlym.

"Are you upset.? "said Constance.

"No, I think it is funny,"said Baitlym.

"Well, wait until my husband returns he will be getting something to eat and then he is going to watch the tel also,"said Constance.

"With three words too, "they are all asleep,"said Baitlym.

"Dear. They are all asleep,"said Shawn.

"Now see that, I spoke to much,"said Baitlym.

"I hope you will calm down you are in a laughting and joking phase right now and try to relax,"said Constance.

"I will I need another pastry,"said Baitlym.

"here it you do not like this I will have it,"said Constance.

"This is delicious. A cut up pastry two of them with warm dark pudding on it, thank you so very much,"said Baitlym.

"I think I will try one,"said Constance.

"Good.?"said Bailtym.

"Very good. But one is enough for me,"said Constance.

"If you do not want it I will take it ok,"said Baitlym.

"A few more bites and it is all yours,"said Constance.

"Thanks,"said Bailtym.

"If you are bored, would you like to work a few hours a day,"said Constance.

"No, I am allright it was just breing one my feet all day,"said Bailtym.

"Dear, do you want to go upstairs,"said Baitlym's Husband.

"No thank you, I am alright,"said Baitlym.

"Here you are this is a new one and no more,"said Constance.

"Thank you, so I guess all this is the new baby,"said Bailtym.

"You have quite a few months to go, but you are very strong, "said Constance.

"You know you are right, I am just so pleased that I am not to sentimental, I think I would need a few drinks for that,"said Baitlym.

"It is a good thing no one likes to drink in this house,"said Constance.

"What would be the reason.? "said Baitlym.

"Lack of money, we may have a drink in the evening but we do not drink a lot." said Constance.

"This is what we all do have in common. I mean something that is extreme good,"said Baitlym.

"I know what you mean it can ruin a family, but it is not going to ruin this family that is why I control the money,"said Constance.

"What about the others they seem to have a lot of cash.? "said Baitlym.

"All are on a budget and the large amounts are invested only,"said Constance.

"Even Craig has one, a strick budget in Newport,"said Baitlym,

"Very strick. The only ones are you not in control here are you and your family,"said Baitlym.

"We have nothing other than the house that was sold,"said Baitlym.

"I know and you did want your very own expensive auto,"said Constance.

"That was nice of you not to complain,"said Baitlym.

"I will not complain just save your money for now on, ok,"said Constance.

"I will now that we are having another baby, I need to save,"said Baitlym.

"That is good to hear,"said Constance.

"I need to go upstairs now, I am very tired,"said Baitlym.

"Remember the doctor is on duty he is an intern if anything is wrong just call him up and they will get me,"said Constance.

"I remember him we met all the staff one afternoon, it is a good thing they are all pedestrians,"said Baitlym.

"They all will be and good night, your children are already asleep,"said Constance.

"Darling why not sit down and watch the show and we can still talk and they need to be alone to talk the both of them,"said Shawn.

"She is tired and so am I we can go upstairs now if you want to,"said Constance.

"Lisa and Don went upstairs with Will,"said Shawn.

"Will is a good help to us and he needs to get away to a private school,"said Constance.

"I know he should but let him want to go,"said Shawn.

"I think he is ready now,"said Constance.

"We should turn off a lot of these lights,"said Shawn.

"There is a main switch behind this wall when we are upstairs,"said Constance.

"Now all are upstairs I know because Don and Lisa were sleeping on the chair with me,"said Shawn.

"I will go see them for myself,"said Constance.

"I will wait right at our door until you return,"said Shawn.

"There it was not hard to do,"said Constance.

"Everything is alright.? "said Shawn.

"All are asleep,"said Constance.

"Here is Lisa,"said Shawn.

"Whey don't I take you back to your room and see just what is wrong with your own bed,"said Constance.

"It is to bed, to big,"said Lisa.

"Do you want a smaller one,"said Grandmother.

"No,"said Lisa.

"I know what you need is some of your favorite dolls and look we can put this big lion and a large bear at your feet,"said Grandmother.

"Then if anyone is in your room no one can find you,"said Grandmother.

"Good,"said Lisa.

"See even now I can not tell where you are when the lights are off or when just one light is on,"said Constance.

"Do you want to try it this way, for right now.? said Grandmother.

"Yes, please,"said Lisa.

"Then I will see you in the morning, alright.?"said Grandmother.

"Yes I will, I love you,"said Lisa.

"I love you too, see you in the morning,"said Grandmother.

"Lisa, here get under the covers,"said Grandmother.

"I want to have breakfast,"said Lisa.

"It can not be, that time. So it is,"said Grandmother.

"See Breakfast,"said Lisa.

"Good morning everyone, Lisa woke me up,"said Grandmother.

"Have some food you too,"said Grandfather.

"The pastries are define,"said Baitlym.

"Did you ask the cook for this with a warm vanilla pudding for our snack time.?"said Constance.

"No,"said Baitlym.

"I will right now,"said Constance.

"Thank you that was excellent last night,"said Baitlym.

"Because of you Baitlym I got a lot of sleep last night,"said Constance.

"That is good, here is some fruit Lisa,"said Baitlym

"Thank you,"said Lisa.

"Your welcome, here is some toast,"said Baitlym.

"All is well is the news nothing to report about the family,"said Grandmother.

"That is a good update we need to stay informed especially of the whereabouts of these young kids,"said Constance.

"Thank you Grandfather now we are at ease,"said Bailtym.

"Yes, now we all well informed, thank you,"said Constance.

"I did hope that that would be of some use, we did receive quite a few faxes from all of them, so gave them an answer,"said Grandfather.

"That was good of you, did you just start that recently,"said Constance.

"No, I have answered Craig and Gale and many others since I moved in,"said Grandfather.

"What sort of answers.?"said Constance.

"Thanking them for the reports that went to the business office, things that needed acknowledgements,"said Shawn.

"Am I thinking the same thing,"said Baitlym.

"Very good, Baitlym, Shawn you need to be put on the payroll, it is true the money is for us and we need to take it,"said Constance.

"I better get this right now,"said Shawn.

"See you have created your own job "said Constance.

"Then I need to break it up with two people, 8-12 then 1-5 it is to much work for just one, how about Bailtym helping me out too,"said Grandfather.

"Good idea,"said Constance.

"1 to 5 is fine,"said Baitlym.

"Then it is a deal, I will also submit this business office,"said Constance.

"Is anyone thinking of the same thing,"said Grandfather.

"Yes, but Grandmother should share the hours with Urnlee when she gets home,"said Baitlym.

"Good job of it Bailtym,"said Grandfather.

"Yes, I have a wonderful wife, and for Lloyd's I have submitted my name to, "said her Husband.

"What is it called no let me guess, Lord Saddenski,"said Baitlym.

"Should it not be Lord Silenceski,"said Constance.

"You certainly took your time to think of it but I could not take the silence any longer,"said Baitlym.

"Then Lord Silenceski it is, I do have a month to decide so I will submit it again right now,"said Baitlym's Husband.

"Thank you for Lloyd's dear you did wait awhile,"said Baitlym.

"Now I just hope that Lisa is good and does not wake me up so early, is that you little girl,"said Grandmother.

"Ok, I am sorry, my toys worked this morning,"said Lisa.

"Yes, they did but what is more important is that you received a lot more sleep,"said Grandmother.

Chapter 21

Urnlee and her husband Needo are home now for three days and so far they like what we have done on the decisions when they were on their honeymoon,"said Will.

"They are pleased,"said Baitlym.

"They are indeed, we did an excellent job,"said Constance.

"Me too,"said Lisa.

"You too, Lisa,"said Grandmother.

"I will take over the messages for you, Baitlym,"said Constance.

"Thanks I know I can return the favor some day,"said Baitlym.

"Oh, right, am I all red in the face, Constance,"said Urnlee.

"No, said Constance.

"No, why do you want me to say it louder.? "said Baitlym.

"No, I understood it the first time,"said Urnlee.

"Now lets all have enough food it is a busy day,"said Constance.

"I think I am going swimming in the pool would anyone alike to go,"said Urnlee.

"I will, there is a life guard employed by the college everyday so a lot of us may attend,"said Needo.

"Me too,"said Will.

"Not me, yes me too,"said Lisa.

"Ok, I think that is more than enough for swimming see all of you later,"said Constance.

"I nearly called you Shawn by my husband's first name Edlance,"said Constance.

"It is all right it usually means that you are trying to call your father anyways,"said Shawn.

"Does it,"said Constance.

"He was the last man or the first that was in authority so therefore he exists first in you mind,"said Shawn.

"Now it would be Santa, he did more, if I remember correctly,"said Constance.

"That was very good,"said Shawn.

"No, that is more like the truth,"said Constance.

"You two are a joy to listen too,"said Baitlym.

"That is why I am silent,"said Baitlym's Husband.

"Good for you, you are a good man,"said Constance.

"Thank you,"said Lord -----

"Now wait a minute, Lord,"said Baitlym.

"Baitlym you interrupted your husband and yourself just then,"said Constance.

"I know, I apologize, does it sound strange just to call him, Lord.?"said Baitlym.

"I accept your apology,"said her Husband.

"Oh, you are so funny,"said Constance.

"Yes, we are,"said Baitlym.

"Why not go upstairs the both of you and be alone for awhile and rest,"said Constance.

"Si, lets go now,"said Baitlym.

"We both could nap too. We are going to use your elevator, ok,"said Si.

"Yes that is quite all right. It is a good thing the Priest is not here,"said Constance.

"You and I should go upstairs,"said Shawn.

"Goodness sakes,"said Constance.

"Then how about another coffee and soon we will hear about the swimming too,"said Shawn.

"Coffee seems to be ok for now but watch what you say the children might walk in,"said Constance.

"I will remember,"said Shawn.

"Yes, please do I just ordered Baitlym's favorite snack and for tonight too,"said Constance.

"Good,"said Shawn.

"She answered, "Every day and evening,"said Constance.

"Say yes,"said Shawn.

"There all is done,"said Constance.

"Very good now have some coffee, and here is everyone all the swimmers,"said said Shawn.

"Oh, Oh I can not understand all of you,"said Constance.

"Baitlym, you two are back, I was just saying all the swimmers have returned"said Shawn.

"Not all of them,"said Si.

"Now is that time where all good husbands should be seen and not heard from,"said Constance.

"Sorry,"said Si.

"Oh, I get it,"said Baitlym.

"Yes, you did,"said Si.

"Both of you stop right now,"said Constance.

"Yes, both of you,"said Shawn.

"Sorry,"said Baitlym.

"We are going upstairs for a little while,"said Baitlym.

"Good and rest ,"said Constance.

"Will do you want to go to a private school.?"said his Grandmother.

"No, all I have is you now, so I want to be home.?"said Will.

"That is what I thought and thank you so your decision is for Don and Lisa too so now all of you will have tutors here,"said their Grandmother.

"Thank you grandmother, so much,"said Will.

"Your welcome, I want you to get good grades and to be happy,"said their Grandmother.

"We are going to have fun this weekend and next weekend your Mother and Father will be home. They just wanted to be in Paris,"said Shawn.

"Oh, boy I hope they brought us gifts,"said Don.

"Yes,"said Lisa.

"Then next weekend their will be a lot of joy too. Mom returns home." said Will.

"Yes."Mom.

"Mom,"said Lisa.

"Also you have a wonderful new father,"said their Grandmother.

"That is right we do,"said Will.

"Yes, we do,"said Don.

"Yes" said Lisa.

"I am glad we all agree. A very busy weekend that is good, so Shawn what do we do today for excitement,"said Grandmother.

"We can have a cook out and still be in the screen room for dinner,"said Shawn.

"Good so now we have plans for today and tomorrow.?"said Grandmother.

"Look at what we have.?"said Will.

"All new Grandmother,"said Don.

"Three new films for children, ok,"said Grandmother.

"All are from Versailles Film Studios,"said Grandfather.

"So we will be busy this weekend and next,"said their Grandmother.

"That seem to be a lot of fun and good entertainment,"said Grandfather.

"Baitlym you returned and with all of the children put the baby right here,"said Grandmother.

"I could not sleep and besides I do not want to wait up at 4:00a.m,"said Baitlym.

"I do not blame you and I am glad to see all the children,"said Constance.

"They are not all out to stay,"said Baitlym.

"Just let the older ones stay,"said Constance.

"I will take these two upstairs right now so they can rest,"said Si.

"Good idea she looks so tired,"said Grandmother.

"Baitlym have some coffee and we are going to have a cookout this afternoon,"said Constance.

"Does the cook know.?"said Baitlym.

"Yes, I told him, see the message,"said Constance.

"Yes, I do and I see his answer, he does not object at all,"said Baitlym.

"Steaks, children and corn and cool drinks. "said Constance.

"Good idea, Baitlym Grandmother mentioned that I may stay here and have tutors for my education,"said Will."

"I might even listen in,"said Baitlym.

"We can both observe at the mirror on the other side,"said Constance.

"I like that idea,"said Baitlym.

"It will only be interesting subjects for me, a refresher course, "said Constance.

"Me too,"said Baitlym.

"Me too,"said Will.

"Now stop that Will,"said Grandmother.

"Sorry,"said Will.

"Me,"said Lisa.

"Be good, Lisa,"said Baitlym.

"Good,"said Lisa.

"With the rest of the day to get ready we are having a dinner in place of a lunch so the cooks are starting right now,"said Constance.

"There is a phone call, Princess,"said the Butler.

"Thank you, hello yes, Urnlee, ok, sure, see you then, good bye and we love you both,"said Constance.

"They are both fine and are going to be home on Sunday, she does not think she is going to call again there is so much to do,"said Constance.

"Leave it to her to have a short call and to keep her marriage going. I wish I went to Paris too"said Baitlym.

"There were to many people around them both, so she ended the call. Baitlym you still could go to Paris,"said Constance.

"She is clever and wants this marriage to work,"said Baitlym.

"I know, he showed interest at the right time for her,"said Constance.

"You are right, she was beginning to be a little upset with being a widow,"said Baitlym

"After my baby is born she is next,"said Baitlym.

"We will be ready to help,"said Constance.

"I know we are all going to be a help to them I am sure of that, I am in very good health because of her,"said Baitlym.

"I know you are and all of us are too,"said Constance.

"We do owe her a lot and we are going to make sure they are together and very happy too, even if it means they both live somewhere else,"said Baitlym.

"I think they will be able to receive a lot of privacy, they are going to live in the smaller building on the other side,"said Constance.

"That will do it, I am sure of it,"said Baitlym.

"This plan will work.!"said Constance.

"Maybe until they want to be with others or they want to raise their own without many of us,"said Baitlym.

"Maybe that is not a bad idea for each family to have a condo inside this large building,"said Constance.

"We could get away and be with our own adults,"said Baitlym.

"We will think of that when the time comes,"said Constance.

"That is when the children want privacy too,"said Baitlym.

"That is right now, anyways,"said Constance.

"We do let them go to the other buildings but it is going, going to take awhile, "said Baitlym.

"We can not leave them alone I know,"said Constance.

"Speaking about being one ones own, Si suggested that we all take a condo now so the adults can meet in the great room and have some privacy,"said Baitlym.

"It is up to Urnlee if she moves back in then there will be a full house in this building,"said Constance.

"My husband and I and the children can use the first floor apartment,"said Baitlym.

"The suite was painted just has week and the other suites too when everyone moved out,"said Constance.

"I will move today and if it is not what I wanted maybe someone can take our place,"said Baitlym.

"With Lisa, Don and Will they need to be on the second floor,"said Constance.

"I know Lisa is finally using her bedroom, hopefully she will continue with that. So I will move, "said Baitlym.

"With the baby you do need the first floor. Or you can stay with us and use the elevator,"said Constance.

"No, I think I will like that apartment, It has a balcony and apart of the second floor too,"said Baitlym.

"That is right and I can take the third floor for Shawn's library connects to it and he can use an office space,"said Constance.

"This is even nicer and if Urnlee stays there we will have the privacy we need,"said Baitlym.

"There I message the staff and the apartment will be ready in an hour,"said Constance.

"Good and I know for a fact the third floor door is only needing to be locked,"said Baitlym.

"All settled and you do have a kitchen there also,"said Constance.

"Si, as we speak you and I and the children will be on the first floor apartment near the other side of the house looking at the backyard,"said Baitlym.

"Nice and all is final then. Thank you, Constance we do need to keep away from the staircase for a little while,"said Si.

"As long as you too are happy and delighted. I have a call so it will only take a few seconds,"said Constance.

"Lovely, it is finished like the others rooms in this house so I do not need an furniture from our own suite,"said Bailtym.

"So, I know they, Urnlee and Needo approve of the new housing, bcause they both agreed on the phone a few seconds ago, and they are going to be home in about a few minutes,"said Constance.

"They decided to return a few days earlier,"said Baitlym.

"Mom is home,"said Will.

"Mom,"said Lisa.

"Mom and Dad,"said Don.

"Dad is home,"said Will.

"Hope they are not to tired,"said Constance.

"What a delight when I heard I was going to stay in the main house,"said Needo.

"Oh, you are to funny,,"said Shawn.

"Welcome home Needo. and Urnlee"said Constance.

"Yes, welcome home, "said Baitlym and Si.

"Mom and Dad "said Will.

"Mom and Dad,"said Lisa.

"Mom and Dad,"said Don.

"Let the staff take your things and do you both want to go up stairs to rest,"said Constance.

"Mom,"said Lisa.

"Dad,"said Don.

"I am so glad you are both here,"said Will.

"Yes, me too,"said Lisa.

"We can talk for a while in the living room,"said Needo.

"Yes, we stayed one day in Paris and saw Gale. He allowed us to use the Hall of Mirrors in the Palace of Versailles for one evening for dinner alone and now we are here again, it was so exciting, I am still excited,"said Urnlee.

"I know why the both of you did not tell us it was because of the security,"said Shawn.

"That is right too,"said Constance.

"Your correct the both of you and now are you doing alright I need to ask my patient,"said Urnlee.

"I am fine, Versailles must have been beautiful,"said Bailtym.

"It was, we both wanted to share this with all of you but it was urgent to keep it quiet until we got home,"said Urnlee.

"We do not mind, I hope there was a lot of photos,"said Baitlym.

"There is we photoed them by computer so they should be ready in a few seconds."There your vitals signs are fine, "said Urnlee.

"I have been taking her signs since you were gone, "said Si.

"Good and you got your new name again,"said Needo.

"That is right, finally,"said Si.

"Yes, we have done a lot also since you both were gone,"said Constance.

"There has been good things happening to all of us,"said Shawn.

"That's right Dad, I am going to stay home and study,"said Will.

"You better get good grades,"said Needo.

"Yes, you better or I am going to ship you off,"said Urnlee.

"Me too,"said Lisa.

"We need some refreshments,"said Constance.

"Lets all sit down and talk for a few minutes more,"said Shawn.

"We need to get ready for dinner and here is some more gifts for all of you,"said Urnlee.

"Lets see your gifts. Jewelry for me,"said Constance.

"I do not open mine yet,"said Shawn.

"Good, games for the children and Shawn a nice hat to wear,"said Constance.

"Jewelry for me, a pen for my good husband and games for the children,"said Baitlym.

"Shawn does your hat fit alright, if not maybe you can switch with Si,"said Constance.

"It does not fit,"said Shawn.

"Here is my pen,"said Si.

"Thank you. How does the hat fit, ok.?"said Shawn.

"It fits good, and perfect, thanks,"said Si.

"Now all of us are delighted I hope,"said Constance.

"All,"said Lisa.

"Here they are. The newly weds,"said Constance.

"Oh, I see the hat works I realized that in the car just as we drove into the front yard,"said Urnlee.

"Wonderful, thank you,"said Si.

"Yes, thank you both,"said Constance.

"I was not sure if you were going to Versailles but with the security I did not say anything,"said Baitlym.

"You are correct and what could me do,"said Urnlee.

"Nothing, until you were home again,"said Baitlym.

"All went perfectly and now you are home do you like your suite now.?"said Constance.

"Yes, I do thank you all and Baitlym do you like the other apartment and the first floor,"said Urnlee.

"Yes, we do and the third floor office is very good for Si, and he locks it up so the children can not get into it,"said Baitlym.

"We do like the our new suite,"said Urnlee.

"We stayed in our own suites,"said Will.

"Good for you children you made it easier for all of us,"said Urnlee.

"Here is some coffee Urnlee is there anyone else,"said Shawn.

"Yes, me dear as long as you are up,"said Constance.

"Uncle, just a little thank you,"said Baitlym.

"Remember tonight all the children stay upstairs,"said Shawn.

"Yes, we can say that now, while they are playing in the other room, it did work out these last few days,"said Constance.

"We do need some private time for the adults,"said Shawn.

"We might be able to do this all the time,"said Constance.

"You I hate to be cruel, but when they are growing up they are to play where we say so and not try to get their own way about things,"said Shawn.

"This is true, play and enjoy yourselves or stay in your room and cry it out,"said Si.

"We will not have any problems they are quite aware of what they can not have if they were to be unmanageable,"said Urnlee.

"If that were to happen not only swimming but there is horse back riding that can be taken away,"said Constance.

"They will not be unmanageable. We forget about the horse back riding and there is plenty more for them to do,"said Bailtym.

"I did not have all of these things growing up,"said Si.

"I did not either,"said Shawn.

"Either did my sisters and brothers they refused,"said Baitlym,

"I had everything growing up and then it was taken away by bad business and my husband and I build it up for ourselves,"said Constance.

"Now they have a turn and it will be controlled legally so they and we will not going to be robbed,"said Baitlym.

"I know how to solve this I bought again a few hours ago Euro train stock and sleep and loitering and when Gale takes it over he will buy us out. He has to do this for us so we are always protected,"said Needo.

"That is right, he bought us out and just before he took over, "said Constance.

"We are in good hands when we are finshed with this project and want out, "said Si.

"You know I just thought of that, when Chardin's husband died Gale made sure she and all of us took over, so he might be thinking of taking over again,"said Constance.

"He will help us I am sure,"said Bailtym.

"Good point but first we need to help him. We have to think of all of that stock he should buy from us and we need to purchase it all before that happens so what is left right now.? "said Constance.

"Right now, here I just issued it so now the last has been purchased,"said Shawn.

"Remember that our Euro train pharmacies and Versailles fast food is new and we can unloan that to him personally. It is so good our meetings have started "said Baitlym.

"Then there is nothing else to purchase and all Gale needs to do is to buy us out,"said Shawn.

"I know one thing when he was here for the wedding there were many new people around us but the next time he is contracted his name is Paul,"said Constance.

"We did use Paul when we visited,"said Needo.

"That was his wife that started that, Princess Duless. I need to get rid of your name too, Needo,"said Urnlee.

"Then call me instead of Prince Friendtus Needo, it was always Neeus to my undergrad and graduate years. I know it is not much better,"said Needo.

"Ok, then Neeus, I remember that year you played soccer and the crowds were screening it,"said Urnlee.

"I hope so, it was the last screen for fame in football too, until I married you,"said Neeus.

"Thank you, I love you so much,"said Urnlee.

"Did you know, I -----,"said Neeus.

"I am not going to ask what they both whispered,"said Shawn.

"I have a secret for you and I do not need to whisper it,"said Constance.

"I know we need some more coffee,"said Shawn.

"This is the truth yet you will hear from me tonight, and some new orders too,"said Constance.

"Do you need new orders Si.?"said Baitlym.

"It might not be any good to whisper,"said Si.

"I do know it depends,"said Baitlym.

"Now lets set the event for all of us with a toast to our happiness,"said Shawn.

"Good idea and that will make an end of a perfect evening,"said Constance.

"Here is to all of us that we make good decisions from now on and our happiness and life is a good and healthy one,"said Shawn.

"Here, here,"said Neeus.

"Yes, indeed,"said Urnlee.

"Now good night all,"said Neeus.

"Night,"said Constance.

"Night,"said Urnlee.

"Night,"said Shawn.

"Little Lisa, now I know it is early in the morning,"said Urnlee.

"Food, please,"said Lisa.

"You have your rob on and slippers why not go down stairs and get some breakfast for yourself, ok,"said Urnlee.

"Grandmother is downstair,"said Lisa.

"You can go it is alright,"said Urnlee.

"I will bring her,"said Neeus.

"No that is alright, I will go,"said Urnlee.

"Thanks,"said Lisa.

"Here is Lisa,"said Urnlee.

"Good morning my dear and how are you this morning Lisa,"said Grandmother.

"Good,"said Lisa.

"How is grandmother? "said Urnlee.

"Do you want to go upstairs,"said Constance.

"I want to, I am so tired,"said Unrlee.

"Ok,"said Lisa.

"Ok,"said urnlee.

"She is very tired Urnlee was at Versailles yesterday,"said Constance.

"The Palace of ---,"said Lisa.

"Yes, Versailles, the Palace of Versailles, here is a picture of it on this wall,"said Constance.

"Oh, the painting,"said Lisa.

"Yes,"said Grandmother.

"It looks like this house right here,"said Lisa.

"True but Versailles is a little bigger, our house is half as big,"said Constance.

"No one realizes how long it took Shawn we had all of the supplies by our own construction company so it would not cost to much,"said Constance.

"I do remember that Ed had a demo going on in many places and when he had enough materials he went ahead and would build just as much as he could,"said Shawn.

"It took twenty five years to build and materials were cost nothing and the security did and with the latest and waiting these last few years the updates are the finest,"said Constance.

"The actual size is now, that is including the family plots that are all underground,"said shawn.

"Yes, and thank you for whispering that last part,"said Constance.

"Please more,"said Lisa.

"Oatmeal it is,"said Grandmother.

"Thank.you,"said Lisa.

"Your welcome, you do not need to whisper Lisa, Shawn did you have enough also too,"said Constance.

"Yes I did and I am going to the library thank you ladies I will see both of you later, and I am going to take my coffee with me,"said Grandfather.

"Bye,"said Lisa.

"Bye my dear,"said Grandfather.

"He is going into the library if you want to you may visit him,"said Grandmother.

"Morning all,"said Will.

"Will hear is your breakfast, "said Grandmother.

"Thank you and Urnlee would like you to go upstairs to see her,"said Will.

"Lisa go see your Grandfather when you are finished, ok,"said Grandmother.

"Yes,"said Lisa.

"This elevator, it is so slow"said Grandmother.

"Please sit down, this did not even wake up Neeus, I just had my first morning sickness, "said Urnlee.

"My dear, it is right on schedule,"said Constance.

"I am all right now,"said Urnlee.

"I think I will make sure you have something to eat when your husband wakes up so why not just rest or are your getting hungry,"said Constance.

"What is,"said Neeus.

"Good morning dear,"said Urnlee.

"Here is your tray and I want you both to talk,"said Constance.

"Constance wanted me to tell you something,"said Urnlee.

"Wait until I get my first sip of coffee, and thank you for getting it my dear,"said Neeus.

"My dear, I know we got married a while back and in Versailles was a blessing by the Pope on his visit to see Gale and us,"said Urnlee.

"Ok, and what did you want to tell me,"said Neeus.

"Today it is offical I had a test taken and I was sick too and I and we are having a baby,"said Urnlee.

"Wonderful."Who else knows.?"said Neeus.

"Constance and I told her to tell everyone, she was there when I took the test and she brought the children down stairs for me,"said Urnlee.

"Sorry,"said Needus.

"You were asleep and you would not wake up, "said Urnlee.

"So when is it,"said Neeus.

"I guess in nine months I am not sure I did not take the second part of the test. It is over there just open up the bottle and place it inside,"said Urnlee.

"Like this,"said Neeus.

"See take off the long stem and the attached test end goes into the bottle,"said Urnlee.

"Good now the top of the bottle is on tightly,"said Neeus.

"Now watch to where the water level stays, when you make sure the top is on and is tight the seal for the liquid breaks and enters the test and the water level does indicate what month, "said Urnlee.

"So it does indicate the over this amount is six or more months,"said Neeus.

"Yes, the less months you are the accurate the reading. Over six months you need to buy another test or send for it as a discount,"said Urnlee.

"So you never get money for this as a discount.?"said Neeus.

"You should always get the last test to find out the day of the delivery,"said Urnlee.

"So the six month test would tell you your last day,"said Neeus.

"It will tell you of the water break,"said Urnlee.

"So we do not have an official date yet,"said Neeus.

"That was a law created by my nursing and the medical professional use that criteria for it test development,"said Urnlee.

"The first test applied because you were in your first month,"said Neeus.

"Right and the next test to be mailed to us is applied to the registry for women having a baby and not due to the false pregnancies that may accur,"said Urnlee.

"So this is positive,"said Neeus.

"Yes, it is and we will wait for the test because of the registry. My doctor would be told because I will see him today when he sees the children,"said Urnlee.

"He is your doctor and a pediatrician too,?"said Neeus.

"You may see him too, he is also a general practitioner,"said Urnlee.

"So if I have a cold, he will see me.?"said Neeus.

"Yes, he will,"said Urnlee.

"I have not had a cold since I left my mother's house,"said Neeus.

"Or since you were in boarding school where the atmosphere is different,"said Urnlee.

"How do you know this.? "said Neeus.

"As a nurse it is my job to know,"said Urnlee.

"So you do not act like a nurse around any of us,"said Neeus.

"I do not have much of a working career and most of it was in a private practice in a Europe residential environment,"said Urnlee.

"So you act professional only when the doctor is here,"said Neeus.

"I have too if he thought I was not a good nurse he could take my license away. Why do you think I was so upset when Ed died he was my patient too and it is not a recommendation when a patient dies,"said Urnlee.

"But he was dieing of cancer,"said Neeus.

"I know but it still is a negative while on a resume when Chardin called me up saying she did not feel good I immediately got the doctor and she ask for one also,"said Urnlee.

"I never did think of these things, I am, so sorry,"said Neeus.

"Now that I was married to one man in this house and now if things go wrong the law is going to look towards me,"said Urnlee.

"I hope you can forgive me,"said Neeus.

"I can will the police if anything else happens, why do you think I did not want to get marry to Ed,"said Urnlee.

"I did not ever think of that at all,"said Neeus.

"I have and it took to good looking men to make me say I do,"said Urnlee.

"You will be alright I hope you are ok now,"said Neeus.

"I am fine, it is impossible to be otherwise when Ed died I was given a house and an automobile and a few new checking accounts,"said Urnlee.

"You will be ok,"said Neeus.

"When Constance found out I did not spend any money I spent it on the children and bought them stocks, she bought me a new automobile,"said Urnlee.

Chapter 22

"Good news here is another test to find out if it is a girl or a boy lets use it I just remembered it was in this draw,"said Neeus.

"Good I can use the urine or the blood with a small twist of the cap to my finger,"said Urnlee.

"Oh, I sure it is a boy,"said Neeus.

"I think so,"said Urnlee.

"Put the cap on the the liquid will show a color on the bottle,"said Neeus.

"See here it is, it is a boy. You are correct "said Urnlee.

"I am correct all the time,"said Neeus.

"Are you stating a fact or a funny joke,"said Urnlee.

"Both,"said Neeus.

"Very funny then and we do need to talk in a group some how we all need to control the money,"said Urnlee.

"Why,"said Neeus.

"So it can not be use or just for me with a committee in case anything might happen I have my own and I do not need to spend it down maybe just save it for the children,"said Urnlee.

"We can talk about it at our new meeting this evening. It is just in a few minutes anyways,"said Neeus.

"Good I have to get this done right now tonight,"said Urnlee

"I have an annoucement to make I did not know how Urnlee has taken this all in and remained quiet until now, as a nurse the quilt can be serious when there is a death,"said Neeus.

"I am so sorry,"said Constance.

"Please do not feel that way,"said Shawn.

"No, please do not do that,"said Constance.

"I told her that. Dear you do not have to be guilty,"said Neeus.

"I think I understand you want to be in charge of the children monies to help them out if something happens. Said Constance.

"That is correct. I do need a committee,"said Urnlee.

"Also if there is anything given to you, to control it, so it does not look like you are having a lot of fun,"said Constance.

"May I say something and from someone that just started working here using the text and phone,"said Baitlym.

"Please do,"said Urnlee.

"If I work using the phone for ten years then I am valuable besides the publicity. But anything that I inherit is controlled and I have a small check,"said Baitlym.

"I have had small amounts myself then we this company started that is the money that you have been seeing,"said constance.

"Constance gets my money along with my family when I am dead but I give her a check each month because she is a value to me and she helps me sells or rent my estates,"said Shawn.

"That is correct I was with him when his mother went into her final home by the shore and he rents all of the other homes and I met all of the clients,"said Constance.

"This is working,"said Shawn.

"Yes we all had our pictures with our clients welcoming them into the castle as the renters,"said Constance.

"You were busy even on your honeymoon,"said Urnlee.

"You are busy, and probably were unaware of the nursing qualities for yourselve but all is there when everything is perfect,"said Constance.

"Now stop thinking of yourself as a useless person when we need you just as you are,"said Neeus.

"Thank you I just wanted to explain,"said Urnlee.

"Very well too, your case is understood and we will controll,"said Baitlym.

"If you are worried about anything you inherit, you will just have to report all to a lawyer once every six months or monthly if you are not comfortable,"said Constance.

"For any large amount there is a committee first,"said Shawn.

"Also a small amount to any stranger needs to be approved of,"said Baitlym.

"No one can have a small check for blackmail,"said Urnlee.

"That my dear is something you do not need to worry about that would have happened when you were engaged to my son,"said Constance.

"If I gave Likus a check or to your sister-in-law Baylib for six months I am approved and when the six is over they have to ask some one else,"said Shawn.

"This is a fact if I leave my husband we are on our own and I have to stay here to provide for my children. "said Baitlym.

"That is the agreement to the Belgium government and the committee can decide not to be in favor of any kind of law or agreement with its people in business,"said Shawn.

This is the law,"said Constance.

"A very good one,"said Shawn.

"I did not say anything while your husband Ed was alive because we were being paid by Gale and the Belgium government and because of Ed in Bavaria put this business together for us,"said Constance.

"It was by your grandson, who is in control,"said Urnlee.

"If there was a take Gale is in charge, then my grandson and then me,"said Constance.

"If something happened to all of them then, it is controlled by Ed's wife Princess Ownsite will be in charge as President of the company,"said Baitlym.

"That is nice there is never a chance for me to be in charge,"said Urnlee.

"We are not in charge we just give our photos to the press and collect a salary and let the committees do the work,"said Bailtym.

"The reports tell us what it is, when the prices go up we and the committees are notified,"said Baitlym.

"I am very much relieved at this point,"said Urnlee.

"I am here if you want me to take over years from now, remember there is your children Will, Don and Lisa, "said Baitlym.

"I never thought of that,"said Urnlee.

"It is a good thing we got all of this out before you got the flu out of all this stress,"said Baitlym.

"Well, you are a help to us and now we did help you and you can be more relaxed now,"said Constance.

"Besides this business has anyone trying to control or steal we are a Eurotrain under the Atlantic now so we are protected by the Federal and International laws,"said Baitlym.

"That is why the press in always looking to this house, this castle to see what they can use in the news,"said Constance.

"When you were going again to Paris and Versailles we did not mind and beyond these walls indeed the press is always looking for something,"said Shawn.

"We do have it made. I am very lucky to have you Urnlee,"said Neeus.

"It is impossible to collapse a large business this way, the energy and its electrical is very separate,"said Si.

"Impossible,"said Constance.

"There lets all relax and have some refreshments it has been an interesting day. Did I ever learn fast, from Detva and Ed that the gentlemen are in charge if worse comes to worse"said Baitlym.

"Tell Urnlee what happened when you mentioned that you could take over,"said Constance.

"They arranged for all of us to be at a castle in Belgium near the border for a picnic and released the mote and told me I was in charge,"said Baitlym.

"We did not know it was to be cleaned and given new water,"said Constance.

"I cried all day long until I could not see them with my own tears,"said Baitlym.

"She did and they finally agreed to tell her when she would not stop crying,"said Constance.

"Did you finally stop,"said Urnlee.

"Sure, when I was told that I did not have to call anyone,"said Baitlym.

"After that you no longer even gave advice. Now wonder why you are so proper and just listen,"said Urnlee.

"With boys that are still good brothers in control, I always let them start the day and decide on what to do,"said Baitlym.

"Wise idea when you are out numbered,"said Urnlee.

"Now I just found out from the nannies that all the children are watching a movie so it will be over in time for bed,"said Constance.

"That is good,"said Baitlym.

"I will need some more of that coffee and I know that this has been an eventful evening. Now we will all relax,"said Constance.

"Here is something with the stocks who would want to buy a large amount of shares this time around,"said Shawn.

"I will,"said Urnlee.

"She may do so but it is here turn to put them into her name with the company money,"said Constance.

"Right Urnlee never buy a large amount without telling if you do the company will pay you back,"said Baitlym.

"This stock she should keep in her name,"said Constance.

"Done,"said Shawn.

"My wife a large share holder, you are getting important Urnlee, will it be my turn next,"said Neeus.

"Yes, put his name there to be next and the same amount when it reaches that limit,"said Constance.

"Done,"said Shawn.

"So that is it,"said Urnlee.

"Yes, I am sorry I did not give you a chance to do this but now you have your stock and the company wants you to hold on to them,"said Constance.

"Why not let her own when it is time to sell to Gale,"said Shawn

"A very good idea,"said Constance.

"Yes, I love it and it gives me a chance to represent much later,"said Baitlym.

"Then me,"said Si.

"Then me,"said Neeus.

"Good Shawn did you mark that order of representations,"said Constance.

"Remember, by this time there will be Don, Will and Lisa,"said Urnlee.

"Also Likus and his wife and Detva and his too,"said Shawn.

"Which reminds me Detva might be home if his visit causes Gale to run the business sooner,"said Shawn.

"Good, now I am so please with this meeting, no we should give Detva Gales turn so he should stay there until the transfer,"said Constance.

"You are right again we do not want this to be a taken away, I think Ed bought all the stock,"said Baitlym.

"Yes, I did why,"said Constance.

"We should buy it and buy out everyone. Then invest in the 24 hour and then give that money to Gale,"said Baitlym

"That is right he did,"said Constance.

"After we had made a fortune in a few hours we invest by giving Gale the money,"said Baitlym.

"I remember that Ed did that several times and now can do it,"said Constance.

"I pick the 24 hour investment program and it is good for only a few minutes and we get the money,"said Shawn.

"Does Ed have any stock right now and the others. No, just Baylib and I just transferred that to Urnlee,"said Baitlym.

"Ed turned over his stock a while back and so did the others, according to this report,"said Shawn.

"Good,"said Si.

"The stock is finished, if we wait another 5 minutes we get them full amount and more with interest,"said Shawn.

"There how is it now,"said Baitlym.

"Urnlee, you are now the riches woman in the world, I put your story in and photo,"said Shawn.

"Thank you, Urnlee so much and now we transfer it is our own joint account so we all have to decide when to use it., while it makes money for all of us to have a individual account this is so exciting,"said Constance.

"Now the check is to be cut because we now have the equal amount of money,"said Shawn.

"We get an individual account for us all and Gale has his,"said Constance.

"You do remain in this position until you want out,"said Baitlym.

"I need my husband to represent me and then Baitlym if she wants the job,"said Urnlee.

"Then now it goes to, Si. With Urnlee excuses to the share holders and public,"said Shawn.

"You are getting very good with this Shawn,"said Constance.

"This is how I made my second fortune, we however are right in time for this business adventure or commitment,"said Shawn.

"We now have a fortune of our own is that true,"said Baitlym.

"Yes, and I insist Baitlym if you want to have a business please let it be here in Belgium ok, I do not need to loose another one of us in the family, please,"said Constance.

"Thank you, Grandmother, .I do not intend to leave this house yet I think many of us should keep on making these financial programs of earning this money very fast while half of us keep on buying the stock,"said Baitlym.

"Good decisions,"said Urnlee.

"Yes, it is you are a good wife,"said Si.

"A very good business woman,"said Neeus.

"A very good and wonderful Granddaughter,"said Constance.

"And may I add a very good trillionaire,"said Shawn.

"Thank you, all of you, I am very rich very rich now,"said Baitlym.

"Yes, you are,"said Constance.

"I can enjoy and relax and not worry about my children,"said Baitlym.

"Yes, you may,"said Urnlee.

"Now I think the public and the press is going to wonder about why the sudden increase and yet it was never before,"said Constance.

"Yes, why is that,"said Shawn.

"We have been making these money yet it is going into the security of the Euro train and its employees have had many increases earnings,"said Constance.

"All this time, for them and it had to be,"said Bailtym.

"That is right and we waited for many years and now we are allowed to have ours,"said Constance.

"Because it is the company is first we can not put it is use on the outside unless it is approved of and I do not think this money will be approved for that purpose,"said Shawn.

"We can invest in what we have done for each of us only.?"said Constance.

"Right thank you, dear,"said Shawn.

"We have to invest in our own stocks,"said Urnlee.

"We can let Don, Will and Lisa worry about other stocks right now the company is still very young "said Baitlym.

"They will never be able to bankrupt us or them anyways,"said Shawn.

"That is good too know,"said Baitlym.

"They can only help,"said Urnlee.

"They will have a complete committee right,"said Neeus.

"Yes, and we do to, if Gale does not want a deal it is over,"said Constance.

"That is a problem, you mean he will take charge after that,"said Urnlee.

"That is right,"said Constance.

"First we have to make money of each of us, then give that to Gale, then we have to complete that again for us,"said Shawn.

"So we are able to make this money then he takes over,"said Urnlee.

"We were always in charge all we needed to do was to ask for the position publicly,"said Constance.

"If was Gales intensions for Charedin to be in charge to keep busy and now we have Urnlee,"said Neeus.

"Yes, and just be yourself and represent us and we will do everything,"said Baitlym.

"Certainly I do not mind representing us at all,"said Urnlee.

"Thank you, I do want my children to think that I am a house wife only I am sure all of you do not mind that,"said Baitlym.

"No, we are all in an agreement with you,"said Urnlee.

"This is how I understood the business by watching,"said Constance.

"I know I will get by,"said Baitlym.

"I do have to say when we were married she did not want to work with me at any time and did mention about working at home only as a housewife,"said Si.

"Good for you, Baitlym,"said Urnlee.

"Yes, it is a fulltime job,"said Shawn.

"Now the few times that we are in charge we should include the others in even Newport and Likus ok,"said Urnlee.

"Yes, the stocks as an invest is running by all the names right now it only takes a few minutes to do,"said Constance.

"Remember when Ed did this a while back he even included us and our staff here as well to enhance their own value,"said Baitlym.

"Yes, and the computer gave everyone an account that duplicated the stock amount so the individual could sell at the same price that was earned,"said Constance.

"We should do that for all the ones who are not living here so we can see what is happening with the accounts,"said Urnlee.

"Right then they are in charge and might want to protect the money for a while,"said Shawn.

"It could earn more and then sell,"said Constance.

"I think I will have Ed buy and hold it for awhile he did that the last time,"said Baitlym.

"That is good, then he can invest and sell it to Gale,"said Constance.

"I see the accounts are working and now Ed is in charge of the larger account and all of us were paid,"said Shawn.

"Right but he knows he is not in charge of the company right now." said Constance.

"Look, the computer put it in Urnlee's hands again right after it made a fortune,"said Baitlym.

"Look, it the computer the stock is right at home here in Belgium and now it is hitting the roof many know of the status,"said Shawn.

"What is happening,,"said Si.

"There seems to be a great interest, this is how many people programmed their computer and are acknowledging this,"said Shawn.

"They are approving of the merger of stocks and clients,"said Baitlym.

"Are they selling too,"said Constance.

"Yes, and apparently Newport and Ed are buying up,"said Shawn.

"Please do not stop,"said Baitlym.

"When this is over we should here from our individual accounts again and they we are still in charge,"said Constance.

"There all new purchases of stocks and we are in charge now,"said Shawn.

"This is not against the law we because of the Euro train sleep and loitering. We have our own stock exchange so we buy when no one does,"said Constance.

"What about the other exchanges.? "said Urnlee.

"We included them in the beginning and their stock went back after the first large amount of cash,"said Shawn.

"It works out the stock is insured and we give them what they invested after our individual amounts ,"said Constance.

"So it evens out to the other exchanges and we are allowed to buy, then others sell at a good price and then we rest for a while,"said Shawn.

"There are thirty other companies that do this,"said Constance.

"What someone buys is what they get when we start to purchase,"said Baitlym.

"I realize the public could still sell and invest the money the way that was just done, "said Urnlee.

"But never with us,"said Baitlym.

"I think that is against the law, unless a person gives us the money we earn it and they get a percentage only,"said Constance.

"That part is correct and legal. The only one that took in strangers was Ed and they gave him the land deeds and money to do the Euro train from California to Canada,"said Baitlym.

"We can not have that right it is for Ed or Gale who are the innovators of this project,"said Constance.

"We have accomplished a lot this evening and we need to do more like this,"said Shawn.

"We are, Urnlee is in charge now of the money and all of us have invested and we are on our way to control and the success that the Euro train needs.

"I suggest that Urnlee is the new President of the corporation and Constance is the Vice President,"said Baitlym.

"We have been recording all of these meeting so Baitlym should be the recorder and I second all the motions,"said Shawn.

"Secretary is for Shawn at this time,"said Constance.

"All financial reports to Si,"said Baitlym.

"If we have no knowledge of the proper names and not enough of family to handle this so we can get my secretary to help with the rest,"said Constance.

"It is all recorded right now and that is the main thing for us that we are aware of what was said and done,"said Baitlym.

"So we need some more coffee and then a good night, how are the little babies doing,"said Urnlee.

"Good it is my week to check up on them and they are ok, and no colds or anything else,"said Baitlym.

"They are fine I checked on them about an hour ago,"said Constance.

"Good that is nice, I do not think I am going to visit unless the doctor is there with me, they need to know I am a nurse first and their relative second,"said Urnlee.

"Good decision, how about that little baby in the middle of the room she is so cute,"said Bailtym.

"With the blonde hair and curls,"said Constance.

"Yes she is a cute baby,"said Urnlee.

"Baitlym, did you get the second test yet,"said Urnlee.

"No, I did not. I am going to talk to you just as it arrives, ok,"said Baitlym.

"Yes, as soon as it arrives,"said Urnlee.

"Did you tell me that it arrives about six month after,"said Neeus.

"I could arrive earlier,"said Urnlee.

"You two girls will let me know also,"said Si.

"Very funny my good husband,"said Baitlym.

"Now lets all go upstairs and say good night,"said Constance.

"I know as soon as I awake Lisa will wake me up for some food so I need to get to sleep sooner,"said Urnlee.

"Go to bed right now Lisa it is very early,"said Urnlee.

"I am here we are going down stairs right now,"said Grandmother.

"Thank you, Constance,"said Urnlee.

"We need a routine around here Lisa if you need to have breakfast go to my door and walk into my bedroom and we can go down stairs together,"said Constance.

"Ok, I am hungry,"said Lisa.

"I know so here we are "said Grandmother.

"Where is Urnlee,"said Si.

"Here is she on the elevator,"said Constance.

"Baitlym is having her baby, we need to call an ambulance now,"said Si.

"I will call, I have my phone and I will see you upstairs,"said Urnlee.

"See that she is comfortable the contractions just started, she is only a few days away from delivery,"said Urnlee.

"She wanted that third test and why,"said Si.

"She feels so large that she did think it was twins,"said Urnlee.

"Here is the ambulance dear,"said Si.

"Ok, I do hope anything is alright,"said Baitlym.

"Sure everything is fine right,"said Urnlee.

"I will go alone.?"said Si.

"That would be good and we will see you both later, the doctor is in the hospital,"said Urnlee.

"Here we go, dear,"said Si.

"Ok,"said Baitlym.

"Constance, will you go with us,"said Si.

"Yes, I will, "said Constance.

"Lisa, here is some more food,"said Urnlee.

"Neeus, I am calling, to fine out how is the children are the nannies alright.

Good I will talk to you later "said Urnlee.

"All is ok,"said Lisa.

"Yes, Baitlym and her children are just fine. Do you want more food.? Lisa"said Urnlee.

"More juice,"said Lisa.

"There you are,"said Urnlee.

"Baitlym is ok,"said Lisa.

"Yes she is,"said Urnlee.

"Now another.? "said Lisa.

"No, that is all,"said Urnlee.

"Good morning Lisa,"said Neeus.

"Morning,"said Lisa.

"Neeus could you bring her upstairs to get ready for the day,"said Urnlee.

"Yes, sure I will,"said Neeus.

"Is Lisa ready I will bring her up. I hope Baitlym will be alright ? "said Will.

"Thank you, Will. Everything is alright,"said Neeus.

"Thank you, Will. She is alright, "said Urnlee.

"I could not move, I needed the elevator myself, and I am a nurse,"said Urnlee.

"You gave her to the hospital and the doctor, you did the right thing,"said Neeus.

"So Baitlym is with her husband and Constance for the first day, we will do it that way alright, "said Urnlee.

"Another wise decision you made,"said Neeus.

"Thank you dear, we will be in the living room and Baitlym's children will be with us all day long,"said Urnlee.

"We have the nannies and Shawn will help too,"said Neeus.

"Right, and he may bring Baitlym's clothes and some for Constance and Si if they both wish to stay over night,"said Urnlee.

"Thinking all the time I did not know why you are so upset too with yourself,"said Neeus.

"Blame it on your own newborn when you see each other,"said Urnlee.

"No, I will not and I will remember that is a concern for us both "said Neeus.

"I'm sorry I just did not, everything may occur very fast and she was not in danger or the baby so I must be a more aware of a large number of people in a large house any thing can happen,"said Urnlee.

"Yes, and I will help you,"said Neeus.

"Thank you, so much, Neeus, I love you,"said Urnlee.

"I need to tell you something when I move in I said,"I was not working is true and my company is all right."Yet there is another job when I went to work everyday and the,"said Neeus.

"I hope you are not going to tell me that you are a spy.?"said Urnlee.

"No, I did however go the local police station to work because of the castle was the reason so I could bring the police in,"said Neeus.

"Wait do you think you are doing this here too,"said Urnlee.

"Well yes, and I can bring them in by the trap doors and into the living room from the outside while many are searching the grounds,"said Neeus.

"Yes, you may if it means you want to leave each day and you may take Si if you mention it to him,"said Urnlee.

"You do not mind me leaving each day,"said Neeus.

"No, it is part of life and go for it. You have another back entrance and also your own apartment, for the funeraltory when it is used,"said Urnlee.

"Thank you dear so much,"said Neeus.

"Your are welcome but you will stay there when you are wanting to be angry with me or the children or we are not getting a divorce and you will live there all of your life time,"said Urnlee.

"It is a deal,"said Neeus.

"I do not want to loose you why not have the police here and in the other buildings and you can work with them use a uniform while the children are young,"said Urnlee.

"That is a deal and I will do that while they are all younger,"said Neeus.

"It will be good to have the security here and in the other buildings,"said Urnlee.

"I can get started in a few days and they can be in here in one the same amount of time,"said Neeus.

"Good, then get it done, use the phone today,"said Urnlee.

"I will and I might have an appointment today.?"said Neeus.

"That well be wonderful,"said Urnlee.

"Now I have my job that I wanted yet I will let everyone think I am at my own company work while I am in my office here in this building,"said Neeus.

"I do not understand,"said Urnlee.

"No one will know I am doing police work and I will work alone." said Neeus.

"How could you work alone without the others.?" said Urnlee.

"I can be with the other police when the children are in school." said Neeus.

"What about the adults.?" said Urnlee.

"This part is up to me, and will you tell the children not to bother their Daddy." said Neeus.

"I will and I am sure the others will not interrupt you while you are working." said Urnlee.

"Thank you are you disappointed with me." said Neeus.

"No, we need the police here." said Urnlee.

"Thank you it is the only way we can have the police and a barracks also so nothing will go wrong." said Neeus.

"You are correct and we do need protection so let it happen." said Neeus.

"So lets have some breakfast and we can help Baitlym's children, I think they are all up and everyone will stay home today." said Urnlee.

"Good morning children, did you have enough breakfast" said Neeus.

"Who wants some more.?" said Urnlee.

"I do." said Will.

"Will, is the only one.?" said Urnlee.

"Ok, I am going to have some thing to eat." said Neeus.

"I am good, right Lisa.?" said Urnlee.

"Yes, Nanny?" said Neeus.

"Baitlym's wants her children in the hospital right now." said the Nanny.

"That means she is going to stay a few days so go with your nannies children." said Urnlee.

"I s she alright.?" said Neeus.

"Let me call Constance, "Hello, is she all right.? Good, we can talk later." said Urnlee.

"How is she.?" said Neeus.

"Your Mommy is alright children, she wants to see you right now lets go with your nannies." said Urnlee.

"They left so fast and into the cars." said Will.

"I know but she is alright so no one has to worry." said Urnlee.

"I hope she is fine, I have told them back and they are brave and so is she,"said Will.

"Will, you're a good boy sit down and have some more food, ok,"said Urnlee.

"I am right now,"said Will.

"Lisa and Don do you want more.?"said Urnlee.

"I am going to help, you have a phone call,"said Neeus.

"There is another call, help Neeus, ok,"said Urnlee.

"Yes, they are, hope she is alright give her our love ok, Constance, ok, goodbye,"said Urnlee.

"They wanted to know if they had gone to the hospital,"said Neeus.

"Yes, and they will be there in a little while,"said Urnlee.

"We can go see her when she wants us to, is that alright with you,"said Neeus.

"We both agreed that we would stay here and help the children,"said Urnlee.

"But she called and wanted her children with her,"said Neeus.

"Mothers are like that and they are not going to stay to long while she is in labor,"said Urnlee.

"Here sit and I will pour the coffee,"said Neeus.

"I am sorry that you could not get to the police office,"said Urnlee.

"They are here in the building behind our apartment,"said Neeus.

"It is a good thing it is the police,"said Urnlee.

"I wanted you to see how easy it is to get into this building without a large army or security to watch,"said Neeus.

"But it was you who let them in, some how,"said Urnlee.

"That is how it is done, but do not worry I am here to watch and protect you,"said Neeus.

"You are a good husband,"said Urnlee.

"Thank you, are a good wife," said Neeus.

Chapter 23

“She had a baby boy,”said Urnlee.

“It happened in the night time. I knew I should have stayed there all of the time,”said Constance.

“Why they did not call in the morning.?”said Neeus..

“She gave birth almost two hours ago and she wanted the baby dressed in his pajamas and all the tests were done before anyone visited,”said Urnlee.

“Neeus, I am going with Constance and Will right now, so you entertain Don and Lisa when they both come downstairs for breakfast,”said Urnlee.

“I am, quickly here they are, right now,”said Neeus.

“It seems that all we do is sleep and have breakfast now we are out of the house,”said Constance.

“I did not go to the hospital due to germs,”said Urnlee.

“So when they come home we can give them a bath, everyone should,”said Neeus.

“Good morning I hate to interrupt but did you both see that Si, is getting a check with an increase in it because of his name is different now,”said Shawn.

“Because of the assassination laws we all get an increase the next time.!”said Shawn.

“That is perfect he did the right thing at the right time, and good morning Shawn how are you doing.?”said Urnlee.

"He did, and good morning and thank you for the good news did you text him, yes I did and gave him the copy,"said Shawn.

"Good she will be able to see it today at sometime if he wants to show her,"said Neeus.

"He has one of the copiers,"said Urnlee.

"Yes, it fits into his jacket sleeve pocket,"said Neeus.

"Do you have one.? "said Urnlee.

"I do and there is one for one if you want it,"said Neeus.

"Could you order me one too,?"said Shawn.

"Sure, it could be here within the hour,"said Neeus.

"That is nice thank you both for thinking of me, and how much is it,"said Shawn.

"It is the accounts money for the family right.?"said Neeus.

"Yes, it is. I am going to use the machine in the library,"said Shawn.

"This is good for Lloyd's then he askes them for the money at the office,"said Urnlee.

"He left right away,"said Neeus.

"He is going to get extra money from the bank,"said Urnlee.

"We do not have Exile here in the building, do we,"said Neeus.

"No, the bank might be in the gate house for the locals in the back some point in time, I do not know, I will put that on the test for tonight,"said Urnlee.

"Good, I can not wait until Constance sees this,"said Neeus.

"I only did think of it right now because we have been talking,"said Urnlee.

"So far you and I have two important ideas for our meeting tonight, both for this evening too,"said Neeus.

"We are quite the team if I do this again, then I will be a pro,"said Urnlee.

"That is right but remember we are never finished with an idea,"said Neeus.

"True do you know something.? "said Urnlee.

"Yes, both gates and not the front,"said her husband.

"Perfect and the two are in good places, that can not be seen,"said Urnlee.

"That is right, so we are prepared for a good evening,"said Neeus.

"Baitlym has given too,"said Urnlee.

"I get to have another name and this time, I am not going to tell you so I can return to Shawn,"said Uncle Shawn.

“That was good, very good,”said Unrlee.

“Thank you I will have some more coffee but first I am going to see the children up stairs,”said Shawn.

“Mine are napping including Lisa,”said Urnlee.

“I wish I did,”said Neeus.

“Maybe tomorrow, I should have told him to ask the nannies.?”said Urnlee.

“I am sure he will do it,”said Neeus.

“He might.?”said Urnlee.

“Here is Constance and the others,”said Urnlee.

“How is Bailtym and the baby.?“said Neeus.

“All is wonderful he looks so much like Ed. Edvard in Bavaria,”said Constance.

“Oh, Si, and Will, did you have fun,”said Urnlee.

“Good, all is fine,”said Grandmother.

“Excellent,”said Si.

“He looks like my brother, Ed,”said Urnlee.

“Hello everyone, I check the children Urnlee all is fine. Constance my wife you are back, that is good,”said Shawn.

“My husband, you should see this baby,”said Constance.

“I will go with you the next time you go there but I will not stay to long,”said Shawn.

“Lisa and Don are you hungry go upstairs with the nannies first then have a bath,”said Unrlee.

“We have made good strides so for this evening should we start the meeting now that the children are home and will be with the nannies,”said Neeus..

“Si, are you going up there late to sleep over, to be with her in the morning.?”said Urnlee.

I am going to have dinner and then be in the group because Baitlym wants to know what is going on,”said Si.

“That is nice of you,”said Constance.

“Now here is what can be done for our group,”said Urnlee.

“What.?”said Neeus..

“What is to be is to be,”said Constance.

“That is right, lets give the press a chance to do some harm and we can go for the lawsuits and the real cash,”said Urnlee.

“Grandfather I want you and Constance to check the press on us and see what we can do,”said Urnlee.

"Ok,"said Shawn.

"It is a perfect plan, it is what Ed did in Bavaria and made a fortune,"said Constance.

"It happened right after the stock mergers and your accounts went to the roof,"said Shawn.

"You remember,"said Constance.

"Do you remember the secret boy friend no one knew about,"said Shawn.

"Yes, but I, "said Constance.

"Well, here is the check that is yours I have waited for your family merger. Now here is what I own you and now this account is closed,"said Shawn.

"What do you mean.?"said Constance.

"This amount to cover up my name in the press made this amount just for you, Constance,"said Shawn.

"That was you.? "said Constance.

"Yes, it was me, and here is your check,"said Shawn.

"What if I did not see you at all.?"said Constance.

"Then this check for this amount I would have to give it to you at this time now that there is a first merger for the stocks,"said Shawn.

"So we would be meeting for the first time this evening, right,"said Constance.

"Right I hope you still love me,"said Shawn.

"Yes, I do, oh, my goodness, Urnlee look One Trillion,"said Constance.

"Are you pleased,"said Shawn.

"Yes, I am and I do still love you,"said Constance.

"Oh, I can not believe this, you have one good man, who loves you very much Constance,"said Urnlee.

"You have worked very hard for me,"said Constance.

"Yes, I know and I can do it again,"said Shawn.

"The meeting is over, Shawn lets go upstairs right now,"said Constance

"All right,"said Shawn.

"Now that they are upstairs I want to know if you want a trillion,"said Neeus.

"I love you anyways, but if you want to invest for the children then you should,"said Urnlee.

"Let me see did you take out the money or leave it in,"said Neeus.

"I left it in, I guess everyone wanted their check and I forgot to ask for it, I guess,"said Urnlee.

"If me see and I can out it into our own account together and make some money,"said Neeus.

"I will let Constance an Shawn know this so they can get the same deal for this family too. There I let all of them know,"said Urnlee.

"Good now we can all get rich,"said Neeus.

"We too,"said Lisa.

"Will why not take Don and Lisa to the dining room and have some food and I do not know Lisa I think you are too young,"said Urnlee.

"Good Don and Lisa there are snacks in the dining room,"said Will.

"We can let them stay up and sleep on the couch it is a weekend,"said Urnlee.

"Sure they can stay up we are going upstairs right after they have their snacks and we have some too,"said Neeus.

"Si, left for the hospital a few minutes ago,"said Urnlee.

"Oh, what about his account.?"said Neeus.

"Strange that you should ask, Shawn wants know if you want him to do our money accounts because he just finished with theirs and Si and Baitlym's too,"said Urnlee, "said Urnlee.

"Yes and thanks,"said Neeus.

"So how is that done,"said Urnlee.

"We put the money in together and it separates when it has been completed, he might even be asking for a trillion for each of us too,"said Neeus.

"I will make sure of that right now,"said Urnlee.

"Good, now we wait. All the accounts are used,"said Neeus.

"He is trying,"said Urnlee.

"We, You and I can not get out even if we wanted to,"said Neeus.

"The individual is still a group deal,"said Urnlee.

"That is it,"said Neeus.

"While are walking to our apartment I put Lisa with us so not alone. Don has his room near his grandmother so he is all right,"said Urnlee.

"So the meeting ended, yet Shawn is still working,"said Neeus.

"So it is on the computer with instructions when to end it, and I do know there is a phone call in case of a stock disaster,"said Urnlee.

"How did you know that,"said Neeus.

"Because it is the only phone call that rings and does not stop until you here the message,"said Urnlee.

"Here is Lisa now,"said Neeus.

"Do you want to go to bed now, you had your shower I see and you are nice and warm right now,"said Urnlee.

"Yes please, do I have to go to the hospital. ?"said Lisa.

"No, do you want to wait until Baitlym comes home and you can see the baby then.? "said Urnlee.

"Yes,"said Lisa.

"Don and Will thank you for saying good night to us, are you going back to see Grandmother right now.?"said Urnlee.

"We are returning right now,"said Will.

"Night,"said Don.

"Night,"said Urnlee.

"Was that the boys.?"said Neeus.

"That was Don and Will I did not want to turn them away but I know Don likes to make the rounds and say good night,"said Urnlee.

"We do have to consider him and I will tell them or you that we must all say good night to all of us so he is not worried,"said Neeus.

"We are going to do that because I do not want him to wander off,"said Urnlee.

"He probably would not, he is on a mission and is determine to see that we are all right "said Neeus.

"Yes, he is a good boy none of them have displayed to much emotions about their parents,"said Urnlee.

"Why is that.?"said Neeus.

"This building is designed for that and there is to much for them to do,"said Urnlee.

"They are busy and the tell is on, and it is a very good parent anyways. "said Neeus.

"What about the horses they are still in the other building,"said Urnlee.

"They were born here and there is a rider who is apart of the police, and he exercises them,"said Urnlee.

"I did see him and he is now apart of the force,"said Neeus.

"Good, we need the involvement from the other building,"said Urnlee.

"That is what they are here for,"said Neeus.

"As traffic, that gives me an idea for a campaign, I lived in the states and know about the driving, now we can say the Euro train saves lives or use this 95 or 91 like."95 saves lives use the tunnel, I-95 Eurotrain,"said Urnlee.

"That is there work a big part of it and always is, and we now have a good quote. "95 saves lives "I like that and for the other tunnels entrances in Europe it can work too,"said Neeus.

"It is the correct time to advertise this and to use the train under the I-95 it is now a good ad for us to use,"said Urnlee.

"It is the best I have ever heard,"said Neeus.

"Thank you,"said Urnlee.

"Now I have to say, this is a hold up now, stay in that chair and we want the safe in this room opened,"said the Robber.

"We have a main safe with the security guards there is not values or money here at all,"said Urnlee.

"Dear wake up, why are you talking to a stranger, talk to me.?"said Neeus.

"What, what.?"said Urnlee.

"You were talking in your sleep,"said Neeus.

"What did I say.?"said Urnlee.

"I do not know but it was not fun listening to you.?"said Neeus.

"I know we were being robbed and I was ready to call the security,"said Urnlee.

"We could both give a commercial that way for still advertise sleep, loitering and the Euro train at the end. You do not mind do you, you are all right "said Neeus.

"No, I am fine just put that info in the phone for this evening,"said Urnlee.

"You and I could do the ad and right here in the building too,"said Neeus.

"Let us relax for a minute or two, and we can use the living room for now on the second floor then the children will not be so upset,"said Urnlee.

"I will write, I mean talk that message also,"said Neeus.

"Good lets have something to eat and Lisa will be here very soon,"said Urnlee.

"We can and I did already you eat I did not want to much of anything,"said Neeus.

"I see you had a few desserts, cream filled too,"said Urnlee.

"Very funny, there is enough for you,"said Urnlee.

"I know,"said Urnlee.

"Also I wrote Urnlee had another idea, an ad,"said Neeus.

"Thank you,"said Urnlee.

"Sorry about working your subconscious, but I can not write this subject matter and give credit too,"said Neeus.

"Thank you again, and it is hunger,"said Urnlee.

"Ok, I did not think of that,"said Neeus..

"Oh, it was both, first hunger, then it was in the form of a tease,"said Urnlee.

"You are right, here is Lisa now You are here for your breakfast or can I have it." said Neeus.

"Oh, a kiss for both of us,"said Urnlee.

"Thank you for the kiss and this is for you,"said Neeus.

"Thank you, Lisa,"said Urnlee.

"It is good,"said Lisa.

"No, thank you it is for you,"said Neeus.

"You wanted it, so I will give her another,"said Urnlee.

"Ok, I do love this mellon,"said Neeus.

"I know what you were saying. Good bye for now see you later I am going to close the door right now we might go back to sleep,"said Urnlee.

"Good bye, Lisa,"said Neeus.

"Bye, Daddy,"said Lisa.

"Lisa any more, then here is your cereal and toast,"said her Mother.

"Thanks,"said Lisa.

"You are welcome,"said her Mother.

"Who is that, Yes,"said the Officer.

"Excuse me, your Ladyship is the General here I have message for him,"said the Officer.

"No, he went to the office it is right at the end of the hallway,"said Urnlee.

"Yes, I know where it is your Ladyship again I apologize for disturbing you,"said Lady Urnlee.

"Officer,"said Lisa.

"Yes, he wanted your father, he had a message for him,"said Urnlee.

"Ladyship,"said Lisa.

"Yes, that is my name, and yours is Lady Lisa,"said Urnlee.

"Princess too,"said Lisa.

"That is what the newspapers and the tel call you,"said Urnlee.

"So why not television,"said Lisa.

"That is a good question because now the television can locate anything that you lost and it is only for emergencies,"said her Mother.

"Ok. More toast,"said Lisa.

"Lady Lisa is that all,"said her Mother.

"Yes, and thank you,"said Lisa.

"You are welcome,"said her Mother.

"Good,"said Lisa.

"You watch the tel and I will be right back,"said Urnlee.

"Eurotoons,"said Lisa.

"This is good, Lisa your Nanny is her she will bring you to the second floor living room ok,"said Urnlee.

"Ok, and toons too,"said Lisa.

"Yes, Eurotoons for her Nanny and thank you,"said Urnlee.

"Bye said Lisa.

"Bye, now we are alone and I am going to have a shower,"said Urnlee.

"Alright. I got the officer's message,"said Neeus.

"Good, I hope it was important and that he was not to be blamed,"said Urnlee.

"No, he was not, and it was very important. All the other buildings have barracks in them now,"said Neeus.

"I hope this does not hinder the performances of the troopers of the other building and they are not anger at anyone for not having an estate also,"said Urnlee.

"No, but this is why all of them have an attitude because they even are having their break in the building or outside in the garden,"said Neeus.

"Really, I am glad I do not drive anywhere,"said Urnlee.

"Are you near the office door now,"said Neeus.

"I am dressed and I am going down the hallway,"said Urnlee.

"Are you near the door,"said Neeus.

"No Neeus, I am not,"said Urnlee.

"Now,"said Neeus.

"Yes, I am, I see your building front, all in blue marble that is really a room for the cerimonial for a title for this land and five other countries only,"said Urnlee.

"Good, here you are. See the garden and now look at the garden at the wall and the steps,"said Neeus.

"Oh, why for goodness sakes,"said Urnlee.

"Now you are allowed to know this but do not tell anyone just yet,"said Neeus.

"Of course I will, I see their automobile and there is another one,"said Urnlee.

"Then I can not show you other things, and you might not earn your millenarian title or uniform, "said Neeus.

"But what about Constance she must be given hers now,"said Urnlee.

"Give me the field glasses and we are very soon in this room,"said Neeus.

"I hope so,"said Urnlee.

"Come in, Constance,"said Neeus.

"Constance you look, beautiful,"said Urnlee.

"I have had her with me getting ready as a security precautions and thank you for wearing what was put out for you by your maid, we will be celebrating all day and maybe Edvard might be here from Bavaria,"said Neeus.

"I hope so. they are talking her picture right now and look at her grown,"said Urnlee.

"White with a red ribbon and her metals too,"said Neeus.

"She looks so beautiful too,"said Urnlee.

"All of the protocol names and her gown will be mentioned in the news and on the tel too,"said Neeus.

"So I am the only one here,"said Urnlee.

"Yes, I want a far away look wanting many to see and want her. She is done. Now Shawn will enter,"said Neeus.

"My dear you look beautiful,"said Shawn.

"This is so good why not letting this be done with Baitlym, oh say no more,"said Urnlee.

"Right, the doctor said, "It would only increase her labor and nothing else,"said Neeus.

"Good idea,"said Urnlee

"Urnlee, look a militarian metal from the police and I heard this will increase Baitlym and she will be home sooner,"said Constance.

"I think it is going to make the baby arrive sooner and nothing else remember a mother and her children have a stay in the hospital for two weeks now,"said Urnlee.

"That is right it is because of Princess Ownsite,"said Constance.

"There is a party all day long,"said Urnlee.

"That is good we need to celebrate,"said Constance.

"Yes, we do and the stories are hitting the news right now the law suits are for Urnlee the press has stated that all of the children in this house are hers,"said Shawn.

"Let this ride,"said Constance.

"Why are you whispering they are,"said Urnlee.

"Love that joke dear,"said Neeus.

"Even Baitlym's. "said Constance.

"Oh no they can not do this?"said Urnlee.

"It does get worse as the years go by and if Baitlym does die, they will try to get back the money. Said Neeus.

"I did not think of them, Baitlym's children, they can not do this, "said Urnlee.

"The press will and in years from now they will try again about any topic that they have written about,"said Neeus.

"Then Baitlym better stay alive,"said Urnlee.

"You both will, both of you are in good health,"said Neeus.

"It does sound so awful,"said Urnlee.

"Oh, now I have some homework here is my check book,"said Constance.

"Why,"said Lady Urnlee.

"We are not celebrating yet, it is in formal this evening anyways,"said Constance.

"Then what are you indicating, Constance.?"said Urnlee.

"The presses have been doing this you and Ed were married even claiming it was young Ed,"said Constance.

"This is terrible,"said Urnlee.

"I know young Ed received an account and your husband Ed took control of yours and when it was mention is the day you get the money and that is today,"said her Mother-in-law, Constance.

"It is tragic and you grandson knew it when he was here,"said Urnlee.

"This is Lloyds' and now you have to take this check and this is what you are going to invest for you and your children,"said Constance.

"Oh, this must have been years of investing.?"said Urnlee.

"I know and now it is finally yours,"said Constance.

"Are you upset,"said Neeus.

"Yes, but I understand now, oh no,"said Urnlee.

"What,"said Constance.

"What,"said Neeus.

"This baby might be Ed's and also Baitlym's according to the gossip,"said Urnlee.

"This is good, I never thought of Baitlym's children,"said Constance.

"What are you thinking of now, yourself that just got married,"said Urnlee.

"So this is why Baitlym introduced me to her children as my children when Chardin was alive,"said Urnlee.

"Funny gentlemen, if I were you I would not gain any more pounds according to our cartoon Ed is still long enough to reach around my bedroom door,"said Constance.

"Listen con or convict, I still love you,"said Shawn.

"This talk has been going on for a long time and even involved me years ago,"said Neeus.

"What is going on.? "said Urnlee.

"What, I will tell you what Ed has been keeping from you to earn all of that money and you will invest it. Because this is the way my sister and I earned at the castle so we would have enough money and you were no longer involved,"said Neeus.

"That was years ago. I also told you to stay there, "said Constance.

"You mean I was the one who gave you two your fortune,"said Urnlee.

"Yes, why do you think I wrote out this check, and I love you, Urnlee,"said Neeus.

"My check also here it is,"said Shawn.

"You and me,"said Urnlee.

"Baitlym,"said Shawn.

"My dear, this is how families in Europe survive by helping each other eventually. The recorders of Catherine the Great we are not allowed to see, yet she did earn money by law suits too,"said Constance.

"Yes, but I am not Catherine,"said Urnlee.

"No, but if I get drunk tonight I can take away your press that me are giving you right now to earn that money for us to survive and your business too. Do you want me to get drunk.? "said Constance.

"No, we would loose a lot of money so do not do that at all,"said Urnlee.

"Spoken, like a true Princess,"said Constance.

"I was a little nervous just then, "said Urnlee.

"I will become sixteen or thirty six if you want me too,"said Shawn.

"Then I will have to get drunk and take away you and this means the news too,"said Constance.

"Now we will all keep quiet and lets go to the large great living room and celebrate with coffee,"said Neeus.

"Hoping, get in a group and I will say I hope the walls have ears too,"said Constance.

"There is enough of the cupids,"said Urnlee.

"That is us too,"said Shawn.

"I did get that one instead of st but cu,"said Urnlee.

"What do you mean you have Neeus,"said Constance.

"I mean,"said Urnlee.

"Yes, I mean, not drunk to think,"said Constance.

"You earn this award for sure,"said Urnlee.

"I know all of my ideas are good and finally we do make a great deal of money. Ed always told me that,"said Constance.

"Oh, my "said Urnlee.

"Oh me,"said Neeus.

"Oh yes guys and look at the reception table they must have planned this all night,"said Shawn.

"Yes, I did,"said Neeus.

"You are mine, and I love you for all that you have done for us and this is a good tribute to Constance,"said Urnlee.

"Remember your award is with your new baby in your lap, ok, "said Neeus.

"Yes you are right, but first the baby picture alone, ok,"said Urnlee.

"Baitlym is on the phone, she is happy and in pain and does forgive us all for making the labor faster,"said Constance.

"I am glad we are forgiven,"said Urnlee.

"Not to angry,"said Neeus.

"No, just in pain so she got a shot just before I hung up. Si, is there as we know and can not believe what you have done for me Neeus, with this award,"said Constance.

"We are grateful for all that has happened and a day like today makes it all worth while, We are praising one of us today,"said Urnlee.

"We are and I am so thankful,"said Neeus.

"A great woman who watched and protected Ed and his wife, Princess Ownsite for without Constance helping that couple, we would not be here today as a family,"said Urnlee.

"We know it is early and the party will end late tonight but lets us give a toast to a great Lady, Her Royal Highness Duchess Constance Mogeesom with her fortitude we are all here to serve,"said Neeus.

"Hail to Constance,"said Urnlee.

"There now we have done it we gave our blessing to a wonderful woman who has done to much for all of us,"said her Husband.

"Thank you, everyone,"said Constance.

"All at this table has promised me that we will talk, after this breakfast,"said Neeus.

"Neeus, I am looking at this table and I see all of my old friends and the children looked so grand and enjoying themselves too,"said Constance.

"This is your day dear,"said Shawn.

"Constance I have found out that there is four other gowns like this one for you to use during the day and evening,"said Urnlee.

"Good then there is some to alter and save this one and auction off the others some day,"said Constance.

"You know as you wear the second, third and fourth you could have your seamtress make them all different for the late evening,"said Urnlee.

"Did you tell them too."I hope so it sounds like to good idea,"said Constance.

"She wants you to get into the second gown, right after this breakfast,"said Urnlee.

"I will, I know her there will be a evening dress too of the second one,"said Constance.

"Are you sure.?"said Urnlee.

"After what your team did for me I do expect there is a third in no flare for dancing as an evening gown and fourth of course is in pants,"said Constance.

"It is fascinating.!"said Urnlee

"The second will be in a slit at the beginning for dinner,"said Constance.

"This is when we are waiting for dinner, up stairs for a while,"said Urnlee.

"I am glad it is a little to cold outside to do anything there,"said Constance.

"I will make sure the guests are on the porch only for fresh air,"said Urnlee.

"Good, and they will have a good time of it,"said Constance.

"I seems to be over, and all are in the living room and resting upstairs before the dinner and music,"said Neeus.

"It is a success, I did not think it could have been any better, did you think of Baitlym for this,"said Constance.

"Yes, I doctor told me see needed a good feeling of home and an excited one in fact a celebrating time,"said Neeus.

"You are indeed a good and loving man for Urnlee,"said Constance.

"Lets go upstairs and rest and many are sitting down and talking,"said Neeus.

"I will stay and you go upstairs look at the children and I understand most of them are watching this on the tel,"said Urnlee.

"I will stay with Urnlee,"said Shawn.

"Go now and then we will go up when you both return,"said Urnlee.

"This is quite a day,"said Urnlee.

"They were all here for your wedding too,"said Shawn.

"What did she mean when Constance said."She did not she them and as titles in a long time,"said Urnlee.

"She is referring to the amount of expensive jewelry all of us are wearing, here is my cousin,"said Shawn.

Chapter 24

"Good evening to you both, Hello again, I have not seen you since my wedding,"said Urnlee.

"She is my cousin as you know Urnlee, tell us what all the jewelry is worth cousin I do believe you and all the others are deeply indebted to Neeus your husband for this event. Actually the both of you,"said Shawn.

"We are very appreciated for this pleasant gathering and as an historical time for us all of us, this jewelry has not been out of my vault in 25 years and is worth one billion,"said his Cousin.

"Oh, my goodness let me do just one thing right now. Please Neeus more security for our guests, yes it is the jewelry,"said Urnlee.

"That is our Urnlee, always working and now I need to take her over to another situation for the security needs our attention see you and talk later cousin,"said Shawn.

"I need to tell Urnlee just one more thing this goes to Baitlym when I die because you father gave this to me because I married the right man,"said Shawn's Cousin.

"It is true, she was going to marry someone else and is very grateful today for the family telling her what he was,"said Shawn.

"Oh, now that we are away who was it,"said Urnlee.

"First I need to show you these doors need guards and the staircase as well to the second floor and guarding the third as well,"said Shawn.

"I will tell Neeus right now and make sure there is overtime too,"said Urnlee.

"Good it is done, do not worry about her husband that was not. He did like to enjoy other women had several religions and would abuse just one son who worked very hard at the family business,"said Shawn.

"Here is Neeus and Constance,"said Urnlee.

"It is our choice to go upstairs right now,"said Urnlee.

"Here we go upstairs, right now,"said Shawn.

"Those two did seem to be talking about us.?"said Urnlee.

"No need to, this day is for Constance,"said Shawn.

"Wait, you were talking about my Ed,"said Urnlee.

"I was but she needed to get off the horse back riding and start you manners she was a tomboy growing up she gave you a complement for you are in charge of the Baitlym's account, "said Shawn.

"Then there is nothing else to know about.?"said Urnlee.

"No, nothing, I am sorry I told "said Shawn.

"I am not blaming you,"said Urnlee.

"I can wait right here for you outside the apartment door,"said Shawn.

"The children are ok and I will check upstairs in the large nursery,"said Urnlee.

"All is ok.?"said Shawn.

"Yes, perfect,"said Urnlee.

"Did you just change right now.? "said Shawn.

"Yes, Constance is coming up stairs I want her to wear this knight shirt of gold mish for a little while, it is her day,"said Urnlee.

"What do you two want.? "said Constance.

"I want you to wear this picket fence or whatever you call it is your day and evening,"said Urnlee.

"I will but I am not singing tonight,"said Constance.

"Please, do what I say.!"said Urnlee.

"Alright, for a little while because we had dinner but after you must wear the other one because you are not the celebrity, tonight,"said Constance.

"Alright, I will,"said Urnlee.

"Ok, it is a deal, this will make you stop and take notice who is in charge,"said Constance.

"It looks like you have half a shirt and a full backside and no front just one side for a sleeve and you are able to go to the bathroom to sit down,"said Shawn.

"I think he got it all, then,"said Constance.

"Then one must be a very large man to use this,"said Urnlee.

"Right,"said Constance.

"Then let me know when you want to get into the pants suit ok,"said Urnlee.

"So I guess Urnlee, you are not going to sing tonight.? "said Shawn.

"No, I think Constance should after all, she lost the war, I did not,"said Urnlee.

"Good one I hope the ears are listening so we have a great day and evening now at the media,"said Constance.

"Should be after all I did not say to you what I had thought of the bargain Ed had missed marrying me instead of Chardinrey and me at the same,"said Urnlee.

"Oh, did you ever think of wondering what the name of the restaurant is right now in the capital,"said Constance.

"What Billings,"said Urnlee.

"I wish it could be at least that consoling,"said Constance.

"Then what.?"said Urnlee.

"For our gentlemen folk, it is Lisa,"said Constance.

"I will have duel or kill him myself,"said Shawn.

"You can not even have a lawsuit, and last month for the brave, it was Duless,"said Constance.

"Does Neeus know of this because he might get a new name.?"said Shawn.

"Even if he called himself, Duke it would not apply, we can not go to that direction at all,"said Constance.

"How do we get the sign off the property.?"said Urnlee.

"It can not be done by the police even as of today,"said Constance.

"It is ok, to be called Lisa, but what about other times,"said Shawn.

"We are earning money right now the way he did so it is Lisa right now,"said Constance.

"Then we now have a good idea, we have to talk to him on the phone more often,"said Urnlee.

"You might have an evening to tonight he might arrive and we will all give him nice greeting and an embrace,"said Constance.

"What was his nickname as a girl when he was growing up.? "said Shawn.

"Nothing other than Ed was in the hospital and never spoke to him angrily again,"said Constance.

"What happened,"said Urnlee.

"Meanly after all Ed was my husband.?"said Constance.

"Right,"said Urnlee.

"After the lawsuit that was first, Ed said to the press."Next time, it is not in court because they are rich, "said Constance.

"The last I. O. U. with Ed as his son he called the,"teacher an I. O. U., also,"said Constance.

"So the damage was very bad.? "said Urnlee.

"Lets say, with other nations it was still being very colorful,"said Constance.

"We do not do that,"said Urnlee.

"No, and even we do not drink either,"said Constance.

"That is why, we received this job from Gale,"said Urnlee.

"Yes, or it still can be called, "Versailles,"said Constance.

"What did happen to Ed that caused surgery,"said Urnlee.

"No surgery it was done when he did not go out of the house and while he was watching the tel,"said Constance.

"But, Ed looked fine to me,"said Urnlee.

"But to his enemies Ed did not,"said Constance.

"What about Ed his son that is going to be here this evening,"said Urnlee.

"You are a nurse, Ed does not care he has his Ownsite and before that he had the tel and still has both,"said Constance.

"Giving Ed his inheritance sooner was my idea, so he could go out with important woman, celebrities,"said Constance.

"That is why Gale never visited, he gave me the idea for Ed to date and he gave me the idea that Ed can have a fortune doing the tunnels and his father and Princess Chardinrey had no money of there own,"said Constance.

"You mean it was yours anyways,"said Urnlee.

"That is true and that was the last of the gossip,"said Constance.

"Ok, then we are going to have a good time tonight for this is your evening and Constance you deserve it, we all love you,"said Urnlee.

"Thank you both,"said Constance.

"Go for it Constance. Shawn, now that we are alone, do you know what happened to Ed,"said Urnlee.

"His son was not the only one to fight unfairly to Ed and his father, after that he would stay at home,"said Shawn.

"When we dated he was just fine and wonderful,"said Urnlee.

"Remember Urnlee, twins should not have surgery when in a castle or the staff and all should be prepared to do the same,"said Shawn.

"Guessing and as nursing I would think Ed his father would stop teasing yet I think he was going to outlive his insecurity and immaturity and his son outgrew both,"said Urnlee.

"Wise to a perfect reasoning,"said Shawn.

"I loved Ed but I never saw this immatureness with him at all,"said Urnlee.

"Now here we are at the throne room,"said Shawn.

"Ok, you go an entertain someplace else and I will stay here,"said Urnlee.

"Hello, my love,"said Neeus.

"There you are Neeus, I am going to talk to the others in the next room where is Constance. ?"said Urnlee.

"She is in the Great Hall where there is a lot of guests for her to meet,"said Neeus.

"I will talk to you later,"said Urnlee.

"Hello,"said Princess Ownsite.

"I can not thank you enough for being here. Ed and Princess Ownsite. Here is Constance,"said Urnlee.

"We are all talking about you Edvard and Lisa is now the Lady in charge,"said Constance.

"Good, and as I once told dad when he was never a titled gentlemen he was going to understand that a business is run together or not be apart of at all was what he had found out from me,"said Edvard.

"Yes, Constance was telling me,"said Urnlee.

"What I never heard from my father, if he was a twin or not, and that it will make no difference at all,"said Ed.

"We are here to celebrate a great victory and a great woman that is why I had Ed call Neeus and make sure there was an award ceremony,"said Ownsite.

"Yes, I needed to have it a secret because of the nature of the award,"said Neeus.

"This is all so lovely celebrating a beautiful woman and her love for her family,"said Urnlee.

"This is a great hour and evening,"said Neeus.

"Thank you all for being here this evening and I hope you have enjoyed yourselves,"said Constance.

"I am sorry to say Lisa, we all need to go to bed now,"said Urnlee.

"We are all delight to have you,"said Constance.

"Detva can you take Lisa to her room and we can say good night at the door and see you in the morning,"said Urnlee.

"Sure here we go Lisa. Good night I will see you in the morning ok,"said Detva.

"Thank you, and Likus for hosting the guests for,"said Urnlee.

"Your Welcome, I will see all of you tomorrow, good night,"said Detva.

"Well Neeus. Here you are and I did not crack under the stress about Ed and defending him even when I found out it was Ownsite who called you,"said Urnlee.

"Yes, she did arrange it but It was done security not to get anyone upset, it was for security purposes only,"said Neeus.

"She just called and mention it, to do it something for Constance,"said Neeus.

"When were they called.?"said Neeus.

"Over an hour ago, they were here for the entire day, either was Likus or Detva,"said Neeus.

"I am sorry I am just glad I waited to talk to you?"said Neeus.

"That is ok, we had mostly everyone here,"said Urnlee.

"Tomorrow Baitlym will be home so there is going to be another problem she was not included,"said Neeus.

"I know the doctor said he could go for a few hours but she was not feeling any good, so she needed the more rest,"said Urnlee.

"Right and for security reasons no one would ever think we would have a party,"said Neeus.

"Your right I was a good idea and a lovely and thoughtful one,"said Urnlee.

"It was and now we need to think of tomorrow and your health too,"said Neeus.

"Ok, good night, before you know it Lisa will be waking us both up,"said Urnlee.

"Could this be a few more days for you Detva,"said Grandmother.

"I wish it could be but I am in charge of many building and it is just what Gale wants in France for himself and us. Besides all I needed was to see you in the throne room at last and an early breakfast too,"said Detva.

"Five is early but I made sure we were not celebrating all night,"said Grandmother.

"I hope to see you again some time with the children and your wife did you hear me.?"said Grandmother.

"Yes, I did and we will be here soon I promise you,"said Detva.

"Ok, and drive carefully,"said Constance.

"Where did you come from, Constance,"said Urnlee.

"I drove the small car from the garage the large garage with the auto casings are, where Detva always leaves his car, "said Constance.

"Why what is the matter,"said Urnlee.

"I never know if anyone will return now since Ed and Chardin died,"said Constance.

"I know what you mean and it is a good thing that their school is here,"said Urnlee.

"Will is going to leave for school and he is looking forward to it so much,"said Constance.

"So we are letting him go and Baitlym is to bring someone else in,"said Urnlee.

"It seems quite amazing with a new life,"said Constance.

"I am sure that Will thinks the same way yet understands but does not explain it to us, the way he feels, and sees life, "said Urnlee.

"Why he is leaving to make way for another,"said Constance.

"So did all of the others and you are able to see it all what a wonderful and beautiful opportunity for a grandparent to see this happen, and there is not destruction of a good business too,"said Urnlee.

"I know this is what Europe is now a days the ones in charge are the ones who know they are going to do good work,"said Constance.

"The others,"said Urnlee.

"There is a law if you can not do the work for a while they have a replacement especially in the family business,"said Constance.

"A very good plan,"said Urnlee.

"That is why I want to give one duty to everyone in the house. We have suggestions and put all messages on the phone, "said Constance

"The only job we have as of today, and the ones that are hired can do what we have been doing,"said Urnlee.

"Right, now that Baitlym and you will have a new baby to take care of you will need your husband to share his responsibilities with others at the work place,"said Constance.

"I think Likus and Detva are doing that right now,"said Urnlee.

"This is true because they would have not shown up,"said Constance.

"So we have to do the same,"said Urnlee.

"Do what,"said Neeus.

"We need to lighten the role in the work place and to give the secretaries our responsibilities. If we have a message we discuss it in our evening meetings,"said Urnlee.

"Then I am forgiven about yesterday,"said Neeus.

"Of course, it was a surprise and you had to worry about security,"said Urnlee.

"I loved my surprise,"said Constance.

"It was heaven, we all had a good time,"said Urnlee.

"Then I am forgiven,"said Neeus.

"Of course you are and you did a very good job of preparing this event,"said Urnlee.

"You did do an excellent service to me, your countries and our guests, "said Constance.

"I am apart of this country now and I hope I can do something like this again,"said Neeus.

"You are out of luck, I think the next one is Baitlym's christening for her baby,"said Constance.

"I can not think of another award except for in your own department with the police,"said Urnlee.

"Let me know,"said Neeus.

"We will, this is a challenge that even we are not quality for,"said Urnlee.

"She is right, and we do not know of these things,"said Constance.

"Then alright, I am going to the office right now and I will see you both later or maybe even for lunch, I will call,"said Neeus.

"Ok, see you soon,"said Urnlee.

"By the way, Constance for Lloyd's and the media I change my name to Neeus Barkus,"said Neeus.

"Why, that.? "said Constance.

"So Ed would not have the last and hardest laughter,"said Neeus.

"So that is two words for we do need to know,"said Urnlee.

"Both capitalized and yet joined, I am not NeeusRooftin my twin that could burn this house down so we need to worry about this when in the news about the jealous too,"said Neeus.

"Good one, we are on our way in get some financial help again,"said Constance.

"What about my name? Oh, then I know when I am Scurnlee,"said Urnlee.

"Good but you will not keep it that way, now good bye,"said Neeus.

"Good bye, Urnlee come over and have some coffee,"said Constance.

"Lisa you are dressed and I see you have had your breakfast,"said Urnlee.

"More toast,"said Lisa.

"Toast, I wonder if she knows I was just roasted then,"said Urnlee.

"I do think so, but we will not really know about that,"said Constance.

"This is turning out to be an interesting morning,"said Urnlee.

"Yesterday was wonderful but I do not think I need another exciting day like that in my life,"said Constance.

"So you have hooked the brass ring onto something are you going into the office for a few days at least,"said Urnlee.

"I never had a brass ring with my two expected marriages and I was able to do great thinks and did not due to,"Thou shall not steal."and allowed other to do the work,"said Constance.

"So you have had the opportunities and wanted to be a house wife instead,"said Urnlee.

"Also a fantastic and gracious hostess too,"said Urnlee.

"Thank you dear, you are doing quite well in that category yourself,"said Constance.

"I have been paying attention to you and the way this house is run,"said Urnlee.

"You know that this house when and if we are ruin and broke can be run by it self and the computer system can be let out to the city,"said Constance.

"Why not let the police rent it out, no we have an entire rented building with a fees that will pay for itself,"said Urnlee.

"I will message neeus right now to arrange that, or why not you to it for me.?"said Constance.

"There I will mention it was your idea,"said Urnlee.

"He was busy, and I did think you could speak to him for a while,"said Constance.

"That is show biz, right Lisa.?"said Urnlee.

"He is sawsome,"said Lisa.

"He is,"said Urnlee.

"Not a roast,"said Constance.

"No, he is not Bugs vs. Space Heros,"said Lisa.

"That is a roast show for the cartoons they even suggest another to play a role on whatever instead of who is,"said Urnlee.

"I wish I could get to Ed with that restaurant ,"said Constance.

"Why not Liccus and that is his name of my next child. I also will let Ed who is our real President be the Godfather and Ownsite is the Godmother,"said Urnlee.

"We will have to let him know now and put the name on that building right now,"said Constance.

"See if we can get the name changed first,"said Urnlee.

"We have to find out if we still have authority too,"said Constance.

"Try now and see if they will cooperate.?"said Urnlee.

"I will right now and there is, ok hello,"said Constance.

"Lisa, here is your orange it is ready so have it now, ok,"said Urnlee.

"Thank you so much, Good bye "said Constance.

"What happened.?"said Urnlee.

"I did find out if we can and we may change the name to Liccus and now he needs to get permission again,"said Constance.

"What now.?"said Urnlee.

"I am going to call Ed so it looks as if we are not angry at him and let him know that too,"said Constance.

"Call now.? "said Urnlee

"Hello, Ed,"said Constance.

"Lisa here is another orange, have this while Grandmother stepped away, ok,"said Urnlee.

"There that is done it is Liccus, until and I can not believe this Likus and his family bought the building and it is going to be living there within three weeks,"said Constance.

"It is on the news along with me, see who is living in Venice, it is Her Majesty Princess Vensole and her children and husband,"said Constance.

"Look, it is Seebees,"said Lisa.

"Apparently she told Likus on the phone and he arranged a friend to buy her out of her business in Newport, and Craig her brother is helping out,"said Constance.

"While I can not believe the ingenuity of them,"said Urnlee.

"You are thinking for too and my next guess is Likus wants to live one the shore and restore a castle there are three for him to choose from,"said Constance.

"Wait a call, hello. Sure I will,"said Urnlee.

"What is going on.? "said Constance.

"Neeus, wants to thank you for the babies name and Ed talked to him a few minutes ago. We should watch the tel also,"said Urnlee.

"Good, they are coming home, I need to call Craig,"said Constance.

"Lisa are you finshed now, more juice.? "said Urnlee.

"Yes, please,"said Lisa.

"Craig has five children all in private schools and many of them want to go the universities in the north,"said Constance.

"What else I know there is more.?"said Urnlee

"He mentioned he is going to stay there but he did state he was sending us a few good lawyers,"said Constance.

"When they graduate, that is good for the corporation,"said Urnlee.

"He loves it there,"said Constance.

"Of course there is not any take over, he is the only one in charge and he is not Prince Craig to them he works alone in the building and commuciates by phone and the entire payroll is watched by him too,"said Urnlee.

"I know he has responsibilities,"said Constance.

"He did say he would visit again, right. ?"said Urnlee.

"Yes, he did,"said Constance.

"Then we need to respect his privacy and the families security is not jeopardizes, "said Urnlee.

"Knowing of yesterday and our celebration we were fortunate to have the police service that was available,"said Constance.

"Discuss it with their captain and if there is need a metals, they at least should be given a bonus for yesterday's services,"said Urnlee.

"I will call Neeus right now and he can discuss this with his captain. I do not want to pull ranks right now and besides it is not an emergency,"said Constance.

"Good and professional decision and a correct one,"said Urnlee.

"Hello, Neeus,"said Constance.

"No, nothing for me, thank you,"said Lisa.

"Lisa, you are a very good girl, thank you too,"said Urnlee.

"He is talking to him right now,"said Constance.

"Why is it, three times you went on the phone and the third time Lisa refuses herself from wanting more food and yet I ask her each time you went to door with the phone. What is this.? "said Urnlee.

"It does not matter if each of us have a separate building to live in, this castle is made for one man only. This is Europe,"said Constance.

"He is in front on the throne and we are dismissed to our suites and then he sends for us or we leave,"said Urnlee.

"That is life in these buildings, all are a residencies for one,"said Constance.

"Then that is the true life, one building one person or owner and his family,"said Urnlee.

"We do have a good reason for staying and leaving and when leaving it is to help with the business,"said Constance.

"We do have a 100% so far and when anyone returns here we will consider it a vacation from the business ok,"said Urnlee.

"We are going to do that it must be hard to move and returning should be a commiment to our employees as our children,"said Constance.

"Now Lisa you are ready for school and here is Will and Don,"said Urnlee.

"Good morning boys, work hard and see you when you return from school,"said their Grandmother.

"Bye,"said Don.

"Good bye,"said Will.

"Me, bye,"said Lisa.

"Good bye and enjoy your classroom and study hard,"said Urnlee.

"Good bye, is Baitlym's children going to the hospital this morning.?"said Constance.

"Just this morning, for about one hour and then to school,"said Urnlee.

"So are you working to do anything with your award,"said Urnlee.

"No, I will stay out of their way,"said Constance.

"That is the right thing to do,"said Urnlee.

"Yes, I think too and we need to remember it is next stepping on or keeping a distance for it is "Thou shall not steal,"said Constance.

"Good thing to remember and I will it is good advice too, before anyone of us does out into the community and takes away,"said Urnlee.

"That is right, and our salaries in the business is earned by making sure there is no embezzlements or a rise in prices too,"said Constance.

"I am going to get dressed now here is Shawn to keep you company I will be back soon,"said Urnlee.

"Good morning, Shawn,"said Constance.

"Good morning, to you both,"said Shawn.

"Good morning, see you both in a little while,"said Urnlee.

"Shawn we are going to have Likus back with us, look right now at the news,"said Constance.

"This sure does save a phone call, I can not believe it,"said Shawn.

"Yes, we are having Likus back here with us and then Seebees who is not Princess Vensole,"said Constance.

"Good for her, she got rid of that name, she will like that because the media will leave her alone and have it print nice things about her now,"said Shawn.

"Yes, they do have to do that for a long while then the public will no longer be confused,"said Constance.

"It is just what she has wanted for some time and now it is there for her,"said Shawn.

"I know she is avery senitive woman and needs praise,"said Constance.

"So how is my sensitive woman are enjoying last night or do you need praise, I am very proud of you.? "said Shawn.

"I am very delighted and last night was a very exciting evening for me,"said Constance.

"Now you are pleased with everything being back to normal,"said Shawn.

"I am glad it is ok but that life was never me, "said Constance.

"I guess not I remember from this house no one knew what you were doing,"said Shawn.

"That is the way I like it, for the holidays is fine with me,"said Constance.

"We can relax now and the excitement is over for now,"said Urnlee.

"I think so, other than a little one a new born is about to come home soon,"said Constance.

"Who will be home soon.? "said Urnlee.

"The baby,"said Constance.

"Right and the apartment is all done up for the new arrival,"said Urnlee.

"That is right too she did that about a week ago by herself,"said Constance.

"When she gets home she should give herself a new name for the security purposes as well as for the children's sake,"said Urnlee.

"I know and we know that it is for Lloyd's but it does put the direction to us and we are the ones who need the protection yet the business is sound there is another way to get money,"said Shawn.

"No, because we can only involve ourselves so as it hurts just us, we do control the media and the hurtful stories are not that effective,"said Constance.

"With today more people are more protective of their children and themselves,"said Urnlee.

"They do take notice and will use more security measures,"said Shawn.

"One talk show host guess mention,"We use more names."The host did indicate how it was that he would still want to be our neighbors,"said Urnlee.

"There will be more names. You watch the tel that late.?"said Constance.

"No, it was easier to turn it on then the light switch when Lisa entered the room,"said Urnlee.

"This is part of the one person building but I do not want to loose anyone so we must have a coffee and what do we need to think of what for this evenings meeting,"said Constance.

"We can start on remembering the day you must talk to the police department here in the building that gave you this award last night,"said Urnlee.

"I will include in the message if there is another department outside of this home to talk to and to thank"said Constance.

I have a better I will ask Neeus to tell all those departments to meet you hear on the front lawn and to cheer you for being so brave,"said Urnlee.

"As a gift we can give them a pen set, after all that is the proper instrument to stop destruction and very appropriate"said Shawn.

"Sure I will, and do we feed them there might be to many or to crowded in fact,"said Constance.

"Giving them three paid hours is good enough and we will put it on the tel after and during for security purposes,"said Urnlee.

"They would in fact enjoy the hours with pay and go directly to lunch,"said Constance.

"Very good that is more enjoyable a full morning hours of work with pay and to lunch time,"said Shawn.

"The overtime will make many return early so would be be a better incentive for that day,"said Urnlee.

"It is just a photo in front of the castle with all the police for me to give a thank you,"said Constance.

"A 8:00a.m. to 9:00a.m. with the photo at 9:10 a.m. then they leave,"said Urnlee.

"An easy yet a good schedule with overtime and they start work at 12:00 a.m. Said Constance.

"One more option, which is the best to do, with one full day off with pay to be scheduled some other time because they are doing this photo for us,"said Shawn.

"We can arrange after that one day for Gale in Versialles to have the police visit the Palace in one month, and other day for Ed and we get back the media from him too,"said Urnlee.

"We can photo Venice with Princess Vensole and her family and then give the press back to us,"said Constance.

"Then Likus has a photo and his family mentioning it is good to be home,"said Urnlee.

"Also how he was not brave and strong enough to do the work as his brother Craig is still loyal to the family,"said Constance.

"That weakness will be used to controll getting the media,"said Urnlee.

"But what about years ago and the media was watching Hollywood and not us,"said Shawn.

"Besides Versailles and the Hermitage cable is responsible for that with its own library of films of each actor and actress, "said Urnlee.

"We will give them a movie of us it is time too,"said Constance.

"Right after your award we need good footage of that day and evening too,"said Urnlee.

"Sounds very good and we can do it,"said Shawn.

Chapter 25

"There is just one problem today.?"said Constance.

"What is it.?"said Urnlee.

"Baitlym's your baby is smiling at me and Urnlee I know he is not looking at me at all, because he is smiling at Shawn and saying his name,"said Constance.

"We will all go over to them and they will choose,"said Shawn.

"No, just Shawn and I will and we will pick them up immediately and then give them to their mother's,"said Constance.

"Now that we are hear I am going to sit down with this little one and we are going to have a nap,"said Shawn.

"How many of the children are in the pre-school,"said Baitlym.

"Many in the next grades so that leaves only three more and then they are all leaving the second floor together each morning, it will be a sight to see,"said Constance.

"Here is a one little baby and I am going to give them to his nanny,"said Urnlee.

"This house is filled with children and many of them come running up to me in the hallways and start of say Grandpa,"said Shawn.

"It is good and wonderful and some day they will not be running they will be walking up to us or me and ask how things are and it is going to take us by surprise,"said Urnlee.

"I know and it will be a great day for us all if they go into the business, "said Shawn.

"They are there now us and the younger children are to see how the business grows with our help,"said Urnlee.

"Everything is going in the right directions,"said Constance.

"I know of one more thing for tonight do we own our Exile rentals of the tunnels system ourselves.?"said Urnlee.

"We are in controll of all,"said Constance.

"Then this should be done right now, with a good drivers reports from each state we give a new car to those who have had an accident,"said Urnlee.

"We do own all the dealerships now that are on the Federal highways systems so when any happening the motor industries the autos are still sold at the right prices,"said Constance.

"I get it, when the criteria is perfect when buying a new car we now replace them when in an accident,"said Shawn.

"The cars are replaced after one year, right if the owner does not want to sell, he can have a new one,"said Urnlee.

"This is correct even they do not mind the taxes. We do have an obligation to the citizens now with all of our earnings we can buy out many large condominiums,"said Shawn.

"Along with the properties too and give them the tax and monthly fees for a long while paid for in fact,"said Urnlee.

"We will have to consider the properties nearest to the tunnels only because to its get the population there to stay,"said Constance.

"Just near the tunnels is good and it helps people use the transportation system too,"said Urnlee.

"First lets start with Paris to Moscow, so Ed will help too,"said Shawn.

"Constance you should controll this one and give Ed that message before he does anything else with that restaurant somewhere else.!"said Urnlee.

"By the way who do we get represent us in Newport buying the properties too,"said Shawn.

"I got it, we can ask Baylib if she would do this for us,"said Constance.

"He will be here shortly, give him a message,"said Urnlee.

"Here is Lisa, "said Constance.

"Want to have another dinner with us,"said Urnlee.

"Awesome,"said Lisa.

"I got your message and Baylib wants the work and her husband as well. They were both wondering if they could do the project in Newport too,"said Neeus.

"Sure it is good for Lloyd's also,"said Constance.

"Awesome,"said Lisa.

"Yes it is Lisa, you are correct,"said Urnlee.

"If helps having her watch those cartoons we get filled in too,"said Constance.

"We do and it is good for you to be educated first yet the school does have its limitations,"said Urnlee.

"She will grow out of it soon,"said Shawn.

"You are right about one thing, the school will limit this but it does not harm that much,"said Urnlee.

"No, but remember, it is a representative we are wanting and we will be patient with her,"said her Grandmother.

"She is my little girl and she is the best I love you so much we all do,"said Shawn.

"We are flexable, we are getting an education too. We all love you, Lisa"said Urnlee.

"Lets see my dear how are you, and I love you too.?"said Neeus.

"I am fine and thank you and it is good news about your sister,"said Urnlee.

"It is awesome, right little Lisa,"said Neeus.

"I would stop this about encouraging her, but I think we just did another commercial including the auto exchange program when hitting another vehicle we as a company just replace the car,"said Constance.

"What about the insurance companies.?"said Urnlee.

"It is our autos they purchase from us a certain auto one of our smallest cars,"said Constance.

"Just using it for the tunnels only, that is all,"said Shawn.

"So it could work and we have another idea completed,"said Urnlee.

"The dinner is good and now I know wee have stopped the filming it is enough so all is ok,"said Neeus.

"Now that your sister is willing to help everything is fine with us,"said Urnlee.

"It was our last and greatest decision and I am sure they can keep the homes they work from too,"said Constance.

"They can rent them out if they want to live in Belgium too,"said Neeus.

“That would be good,”said Urnlee.

“Which or where should they start first,”said Neeus.

“Paris to Moscow,”said Constance.

“Good,”said Neeus.

“Ok, then it is settled, she indicated they would start tomorrow looking for a place in Moscow,”said Constance.

“I guess she and going to live at home in Austria to get the halfway section approved first,”said Neeus.

“That will save some money while using the jet to photo the land,”said Urnlee.

“No, do not give her the jet, she must use the agentcies,”said Neeus.

“Grenaire or Exile, what we discuss,”said Constance.

“That is right too, we must think of the security and not give out anything like photos,”said Constance.

“I do not think she will ask that,”said Shawn.

“Know she would not, knowing of the problems we could have,”said Neeus.

“I will remind her about security risks involved and she and her husband will obey us,”said Neeus.

“She will do the right thing, I will talk to her all the time on the phone and she will report what she is doing to make sure it is the right thing,”said Urnlee.

“Keep us informed, we do not want her to do the wrong thing,”said Constance.

“It is perfect now thank you again Neeus, you have done so much so far in such a small amount of time,”said Constance.

“Your welcome it was my pleasure and a privilege to help out,”said Neeus.

“What about me.? “said Shawn.

“You, I thought you have received the best deal here,”said Constance.

“You are right, I should watch out for what I say,”said Shawn.

“It is a deal,”said Constance.

“With this mind I wonder if I need to give birth to more babies,”said Urnlee.

“No, you are good and I love the way you are right now,”said Neeus.

“Ownsite gave birth to 14 babies,”said Constance.

“I know, at the very beginning of their marriage too,”said Urnlee.

“That was amazing what she did for him,”said Shawn.

"They had strong bonds between since they met,"said Constance.

"Making sure they had an engagement was not easy with Ed he was quite a renegade or wanting his own way to travel and leave home,"said Shawn.

"He controlled himself and they are happy and together now and loving life,"said Constance.

"It sounds so wonderful yet things were a bit uncertain when the tunnells were completed then he knew he could go home to Europe,"said Urnlee.

"My routes are where my parents settled in Europe mostly in Italy then he insisted on going home to Denmark and then we capitalized on his title when we all moved to Belgium, "said Neeus.

"But your early childhood was in England,"said Constance.

"There is very little I can remember why Grandmother staying because she never wanted to leave the house,"said Neeus.

"I do remember your parents visiting my husband and your father said,"The only reason why my wife wants to go to this building was it had a lot of Hollywood actors and actresses living there with their children.,"said Constance.

"If I knew of any I would give a call to them but I was just a baby then,"said Neeus.

"That was your parents home,"said Urnlee.

"Yes,"said Neeus.

"My parents lived there too and we stayed awhile and left after Ed was born. After he married Chardin they stayed here with me,"said Constance.

"Awesome,"said Lisa.

"Yes, it was awesome to live in a chateau with apartments inside A u-shaped building,"said Constance.

"When Ed started to build this house he had in mind all of us to stay and work in the business and to help Gale,"said Constance.

"What sort of good guy gives away his business and allows them to earn so much in such a short time,"said Neeus.

"I guess it is some who appreciated someone else doing the work to make sure it was done that people could use sleep and loitering because he would want to have a better healthier life living in the Palace of Versailles,"said Constance.

"Now he is a good, healthier and better guy because of that building,"said Neeus.

"Now I guess we have had enough for now and so we will have coffee and the living room and then we are going to bed early for a good night sleep,"said Constance.

"I think there is a new movie for them to look at it is called."Versailles on the coast and the water glazier,"said their Grandmother.

"It is a good cartoon of how the city tried to stop the glazier from destroying the building,"said Neeus.

"The building is unoccupied for the winter and no one is inside of course,"said Urnlee.

"About the summer homes now that both are vacant why not use them,"said Constance.

"We can split ourselves up and stay in both this weekend or how about tomorrow morning we go there and open them up for ourselves,"said Shawn.

"It is a warm night we have the street lights on those buildings so we will go now, for a good long weekend,"said Constance.

"First we will have the staff go and open up the buildings,"said Shawn.

"Right this is good for security and we need a little vacation,"said Constance.

"Just all us go and we will send for the other children in the morning,"said Urnlee.

"The soldiers are there and the navy and the police too,"said Neeus.

"Good you can notify them now,"said Unrlee.

"This is going to be grand and so fantastic,"said Constance.

"Awesome and so spontaneous,"said Neeus.

"Awesome,"said Lisa.

"Yes, it is going to be awesome and a very good vacation,"said Urnlee.

"Here, I now can see the castle at the sea and I guess we are all staying at one building tonight,"said Neeus.

"I guess so we are all together this evening it looks that way,"said Urnlee.

"Constance is with us, see she intends to visit during the weeks to see how we are,"said Neeus.

"Good lets go inside and wait for her and we are going to be screamed at for speeding,"said Urnlee.

"If you should ever wonder these officers and I will say it while we are all inside they are the ones that can give you a ticket,"said Constance.

"That is why you gave her the children and took the small convertible,"said Urnlee.

"Yes, but this is the one that is for sale,"said Neeus.

"Lets go upstairs and get ready for bed and we are going to have snacks in our apartments,"said Constance.

"The staff brought a lot of food for a few days and we can have sandwiches for right now, tonight,"said Constance.

"All children are asleep I can not believe it and the others will be here in the morning, "said Urnlee.

"I guess it is the salt air, have some food and we can all go to bed, good night,"said Constance.

"Urnlee lets have a bit and go to sleep ok,"said Neeus.

"I will, just do one thing for me tomorrow morning, I want to sleep late so make sure Lisa does not wake me up, ok,"said Urnlee.

"Sure good night,"said Neeus.

"Good night," said Urnlee.

"Lisa what time, we can go downstairs and have a breakfast and do not wake up Mommy,"said Neeus.

"Good morning,"said Constance.

"Constance, you are awake what is wrong.? said Neeus.

"I did not wake up anyone and the police are outside I am glad you both finished your breakfast and are dressed because I have something for you to see Neeus, "said Constance.

"I should go out there alone,"said Neeus.

"Yes, you should,"said Constance.

"Grandma more juice,"said Lisa.

"Sure Lisa and here is an orange I will cut it up,"said Grandmother.

"I do not believe it and how long has it been there,"said Neeus.

"It came by my window about two a.m. and the police got all the people off that wanted to go to a hotel in town,"said Constance.

"But it is a cruise ship right next to our castle our house is it going to be leaning on the castle itself,"said Neeus.

"No, and that is not all, the other new building has one,"said Constance.

"We own two cruise ships as of today,"said Neeus.

"Here is their fax, turning them over to us,"said Constance.

"The ships can move out.? "said Neeus.

"Both can move, it is the Emos satellite that we purchased when Ed did the tunnels with the Euro train that needed its directional systems,"said Constance.

"Why did this happen why did it arrive here,"said Neeus.

"The navy is in both, but it was the space module that went wrong,"said Constance.

"Urnlee must be told,"said Neeus.

"I know and this is what I want you to do bring Lisa upstairs and let her go into the bedroom alone ok,"said Constance.

"If would be better if many found out by themselves and we were entering the room when each one wakes up, I will go tell Shawn,"said Constance.

"We will go now, and I will wait and listen for Urnlee to talk to Lisa,"said Neeus.

"She is inside good, I will talk to Shawn, stay near the door,"said Constance.

"Hello Lisa,"said Urnlee.

"Boat,"said Lisa.

"Boat good, did you have your breakfast.? "said Urnlee.

"Yes, see it is mine,"said Lisa.

"What is that.? "said Urnlee.

"Good morning Ladies and how is Urnlee,"said Neeus.

"What is that at the window.? "said Urnlee.

"It is a ship and you can see it by our bathroom window too,"said Neeus.

"I do not believe this is it going to leave soon.? "said Urnlee.

"No, the ownership it was just fax to us,"said Neeus.

"I do think this is an error by someone the captain,"said Urnlee.

"Good one I never did think of that, but it is the satelite because both buildings have a ship near it,"said Neeus.

"It can move when the Emos is working.?"said Urnlee.

"Yes, do you wan to go outside and see,"said Neeus.

"Oh, this is something I can not believe my eyes look at it over the lawn,"said Urnlee.

"Most of the passengers are in the hotel, the new in fact is taking these people one day earlier,"said Neeus.

"You must wave to them because they are applauding you dear,"said Neeus.

"Ok, hello, look dear there are war ships in the sea,"said Urnlee.

"Say a few words your ladyship,"said a Reporter.

"There is not need of being frightened we have been given the titles to the ships and when they are finally at sea.

"What is going to happen now.? "said the reporter.

"I think it is just better to enclose them, after the passengers get on a new ship in a few days,"said Urnlee.

"What about the future.?"said the Reporter.

"We can study and repair them and for the situation on board we will retire these two models so the world may feel safe again. Thank you all so much so for your concern,"said Princess Urnlee.

"Thank you Princess now we have conclusive ---,"said the Reporter.

"That was very nice and thank you for speaking to them.?' said Neeus.

"Urnlee, that was a very good speech I saw it on the tel,"said Constance.

"Moarning the ships so then they will be safe is an excellent idea and quite a few new apartments as well for us is quite a remarkable achievement for this property,"said Constance.

"I do mean it they will stay right there to keep the public safe,"said Urnlee.

"Look, a new fax from the shipping lines,"said Neeus.

"What does it day.?"said Constance.

"Great idea for a safe world and we will do the repairs for you new extension to your homes,"said Neeus.

"Great idea to customize these two ships for us and their shipping lines look good too,"said Constance.

"I meant what I said if these are our ships they are going to stay right here,"said Urnlee.

"Your are right again,"said Constance.

"Now remember that because when we find out that those ships are yours they still stay right here,"said Urnlee.

"For all the little ones it will be a very good building as a enclosure for them they will have very good summer also,"said Neeus.

"You are correct Neeus and I do not intend to change my mind about this at all,"said Urnlee.

"I know we were going to have all the children here then the other ship will be done first,"said Constance.

"For me,"said Lisa.

"Yes, that is correct Lisa you will have a ship too,"said Urnlee.

"Yes, Lisa that is yours,"said Constance.

"Was there any other child that not traumatized by a ship also.?"said Urnlee.

"Not that I am aware of,"said Shawn.

"No,"said Neeus.

"Then that settles it, we are going to give the other ship to the newborn baby when Urnlee gives birth,"said Constance.

"That is a wonderful idea the little one has earned it we were all praying for the children to help you out and Liccus and Lisa did when you saw the ship in the frontyard,"said Shawn.

"Perfect I am so glad he is mine, congratulations dear hoping we do get a great deal of mail,"said Neeus.

"Hear you loud and clear Neeus as if we all are on the same page,"said Constance.

"Right we can agree on this, we set sail on a true course with this one. A bad mistake made and we will move on,"said Shawn.

"Sure we are and now some coffee for all of us and there are new toys for the children to use and this weekend lunch and dinners are all planned,"said Constance.

"We must be sure that all the guests are in the hotels right now.?"said Urnlee.

"They are the ones you saw in front of the castle were the last and all were waiting for the limousines to arrive, sorry I did not tell you,"said Neeus.

"Good so now we do have some privacy,"said Urnlee.

"I guess the staff situation there is up to the ship lines who stays and who does not until the ship is handed over,"said Neeus.

"I wonder if anyone one or a few married could stay there as a live in year round,"said Urnlee.

"You mean a few cooks and servants such as a maids and the maintenance also,"said Constance.

"I know why not let the ship lines have their schools there and we can be entertainment too,"said Shawn.

"How about a gambling casino that can afford the fees and even help the staff pay for their work and apartments,"said Constance.

"Good ideas,"said Shawn.

"Oh, give me a phone and I will call each ship and talk to the captains and then they will inform their boss themselves,"said Constance.

"A Versailles theatre and Versailles gambling and it pre-school,"said Urnlee.

"Awesome,"said Lisa.

"Yes, it is awesome Lisa and completely productive,"said Urnlee.

"Why we can have the completed businesses of Gale's right here and in the other ship, two fortunes,"said Shawn.

"There is a clear picture of what has to be done,"said Constance.

"What is this.?"said Shawn.

"Why it is a message from Ed,"said Constance.

"I am sure no one is injured,"said Urnlee

"We are all given this large check of 500 hundred million for the four of us to do what is needed if there is a law suit if we can not keep the ship because both are unsafe.?"said Constance.

"So we do have a good child right now, lets do hope the ship are given to us,"said Urnlee.

"We might hear from them in a few hours, lets see what this call is,"said Constance.

"It is good news I bet,"said Neeus.

"Yes, so thank you very much, it is official we own both there is gambling and the staff are finally calm down knowing we will allow them to stay just a few want a transfer,"said Constance.

"What about the ship itself.? "said Neeus.

"Just in a few words it has a wait on it that was lower into the water and in the sand at the bottom so it can not be moved,"said Constance.

"Was anything mention about why it will stay or the cause,"said Neeus.

"The cause is why it will stay, it is unsafe,"said Constance.

"I can not believe this is happening.?"said Urnlee.

"It is and you were right Ed's call was a positive,"said Neeus.

"Thank you dear, good morning Will, "said Urnlee.

"Good morning, you need to go outside right now and Neeus and Shawn will go with you come on right now,"said Urnlee.

"My ship,"said Lisa.

"Ok, here we go right now what is going on,"said Will.

"They will be back soon,"said Constance.

"Here they are, it must have given Will a shock,"said Urnlee.

"Oh, I am, I can not believe it. When can we go on it.? "said Will.

"I looked and I ran inside.?"said Will.

"My ship,"said Lisa.

"I am going to see it again,"said Will.

"Did any of you see the U.S.S. Stipends in the front of the ship, it is bordering it right now,"said Shawn.

"We can see from the this room just open up the French doors and we can go to the windows if we want to, "said Urnlee.

"Good I will go get Don he is still asleep,"said Grandmother.

"Alright look at that ship in front and there is a cloud over us there and the sun is showing from our left windows,"said Urnlee.

"That cloud is the ship and is also covering the cruise ship too,"said Will.

"You can see the ship on this side this left side for miles,"said Urnlee.

"That is why I returned to tell you what is going on,"said Will.

"Here is Don, good morning,"said Urnlee.

"Neeus, Constance and Urnlee we should invite in a delegation into this castle now,"said Shawn.

"I will maybe the Captain can give me the phone number,"said Constance.

"Hello, Captain. We would like a delegation from the other ship and others if it is possible. Good, and thank you too,"said Constance.

"What,"said Urnlee.

"They will arrive in about one hour,"said Constance.

"There is another bit of news a makeup company wants you Constance and not any one else to represent them and to give our other businesses "said Shawn.

"Stop right there I will now and they want to give our businesses employees all the surgery and shots for a new body and face so I am going to represent,"said Constance.

"Good because they want to work in both ships and have their employees live there and have a school also,"said Shawn.

"Why want advertise about this so others might call with offers from their companies, I am so glad someone is thinking about these ships,"said Urnlee.

"I will right now did they leave an address.?"said Constance.

"Yes here is the phone,"said Shawn.

"Email and call right now,"said Neeus.

"I will they are answering, "Hello, yes I am, yes and would you, please advertise this offer right now as a done deal. thank you, good bye, "said Constance.

"For employees too,"said Urnlee.

"That is right, I want everything for them they have worked very hard,"said Constance.

"Yes, I have,"said Shawn.

"Yes, I do agree,"said Constance.

"Then our first raise, "said Urnlee.

"Yes, I second it,"said Neeus.

"Then you two,"said Constance.

"Right now do not give any franchises out we have two ships that need to be run,"said Shawn.

"You are ok, all of you,"said Constance.

"Awesome,"said Lisa.

"Awesome,"said her Grandfather.

"Awesome,"said Will.

"What else did you see on the cameras outside, Will,"said his Grandfather.

"So you know where the station house is that is now a villa. or castle, whatever it is it was suppose to be a castle by now,"said Will.

"Sorry it was my last building, I think,"said Constance.

"To restore, I put it in the phone. So Will what about the station.? "said Shawn.

"Are you ready for this the ship that is over our house is< I can only see the front doorway and its little side walk of stone,"said Will.

"The front door,"said Constance.

"I have to tell your right now that if a submarine wanted to go by it or another ship they need to get very close to the border of the nearest coast.,"said Neeus.

"That is not even Finland, I am going to get a job there as a soldier,"said Will.

"So am I,"said Lisa.

"Actually for both of you I need you both to stay with Grandmother, but I think you can be on ship part time when it is near the dock,"said Urnlee.

"Also actually this is the dock, Urnlee this ship which is half a submarine and carrier ship for planes and allows the other ships to refuel so it can not fit into the English channel,"said Neeus.

"Right, this ship does block the England channel so no one can get in or out of France again,"said Shawn.

"Then there is another one of the largest submarines in the world for Scotland to Norway that is how long it is because no one gets out for a small or large war again,"said Neeus.

Chapter 26

“I can not believe this,”said Urnlee.

“The only way is by plane and it can look like the coast of Finland in three minutes if it has so many do surrender,”said Neeus.

“That I heard was on a Venice type poles that lower and then the waves would cover the ship again when most of it is under water,”said Will.

“Right it is on metal or steel poles and can lower or raise at different times,”said Neeus.

“Now we are going to have a delegation or a navy conference at this house so we have to respect they might have dinner here,”said Constance.

“We are unprepared,”said Shawn.

“No we have enough hams to serve for some reason there were any brought with us,”said Constance.

“All were in the smaller kitchen,”said Urnlee.

“So we are prepared at least one dinner,”said Constance.

“No, I just think we have to move from here and return,”said Shawn.

“If we are the guests on each ship we might just save the industry, and allow them to stay because the navy might take them over,”said Neeus.

“There are seven of us, Shawn, Don and I will go next door on board and stay as their guests even if it is all summer,”said Constance.

“Will, Lisa, Urnlee and myself are going to leave right now,”said Neeus.

“So what if it is a plot as a good well planned kidnapping,”said Urnlee.

“Then most of us are going to say, “I wish I was never born or later on we know we have lost our first fortune,”said Constance.

"So what is it,"said Will.

"We go right now and do not mention kidnapping we are there to make sure we keep these ships,"said Constance.

"While we are in the cars we will talk,"said Urnlee.

"Yes, good bye and we stay as the new owner,"said Constance.

"Now Constance we are at the door, before they have put in the navy guards,"said Shawn.

"I see someone,"said Constance.

"Hello, this Princess Constance,"said Shawn.

"Please enter,"said the Staff.

"Thank you, is your Captain here.?" said Shawn.

"I am the Captain, I apologize for not seeing you all sooner,"said the Captain.

"Your accommodations are ready because all the guests are now gone,"said the Captain.

"We do not intend to stay to long,"said Constance.

"I know your suite and to relax and we may have a tour and I myself and my ship thank you so much for this opportunity, and please call me John,"said the Captain.

"Thank you and please use our first names too,"said Constance.

"Look the ship has left,"said Shawn.

"Will is going to be very disappointed he wanted to see that, oh the phone, excuse me, yes, good then give me a report in an hour and tell Urnlee I, we are with the Captain. John has been very nice" said Constance.

"Your tour may begin right now because we can start with a lunch in the main dining room,"said John.

"Sounds good to me,"said Shawn.

"I am going to use my phone to record,"said Will.

"This elevator has a lobby to it and we go right to the dining room,"said John.

"That sounds fantastic, John,"said Constance.

"You can see the entire ship from here and now near the first floor you can see the gift shops,"said John.

"This dining area is perfection,"said Shawn.

"Please be seated, now I am going to have lunch with you and the gift shop have gifts for all of you, and my gifts are there as well and there will be more, "said John.

"This is quite enough already,"said Constance.

"This is however, is my luncheon with all of you, then a lovely lady will give you all a tour of the ship and then we will meet on the deck in one hour ok,"said John.

"In one hour I will look forward to it,"said Constance.

"Thank you. Said Shawn.

"I did not want the children to hear but when all of you return to your cabins there will be some gifts,"said John.

"Thank you again. This does seem to be a wonderful day,"said Constance.

"This lunch is very grand,"said Shawn.

"It is the theme of today but the clients went to another ships. So we have lots of food to give to you each week so you never have to shopping. We all ready gave your staff their lunch for three weeks too,"said John.

"That is a good vacation at the beach." said Shawn.

"Where did the passengers go.?" said Constance.

"Where were four ships there already so the transportation was available." said John.

"That is right there would,"said Constance.

"Now we may leave for the cabins children and I have a gifts you both,"said John.

"It take just a few minutes to get the suites and there is also more food for all of you, my secretary will call and then let her know when you are ready for the tour." said Captain John.

"Mom, Mom and Dad the both of you would never believe what I got from the Captain." said Will.

"What did you get.?" said Urnlee.

"A genuine private officer's cap," said Will.

"That is authentic. There were antiques for sale on board the ship we were on,"said Neeus.

"All of these gifts are authentic and the staff that gave jewelry all are priceless,"said Constance.

"They already appreciate what has been done for them,"said Shawn.

"I would rename that restaurant Shipdolls but I will not." said Constance.

"Then rename it or most of us do not want a personal war.! "said Urnlee.

The End.